COAST TO COAST

COAST

AUSTRALIAN STORIES

TO COAST

1967-1968

Selected by A. A. PHILLIPS

ANGUS AND ROBERTSON

First published in 1968 by
ANGUS & ROBERTSON LTD
221 George Street, Sydney
54 Bartholomew Close, London
107 Elizabeth Street, Melbourne
65 High Street, Singapore

National Library of Australia
registry number AUS 68-3167
SBN 207 95092 X

Registered in Australia
for transmission by post as a book

PRINTED IN AUSTRALIA BY
J. C. STEPHENS PTY LTD, MELBOURNE

Acknowledgments

Thanks for permission to republish stories in this
collection are due to the *Bulletin* for "Guardian Angel"
and "Mr Butterfry"; to *Westerly* for "Paterson's Flats",
"Dry Season" and "For the Good of the People";
to *Meanjin* for "The Vineyard", "That Part of the World",
"The Three-legged Bitch" and "Penitence";
to *Southerly* for "Old and New" and "Five-Twenty";
to *Blackwood's Magazine* for "A Long Time"; to
Quadrant for "The Grand Passion"; to the
Toowoomba Chronicle for "The Road";
to *Overland* for "She Let Them Know" and
"Thicker Than Water"; and to the *North
American Review* for "Sanctuary".

*Published with the assistance
of the Commonwealth Literary Fund*

Contents

ESME GOLLSCHEWSKY

Guardian Angel

IN HIS chair at the window he leant forward intently, watching the thin sliver of smoke that rose above the athel-trees marking the boundary of the oats paddock. What could she be burning over there? Not grass, at this time of year.

"A fire over there between the oats and the road." A question, in the form of an observation. And she understood it as such, answering sparely as usual. She'd never been a loquacious woman.

"Yes, I picked up the dead wood lying around. That's the stack burning. I set it off last night."

"Picked up the dead wood?" He could hardly believe it. The act of a penny-pinching share farmer, that was. "Why?"

"We want grass."

"Always did, didn't we? Tell me a farmer that doesn't."

"Our stock's nearly doubled the last coupla years." She flipped over the mattress of the bed, hands much stronger than they looked. Hands and wrists. Sure in their work. She never skimped a job, give her that. Mattress turned every day regular as clockwork. Always sending away for new treatments, laboriously composing the letters. She'd never had much schooling, you could tell. But made up for it in shrewdness, make no mistake.

He peered resentfully at the pencil smoke, darker than the mist hanging over the river. Something downright wrong about a fire burning on a man's property without his either lighting it or giving orders for it to be lit. And stock had no right to double in number without sanction from the owner. Who had arranged the servicing of his cows? Such things a man should know.

Because the affront to his pride was indefinable, he wished he could, in some way, get back at her. But she gave him no opportunity. Deftly she set the room to rights, not glancing his way as he sat in the thin wash of wintry sunlight, face turned outward from the room in which he now lived.

His feeling of fretful discomfiture increased. The outlook from his window was curiously unfamiliar—and yet he'd been aware of changes going on for some time past. But vaguely. This morning, with his attention caught by the smoke, everything seemed to have crystallized. Take the pullets scratching under the orange-trees where the earth was cool and damp. There was a helluva lot more than in his time, and pure-bred Rhode Islands at that. His had been wild-eyed, scraggy, long-legged chooks, few in number, sneaking into the kitchen after scraps and leaving grey-white dollops on the floor; or crawling up the leaning stems of the pawpaws to pick holes in the ripening fruit. They were scavengers, and, dressed for the table, stringy and tough.

Must be fifty or sixty of those plump red pullets rolling around, washing their feathers in the loose soil. All very well to go in for chooks in a big way, but what you gonna feed 'em on, eh? The price of feed these days . . . a silvery thread of saliva swung from his mouth to catch on the grey flannel shirt, leaving a snail's trail across his chest.

"Chook feed," he grumbled threateningly, "is a turrible price." He had gone to agricultural college until he was eighteen, but like most farmers' sons tended to disguise the fact in his speech. One taunting cry of "Tonk!" and country boys felt they were ruined for life.

"If you buy it." She sniffed. "I grow my own. And sell some besides. You never did grow enough stockfeed. No milo or sweet potatoes or pumpkins for the pigs—a few miserable sticks of cassava and you expect to rear pigs on that! But who could tell you? You always knew best."

"I was reared to it." His offensive tone said, "And you weren't."

"Reared to what?" She laughed mockingly. "Reared to think you only have to own a bit of ground and you're the big grazier? To ape the big man?" She slapped a pillow into shape and set it exactly where his back would rest. "Order a hundredweight of this and half a ton of that to keep the cows alive in bad weather. A bag of this and a bag of that to keep the chooks from starving. I grow my own, like I said." The corner of the bedclothes, tucked in securely all round so they wouldn't slip, was flipped back ready to receive him. "I'll leave you a Thermos of tea. I'll be away all morning picking corn."

His ungainly head swung about and stared at her in astonishment, deep-set little eyes grown smaller with suspicion. "What corn?"

She raised her voice in the irritating way she'd acquired since his illness as if his hearing was affected. "Ruben ploughed the four-acre last September. I borrowed Hagermann's planter and put the seed in. It's a fair crop. But I want it in the barn in case the weather breaks."

He ran a distorted hand over his shaven head, absently feeling the bumps and hollows her ruthless razor had exposed. Knobs he never knew he had were disclosed after she took over his barbering. "Quicker and cleaner," she said, simply shaving it off. "You know an aunt of mine, bedridden, got a nest of mice in her hair one time. After that they made her brush it out every day." How was it possible for an entire crop to be sown and ready for harvest on a man's land without his knowledge?

"That barn's pretty well fallen down," he said evasively, dodging the issue after all. "It won't keep out no weather."

"I had it repaired. Last autumn."

So there was nothing else to say.

She stood for a moment, bony, callused hands hanging from the shrunken sleeves of her red cardigan. Pity for her touched him. No doubt of it, she'd done a man's work this past year. Say the last couple of years—maybe five, if you were fussy. He hadn't really done much for a while there, even before he got crook. He'd already started leaving things to her. Married nine years last Christmas. Yes, her hands showed it. His own were whiter than they'd ever been in his whole life. Whiter and plumper. But was that his fault? Arthritis didn't mean a man couldn't eat, did it?

Yes, she could work, he'd give her that. And nothing much of her, come to look. A quick little sparrow of a woman. Looking round the room now to see if she'd missed anything, but she never did. Thorough. That was her.

"I'll come back and help you into bed before I go to the corn paddock," she said, turning away.

The blue dog emerged from under the bed to follow her. "Crikey," he wheedled, and clicked his tongue, "here, boy. Come on, Crikey. Come, boy," but the dog ignored him, padding after her down the long hall, nails scratching on the linoleum. Ever you see such a bastard?

He picked up a saucer containing scraps of sausage meat from where it stood on the table beside him. With some difficulty—for, though plump and white, his hands were tortuously out of shape— he picked up the scraps and laid them on the window-sill. Later the birds would come. It was something to look forward to.

Funny, how when she left a room the quietness was intensified. The silence kind of deepened. Yet she was quiet enough when she was present, sometimes not speaking at all, working silently. But it was always the same. Like a hush. He could hear the familiar morning sounds through that hush: the windmill's slow creaking, distant fowls cackling hysterically after laying their eggs, the sow's demanding squeals, the butcher-birds and magpies in the macadamia-trees, far away a tractor growling, and now, above all other sounds, Crikey barking and woofing like a damned lunatic around her legs as she went about the outside chores.

That Crikey, he thought venomously. Ever you know a dog before to leave its master and take to somebody else voluntary, a woman at that? But he'd said all along the dog was no good. Never did show a grain of sense even as a pup. Still, Crikey was his dog, and somehow a man expects his dog, at least ... he'd heard once of a kelpie that lay under its master's sick-bed for months and wouldn't leave it until he died, and there was that Alsatian they hadda shoot because it wouldn't leave a kid's grave and kept scrabbling at the loose dirt, unnerving everyone who saw it. You wouldn't catch Crikey at anything like that. Frisking out there round her skirts instead of being faithful unto death in this room.

She came into view carrying a heavy bucket of pigswill in each hand, shoulders dragging under the weight. The slops had splashed out on her. The sow squealed frantically, thrusting her long snout over the top rail of the sty. He could see her enormous hairy ears flopping forward, the great girth of her looming behind. She was heavy in pig and always ravenous.

That was another thing. He frowned. They'd never bred pigs before, being content to buy a few weaners and raise them. Say the sow had fourteen young when she farrowed. Made a lot of pigs' mouths to fill. Was she counting on carting all that feed to the pens herself? Or putting in automatic feeders? The place, you might say, was in full production. It'd been built up. He sighed.

In her inexorable way she was changing everything. With Ruben's help. He'd painted the house. Always had him hanging around doing something, working to be sure, for she wasn't one to tolerate idleness in anyone, even a pet like Ruben. But he was drawing wages and that was good money going out. Mending fences, pruning fruit-trees, spraying the citrus, whitewashing outhouses, burning off. No end to it. Like a woman possessed, she was. Or possessing?

It occurred to him that the mental picture he carried of the ram-shackle, rundown property going to seed since his father's time and not improved in his, was out of date. It must look very different now.

Well. He was willing to bet she'd get jack of it. The ground wasn't up to much, all said and done, and on the land you had everything against you—seasons, contrary animals, ever-mounting costs . . . you

couldn't tell *him*—he'd been born to it. It all got a man down in the
end. He'd been only too glad to clear off to town every chance he got.

That was what his illness had robbed him of, the free and easy
life, no discipline, no hard work, no being tied down to regular hours
and monotonous duties. He did what he felt like doing and left the
rest. Christ, yes, that was what he missed. The long, lazy Saturdays
at the pub, the races, the yarning, the cards, the companionship.
The bi-weekly cattle sales at the stockyards, with dust rising in clouds
above the backs of milling beasts, the reek of horseflesh, of animal
urine and manure, the cracking of whips, the freely obscene language,
and, at the end of the day, washing the dust out of your throat with
rum. No, he knew damned well it was never farming as a job he
was addicted to, but the way of life it made possible. A lord's life
. . . that's what she used to say. "You live like a lord. Why don't you
work like a lord?"

He'd been content to enjoy it. Made enough to keep his head
above water. In a bit at the bank, of course—who wasn't? But *she'd*
soon paid off that mortgage.

Did it mean a man had no feeling for his land if he let it run
down a bit? he thought querulously. Neglect, she called it. He'd
thought of it as, say, a bit of easy living for him and the land. No
pushing. Just knowing it was yours and nobody was driving you
and making a living.

Why, then, had he married her? The old, old reason for country
people—he'd needed a housekeeper. To a farmer a wife is almost as
necessary as water. But that didn't explain why she'd accepted him.
Better than slushying at the pub where he'd met her, probably. He
had stayed there over a weekend and she'd shared it with him, nursing him back afterwards from a heavy drunk. Tractable enough,
she'd seemed, anxious to please, malleable. He'd married her confidently enough. She was meticulously clean in her habits.

He had no complaints, then or later. If she had any, she kept them
to herself. Sometimes she tried to organize the work around the
place and he'd had to put her down, keep her in her place. But what
was her place now? She was a kind of boss cocky.

When had everything started to change? There had been his illness when he was so dependent on her. And afterwards a kind of
passive resistance in her attitude had made itself felt. She became, in
fact, an unknown quantity, which accounted for his present wariness,
his uncertainty, his wish to placate her.

She came in wearing an old pair of his khaki pants cut down to fit
her, one of the boy's shirts of which she had a number, and an army
hat. It seemed an injustice that at—what? forty-two—she retained

the figure she must have had at sixteen. No face to speak of, but trim behind, slim hips, and swift feet that sped lightly about their work. Red-eyed with worry and resentment, he deliberately made it harder for her to get him into the bed, jerking away from her, going slack. But he failed to goad her into protest.

"You want your bottle before I go?"

"Not now. Leave it handy." He still disliked her standing near after she'd put him on the commode or while he used the bottle, after all this time. Not that it worried her. She usually whistled unconcernedly while, in an agony of embarrassment, he made water.

"I'm off to the corn paddock now, then. If you want anything urgent there's the cow-bell." A green cord fishing-line was tied to his bedhead, passed through the window, and attached to an old cow-bell hung above the barn. Its clamour could be heard for miles. He'd only had cause to use it once—when he set fire to his bedclothes. She'd seen to it that he gave up smoking after that.

As she bent to tuck in the covers he glimpsed the soft, muzzy growth of black hair between her breasts. You ever know before a woman who grew hair there? Wasn't feminine. He'd told her so, the first time he saw it. But she'd only smiled. He realized later why she smiled. She'd known he was wrong.

"Don't knock the Thermos over, now. Biscuits in the plastic box. Should be home about one. You'll notice I've left the windmill on but don't worry. I'm irrigating the young grapes."

There was never any irrigating done in his time. Lot of fancy nonsense in his opinion. It meant laying out money again. You couldn't irrigate for nothing. Was there no end to her extravagance? And just say anything to her! See how her little pink mouth hardened! A woman who never had a suitcase to pack her things in when she married—just rolled 'em all up in a chenille dressing-gown. That was how much she had. But look at her now! Spend, spend, spend . . .

Crikey hadn't come in this time. He waited at the door, yellow eyes following her, ears cocked, whining softly. When she left he bounded ahead of her. Joyfully. The mongrel!

Again the settling silence. He heard the Land-Rover coming down the track that led from the main road, its bumps and thumps and roars muffled by the overgrown oleanders. He'd never been one for a garden, but anything that grew without care or attention he planted lavishly. The Land-Rover stopped in the yard. Ruben. Always about lately, sometimes far into the night. He lived in a galvanized-iron and bag hut down by the river, picking up odd jobs and seldom having to go far looking for work.

"Get Ruben," the farmers said when they were short-handed.

Good-tempered, childishly generous, always laughing, Ruben was spoken of with tolerance. If not mateship. He'd been in trouble with the police a few times, nothing serious, and with that cherubic face you tended to forget there'd ever *been* trouble. One farmer wouldn't pay up when Ruben finished some contract fencing for him. Ruben had caught the farmer's bull one night and tied a length of plastic cord around its pizzle, letting the bull go again in the paddock. The breeding paddock, with cows on heat.

He'd used cars without permission of the owners, and been up for carnal knowledge of a girl under the age of consent (though everyone knew what Libby Chase was), stealing, and things like that. But the queerest thing about Ruben in his lonely river-hut existence with crab-pots lying about and fishing-nets festooning the nearby oaks, was the fact that no pets would stay with him. No stray dogs made their home with him, and no prowling cats made forays on his camp.

No sound from the Land-Rover of a slammed door, but that was usual since all doors had long since fallen off it. But he heard the crunch of boots on gravel, and Crikey, the pseudo-watchdog, barking aggressively in the distance. Let a stranger come near the place and he slept on regardless, or cracked fleas with concentrated attention. But a familiar figure like Ruben roused his noisy suspicion. That Crikey!

Ruben's head and shoulders appeared in the window, blotting out all light. Ruben was a big, gangling fellow. The sun, stronger now, and having dispersed the wisps of fog hanging about, struck through the upper panes of glass and lit his roughly sheared, innocently fair hair with dazzling brightness. Angelic. That was the look of him.

Yet Ruben was not young. The network of lines about his tranquil eyes was meshed deep, but you didn't notice unless you saw him in bright light, so smooth and brown was his complexion. His mouth was full and wide, lax, but there was the setness of maturity about its very laxity.

"How's it today, Mister Boss?" Easy, drawling voice with the eternal half-laugh, the bubble of spit at the corner of his mouth. Candid blue eyes regarding him benevolently. The childish face with its fleshy features expressing goodwill.

"No use complaining." Perhaps he'd go soon. It wasn't customary for him to come near the house when she wasn't there. Usually he went straight to where she was working to get his orders for the day. The uneasiness he always felt in Ruben's presence was intensified today. Ruben's reassuring smile filled him with disquiet. There was something he couldn't trust about a man who had no mates,

didn't drink, never brawled, always smiled—but why, for Christ's
sake? Ruben was a bit of a nong, everyone said so.

"Where's the wife?"

"Picking corn."

But instead of withdrawing from the window Ruben took out his
Gold Flake tin, extracted a paper, and set it wetly on his bottom lip
while he rolled the makings. Never in a hurry, Ruben. Except at
knock-off time. He'd seen him down tools a good quarter-hour before
time and he'd told her. She didn't sack him, though. Only saw to
it that he worked proper hours.

"She—er—said anything to you, like? Know what I mean? Been
discussing?"

Give him a hard stare. Not that it shifted the pleasant grin off his
face. Even his growled, "No. Why should she?" only seemed to
make the grin grow wider. He added, "You know her." Meaning
her quiet, secretive ways.

"Yeah." Ruben's grin broke into spitty, delighted laughter. "I
know her all right."

What the be-Jesus was he laughing at?

"So she didn't tell you, eh? Said she was gonna. But like you
said, we know *her*. Well, nothing for it but to tell you my way.
Baldock Brothers want to buy you out. Offered a good price. Nine-
teen thou., actually." Like many men who'd never had a dollar to
their name Ruben spoke of large sums with grandiloquent casual-
ness. His serene eyes suddenly grew menacing, but only because
they narrowed against the sharpness of smoke rising from his cigarette. "Not bad, eh? When your grandfather took up this land for nix,
in open selection. She told me. She thinks it a fair enough awfer."

"Might be. But I'm not thinking of selling, and it's not hers to sell."

"Come awfer it. Too bleddy right it is! I'm telling you now, it
wouldena kept a family of bandicoots before she got the reins. You
wouldena got a quarter that for it."

"Had I wanted to sell."

"You ain't got no say, see? Made it over legal to her, you did,
when your arthuritis got so bad you couldn't hardly hold a pen.
Someone had to write the business letters and cheques and orders
for stuff for the farm and that. You were only too glad to hand it
over, holus bolus, to that good woman then."

"You bastard! It's got nothing to do with you." He wanted to
groan with the indignity of it. That he should have to lie here and
listen to this great stupid ox wouldn't be so bad if it wasn't true. Only
it was all different to the way he said. She was submissive then. She
was humble. Kept her place at a word from him. Never presumed.

Wrote no cheques without his supervision, talked everything over first. He checked the orders—but how long now since he'd seen a wages sheet, a bill, a cheque book? "Mind your own business. And get out of here, you dirty swine. I don't have to put up with you and your sticky-beaking into my affairs. Go on, get!"

Ruben beamed at him. But how could such a rotten bastard have a—a *beatific* smile? It just wasn't possible.

"Arright, Mister Mighty Boss. Don't do your narna. Just reminding you of a few facts you seem to have forgot, like. What she shoulda told you herself. Don't understand her. Reckon she's not telling lies when she says she's fond of you. It's got me beat, a woman like that."

"You crazy coot—"

"No. I'm a lotta things, but I ain't crazy." Limpid, gentian eyes, all too reasonable. The terrible reasoning of non-feeling. For the first time he felt a stab of fear. But fear that was unchannelled, amorphous. "We been talking of going north, see? Up to the Isa. Big money there. Me brother's got a proposition if I can get a hold of a good truck. But we gotta have a van to live in as well. Gonna cost a heap. But no risk. There's money to be made there, you can ask her. Catch her risking money?" He laughed admiringly. "She's got a better head for business 'n you'll ever have. But you were always such an arrogant bugger you couldn't see it. But you can trust her—she don't throw no money down no drains. I've learnt that." He nodded vigorously, adding emphasis to his trust.

It couldn't be possible. A man smiling tranquilly at you while he planned to take over your wife, your home, and your farm in one sweep. He shook his head dazedly. "You and—her—"

"Like that we are," Ruben agreed, smiling, and holding up the first two fingers of his left hand, the gesture made ludicrous by the missing notch of his forefinger. "Time for you to know. I kep' telling her 'Tell him, what're you so soft on him for?' Well, now you know."

It was the smiling, untroubled face, the sanguine calm of the eyes, that unmanned him. He heard himself whimpering like a pup frantic to pee. He shut his eyes, but the face was imprinted on his vision, even to the rim of moss on Ruben's big teeth. Tears grew cool on his cheeks.

"No need to upset yourself atall." Words made more monstrous by the genuine kindliness in which they were spoken. Ruben would be smiling and gentle even as his fingers closed round your windpipe. "No hard feelings, I hope? Brooding gets you nowhere, I always say." He withdrew, chuckling. "Best I get going or she'll do her narna. Never knew a woman such a slave-driver. Well, that's the way to get on, they say. Be seeing you."

When the familiar stillness settled again on the room, a butcher-bird hopped on the window-sill looking for crumbs. Ruben must have knocked the scraps of sausage off. The bird lifted its head, emitted a heart-breaking trill, and peered restlessly about before dropping to the floor. He heard the threadlike scrip of its feet on the linoleum. Then the bird flew up, alighted on a chair-back, flirted its tail, and surveyed the man through beady eyes. It dropped a grey-white streak on the nylex-covered cushion and flew away.

He heard them come home at one, punctual as usual. Almost, he could believe he'd had a nightmare, that he'd dozed, and dreamt the interview with Ruben.

He followed their movements by listening. The usual sounds, nothing different from any other day. Ruben whistling as he washed his face and hands at the back door where a bench was set. Blurred voices. Slam of the fridge door. Lid of the teapot clinking. Crikey's sharp yelp of protest. Rattle of cutlery and china, then above everything else the clear enunciation of the news reader as the radio's volume was turned up. Light, quick steps coming down the hall to his room. She put the tray on the bedside table, plain food but appetizing, prepared with the unfussed cleanliness that was second nature to her. But how in hell expect a man to *eat*?

"You want your transistor?"

"I can hear the news." He pulled himself upright as she reached for the grey cardigan hanging on a knob of the bed and helped him on with it. "If I want to. Had a stomachful of news this morning already." He stared at the tongue and salad. The slice of cheese. The brown tea. "Why don't you poison it and get rid of me altogether? I've been crook so long nobody'd know. Or ask a single question."

"What a way to talk! It wouldn't be right.'

Morals, yet! "You think selling a farm over a man's head *is* right?"

"You signed it off to me legal. And you know why? Because you had the runs thinking I'd clear off and leave you when you got so sick. It was a bribe. You'd never bothered to treat me decent before. After the first coupla months you never even slept with me no more. Why? What was wrong with me?"

He stared at her. What *had* been wrong with her? Strange to think he hadn't even wanted her, had dumped her so easily.

"Think I don't know about that slut in Leichhardt Street? About the chooks you dressed and took into her, the baskets of grapes, the bottles of cream? Wasn't I as good as her?"

Well, better, come to that. But how to explain? Even to himself. He hadn't really seen her, and that was the truth. Never used to look at her, or listen to her, or think about her.

"You think there's nothing to be said for my side of it?" she demanded angrily. "Look at it my way. Ruben's got faults, but I'm awake up to them, see? I can handle him. I might even have a kid. It's not too late."

"But it's me you're married to, not him!"

"Put yourself in my shoes."

He tried to, and couldn't. He'd never known how her mind worked, he realized it now, not in all the years they'd spent together.

She said, "Who'll know anything about us when we get to Mount Isa? Who's married to who and all that? You won't have to sign anything, you'll hardly see anybody. I'll look after everything."

He considered. Took a good look at the reality mapped out for him. And, "If it's all the same to you, I'd rather die, I think. Just at first that's what I was scared of—Ruben murdering me in my own bed. Now I see it's the best way out. There's worse things."

"Don't be silly. You're not going to die and that's all about it. I'm not denying Ruben had ideas about doing you in—he'd split a man's skull as easy as a sheep's, that bloke—but I've got principles."

It was too much. He broke. "Please! What harm have I ever done you? Except perhaps neglect—please—let him do it his way. Take the farm, the money, everything, only let him kill me! Please. I don't want to live on."

"You mustn't talk like that. There's the physiotherapy, and that new treatment the doctor was talking about." She was plainly impatient with his mewling. "Dead's dead and living's living. I'm not a person to interfere with that."

"But Ruben will. Please."

"Never."

"Please!" Not in all the critical days of his illness had his courage failed. Never had the prospect of invalidism made him drop his bundle. Never in his life had he wept as helplessly as this, pleading, begging.

She crossed to the window and peered out at the overcast sky. "We've got to get that corn in. It's coming up like rain. The crop isn't included in what I'm getting for the place." She noticed his wet cheeks and the mucus running from his nose, and tossed him a handkerchief. "Wipe your face." Regarding him with a certain tolerant friendliness. After all, didn't she owe it all to him? You could see she was grateful in her own fashion.

"Don't worry," she said soothingly. "I'll look after you."

He believed her.

And all through the cloudy afternoon from time to time he heard Crikey barking, away in the cornfield. Chasing hares, stray cats, birds, or shadows—the week-old scent of a fox was enough to send him into hysteria. Sometimes Ruben brought him back with a whistle. Once he heard the woman's laughter mixed up with the barking as if she were playing with the dog.

That Crikey!

MARIAN ELDRIDGE

Paterson's Flats

"Then if you won't lean on my shoulder, Pa, at least take your stick!" Paterson ignored his daughter-in-law, conscious in the back of his scalp of her disapproval, as unaided, he drove one foot after the other out of his room and down the passage. Like sheep his feet huddled and jammed together, ready to bolt in all directions should his will-power falter. He heard Margaret, busy with clean linen for his bed, thumping obedience into his pillows. Her voice running after him snapped at his heels. "Remember, Pa dear, only to the bathroom and then straight back to bed!" He made a little rush at the bathroom door and shut it against her, locking himself in the bathroom's neat suburban safety. Women!

Breathing heavily, he clutched the chrome taps over the clean pink hand-basin, and saw instead his liver-spotted, swollen hands grown straight and strong as a boy's again, and black from bagging potatoes with his father all morning. He wanted to rinse his hot wrists, splash his face, gulp from his cupped hands. As he reached towards the brass tap that ran rainwater from the tank on the lichen-crusted stand into the crazed porcelain sink (on the wood stove hot water simmered continuously in the heavy black kettle), *her* voice stung him like droplets of steam: "Waste not want not! Mark my words, it won't rain tomorrow!"

Women! His shoulders sagged under a hundredweight of provisos. Deliberately the old man avoided the plug in Margaret's pink hand-basin, poking his fingers one by one under the gushing tap. "We'll do just what the doctor says, Pa, and we'll be back on our feet in a flash." Soapsuds trembled through his fingers. On his feet, she said. Didn't she know he'd been trying his whole damned life? If at first ... He sucked his gums with excitement as a scheme suddenly suggested itself. Steadying himself against the hand-basin, he thrust out his jaw at his enlarged image in the shaving-mirror: Today he would beat that bed.

But hurry. Teeth—he fumbled them from their beaker, wiping them across his lapel before plunging them into his gums. He grinned. *She* would have approved . . . eat with your teeth in . . . shave every day—shave! He glanced uneasily at his razor. If he hung around any longer Margaret would have finished his bed and his scheme would be ruined. Hang shaving.

In his haste to escape he brushed against the passage walls and the doorway of his bedroom. "Sit down, Pa," panicked Margaret, dropping a heap of bedding and pushing him into the chair by the window. "I'm sorry—you *were* quick today."

"Beat you, did I?" Paterson grinned, easing his old bones into the comfort of the chair. Its foam cushions sighed with success. This was the life, here by the window. Above the high brick wall that his son Colin had built to shut out the roar and thrust of the traffic, Paterson could just glimpse the sky. It was a sky white with stones. Stones were a sign of good soil, they said, if you waited long enough. Not an acre of sky could he ever see from that coffin his bed. When Margaret turned around and saw how much happier he was out of it, the dear kind girl would gladly let him stay up for his Akta-vite and—his chest hurt with cunning—by drinking the foul stuff slowly he would have all the morning to sit watching that old dog the wind at work. "He'd a'been a champion only I never got round to training him right," he muttered. Margaret looked at him kindly. There was such a bustle and bleating in his ears that her voice grew distant, like Kate's thin shout from the house to the yards when she'd wanted something, "I'm out of wood!" or "Dinner time!"

"Bother, I've forgotten your Akta-vite," Margaret was saying. Akta-vite! Why couldn't she let him be? "But I've brought you a surprise, Pa. Look." On his plate was a slice of orange cake instead of the usual dry biscuit. The dear kind girl. His jaw trembled greedily. He wished she would go away so that he could take out his teeth to eat it.

Something held her, however. "You didn't manage your shave this morning, Pa," she pursued him. "Listen dear, I have a plan. Why don't I shave you each morning after breakfast?"

Paterson's eyes bulged. Let a woman shave him! "I—I—I—" He began to cough.

Margaret made a little rush at him. "Dear, now I've tired you keeping you out of bed. Lean on my shoulder—"

Bed! His bellow came out as a whisper. "What about that—"

"Of course, Pa, right away—but are you sure you can—"

"*Akta-vite!*"

"Yes, Pa." In the doorway she turned triumphantly. "I told you the taste would grow on you."

A bus drummed along the street, or in his head. They were forever pushing him, Margaret and that doctor. Bed! He dropped his lip. The pillows sat like a tombstone, the green blankets, with the sheet turned down like a nudge to get in, were as thick and springing as new grass, as—Paterson jerked forward—as Klepl's river flats! The rye grew knee-deep, the clover bloomed. But where were the cattle? He struggled to his feet. He knew—in his grandson Timothy's bedroom, in a box called "Farmset". Painfully the old man set off on his second long walk that morning. It was a crying shame the way young Klepl understocked those flats of his. Paterson was forever telling him so. Time and again he'd put off whatever he was supposed to be doing, planting those bloody poplars in a new washaway, or burying a couple of milkers that had died of bracken poisoning or swallowing stones, in order to stroll over to his neighbour's for a yarn, cornering the boy with his advice until young Klepl was forced to take his foot out of the mounting stirrup and listen. "Never mind what anyone else tells you, Will, *you're* the boss now. Those flats should be carrying twice the stock you've got." "Yes, but it says here—" and Klepl would quote some newfangled nonsense from *Farm and Home* or the *Weekly Times*.

This stubborn streak in the younger man maddened Paterson: "Now, if *I* was running those river flats—" But Klepl would twitch his long hands, sliding his eyes like tea in a saucer. "Ar, she'll be right, she'll be right." That *she* made Paterson's heart pound his ribs in rage as with fingers thickened like artichokes he grasped what he could of Tim's farm set. Anyone could see it was Mary Klepl who ran the place. What else, when the woman spent her life beside him, riding every inch of the property, going to auctions, planting out seedlings as fast as he turned the garden beds, prodding Paterson about that saffron on their boundary fence? She'd have been a pretty girl, dressed up and silenced, if it had ever struck her to seek Kate Paterson's advice on women's fashions. Of course, it was Will Klepl who did the actual talking: "I'll come over and give you a hand with those thistles, Pat. Thursday suit you?" Pinned down, Paterson would agree with bad grace, fancying he felt *her* influence in the background, like a bloody conscience. . . .

"What are you doing hanging about instead of getting on with it I'd like to know? You mark my words—" (She was forever at him to mark her words—but twice down the passage was a fair effort, mother, and Tim's bed cradled him.) "In *my* day young people didn't moon about under their better's feet, they hopped in and helped—" glancing at her empty woodbox "—or improved their minds—" flinging her hand towards the cherished old books of her girlhood, those treasures he was always meaning to read "—or they went courting. You mark my words, *the world mirrors a man's face.* Have you washed yours? Got a clean hanky?" He'd forgotten, of course. "Don't polish your shoes on your cuffs! You never think of me feeding and dressing you all these years and you chasing after that Kate what's-her-name every other minute and nothing but a dirt floor in my kitchen! Eh? Eh? Your father would turn in his grave."

And of course she was right. He could never argue with her. Seizing an axe he would flee into the gully where a small creek ran more swiftly each winter, in order to ring-bark a few more of the straggling old gums along its banks that in later years he tried to hold with poplars. Damn her! damn her! as he gashed the sappy wood. It was his farm, wasn't it? His life? She wasn't the only one who dreamed of the thin stony hills turning themselves into a parkland. As for Kate, let her sit there in her fine room at the schoolhouse with her gloves and her parasol and her best hat! She had no hold over him. And if she fancied that he owed her an explanation—"But of *course* I understand how it is on a farm, Pat dear," cried his dearest Kate. "And my afternoon wasn't wasted a bit—look, I made you a scarf."

Oh wonderful, perfect Kate! She called the road "the street" till the day she died. He had been lucky. "Of *course* you're too busy to put a floor in the kitchen," she soothed. "Though I do think it's horrid of Will Klepl to insist you and he net your boundary fence when everyone *knows* rabbits are part of a farm. Now I've heard of a carpenter who could do the whole floor one weekend. I'm amazed that your mother—But if he's too expensive—"

"No, of course not," Paterson lied.

"And then I'll repaint the kitchen. And throw out all those old saucepans. Oh, I have such wonderful plans!"

So much energy . . . Memories flew against the old man like moths . . . His boots thrown off in her kitchen. New bread. Kate kneeling in her garden, her hand suspended above the soil and a seedling limp in her fingers. Himself leaning over the back gate, watching her. He wasn't too keen on gardening himself, fiddling about with seedlings he had to get in before the roots dried out and then chasing after weeds that sprang up thicker and faster than whatever he'd planted, especially after that time he dug in barrow-loads of rich rotted-down sheep manure from under the shearing shed. Poor Kate could hardly bring herself to touch the soil after that.

He smiled wryly at other memories . . . Kate creeping out at day-break to the cold stove. Himself opening his eyes one time just as she slipped her nightdress over her head, so that, although he wasn't in the habit of staring at her as she dressed, her gaze held his until he was sure that when she moved she would run to him, falling back into the warm bed as though she had all the morning to give him. And why not, he argued. Why should she come to him only at night, the last thing after setting for breakfast, shutting the stove, chaining the dogs, like some sort of sleeping draught? He stirred impatiently as she hesitated. What was she waiting for? Just as he moved to fling back the bedclothes, *her* voice startled him: "You mark my words—you mark my words—" so that to save Kate from indiscretion he cried harshly "Get your clothes on, woman! You'll freeze to death!"

For a moment her eyes burned him, then she plunged into her clothes as though she too felt the presence of a third person, fleeing into the safety of her kitchen while he huddled under the warm inertia of blankets. Hang the overdraft, he would buy her that piano. She deserved that. Hadn't she grown up amongst lovely things? The kind *she* had wanted—he really would read those old books, those treasures. He would— Suddenly there was Kate at his shoulder saying in a perfectly normal voice, as though he had just woken: "I've brought you your cup of tea, dear. You work so hard once you're up, you stay there to drink it." Funny how he never resented Kate's little domestic tyrannies! Love curled around him like the steam of his tea. Kate knew how to look after a man. He lay in bed until the cows' anguished bellowing at last forced him out to the milking shed. Damn it, he'd wasted half his morning in bed. *She* would have prodded him out hours before!

Clutching Tim's farm set, he began his slow return down the passage. Kate wouldn't like animals in his room. Swish! swish! with her mop. Hadn't realized farms were so dirty, she said; couldn't bear the smell of his boots. Swish! swish!—"Don't walk on the floor, dear!" As though he would dare! . . . But all the same a floorboard in the passage creaked—

"Is that you, my poppet?" called his daughter-in-law from her kitchen. "Timothy? What are you doing?"

The blood bolted in his ears. Don't let her push you around, son! But she'd beaten him every time.

"Did my poppet remember his teeth this morning?" called Margaret.

With dull rage Paterson levered his teeth from pocket to mouth. Always on to a bloke! . . . "Tickey, eh?" Klepl had said, springing upon him as drearily he pulled together two wool-covered strands of barbed wire where his sheep had been scratching themselves. He hadn't got around to dipping them that year. "Listen, Pat, you're fond of advising me. I suppose you've heard those river flats are coming on to the market?"

Paterson shook his head. "No one tells me anything these days."

"You've lived in the district longer than me. What do you reckon the flats are worth? Truth is, I'm thinking seriously of putting in a bid. Crazy, eh? Selling ourselves to the bank. But I look at it this way. It's a kind of promise I made to myself, to farm a bit of good land one of these days. Bloody hills. Cripple a bloke in the end." Paterson nodded. "And take this little bloke," Klepl rushed on, his eyes bright with dreams as he looked down at his small son. "We've got to think of his future."

Paterson felt suddenly angry. Didn't anyone think of *his* future? It hadn't even crossed Klepl's thick head that Paterson himself might be keen on those river flats. When Klepl, damn him, had at last ridden away, Paterson dropped the broken strands of wire and slowly walked back to Kate, half listening for the piano that often welcomed his home these days. Paterson's river flats. Kate would be pleased. He deserved a bit of good land sometime instead of crippling hills all his life. It would mean selling himself to the bank, of course. He'd had bad luck lately, carrying too much stock through a trusting faith in rain. He would have to be careful. Sell the piano. No more dresses for the girls. And Colin could forget about going away to learn wool-classing. His hands trembled as he pushed the little animals over the thick green blanket. He grinned. The rabbits were as big as the sheep. Soon fat cattle grazed knee-deep. He would cut grass hay in the spring. And put in a new front fence and paint the name over the gate: *Paterson's Flats! She* would have liked that. He listened in vain for something appropriate from Kate's piano—"See the Conquering Hero Comes". He'd forgotten that it was washing day, that since breakfast time Kate had been boiling clothes in kerosene tins on the kitchen stove and carrying them outside to be rinsed in big tubs on the back veranda. Late in the day though it was, she had just finished, and he watched her as she bailed the last of the greasy water over the brown patch they called lawn. She straightened her back when she saw him. Her smile and her voice were tired. "Won't it be wonderful when we put in that hot-water service next autumn? I'm so glad you let me write away to the plumber, dear. You can't imagine how much I've missed a proper laundry and bathroom."

He smiled faintly. He could never argue with her. He was beaten before he started. She came up to him. "You look sad. Have you been working hard? Sometimes I think I should have learned more about farming, gone out with you and picked up stones and helped you plant poplars—but so much dirt everywhere! I've been scrubbing and polishing for *years*—"

He began to laugh. He put his arms around her and leant his head on her shoulder, fumbling for words. "You're perfect, perfect. You're all I ever wanted of woman—"

Laughing until he was tired. Life was too strong for him. He needed a shoulder to lean on. Wherever was Margaret? Wasting time in her kitchen. She had already forgotten his Akta-vite once that morning and here he was still out of bed. He stood up. He would have to climb in by himself. Paterson's flats! He sank into the springing clover, drawing the green blanket right up to his chin. Sapped of energy, he closed his eyes to the truth: great hills and gullies wherever he thrust his legs.

M. G. VINCENT

The Vineyard

A WINTER's gale raked the plains and the despoiled ridges; but on the sheltered north-easterly slope of "Sugarloaf" the vineyard slumbered, warm in the midday sun. From the hilltop the young woman looked down, balanced precariously against the wind's assault. The ends of a head scarf whipped against her neck, and the luncheon basket on her gaunt arm bobbed about like a coracle in rapids. A few paces away her little boy, pretending to be a dog, lifted a wobbling leg against a fence-post while the two labrador retrievers waited, their brown eyes beseeching the boy to forsake tom-foolery for exploration. The wind attacked them; pinned their pendant ears erect like the velvet wings of gigantic black moths; whipped the spittle from their grinning jaws; but the expression of their eyes was safe from its fury and their beguiling glances continued backwards and forwards from the boy to the vineyard.

Pamela, glancing at this pantomime, was aware immediately of its import, and an intricate network aged her face as though acid had etched the dim tracery of constant apprehension.

"Colin!" she called to her son. "Hurry up! Let's get into the packing shed out of this dreadful wind before we all get bronchitis!"

"It's not dreadful!" he yelled, but she did not hear because as her words exploded without volition, she was standing again in the apple-tree at her parents' home and joining with the wind in revelry at two o'clock in the morning. The voluminous silk underskirt of her ball gown titillated every nerve from thigh to ankle, and in her mind the singing spun deliriously without knowledge of the hiatus of decay and death, which came to her a year later when she married the young R.A.A.F. pilot. From that time, all she sought was a refuge from conflict.

"Come on, come on!" she demanded. "This is a dreadful wind."

"Nothing dreadful! Is it boys?" The "boys" looked at him with joyful devotion. They wagged their tails and panted. They gave him the invitation again, turning to the vineyard. "We want to play in the binyard!" he yelled.

"But we're going to the packing shed for lunch," she protested. "We're going to mend the cases. If you're good you can hammer some nails." Regret was immediate as she visualized a nail disappearing into his hand. "Oh, there's only one hammer. Well, you can hold the nails for Daddy, because it's very, very dangerous for him to put nails in his mouth."

"I wanna play in the binyard," his refrain bleated. Holding on to the top fence wire he stuck his head underneath and, using the lower wires as a cradle, swung vigorously. "We'll be safe," he persisted. "No lions bears tigers robbers. No bad germs. Look down! There's even no wind. There's nuffin!"

She looked down once more. Certainly there was tranquillity; but was there safety? In this dormitory lizards slumbered; perhaps snakes, too. And in the friable loam ants laboured. These would do him no harm. But what else was there? She searched the sky but found neither bird nor insect. The plaintive blue jays, the garrulous starlings and soldier-birds were no doubt raising a clamour in the timbered swamp paddock, and the swallows kept close to the house eaves. To make sure that nesting magpies were not foraging for food, she pulled the lever which manipulated the rattlers. Hundreds of rusting tins danced along the rows of wire.

"There you are," he said in triumph, "what did I tell you?"

"Well, I don't know," she demurred. "Perhaps Daddy might come down for lunch, so if you promise me *not* to go out of the vineyard . . ."

"Why should we?" he asked amazed. "That's where we want to go, isn't it boys?" The dogs yelped obediently, twisting their bodies in convulsions of ecstasy.

"Just one minute," she cried. "If he can't spare time you must come up immediately I pull the rattlers. Immediately! If you don't I'll chain them both up for two days!" This announcement put a stop to their antics, and they looked at her with such abject meekness that for a moment her eyes held flecks of rejuvenating amusement.

"Come on, boys!" Colin shouted, his ardour undiminished. As though one person, they plunged through the wires, precipitating a ten-legged bundle down the headland.

Aware of their jubilation, she tried to repress the irrational fear which she had long ago given up all hope of expelling. Like a secreted radar, it had scanned her husband's war service, imprisonment, release, rehabilitation, and recorded every shadow on the embedded screen. Through the years of toil and penury, and even now, when she could look down with such pride at the pattern imposed upon the pastureland by his seven years of labour, a sinister signal threatened family, fields and harvest.

"If I feel so frightened, the danger must be there somewhere," she grieved.

On the marsh's fringe the slender saplings lashed at a patch of racing bulrush plumes. It seemed to her like a scene in a nightmare, the plumes a flock of flaxen sheep scourged implacably by scintillating scimitars. The frenzied flight never lost its impetus but never gained ground. Dimly she groped for clarity, feeling, rather than thinking, that the urgency which beset the striving individual accomplished nothing more than his final atrophy.

"That is what I am like," she thought. "If only I was like the vineyard! There it is, resting after the harvest, and content to just feed." High above the frosts, sheltered and warm, it seemed petrified, but its greedy roots were absorbing the riches of the cunningly contrived trenches, the lime and phosphates and the humus of the newly turned-in green crop of field peas and the lupins' purple spires. Their beauty had been a sacrifice to the vines' gluttony, she considered, seeing again in retrospect the whirling hoes of the tractor which had left the twelve acres stretched like a parchment, with an epitaph in convoluted writing black on the silver trellis lines.

With an effort she ended her contemplation and hurried towards the packing shed, casting backward glances in a vain effort to locate the boy and his companions.

Her husband's greeting was jocular. "Thought you were never coming. That wind has dried me right out. I can feel the roots of my tongue knotting around my windpipe. Just as well the vineyard's sheltered."

"It's simply beautiful down there," she told him. "Let's go down for lunch. Colin's there with the dogs."

"Good idea," he replied with an alacrity she accepted as a benison. "I'll go straight down . . ."

He interrupted. "Whoa there. What's your hurry?"

"Well, I've left them alone . . ."

"Weren't you brave!" he said drily. He grabbed his hat from a nail and joined her. "Silly ass," he said.

She thought: "Perhaps the bad years have gone at last. When I tell him about the baby I might be able to ask if he thinks we're all set now."

As they went into the vineyard her eyes searched for and found the boy, and she called out to him.

"Now look what you've done!" mumbled her husband as the boy and dogs sped towards them. He braced himself, but staggered under their onslaught and came down on his knees. "Fair go!" "Poor Daddy," she murmured, settling down beside him. "Mmm," he replied, dreamily defending himself and reaching for a sandwich. "Where's the fodder?"

It was some time before he spoke again. Then he said: "That six-acre paddock'd make a good little vineyard."

"Oh surely you're not . . ."

"Give me time to finish! Young Col can lay one out there when he takes over, and then he can gradually replant this."

She crossed her fingers and almost said: "Perhaps he won't want to. Or something else might happen." Looking at him she was thankful she had refrained, for today he looked like the young airman she had met at the gay party; the man she had told herself would never return. Often, waiting for him to come in from his fanatical slaving, she had wondered if only his body had come home, and perhaps his memory of things better forgotten: but she had never been able to ask. It had not occurred to her that perhaps he was planning for the future, without a thought for the past.

Lying on the warm soil, she looked at the sky, spread like an illuminated ice-field with white wind clouds skating past in diaphanous skirts. Her disquiet ebbed away and she told herself that he would be pleased about the baby.

"I'm a rabbit," Colin cried out. He began to dig wildly in the loam. The dogs growled deep in their throats, their bristles sprang erect and their tails stiffened. They pushed against the boy and sniffed at the diminutive hole, then thrust him aside and began excavating. Soil sprayed over the protesting man. "Go away with your dogs. Go away if you want to chuck dirt."

"We're rabbits!"

"Well go and be rabbits somewhere else."

Dragging one leg and hopping on the other Colin moved away, followed by the dogs.

Pamela thought, "Now is the time to tell him." She sat up and looked about her. "Where on earth did he go to so fast?"

"Now don't get in a panic. Nothing can happen to him here. He's safe as an oyster in its shell. Look, there he is. Gosh! Now what's he up to? Hey, what are you doing there? Come away from those vines!"

"I'm crumb pruning."

"It's not time yet for thumb-pruning. Come away."

Pamela, her arms tight around her legs, her chin on her knees, watched Colin moving along the trellis. She prayed: "Please help me not to be such an ass. I've been waiting for a day like this for so long, and now he seems his old self, it's me who can't relax. Please help me. Especially now another's coming."

The man stirred, mumbling, "I can't loaf here all day hibernating like the vines. I'll have to get those boxes done. Spraying tomorrow."

She leant forward. "There's something I want to tell . . ." Colin's anguished scream and the dogs' baying was followed by the eerie death cry of a hare. The man and woman sprang to their feet, and as they ran towards the frantic child and quivering dogs the man yelled: " Here, Rex; here, Hunter!" No sound of the tumult rose above the vineyard. It was as though the wind, racing over the hill-top, were a huge lid confining the bubbling to a cauldron.

At last Colin was in Pamela's arms, and her husband was tugging at the dogs' collars so that their eyes bulged and their tongues lolled pink behind the lacquer of saliva. She could not see their victim, and whispered, "Is it dead?"

He stood up and revealed the mangled corpse of a baby hare, its limpid eyes protruding with the fear which survives death. She said faintly, "A *baby* hare at *this* time of the year." In late spring and early summer they sometimes found the babies under the cool vine leaves, secreted there from the fierce sun until the mothers could safely return them to the forms.

"Eeeee," screamed Colin, quivering violently. Suddenly he became rigid: neither sound nor breath escaped. "Stop that!" His father hit him smartly on the arm. The child gulped and began to cry normally, the tears streaming from his puckered eyes.

"Better take him home," the man said. Once again his face had the pinched look of sickness and starvation, the out-thrust bones polishing the tautened skin; and at one corner of his mouth a pulse leaped.

She could not withdraw her gaze from the pulse. "It's back again!" she thought, and although pressed by a fierce desire to keep both man and child within a besieged sanctuary, her mind capitulated and her will dissolved.

"I can't go through it again!" she told herself. She felt the earth roll, and as she sank into the dark mists she identified herself with the doe seeking shelter for the leveret. The vines were bare, and as she fell she murmured, "There isn't a leaf."

He caught and gently lowered her, and said to Colin, "It's all right, son. Mummy's just fainted." He wondered what he could do to comfort the child while he atended to his wife, and was inspired to give him the hare. "I'll wrap this little chap up in my hanky, eh, and you keep him warm. Tonight I'll give him back to his mother when the dogs are asleep. Now sit down, there's a good fellow."

Contented, the little boy sat down, cradling the hare. He began to croon, and the dogs sat beside him, bashfully side-glancing while the saliva still streamed from their jaws.

This reedlike humming was the first thing the mother heard, and she listened for some time before opening her eyes. She felt the sun's warmth, the firm fingers pressed around her wrist, the hand smoothing her hair; then the sunshine left her, and with a great effort she raised her eyelids and saw her husband's face close to her own. For an instant it seemed the face of a giant: the lips a chasm, the nose a promontory, the eyes ponds. The spinning in her head moderated, and as the flow of blood resumed its normal rate she watched the features above her gradually resolve, and at last saw him clearly.

"Are you all right?" he asked anxiously. She answered, "I didn't do it with Colin, but that's what it is. I was going to tell you."

"Oh, so that's it!" he said gruffly. He fondled her hand. Only the constant clearing of his throat told her that he wanted to say more, but could not find the words. At last he said: "That's a relief. I thought you were really letting your imagination run away with you!"

Colin bustled forward with the hare, now protruding from the handkerchief. "I'm keeping it warm!" he said happily.

"And tonight I'm going to put the little chap in a safe place where his mother'll find him," the father said quietly.

Looking up into their unshadowed eyes, she found her image, and within that image fear looked back at her. At last she knew who cast the shadow on that inner screen.

NANCY KEESING

Old and New

A CAR and a station wagon, parked confidently between "No Parking" signs in the station yard, had brought the Henderson family, deliberately too early this frosty June night, down to Jack's Creek to see young Leila off on the eight o'clock city-bound train. They made it an occasion. The Hendersons excelled at occasions, separately or *en masse*, as now, gathered clannishly outside the booking office in a patch of sickly yellow light, standing in swirls of steam blown from a shunting engine that hissed and fretted by the up platform.

It was no less an occasion for having happened many times before, or because young Leila was twenty-five and experienced in putting herself aboard trains, planes and ships, the world over. Hendersons had assembled to meet or farewell family members or visitors for all the generations since the railway first came through, and before that their smart turnouts had been no strangers to the old staging yards behind the coach office. They remembered stifling summer nights when soot, steam and grit hung suspended in still air above Jack's Creek railway yards to settle slowly and softly on hair, skin and clothes; pouring rain when the passage-way outside the booking office was something between a very large puddle and a very small flood and Hendersons wore stout rubber boots, boat-like galoshes or plastic overshoes depending on sex and age sooner than join lesser breeds without the law on firm gravelled platform.

Jack's Creek had a waiting-room but Hendersons scorned to sit there, although they would occasionally put their heads inside the door to show it to travelling visitors. "Isn't it *fantastic*?" Leila's mother, Bunty, would cry. "That *marvellous* cedar table in a *waiting-room*. Goulburn has one too, but badly cracked." There was also a good fire of railway coals. "So *stuffy*," Bunty explained to shivering friends who clutched coats and scarves across their chests and endured howling draughts, "simply a *forcing bed* for flu."

Leila already had the return half of her ticket. There was no need for the clan to stand near the booking office except that the mystical moment when they would all move across to the down platform had not quite arrived. Andrew, Leila's father, stooped from his six feet eminence to examine the label on a young tree, firmly wrapped and tied in a swaddle of sackcloth and propped against the office's drab brick wall.

"Stan's sending another dogwood down to Mary," he announced. "You can't teach some people. She'll never get it to do down on the sea front. She lost one last year he was telling me."

Young Ross, his infant son carried high on his hefty shoulder, studied ritually an ancient poster describing noxious weeds. His wife Patty held little Samantha's red-mittened hand firmly, for Samantha had attracted the masochistic station tabby and was nearly bursting out of her scarlet, mock Eskimo coat in an effort to grab the strong striped tail which puss waved enticingly just out of reach. Patty's dark head was no higher than Ross's armpit. Thankful for his solidity which afforded some protection from the wind she kept near him, but faced away as she spoke urgently to her sister-in-law.

"Not too short, Leil," Patty instructed. "About an inch longer than yours—on me of course. But you know my size. Bright, but subtle. The shops here are getting past browns and greys but if they have bright colours they're crude." Leila, mini-skirted in stark black said, without a twitch of her long, white face:

"I'll do my best, Patty."

"And the stockings. I adore yours, but not for Jack's Creek—but something a bit different, you know?"

"It'll depend on the colour of the skirt won't it, Pat, but I'll try." She flexed her left leg in its long, white stocking with black criss-cross stripes. Patty moved a little backward, nearer Ross's sheltering bulk. More a Henderson every month of her married life—glad to return from her foray.

"Leila darling," her mother called. "You will ring David Jones won't you. Just *explain*. Don't bother to go near the wretches. But *really* what they sent was *quite* unsuitable."

Patient she listened to their messages. To Aunt Molly, as tall as herself, her father's sister who lived in the town. Leila was said to take after Molly with allowances made for thirty years' difference in age and for what dear Molly had been through. Molly, a war widow devoted to causes, whose ravaged features and white, expert hands were as much a part of Jack's Creek C.W.A., Red Cross and Horticultural Society as cups, tea-urns and scones. Young Ross had called for Molly on the way to the station, because, as Molly now explained:

"I've hardly seen you this time, Leil. It was a big dance to cater

for. Pity none of you made it." She added the last sentence perfunc-
torily. Hendersons never attended Jack's Creek dances, the annual
Show Ball excepted, a traditional occasion at which they arrived late
for a state appearance. They would infrequently roll up to outlying
hops in barns or church halls—these they enjoyed. Organizations in
the town merited subscriptions, not patronage. Andrew's active
presidency of the Horticultural Society surprised even himself. How
Moll could stand all those gruesome town functions none of them
could imagine.

"I'm sorry too, Moll. Next time we'll have to manage things better."

"And when is next time?"

"There's not another long weekend before October. So then perhaps. Why don't you come down to Sydney for a while? There's
always a corner at the flat."

"I might."

A moaning cry, so different from the shrill scream of the dear old
steam locos, a cry as if every curlew in Jack's swamp rose and
mourned together, a rush of cold air against legs and faces—the diesel
express on the up line hurtled arrogantly through and, at its signal,
the Hendersons moved across to the down platform, deserted except
for a red-headed assistant porter wheeling a trolley of freight.

"Nice fire in the waiting-room," he said cheerfully. "Lots of folks
in there . . . Nice and warm for the bubba," he added. A very raw
youth and no native of Jack's Creek.

"Thank you," Leila said. No one moved from the spot at which
the appointed carriage always pulled up.

"Is she on time?" Young Ross asked.

"She's jake tonight, mate," said the boy, and pulled his famous
frightful face at little Samantha. He had much to learn. Samantha
smiled sweetly, tolerantly—a Henderson born knowing all. Whistling
"All My Love" shrilly, off-key, he wheeled his trolley away down
the platform.

Andrew found little to say to his daughter here. At home, out at
"Mookerwa", they'd had a good three days and many hours together
bouncing over paddocks in the Jeep. He'd delayed the chore of
inspecting fences until her visit—it made a pretext for going round
the whole place together. He truly felt Leila was home again only
when she had changed into an old shirt and breeches, discarding
whatever the fashion of the moment as casually as a tree its bark.
He had no interest in the bark of trees, but much concern with
sound, well-grown timber. Those people who thought Leila so like
Molly hadn't known his mother. That's where the likeness was.
Mother was a Henderson too, a second cousin. Poor old Moll; a good

sort, salt of the earth, bit of a saint really, and just as well with so
many long, childless, widowed years to fill. But if you knew Leil
and Moll the resemblance was pretty superficial. They were tall, fair,
long faced (and so was he, and so was young Ross, dash it all) and
graceful. They both had *that* from Mother—pride, and the sense to
accept height. Even in these idiotic short skirts Leil was graceful—
she'd the legs for it, which is more than you could say for young
Patty. But then Hendersons often mated with dumps—and bred back
to type. Who would believe dear Bunty was mother to Ross and
Leila? Molly and Leila alike! But as to the precise difference he was
hard put to define it.

You couldn't say Leila had brains and Molly none, for Moll was
an intelligent, able woman who, in another setting could have
managed a successful business with the skill and resourcefulness
she chose to devote to those Jack's Creek organizations which claimed
her attention. You couldn't say Leila had charm and Molly none.
Molly, in her fifties, still had a way with her and had once charmed
poor Bill Allan clean out of his wits and into a very happy marriage
—its war-terminated brevity was not Moll's fault. She'd had at least
one chance of marrying again, or so Bunty reckoned. But the fellow
was a bit ordinary—might not have fitted in too well with the family
and Moll wouldn't leave Jack's Creek. Probably right, probably sensible. But a waste.

And had Leila charm? For him, certainly. But here she was,
twenty-five, and what sort of life did she live in that flat of hers, with
that job? Plant research. Why couldn't she do her plant research in
the grass roots—on "Mookerwa"? He was honest enough to shrug
the thought away. No farmer in his senses could be, or afford to be,
contemptuous of science. Indeed Leila's interest in natural history
came directly from himself and if, occasionally, he regretted that he'd
not gone on to the University when he had the chance, there'd been
a lot of satisfaction in encouraging his daughter and much to be
gained from her knowledge now.

Leila turned to him, away from her mother.

"Nearly time, Dad. If I'm not up again until October there'll be
plenty of time to test some of your notions in the lab. And you're
sure to hear from Dr Komarov long before that and I'll write too.
And of course if he wants any information that isn't in your notes I
can probably answer most questions, soil, aspect and so forth myself.
Anyway, he'll get the samples on Monday morning."

"Komarov," Andrew growled. "He sounds a clever chap. And all
of us were newcomers not so long ago. Still, he may find a bit of use
in an old Australian's ideas."

"I keep *telling* your father," Bunty said, "he should try to get some recognition for all the work he does. *Hours* he spends with those notes of his. All those observations of birds. The insects he keeps. The museums are at him all the time. I have to *protect* him." Her little face darting emphatically in and out of her brown fur collar. Her little booted feet positively stamping.

"Here! Here! Here!" cried Samantha. Half a mile away the glaring eye of the tender bored through mist and shrieked its warning.

"Leil," Molly touched her arm. "About the flat. I might come down for a week. Next month?"

"Just give me time to air the blankets."

"If I can get away." She spoke quickly, in a low voice. "I'm thinking of taking a trip—overseas. I'd like to talk it over. Before I'm too old. Don't say anything to the rest of the family yet."

"It's a wonderful idea—do come."

"We could, perhaps, both confide."

Ross put the baby's face close for Leila to kiss his fat cheeks. She sniffed a piece of fluffy wool from his cap and suppressed a sneeze. Andrew looked around.

"Just the one case?"

"Yes thanks, Dad, and your box of samples."

"No *rug*, child! You'll *freeze*."

A last kiss for wistful Molly, for Bunty, for Andrew. A wave for Patty, Ross, the children. Then on to the train, gratefully. A clean, old-fashioned carriage divided into compartments, three seats to a side facing each other, with a side corridor the length of the carriage. High-backed leather seats and big framed pictures of "The Orient Cave, Jenolan" and "Panorama on the Stonehaven R." Stiff yellow varnished window frame impossible to open. Hot, scratched, pewtery foot-warmer. Worn re-patterned carpet. So far no one else in the compartment. Marvellous.

Outside white Henderson faces smile like multi-mirrors. She waves and the mirror people wave. Samantha blows kisses until, at a jolt, Jack's Creek recedes and is lost at a curve past the end of the platform. Suspension now for three and a half hours between the two places that the word "Home" means. The word "Family"?

Home at "Mookerwa" is sprawling, many-roomed and the rooms large. Its kitchen and pantry cover an area bigger than the whole flat, which has two bedrooms and is not exactly tiny. The "Mookerwa" kitchen is white, always scrubbed, frostily painted. There is a bleached wooden table and whitened benches. When Bunty came to "Mookerwa" she had thought of linoleum tiles. When Ross brought Patty home she sent for sheet vinyl samples. But the immutable

"Mookerwa" kitchen turns stranger women into Hendersons more quickly, perhaps, than anything else—benches and table, sandsoap, the cream enamelled coke stove; in the pantry scoured cream pans and indestructible, deep old Chinese vegetable baskets and enormous wooden-lidded stoneware crocks for bread and flour.

Each "Mookerwa" room has its own character and nothing and no one changes it, despite new loose covers, curtains, mats and pictures. The living-room, dark and tree-shaded, has absorbed (and rejected) nineteen-thirties radio consoles; glazed chintz and, briefly, genoa velvet; standard lamps with ivory silk shades and black cord trimmings. It presently ignores a television cabinet and chrome space-heater. Every room has also its constant, unvarying smell—always pleasant but unique to each set of four walls. The living-room remembers fires despite the frequent use of the new space-heater, and even in midsummer. One bedroom has lilac although no lilac grows on that side of the house. To the bathroom clings an odour of brown, slippery globes of Pears Soap—the globular shape has been unprocurable these twenty years. If you were to set down a blind Henderson anywhere inside "Mookerwa" he would immediately know by his nose in which room he stood, although Henderson wives and their cleaning women experiment with polishes, disinfectants and detergents like anyone else, and as often as anyone else.

On the long deep timbered verandas Samantha's plastic wheel toys make as little visual impression, among immemorial deckchairs and seagrass tables, as once did Leila's tricycle and dinkie or Andrew's wooden wagons. The present house was built by Andrew's grand-parents to replace a smaller cottage. No one knows who, which Henderson or wife, stamped it forever and unchangeably as home.

The flat at Kirribilli is one of ten apartments honeycombing the shell of a white, three-storeyed mansion built at much the same time as "Mookerwa" homestead, but nothing about the place is static and the frequent moves, comings and goings and sub-lettings of its tenants do not altogether explain this quality. Even the little-altered entrance hall alters from day to day, sometimes from hour to hour, although nothing more solid could be imagined than its red floor tiles, cedar staircase whose strong posts are carved like squat Doric columns; its huge, brass-fitted door surrounded by plate-glass portraits of English poets (Shakespeare, Dryden, Tennyson, Wordsworth, etc., labelled neatly, and Martin Tupper but no wicked Lord Byron). A massive metal hallstand holds a hideous but splendid mirror and anchors a liver-coloured marble table whose black iron cabriole legs are each tortured into a claw-foot with wicked gilded claws. The hall door is usually open and the space dances with light although too far

from the harbour to catch water reflections. At night a street lamp
glows through the poets. Yet light does not seem to be the whole
secret of the hall's variability.

Leila's flat is on the first floor. Her bedroom opens on to a segment
of balcony partitioned from its neighbours by plywood walls. Between rows of roofs and the tops of trees a green glass square of
harbour can be seen and the shining top of one opera house sail.
Indoors in the little kitchen, wall shelves carry jars of spices, herbs,
condiments and ingredients unknown at "Mookerwa". Above the
stove in a row graduated copper saucepans hang from hooks. Every
room recalls Leila's student scholarship overseas—woven covers,
pictures, pots, ornaments. She returned four years ago. But here too
nothing is constant for many days together. She often alters the
placing of furniture and objects and her sewing-machine is usually
open in the second bedroom. She designs and sews well and often
unnecessarily replaces curtains, cushion or chair covers.

Family?

In Sydney family are errands, letters, a few never visited aunts
and cousins and Great Aunt Lucy Prentice at Vaucluse. Leila occasionally visits Aunt Lucy who is no Henderson, loathes "the country",
cannot believe dear Bunty actually enjoys life, plays bridge or mah-
jongg with old friends every day and is sure Leila's work must be
quite fascinating provided, of course, that one cares for that kind of
earthy pursuit.

The train rocks farther away—farther and farther away from
family, hurtling through the cold tablelands moonlight towards
friends. Leila switches off the reading light and through the window
looks at the hunched forms of sleeping cattle, grey, rocklike. What
breed? If mixed it does not trouble their rest, any more than does
the racket of the passing train which mutters, Komarov, Komarov,
Komarov.

She and Andrew talked about the laboratory a good deal these past
few days. Dr Komarov, Dr Komarov. Never Vass. Vassily. Or Kom.
Much about his ideas, plans, enthusiasm. Nothing of what, in the up
train last Friday evening, she had planned to speak.

Round the curve ahead the tender sways and screams its signal
in a shaft of steam, a glow of fire. There is a long tunnel here with
Wattstown stop at the other end. The reading-light on again.

At Wattstown the carriage fills. Two very pretty girls and a young
man now share the compartment. The young man, Dan, hoists suitcases up to the wire luggage rack. He is well dressed—U. Australian
well dressed. Brown tweed coat, grey corded trousers, white shirt,
brown tie and stout, well-polished brogues. No bow ties or wizard

pointed shoes for Dan. He is muscular, shorter than Ross but not short. A country boy. The girls match him, casual, expensive. The dark girl in the grey flannel slack suit has to be Dan's sister, the family resemblance is so strong. The tawny, feline little person snuggled into a white clipped-lamb coat wears someone's sapphire engagement ring—Dan's perhaps.

Their conversation, uninhibited and personal, is Hendersonian. They have taken Leila's measure as quickly as she theirs. They know that she will read, or seem to read her book, her white face expressionless, her hands moving only to turn pages—she will not deliberately listen to them. Nevertheless she knows soon that Dan's sister is Viv and the other girl Sue. At every station now the train becomes more crowded.

The seats next to Leila remain vacant. Three tipsy youths have several times looked into the compartment but Dan's pleasant, insolent stare has been effectively daunting and they have crashed off along the swaying corridor. Leila is grateful.

At Walden where steep, weeping sandstone cliffs overshadow the little railway station, the seats are occupied at last, and at the last moment by a middle-aged migrant couple who nearly missed the train. Breathless, stout, strung around with boxes, suitcases, bags, coats and a basket of fruit they settle in agitated spurts, beaming and voluble. Dan is helpful, Viv and Sue polite and agreeable. Everyone stoops to retrieve a dozen oranges which spilled from a paper bag and rolled maddeningly beneath low seats. The incident breaks the ice but does not make friends. The woman thanks everyone in passable English but directs re-packing in her own language.

The three young people talk on, but impersonally now and with constraint. The couple converse too, partly in English and partly in what Leila thinks may be Hungarian but is not certain. It is now warmer in the train. The gradient falls steeply here and the frosty tablelands are far behind. From one of these curves, on a fine day, one can see the ocean.

The woman leans across her husband and taps Leila's knee. She has a pink, merry face. Framed in a kerchief her features would be attractive, but the hat with ribbon trimmings does not suit her.

"These Jenolan caves," she nods at the framed picture above Sue's head, "you have been there?"

"Yes," Leila says, "a long time ago."

"The long weekend in October we are going. One must reserve far ahead. You enjoyed to see those caves?"

"Oh very much. They're very spectacular." Leila had hated the place; its deadness, its still, damp, enclosed air.

"And on the rocks," says the husband, "are the vallabies?"

"There are plenty of wallabies—anyway near the hotel."

"Bush robbers discovered Jenolan," says the man. His very bright, brown eyes move all the time he speaks, and when he smiles half disappear, still darting glances in all directions, into creased folds of skin. "We have an encyclopaedia. We like to read. We hope to see. I would like," he says "to have seen Ned Kelly."

Leila laughs.

"Yes, it is funny," says the woman. "We are curious. Always we wish to explore, you know. We have come so late to this country."

"Too late," says her husband with a sigh. "Too late to be pioneers and too late to be Australians in this century."

Leila cannot think of anything to say.

"Our daughter we have visited for a week," the woman says. "Her husband, his grandfather, he was a pioneer. We were anxious about this marriage, naturally. A very different life for our girl. Very different people. Country people everywhere change more slowly, I think. But she is very good. She likes the old house, you know. For Australia, very old. Not very rich, but very happy, thank God."

"Thank God," says the man. "There are bush robbers' bullet-holes in the kitchen wall."

Three pairs of eyes opposite catch Leila's almost instantaneously. Of course they have been listening, no one could help it. Everyone, the foreign man and woman too, laughs together and Sue, the girl in the fur coat, whistles a couple of bars of "The Wild Colonial Boy". The couple love this. The man has a deep bass voice which dominates the singing.

"We know so many of your songs—cleek go the shears, boys, cleek, cleek, cleek." But after four or five shared songs Leila is suddenly not at ease. It is the girl Sue. Sue is not simple. Sue is unobtrusive and clever and will not jeer or scorn openly, but now steers the singing to absurdity—to choruses which emphasize the man's thick accent and which make the woman seem a burlesque of her own pleasure. Sue is a Great Aunt Lucy—no Henderson. She will make trade with innocence and is not kind.

You cannot protect a happy perspiring man and a woman in an ugly hat who love to sing:

"Oh had I the weengs of a tottle dof."

Dan is puzzled too, restless. He is Andrew, Ross, Molly—uncomfortable, cornered by what he senses but does not comprehend. He looks at his watch and everyone follows his glance outside the windows, to outer suburban streets. His unease infects them all. The singing is over. Coats buttoned, faces powdered.

At Central the train has barely stopped when the foreign couple make cheerful farewells and, loaded with their belongings, expostulating together, push into the corridor and out to the platform. Leila and the other three stand, ready to leave but waiting until it is easier to emerge. No one talks, but they smile at each other. Through the corridor window Leila glimpses Komarov impatient on the platform outside. His presence is half expected, partly feared, rather hoped for. He looks agitatedly up and down the train, everywhere but through the window in front of him to where she stands. He, of course, would have been among the first to jump off the train—eager. Impatient always to have done with one episode and to begin the next.

When she steps down from the carriage he grabs her suitcase and embraces her as heavy and affectionate as a rough tame bear in his brown overcoat. Andrew's sample box is nearly squashed he is so overjoyed at reunion. "Your train is five minutes late, my swan." Her blood assures her that she, too is glad, but it is not her way to be exuberant like this in a public place and behind his shoulder she sees Dan, Viv and Sue—they glance towards her.

"No Vass, no, I'm not tired," she assures him. And "Yes, they're all well, my family."

HEINZ NONVEILLER

That Part of the World

FOR WHAT happened I blame the job. I blame the country, Jack Johnson and myself. In that order. I cannot blame Katherine, for I never
met her and, in any case, she is not to blame. Mainly it was the job.
It created the setting, a setting capable of sustaining a long nightmare.
Yet the job was no more than a microcosm of the city and the country
in which I live. Dreary, unnatural and soul-destroying. I ask no one
to believe me, for every man lives in another country and some do not
live anywhere.

My name is Janos Smith. Janos is genuine, Smith is not. My real
surname is Hungarian or maybe Czechoslovakian. I am not sure. I am
only sure of one thing: that I spent my childhood in a concentration
camp near Salzburg, Austria, with a man of uncertain nationality who
sometimes claimed I was his son and sometimes that I wasn't, con-
gratulating himself for the selfless love he had for me, an orphan boy
he'd picked up somewhere or other. He was a drunkard and a liar and
yet he managed to convince the emigration authorities that he was a
steady labourer, an Austrian, with all his papers in order, and they
permitted him and me to emigrate together to Australia. For four
years he worked with a group of painters, painting Housing Commis-
sion cottages in country towns, then I ran away to the capital city of
the State and began to fend for myself. I was then fourteen years of
age.

By the time I turned thirty I was an old man, bitter and adrift.
Gaunt-faced, with deep and hungry eyes that always seemed to have
a touch of fever, blond moustaches and dry blond hair, I looked like
all men who have no country to call their own. True, I had become
naturalized in due course, but I was still a man without a country.
I want to emphasize this point. I was a man without a country. Such
a man is very lonely; he longs to have a country. He longs to have a
mother and a father, however stupid they may be. He longs to iden-
tify himself with a native earth, a native people. But he has no roots.

He cannot act; he can only let himself drift, his life is meaningless.

I drifted from job to job. Bar steward, greenkeeper, public relations assistant, freelance journalist for a New Australian paper, taxi driver and finally, proof-reader for the *Daily Truth*.

Now that what happened has happened and is all over, I blame no one, really. I can see I should never have accepted this job. It was the beginning of the nightmare. I entered the long and brightly lit readers' room one evening to apply for the position of assistant proof-reader, and instantly a profound melancholy settled on me and stayed with me during all the time I worked there. Finally I realized it was inevitable that I should have progressed from one futile job to another until I entered the building and the room where the most futile job of all was being done. For what is more futile, more unnatural, than to proof-read manufactured news and lying advertisements. I had arrived at the centre of the city and it was the centre of futility, a perfect microcosm of futility reflecting the dead soul of this century.

I stared at the room with its four neat rows of desks, ten desks to the row, at the narrow aisles between the rows, and felt angry and fruestrated. I looked at the bent backs of the forty teams of readers and assistants reading news-copy and advertisements. I needed a job badly. I had no choice. Perhaps I should rather have starved.

I was given a sheet of paper on which there were a number of words to be corrected and I corrected them and was given the job by the boss, a fat and gruffly impolite old man by the name of Mc-Namara. The following night I started as an assistant with Jack Johnson, a permanent reader, and the nightmare got under way.

Johnson was an Australian—that is, a man with a country. He was a little older than I and tended toward putting on too much weight. His face was square, plain and kind, with faded blue eyes and a vigorous mouth that seemed out of place. When they introduced me he asked: "What part of the world do you come from?" and I said, "Nowhere and everywhere," and he said, "That figures," and we understood each other quite well enough for the execution of our monotonous job.

I always believed, right from the first night, that this job was more than I could take and sooner or later I would run berserk and perhaps kill someone—McNamara or one of his staff who were forever running up and down the aisles, dropping proofs and urging us to read faster with casual grunts, glowering looks and even sharp warnings. Yet it was placid Jack Johnson who, a year later, lost control of himself. Perhaps I passed my madness on to him.

But I must be fair. Most of the readers were quite content with the job. They did not at all see it in a nightmarish light. It paid well, did not require responsibility, put little strain on one's health and was secure. A placid man of average intelligence was likely to find this an interesting and at times even challenging job. Few noticed they were slowly going under in the monotony of it, few noticed that a man with a country should not have to find himself redu ced to this.

Jack Johnson said he had never thought about it, although he was a man who showed signs occasionally of a less than placid temperament and a penetrating mind.

"All jobs are much the same," he said.

"But what about being alive and throwing security to the winds," I said, trying to find the words that would bear the weight of meaning.

"What about it?"

"A job should be a way of life," I said. "It may be a hard job but it should have compensations. It should keep one in touch with—with nature. It should enable one to feel more alive, enjoy life more."

"You're not in here all the time," Jack said. "What you do with your own time is your own business."

"But can you live your life in separate halves?"

"I don't know what you're getting at," Jack said. "This is Australia. Once you're out of this building it's nobody's business what you do with your time."

"Wouldn't you like a better job?"

"Naturally, but what can you do about it?"

I thought about what Jack had said, what the others had said, and I discovered that although all of them were men who had a country, they were forfeiting their right to it. A country that is not being lived in truly, that is not being beautified, that is not being loved, such a country is in danger of being lost. I wondered how long it would take—one morning a whole nation of men, with few exceptions, would wake up and find themselves in a strange land.

As the weeks passed and we worked ourselves into a routine, Jack began to open up a little and told me about himself. He was second generation Australian. His great-grandfather had been Dutch. That accounted for his vigorous mouth, which seemed out of place. He had become interested in the Old World only lately because a few months before I began working with him he had married an Austrian girl by the name of Katherine.

He asked me what this and that word meant in German and how it was pronounced; he was good at picking up the right pronunciation. After a while he opened up even more and confided in me. There were things concerning his wife he did not understand and he hoped that I, being from "that part of the world", might be able to explain them to him. He did not say this in so many words but it was what he implied.

He told me in detail of his courtship of Katherine. At first he merely bored me for I have a cynic's regard for romances of the heart, but at a certain point I began to listen with more interest. He began to disclose some of his more intimate thoughts and actions, driven by some internal pressure to talk of them, as though he were trying to untangle a meaning he could not quite fathom.

"She kept hesitating," he told me one night. "I'd asked her to marry me several times but she wouldn't say yes or no and it was getting me down. Make up your mind, I told her. Give me more time, she said. She wanted more time. She said it was a big step to take. She'd only been in this country for two years and she said she would have gone back home already if it hadn't been for me. It wasn't as if I didn't understand but she kept asking for time and it got so bad that I had only to open my mouth for her to say, please give me more time. I just couldn't give her any more time. It was getting me down too much."

"Why did she come out here?" I asked.

"To visit her brother and learn the language and see a bit of the world before settling down. That's when we met. I know her brother."

"Quite," I said.

"I couldn't stand it any longer," Jack repeated, his face turning a mottled red. "You know how a chap feels. I decided to do something about it. And I did. One night after a movie I drove home and said: "Let's get this straight. I'm sick of waiting. Let's go to my flat and see if we're suited to each other. If we aren't, let's break the whole thing off. If we are, let's get married." She turned quite pale but didn't say a word. She knew this was it. I drove her over to my flat and took her up and told her not to worry, it was going to be all right."

Perhaps he suddenly felt that the privacy of our desk had made him say more than he had wanted to say, because he stopped talking. I glanced at him. His flesh was firm and there was goodness in his face, goodness and a certain glow of energy. A woman might find him desirable. He leant over to my side of the desk and brought his face unpleasantly close to mine. He radiated a warmth that repelled me. His eyes were the eyes of an intelligent dog.

"This is between the two of us, of course," he said.

"Quite."

"After all, what's a chap to do in such a situation? I couldn't wait forever for her to make up her mind. I thought maybe she was scared of sex or something. I wanted to find out."

"She was homesick," I said.

"How did you guess?" He was genuinely surprised.

I shrugged my shoulders.

"True enough," Jack said. "She was homesick. But I had to put an end to it, didn't I? As it turned out, we were made for each other and she says she's happy now and glad she went ahead with it and married me. Like they say, sometimes a chap's got to take the initiative in these matters."

He pulled a photograph out of his coat pocket and handed it to me. It was of himself and Katherine outside the registry office.

"That's Katherine," he said.

There she stood, tall and lovely, with a little space between her and Jack. She wore a full skirt with a broadly patterned border and a white blouse. Her neck and arms were bare. Her face reflected a mood of deep longing as if even at that moment she had been homesick; but probably I imagined it and her expression was caused by little more than the shadows of her high, strong cheekbones. She wore pigtails.

It would be ridiculous of me to say I fell in love with her. I am not the sort of man to fall in love, especially with a photograph. But the plaits stirred some deep half-forgotten feelings and memories in me. In the camp near Salzburg there had been a little girl with pigtails. She may have had a streak of gipsy because she was wild and untameable and had the capacity to invent countless games on the spur of the moment. As I looked at the photograph of Katherine I forgot I was in the reading-room of the *Daily Truth*, and remembered that little girl. And I remembered other moments of my childhood. I was standing in a deserted street in Salzburg, listening to someone playing on the piano in one of the friendly rococo houses. I stood quite still in the sun under the many open windows and listened. There was a slight breeze. I can't have been more than eight years old and at that particular moment I was completely happy and almost had a country. The illusion passed soon enough.

Katherine was part of all this. With her skirt, blouse and pigtails, she even looked somewhat like the little girl who had been my childhood friend. Suddenly I was obsessed by a single idea: *She has a country*. And then it struck me how monstrously selfish and ignorant a thing Jack had done in marrying her. All at once I hated him. What had he to offer her in return for the loss of her homeland? A bit of love no doubt and a dose of sex. So Jack thought that this would keep her happy, but would it? I looked at the picture once more. She

had an intelligent face, but her intelligence was not of a kind Jack
would ever be able to recognize or communicate with. It was a quick
and gentle kind of intelligence, depending a lot on a familiar environ-
ment; it was rather like the sunshine on the open shutters of those
windows, and the breeze and the music. Jack might sense its existence
but he was more likely to appreciate her body. To my mind this
body had betrayed her; it had handed her over to the body of Jack
Johnson.

A month or so later I began to notice signs of uneasiness and tension
in Jack's behaviour. When reading proofs to me his normally strong
voice would gradually fade away or grow hoarse. He missed obvious
mistakes and became absent-minded. He contracted a permanent
frown that made him appear short-sighted. He began to brood.
    "How's Katherine these days?"
    "Oh, all right," he said, unwilling to talk.
    So I waited. Barely half an hour later he opened up.
    "She's just homesick, I guess. It's nothing really. Mum came up
from the country the other day and she says she'll get over it. Mum
says all girls tend to get homesick in their first year of marriage even
if they've only gone to live around the corner. I don't like to see her
miserable, though."
    How I envied her her homesickness! I too was homesick but did
not know in which country to place my homesickness. Sometimes I
attempted, by an act of will, to geographically lodge this homesickness in the most likely country. I would say to myself: It is almost
certain that your father was or is a Czech. Well, be homesick for
Czechoslovakia. It is a beautiful country with a beautiful music all
its own. But the fact is, Hungary and Yugoslavia, Poland and the
Ukraine are as likely places.
    "I don't think it's that kind of homesickness," I said. "I think it's
more powerful than that."
    "You're probably right. She says she misses the mountains, the
woods, the snow, her language. She says she can't take to this
country." He was bewildered. "I can't see anything wrong with it."
    "She wasn't born here."
    "Maybe she'll come round yet and feel that she belongs," Jack said
hopefully.
    It was at this stage that I decided to intervene actively. Perhaps there
was a way in which I could help this girl? And all at once I knew
what to do—it was obvious, inevitable, even though I felt a little
uneasy at my almost demonic certainty.
    "I tell you what,' I said to Jack. "I have some books in German.

If you like I'll lend them to you. Reading in her own language might make it easier for your wife to overcome her homesickness. She might feel less cut off from her native land." Even then I knew it was a highly unconvincing argument, but Jack fell for it.

"That's an idea," he said.

Now, I did not have any books in German, so I went to a bookstore the following day and bought several. They were mainly novels by Austrian authors. Jack took them home and reported the next evening that Katherine was happy with them.

"When she's finished them," I said, "I'll bring in some more."

Soon I had to buy more books. I succeeded in finding a book of coloured photographs of Austria.

"She can't stop looking at it," Jack said, perhaps a trifle worried. "Maybe when she has a baby it'll change her. I didn't know she was going to be so homesick. But she doesn't want a baby just yet."

By that time it should have been obvious to Jack that I was pouring fuel on the flame, but still he suspected nothing. I decided to be completely frank with myself. What you really want to achieve, I told myself, is to break up this marriage and make her go back home. Have you any right to do this? And what do you get out of it?

Right a wrong, I told myself.

But how do you know you are righting a wrong?

Well, if things weren't the way I thought they were, I would never be able to break it up. I would never gain possession of her mind.

Possession of her mind. . . .

I must admit that for a while I had serious qualms. I was disconcerted by the exhilaration with which I purchased more and more books. Perhaps the job was to blame. I lived in a nightmare and in a nightmare all things become simple. I could not think of a single counter-argument. I continued to buy books. They dealt in a variety of subjects, all of which were carefully chosen. The psychology of sex, the art of love, the history of Austria—I even discovered a beautifully written autobiography by an Austrian author who had gone to America only to return ruefully to his native land. The months passed by and I stuck to my plan. Once or twice I even laughed at my tenacity. Had I not gained an interest, a hobby, as it were, which gave me something of a purpose in life?

"Those books of yours are doing her a lot of good," Jack told me one night six or eight months later. He had been taking them home to Katherine during all that time without ever asking me what they were all about. He was not particularly interested in books. The *Daily Truth* constituted his main reading. "She's not been emotional for weeks. She's much calmer."

What he took for calmness, I took for the beginning of clear thinking. I smiled wryly. A feeling of pride and even triumph filled my heart. That I should be able to read the mind of this girl whom I had never met! That I should be guiding her towards a maturer self-knowledge!

So I continued buying books. Katherine was quite happy now, Jack told me still a little later. At the same time he looked more and more puzzled and uneasy.

"Why don't women like sex?" he asked me late one night. Then I knew I had gained possession of Katherine's mind.

"Don't they?"

"I don't know," he said wearily. It had been a busy night and his worries had worn him out. He could not refrain from confiding in me, he was too tired to hold back. "Take Katherine, for instance. She seemed to like it a lot at first but . . ." His voice trailed out. He added: "When she was homesick she was all right, she had passion, but now that she's not homesick any longer . . ."

I waited.

"The trouble is, I don't see enough of her these days, what with me being on nightwork and her working during the day. Did I tell you she's taken on an office-job?"

"No, you didn't."

"Well, she has. I asked her why. Don't I earn enough money? I asked her. She didn't answer. I don't know; she's changed. Why don't you come over sometime and meet her?"

"What good would that do?"

I must have spoken too triumphantly because for a moment Jack looked at me almost warily.

"I don't know," he said slowly. "But you're from that part of the world. Perhaps you can tell me what makes her tick. Frankly, I don't understand her any more. She's so quiet. Hardly talks."

"I'm not a psychologist."

Jack laughed. "No, seriously. Why don't you come over sometime?"

"It might make her homesick, seeing someone like me."

"I wish she'd never stopped being homesick. Then at least I knew where I was with her."

"Give her time."

I did not want to meet Katherine. I felt vaguely that it might undo what I had achieved.

"Does she still wear pigtails?"

"In a bun," Jack said. "Why?"

"I just wondered."

"Let me know when you can come over."

"I will."

I could see from the corner of my eye that he was looking at me with an expression of perplexity. Then with a sigh he picked up another proof, handed me the copy and began to read. Houses for Sale, Cars for Sale, In Memoriam—a conglomeration of lies and clichés. I had difficulty in keeping my eyes on the copy. It was all so futile, and yet here we were, eighty people, sitting and reading this stuff in this terrible room, the desks arranged neatly in four rows, ten desks to the row, the staffmen running up and down the narrow aisles like bitches on heat, and Roger McNamara bullying readers who fell behind in their "output". The hum of voices rose and fell, broke and scattered, coagulated, without rhythm, without meaning. Who was it said words and the human voice were made for communication? I looked across the room and through the tall windows that ran along the length of the wall. Clouds were drifting through the night, lit by an invisible moon. Even in this bright room, I could see them drift. They gave me the illusion that not they but we were drifting through the night, that this room, no—the whole skyscraper was drifting through the night like an ancient slave-galley and that we were the slaves, rowing, rowing, rowing, for no other purpose but to die one day and be cast overboard. . . .

It was only three weeks later, on a Friday night, that things came to a head. Jack was hardly himself when he told me what had happened.

" 'I don't ask you to pay my fare back home,' she said to me. 'I worked for it and saved it. All I ask is your permission to go.' Just like that, out of the blue. I argued with her but she wouldn't listen to reason. It's the first time I've ever shouted at a woman. 'Give yourself time to think,' I said. 'Don't rush.' She said she'd had plenty of time to think. 'I can't take it any more,' she said. What am I going to do?"

He was asking *me* to help him! He was asking me with tears in his eyes to help him. Heads to our right and left turned in our direction.

"Let her go. Marry an Australian girl," I said calmly.

He stiffened and caught his breath. There was a moment's silence. I looked at him and realized he had been drinking during the tea-break.

"You're not on *her* side, are you?" he asked heavily.

"I'm on no one's side. But I can't see why she should have to suffer from homesickness all her life just because you rushed her into a marriage." The words were sharp and I meant them to be sharp. I had looked forward to this scene for a long time. It satisfied me deeply to hurt Jack. That, too, was part of the nightmare.

"Janos," he said slowly. "What do you mean, I rushed her into a marriage?"

"You told me so yourself."

"She'd never have married me if I hadn't rushed her."

"Then she'd never have had reason to leave you."

"You're against me," Jack said in a high-pitched voice. "That's what it is. You're against me. You've been against me all the time!"

"Have I?"

His fist came down on the desk and his face went red. A pool of silence spread around us.

"Why?" he shouted. "Why are you against me?"

"Am I?"

"Yes, you are, you bloody bastard! I thought I smelled a rat. I can see it all now. You've been against me all the time. You wanted to break it up all the time. All those books. I can see it all now!"

"What can you see, Jack?"

"You bloody bastard! All those books. They only made her more homesick. What I can't understand is why? Why?"

"You're raving."

"What are you getting out of it? You've never met her. You're not even from her country. You're a Czech or something. I should never have trusted you. You're just a bloody trouble-maker. Time I woke up to you!"

He jumped up and I expected to be attacked at any moment, but he was still shouting with some coherence and the whole of the readers' room froze.

"You bloody reffos shouldn't be allowed into our country!"

"That's right, Jack, blame someone else for it all."

"They should line you up against a wall and shoot you, the lot of you. This is a fine country, it's a bloody fine country and we're making the best of it, then you bastards come along . . ."

"Jack!" I spoke calmly but sharply enough so he would not miss a single word of what I was going to say to him. "Jack—this is not your country. This is my country."

He stared as if I had gone mad, but never in all my life had I been saner. I had spoken in order to hurt him but all at once the significance of my words came home to me and I knew what I had said was true.

"Jack," I said. "There is a country for those who have no country, and this is it."

This was more than he could take. He threw himself on me and tried to strangle me. For a few seconds it looked as if he would suc-

ceed, the silly fool, then I knocked him back and two readers pinioned
his arms.

I laughed. I laughed and looked at them all, at the whole pale-
faced, wide-eyed, sorry lot of readers and assistants. I would have
liked to make a speech but I realized they would not understand, that
what I had to tell them was too new and too complicated for them.
They had allowed themselves to be ruled and regimented and they
did not really have a country, because only free men have a country
and they were not free, they had never learnt to be free enough to
love it, being too busy with sex and security and all the rest. But I
was a free man and so I could take their country away from them
without stirring a finger while they succumbed to their futility. I
would have liked to tell them, but it was too new and complicated
and already the staffmen and Roger McNamara were advancing
toward us.

I walked out of the room and down the concrete staircase and out
into the night. In the fresh air my mind cleared and the nightmare
dissolved as if it had never been. I saw clearly that I had broken up
a marriage, dispossessed a man of his country and taken charge of it.
I had put everything in its place where it belonged.

E. V. WHITBY

Nundalla

No, I'm not making excuses nor apologies, said Grampa sternly. I'm just telling you how things *was*.

In those days we called them blacks; and there was two kinds—the kanakas worked the cane plantations down by Cleveland; and on this side, out from Fortitude Valley, we had the native tribes, and wild and savage and murderous they were, too.

No, and I won't have that either. We didn't take their land away from them. All they did with the land was pass over it now and then to get that red ochre from the creek-bank for their war-paint. Then they would have a corroboree down by the waterhole where the black swans used to breed.

Hungry people must be fed. What we did with the land, was plant acres of vines; and paddocks of pasture for the cows and horses; and maize and pumpkins and sweet potatoes. Oh, the pumpkin pies my Ma used to make! And we had hens. And bees. And my Aunt Elizabeth had a small flock of guinea fowl; she was very clever with poultry.

Well, Uncle Horace had been a schoolmaster, and that's what he said: the starving millions must be fed, land can't lie idle just for a few people to use for their amusement. According to him, the Old World had its revolutions about that sort of thing.

But we called them blacks because they weren't white. And that reminds me—talking about corroborees—I'll tell you about Nundalla, and you'll see what I mean.

There was this corroboree. The tribe had come for their clay, and they had plenty of room around the waterhole to build their fires and have their dance. We didn't stop 'em so long as they behaved.

My dad and the uncles and the hired men, they got our animals in early, closed in the stables and sheds. They fetched in the farm implements too. We cousins were sent to bed early and told we'd get what-for if we went near the windows and porches. A couple of

men patrolled outside with guns; and another man with a gun
stayed with us; and the women set buckets of water ready—we had
shingle roofs and they were afraid of the blacks' fire-sticks.

Nobody really expected them to attack us, but those natives could
get as crazy on stamping and chanting as anyone else would do on
raw rum. So it was best to be ready, see?

Well, nothing happened. You know how sound a healthy kid will
sleep, dead to the world. So when we woke next morning it seemed
to have been a quiet night.

We woke early, and wanted to know what had happened at the
corroboree; but none of us was let out until the men had gone as
far as the waterhole and looked around; and for all they could see
the tribe had vanished.

So we were let out, and we ran down the home paddock. And
that's where we found her. Nundalla. I dunno whether the rest of the
tribe had helped her or whether she crawled there all by herself; but
she *was* all on her own and looking to the white folk for help.

She had been speared, and we never knew how it happened,
probberly some wild flinging of weapons; but she had been sliced
across the belly, a long straight cut like a split in a water-melon.

I guess, a fraction of an inch more, and she'd have spilled her guts
out. It was a near thing. I never seen anything like it except in the
war. But at this time I'm telling you of, I was only a kid, one of the
youngest in the family.

Well, the older girls screamed, and made to faint like their mothers;
and one of the boys ran for Aunt Charlotte, she was the nurse of the
family. But when Aunt Charlotte came, with a bucket of hot water
and disinfectant and a lot of old sheeting, that young black woman
wouldn't have none of it!

She knew what to do, she said. She told us in her gibberish and
broken kind of English. She wanted to stay just where she was, under
the big gum outside the fence; and she wanted some of us children
to fetch her mud from the swamp; and asked would we give her
little-bit kai-kai later. . . .

No, she didn't say tucker. The kanakas said kai-kai. And I guess
the word spread. Anyway, I was there and heard her, and *I'm* telling
you what happened. . . .

Well, I think Aunt Charlotte was glad not to have the job. She
carried her bucket away again, and left us to it.

Now, what Nundalla wanted was not the red clay from the creek-
bank but some blue mud from a part of the swamp. And we brought
her the mud in an old dish. At least, some of us did, the rest couldn't
stand the sight of all that blood. But some of us did.

Now, she pulled that ugly wound together and held it with one hand while she plastered the thick mud on it with the other.

She sat there, near the butt of the tree, and put on the mud a bit at a time, and as it dried put on more, over the cut and above and below, until she was closed up like in a big plaster cast, see?

And then she asked again for food. Well, the show was over, all the others ran away to play, and I was the youngest there, and so the job was left to me.

I had to fetch her porridge in the morning—same as we had, cracked corn hominy—and a mug of tea, all with lots of sugar. Then there was pumpkin and sweet potato and corned beef for dinner, and another big mug of tea. And bread and dripping or molasses for supper and more tea.

And, of course, being just a silly kid, I said a silly thing.

At first, Nundalla looked a bit frightened; and when I took her food, she would look at me in a kind of begging way. And she made me think of our retriever dog. Well, I didn't say that she looked *at me* in that way, I blurted out at table that she looked like a retriever dog! So I got the regular job of carrying her meals. Go and feed your pet, they'd say to me.

I guess I got a sort of feeling that I owned her. I can see her now —a little dark bundle under that giant tree.

I had to duck through the post-and-rails fence to get to her. And beyond that was the swamp—tea-trees, paperbarks, huge ladder ferns, and the loveliest climbing maiden-hair fern swinging in big swags from one branch to another. Jackasses. Cicadas chirping, such a sharp noise. Birds calling. And wild violets, yellow and blue, in masses in the shade of the trees. Well, I guess it couldn't stay that way. They drained it later, and put a concrete canal through; made it into a sports reserve, and called it after an alderman!

Well, Nundalla. You know how a kid is about time. It seemed to me that this had gone on forever; and would go on forever, too. Probberly she was there about ten days but it might have been longer. All I know, I went down one day with her breakfast, and she was gone.

There was the place where she had sat, worn a bit hollow, cleaned up by the ants. And there was the broken cast. That was all that was left of Nundalla.

I looked at the mud cast, and the inside was like a pattern—where her navel had been, and a long puckered mark where the wound had healed in a big ugly scar. And I went home and cried.

They told me that she must be quite better, and she knew where to go to her tribe, and she had gone to them where she belonged.

But I had a feeling like you don't want to give back a dog to the feller that's thrashed it and half-killed it.

Well, that's the story of Nundalla. And that's what I was telling you. If Nundalla had been a white woman, do you think all the white men would have run away and left her in that shape? How did *they* know that *we* would help her?

In my young days, being white was a feeling you had, like being an Eldest Son, or a Good Provider, or a Good Shot; or being a Highly Respected Schoolmaster like my Uncle Horace; yes, and like being a Good Hand with poultry like my Aunt Elizabeth. . . .

See?

MAXWELL PAINTER

The Haircut

I was still trying to get Gilworthy's agreement as we walked down the corridor towards the lifts, but he wouldn't be moved. He is one of those soft-looking but obstinate men.

"It's a system that works, Ian; I know that from experience."

"It might work well enough in the Antipodes, but I doubt whether it would do so here." His voice was plummy. He affected not to notice my use of his first name. His pronunciation of "here" made it sound a lot better than anywhere else.

Arrival of the lift gave me time to dampen down Antipodean backlash. As we dropped from the eleventh floor, wedged among homing typists, I simply asked: "Why not?"

"Because the psychology here is different." Then, amiably but forestallingly: "A fact which you will have to get into your shaggy Australian head before you're here much longer."

There was plenty about Gilworthy which I had, in the months since my arrival, found irritating. His firm belief that "the psychology here is different". His frequent insistence on the importance of "background"—he knew I had none in the sense implied. His ability to kill a bright idea with the air of a man performing a creative action. His use, to me, of the kind of slightly personal remarks which he didn't make to other colleagues.

I was never a shaggy Australian. In fact, I dressed neatly and, it could probably be said, conventionally, worked regularly, and tried to meet the English, so far as such a thing is possible, on equal terms.

Yet in the mirror-lined walls of the lift I saw an endless series of Gilworthy-and-me, diminishing to eternity in an ocean of typists, and every image of me had the line of its collar violated by a little fringe of back hair. Gilworthy's thousand necks were, of course, razor-trim. I saw him smiling sardonically in infinite repetition, but the faces of the girls were all politely blank.

When we got to the street I gave a rather short answer to his

"Good night, old man" and walked off briskly the other way.

At five o'clock it was quite dark and had been so for hours. Traffic ground wetly along. Buses had their windows well steamed-over and inside they reeked, as I knew, of menthol jubes and damp tweed. Saturated, the sky dragged itself low across the buildings, and an aggressive wind patrolled the streets. Occasionally the word "Bar" proclaimed sanctuary, but I was headed for one particular pub some ten minutes' walk away through a tangle of old side-streets. A good top-coat and a smoulder of Antipodean resentment gave me protection from the cold.

Lamp-standards were far apart in the narrow streets through which I walked, and puddles lined the worn flagstones. It was a relief, after a few minutes, to find myself approaching a spill of light from a huddle of small shops. The first of these, as I came up to it, proved to be a barber's. Through the window I could see a hanging light throwing yellowish radiance over the unoccupied barber's-chair below it. The effect was rather that of a gilt throne in some museum show-case, with the same slightly eerie suggestion of the suspension of time. The shop was empty of people.

I hadn't argued back much to Gilworthy. I never do, for it was some past sarcasm of his that had first made me aware how easily the Australian voice, aiming to express indignation, takes on a whining note. As a result I often came away from work in a state of bottled-up resentment, and this feeling now almost sent me on my way; rather childishly I felt that I should have a haircut at some time of my own choosing, and not because Gilworthy had applied to me a ridiculously inapt epithet. But then I remembered the evidence of the lift-mirrors. A haircut really was needed, this shop was conveniently empty, and I could spare the necessary ten minutes or so.

A bell jingled overhead as I entered, and again as I closed the door behind me. It was the customary barber's establishment, but gloomier and more depressing than most, and hardly warmer than the street. There were the usual tools of trade laid out along a bench as well as some cabinets, a hat-rack, and a trouser-polished form. There was a handbasin and, above it, sitting upon an anaemic point of flame, a small water-heater. Cheap smoking materials stood on the counter and on some shelves behind it. A few magazines scattered along the form looked years old. The door at the rear doubtless gave onto a parlour; its glass panel was made discreet by a lace curtain, upon which flickered warm light from the other side. Then someone's shadow fell across the pane.

The door opened and I caught a glimpse of quite a cheerful fire in a corner grate, and it seemed to emphasize how not only chill but stale was the air in the shop. The proprietor came in, skinny fingers engaged with the buttons of his starched coat.

He was bald, stooped, frail, old; but, if displeased to be dug out of his warm snuggery, he didn't show it. Indeed, his face pushed itself into an ingratiating smile, revealing the worn tips of antique false teeth, as he said: "What may I have the pleasure of doing for you, sir?" It was a flourish of notes on a cracked old flute of a voice, elocution rather than speech, an ancient vocal affectation now grown into second nature. The way he held himself was also unusual. He did not so much stand as take a stance; one expressing, in a rather exaggerated way I thought, respect and readiness to serve. Altogether, he seemed not so much a barber being unself-consciously himself, as an actor playing the role of barber in some dated stage-play.

"Can I get a haircut?" It was said brusquely, for I was already wondering whether it would not have been wiser to have asked for a box of matches, or a packet of cigarettes, and then got out. The shop itself was uninviting, and of the barber I had formed an instantaneous impression of dislike. It was not just that I was young enough to wonder whether a man so old could still be clean.

But his "superior servant" manner, his servile elegance or elegant servility of speech and movement, jarred upon me. It was brought fully into play as he helped me out of my coat and ushered me into his chair.

I do not like those who incline the head deferentially towards other men, listen to their lightest words with unction, and display respect towards their very hats and coats and shoes. As I sat in the hard and chilly embrace of the chair, the old barber moved behind me to hang up my overcoat, with enough care to suggest that he was concerned about its *comfort*, settling it into place with a couple of little obsequious pats; and I wondered whether he knew that I was watching him in the mirror.

"Your coat is not very wet, sir; has it stopped raining?"

"Temporarily." It was a reluctant mumble. Were the wraps and instruments clean? It seemed doubtful. I was not disposed to be chatty—certainly not to be drawn into making banal remarks which would be received with flattering attention.

"It is proving to be another hard winter, sir; don't you think?" And he waited, fingers of one hand lightly rubbing the back of the other, for my answer. Waited with every appearance of interest until I grunted something, then turned obliquely away to the basin and began scrupulously washing his hands.

Which at least was reassuring. But he wouldn't turn his back to me, and his stance, although he was stooped sideways over the basin, still expressed a degree of deference. If the whole show was intended to please, it had the opposite effect on me. Perhaps I lacked, in Gilworthy's word, the "background" to appreciate it. Somebody else might manage to do so; and Gilworthy probably would. He and the barber would be able to arrive at a psychologically symbiotic relationship; for Ian (as he didn't like me to call him) had a taste, or so I liked to think, for situations involving the humiliation of others. I was keyed-up about him at that moment; for once in the chair it seemed to me that I was sitting in this uncongenial shop solely because he had, probably as a way of turning my mind from the point I was trying to make, called me "shaggy".

As he took a towel and dried his hands, the hairdresser showed his old-ivory teeth again and said: "Coming from where you do, sir, you must notice the cold even more than we do. Sydney, is it not?"

But I wasn't going to award any prizes for picking an Australian accent. The Sydney part of it was probably just a lucky guess. Still, the English are experts at this sort of thing—classifying people and allotting status on the basis of pronunciation. Although the game is not as easy as it used to be. In the end I just said: "Yes."

Then, dropping the towel on the end of the bench, he said solicitously: "I'll put the radiator on for you, sir."

Actually, all I wanted him to do was cut my hair quickly and let me get away. Gilworthy would have told him so. For God's sake, man, get on with it; I haven't got all day—that or some similar rudeness, plummily uttered, and the barber would have reacted like a dog given a stern but not unfriendly cuff. I doubted whether, if I tried to stir him up, the results would be quite the same. Yet why not? Keeping the tone consciously dry and a bit sour (the Gilworthy touch) I said:

"We could certainly do with it. The place is not precisely over-heated. And I'm also in a hurry."

No, he didn't like it from me. Then so much the worse for him. I replayed in my mind the speech just made. Hadn't a slightly apologetic note crept into an utterance intended to be incisive, with ludicrous effect? Oh, damn it, I was becoming so self-conscious about the way I looked and sounded, most of all in the eyes and ears of Gilworthy, that I was almost afraid to express myself in my own natural way. I finished on the Sydney note of: "I'm easy. Suit yourself." It didn't sound very gracious.

It began raining again. I could see the drops running down the

window. There were no, or few, passers-by. The light went out in
the shop across the street (a small travel agency, windows full of
sunny posters—come to Jamaica, to South Africa, to Australia). The
barber got his radiator out of a cupboard, dumped it on the floor,
unrolled some old inflexible flex, and stood with the plug in one
hand. Then he bent over, painfully and slowly, stretching out his
arm and jabbing about in the shadows under his bench. Not finding
the socket he crouched lower and peered into the dark place.

His starched coat showed an old split seam in the middle of the
back, and the split widened as he crouched further. Some wisps of
white hair fell away from his skull. I saw a vein pulsing at the side
of his head, and his collar biting into folds of flesh at the back of his
neck. It was alarming and I slid a foot towards the floor. "Let me find
it for you."

It had the wrong effect. He flapped an arm in almost senile agitation and panted: "No, sir! No, sir! It's just here." But it was several
seconds before I heard the click of the switch. In the meantime I
returned my foot to the foot-rest. It wasn't my radiator, my power-
point or my business.

For a while there was no sign of the power's having been applied.
The first evidence of it was a metallic smell. A tiny glow followed,
then the ancient appliance gave a series of clicks and began to generate
heat.

"An old 'un, sir, but it goes. It will very likely go longer than I do."
This seemed quite probable. The old chap's coming up had been
more painful than his going down. He sank onto the form behind
me and slumped a little sideways. One hand rested on a copy of
Country Life, and that arm was propping him up. He was panting in
a shallow, quick way, but was trying to suppress it. I peered at him
in the mirror; watched him undo the buttons of his white coat and
grope, finger and thumb, in a waistcoat pocket. "Are you ill?" I said.

He certainly looked it. Waxen, washed out; eyes behind their
lenses like slugs in aspic. His finger and thumb inside the waistcoat
pocket moved in a regular kind of way. I imagined that they had
found some small thing—a pill or capsule—and were abstractedly
rolling it around between their tips. Then he said:

"I thought for a moment it was a turn, sir. I've had one or two
before. They say I shouldn't bend over." He grunted, then after a
few seconds straightened up a bit.

"It's just a condition, you see. Something I have to keep an eye on."
He stood up carefully. "So long as I watch it, that's all; so long as I
keep an eye on it." He buttoned up again. The capsule or whatever
it might have been remained in his pocket. Perhaps it had only been

a coin or a small charm of some kind. We were gazing at each other in the mirror but I doubt if he really saw me. It was very quiet; in fact, the only sounds were the simmering of the water-heater and the muted noise of traffic from the main street some hundreds of yards away. We remained motionless and silent for a while, then he seemed to bring himself into focus and said:

"And now the radiator; is it well placed for you, sir?"

"Oh Lord, yes! Don't touch it. As a matter of fact"—to take his mind off the thing—"I really am in a hurry. Perhaps I could call back tomorrow."

Again it was the wrong thing to say. With many apologies for keeping me waiting he began with pallid sprightliness to get to work.

And was making a respectable enough job of it, judging by what I could see in the mirror. I might now have begun to feel sorrier for him, and even to like him somewhat, if he hadn't gone on to undercut my sympathy by the tenor of his talk. It was mostly about how much better situated he once had been than he was now. When younger, he had risen high enough to be of service, as regards the trimming of hair and the removal of whiskers, to many quite well-known men. A baronet had been grateful for some advice about thinning hair. He had for some time attended regularly a bedridden knight in his own mansion. He had once had the honour of shaving the corpse of a lord. He had been able to a large extent to choose his own custom. Of course, the notables he mentioned had constituted the peak of his clientele, which had had, of necessity, to include rougher-hewn material at the base. Even there, however, he had tried to be selective. I can't now remember the list of the varieties of men he was on the whole quite pleased to serve. Most Western Europeans were on it, so were Americans, and Colonials of the right colour, and there were some others. I thought sourly that he made it seem so inclusive that one felt like warning him against an excess of tolerance and democracy. The contrast between all this and his present situation was ridiculous.

A one-chair business in an old shop dismally painted out in cream and brown enamel; a small stock of cigarettes, favouring the cheaper brands; some inadvisable-looking smoking mixtures in glass jars. How much money would actually lie in the cash-drawer behind the counter tonight? Things had changed.

There is a kind of chiacking which does not always export too well.

"And Australians?"

"Sir?"

The cut was well advanced; in fact, almost finished. I watched
the affected elegance of his hand-movements, then repeated:

"Rough old Australians. You don't mind serving them?"

He took it seriously. The mirror reflected, suddenly animated in
denial, his pallid face and worn false teeth. The effect was macabre
—a ghost aghast at a lapse of taste. Also his voice squeaked a little.
I saw the possibility of getting beneath his surface manner, of pro-
voking some give-away response; perhaps, who knows, a touch of
the Cockney. Which would leave me laughing.

"Some people might say that Australians"—I must have been trying
to play Gilworthy and the barber off against each other—"lack background." Strangely enough, I think I wanted to hear it denied, but
he just made a kind of "mm-m" sound and concentrated upon the
last few snips to my hair. He was quite composed again.

"You never thought of going to Australia yourself?"

"I? Oh no, sir!" He was quite decided about that.

"You would have found it very different from here. What's your
name?"

"Perch, sir."

"No, your first name."

"Roy, sir?" For the first time a bit off balance.

"Well, Roy, in Australia your regular customers would call you
that, and you would call them Jack or Harry or whatever it might
be. Even a knight"—this was drawing the long bow—"might let you
call him Perce rather than Sir Percy. What do you thing of that?"

"It doesn't appeal to me, sir. I daresay it's very democratic." The
voice was cold, and it insisted on the "sir". This was reproof, and
it brought me snapping back.

"What's wrong with that? You'd still get a tip for a good job,
and you wouldn't have to kowtow for it." It was the same old backlash, but here I didn't have to suppress it as I did with Gilworthy.

"Sir, I hope that I never . . . that I always willingly . . ."

He suddenly sank into agitation that seemed out of proportion to
my words. His hands trembled as he combed my hair; then he put
the comb down on the bench and turned away from me, just standing
and gazing obliquely away. I felt uncomfortable but saw no need to
apologize. He still just stood and looked away, but seemed a bit as
though shivering under the stiffness of his starched coat.

"Why don't you admit it? Nobody gives service for anything but
money."

He still kept silent for some seconds; then said in a distressed but
determined way:

"I'm sure that any gentleman I've ever served has realized . . . it's

not a question of money at all. If it has been . . ." His voice trailed
away and then picked up again. "You mentioned background, sir.
If you had it . . . if you had even the inkling of what it meant . . ."

This in its way was more severe than anything I had ever taken
from Gilworthy.

"Look, get the wraps off, will you?"

He did, and I got up.

"Haven't you got a brush?"

He picked one up and began, I suppose from long habit, to try to
use it with a showy stroke, as if it were a craft instrument of some
kind. But his hands fluttered too much and the movements were
ineffective. I took the brush from him, whisked it over my lapels
and sleeves, then thrust it back at him. He fumbled taking it, dropped
it, watched it bounce and come to rest with its handle resting against
the wire guard of the radiator; he looked at it in an abstracted way.
A smell of hot shellac became evident. I jammed my hand into my
coin pocket, saying, with emphasis on his name:

"Don't worry, Roy; I'll pick it up for you in a moment."

Down he went, quickly. The same seam opened in the back of the
starched coat, the same strands of hair fell away from his skull, the
same vein pulsed. At that second the memory of his "condition"
came back to me, and with sudden anxiety I moved to intervene.

He took a quick panting breath, clutching at the handle, failed to
grasp it, gave a kind of sob and slipped forward, falling with a crash
across the radiator, pinning it under him.

He lay there still and I stood appalled. Then as the smell of
scorching cloth joined that of shellac, I acted: jerked the plug from
its socket, rolled the old man over onto his back. There was a brown
scorch-mark across his chest, in which was picked out the pattern of
the grille. He looked terrible, limbs sprawled, jaw gaping open,
glasses knocked askew. A comb had slipped from his top pocket and
lay upon his shoulder. It didn't move, because he wasn't breathing.
His white face seemed to have taken on a new pallor. I was in no
doubt that he was dead. Whether he was or not, I should have to
call help.

I tapped briefly at the parlour door and then opened it. The fire was
still burning brightly; there was nobody there. Crossing the room
I went down a dark passage and into a little kitchen. Nobody. There
were stairs in the passage but I could see no sign of a light switch
so I just went up in the dark. Past a bend I went slowly on in complete darkness. At the top I could see nothing but had the feeling of
being enclosed. Arms outstretched, I shuffled forward. My fingers

found panelling and then a knob. Absurdly, standing before the unseen door in stifling darkness, I knocked; then turned the knob and went in. There was a glimmer of light from two windows over-looking the street. Then I found the switch.

The light-shade was of dusty silk, with a glass-bead fringe. It hung above a big old double bed. It was a drab and gloomy room with yellowed lace half-curtains on the windows, faded brown wall paper, shabby furniture. A table by the bedside held a tumbler a quarter full of water with a skin of dust on its surface, as well as some medicine bottles and a candlestick. Above the mantelpiece there was a wedding photo, but the room contained no sign of a woman's presence. The situation seemed clear enough; his wife had been buried long since.

There was only one other room. It seemed pointless to go in but I did. It was full of broken furniture, trunks, pictures stacked on a sofa, piles of old newspapers and a mirror with a tobacco advertise-ment painted on it. I went back downstairs and this time noticed a telephone fixed to the wall in a dark corner.

He was exactly as before, looking very convincingly dead. No one seemed to have entered the shop. I went to the door and looked out, jumping nervously as the bell clanged. Nobody walked the dark pavements and no vehicle moved close by, although traffic still rumbled in the main street. All nearby shops were now shut. I felt a great temptation to slip away, just walk out, and hurry on to my destination and there have a still drink. Let somebody else find the body and report it. But there was an element of risk in that. I knew what I should do and would have to do—telephone the police, stand guard over the barber's pathetic stock until they came, make a state-ment. I went back inside and pushed a bolt in the door.

The water-heater still simmered away. The barber lay silently among my hair-clippings. I went through into the passage and tele-phoned, then came back into the shop and turned off the point of gas.

I picked up Roy Perch's clothes-brush.

Lastly I put the price of my haircut on the counter. It seemed absurd to leave a tip, but I caught myself wondering whether Gil-worthy would have done so.

D. E. CHARLWOOD

A Long Time

IN THOSE days two things drew me to Tal-y-cafn: there was a girl, who lived in fact at Rhyl but who had come with me to the village, and there was the valley of the Conway itself. I have put the girl first and perhaps in those days she was so, but as the years passed the memory of her almost vanished. I married and I heard that she had married too, and eventually she only came to brief life when some one spoke of the Conway, or the town of Rhyl—and in Australia few people spoke of either.

But the country I never forgot. I am not sure why that was so. It had lain hold on me as no place had ever done, almost as if I had come home to it—yet I could not even claim Welsh ancestry. It may simply have been that in the summer of 1943 my mind was hungry for tranquillity: I had come from a squadron in Lincolnshire which had been decimated on the Ruhr raids of the previous winter; then, in sudden contrast, I had found myself alone in that most beautiful of countrysides.

I came to know many places well, but it was one which I saw only briefly that I remembered best. That was a cottage called Rowlyn Uchaf, or Upper Whirlpool. For twenty years afterwards I used to imagine going back to it out of the mountains, and recapturing some special quality of peace I felt had existed there.

The other places, the lesser places, I remembered with affection— the village of Tyn-y-groes, for instance, where Mr Jones the constable had translated Welsh place-names for me on summer evenings. And towards the mountains there was another village called Roewen, and in it a café named The Shirley, reached by a narrow bridge over the "white flowing water" that gave the village its name. Nearer Tal-y-cafn there was a farm called Esgairheulog where one evening I had met a farmer leaning on his gate. We had discussed sheep and potatoes and Welsh singing. Where could I hear some good singing? Well now, if I so wished, I could go with him to his church at Eglwys-Fach.

"The name means 'small church', but indeed it is much too large for us."

So later I had gone to Eglwys-Fach, had gone twice in fact.

Near Esgairheulog a high escarpment rises above the river and there, on the brink of the valley, one could look out to Snowdonia. Often I had sat there at evening, perched five hundred feet above Tal-y-cafn village. Looking to the left it was possible to see, by a bend in the river, the earthworks of the Roman fort at Caerhun. A church lay hidden in trees at the edge of the fortifications, a place as quiet as a hermit's cell, its white walls curving into a roof beamed with blackened oak. There I had once heard a reading voice of such perfection that I had never forgotten it.

All these places I could visualize years after the girl deserted my memory. But chiefly it was to Rowlyn Uchaf that my mind returned; it remained, for some reason, a refuge at the other end of the earth waiting to be regained.

In 1943 I had come to it in this way: I had walked from the Ferry Inn at Tal-y-cafn to Roewen and then over the mountains to Carnedd Llewelyn. In the valleys it had been oppressively hot, and by the time I had reached the peaks I could see thunder clouds massing near Anglesea and mists coming in behind me.

On Carnedd Llewelyn I sat for some time by the precipice overlooking Ffynnon Llugwy. While I was there the mists blotted out vision on all sides. I made no attempt to move until a break came, but then, making the best of it, I began to run.

I ran all the way to Foel Grach, and from near there I swung down a slope that ended in a precipice above two lakes, Melyn Llyn and Llyn Dulyn. I had heard of this place; I had heard that thereabouts five aircraft had crashed, two of them German.

Beyond the lakes the ground rose to a curious chain of hills. When I had clambered on to them I could see the length of the Conway valley. Although I was in sunshine, the sky to the north was black, and a cloud of immense height was moving down the valley, cannonading as it came. I looked ahead for shelter and saw not far off two farmhouses, marked on my map Hafod-y-garreg and Hafod-y-gorswen. I walked quickly towards them, but before long saw that they were roofless and deserted.

The cloud was now only a few miles off, and I could see rain obliterating everything in its path. It was then that I noticed this other cottage, Rowlyn Uchaf, about a mile away against a hollowed flank of a hill.

I began running again, pacing with the cloud, but across its line of movement. I was about half way to the cottage when the whole range shook with thunder and the nearer peaks were blotted out. The thunder rolled among the mountains, crashing and echoing. In strange contrast all the country about me was bathed in yellowish light.

I went on through long grass, past sheep and over fences. Between me and the cottage a stream flowed towards a wood. I pushed through trees, crossed the stream on stones, and climbed a hedge. As the rain began to fall I stood facing the back wall of the cottage. A door led directly into a kitchen from which I could hear light-hearted voices speaking in Welsh. The rain was already streaming down, hissing on the ground. I called out, "May I shelter, please, from the storm?"

The voices ceased. After a moment a man's voice answered, "Come in."

In the dim light I saw the glow of a fire on the faces of a young man and woman, and on an old woman sitting in the chimney corner. The two women were immediately silent and scarcely looked my way; only the man turned towards me. I explained uneasily that I had come from Carnedd Llewelyn and was on my way to Tal-y-cafn where I was staying. He seemed surprised and said something in Welsh to the young woman. I thought she might have been unable to speak English, but she said, "You have walked a long way."

As my eyes became accustomed to the light I saw that the floor was of polished stone, large blue-grey slabs from the mountains. Against one wall stood a dresser of very dark wood and on it a willow pattern dinner-set and some pewter mugs. Beside the dresser stood a grand-father clock, its tick audible above the rain. There was no ceiling to the room, but the underside of the roof was whitewashed. It must have been fourteen feet at the gable.

The young woman was standing at a table near the only window, mixing something in a bowl, her eyes on the gloom and rain outside. Her mother, or mother-in-law, sat motionless before the wide hearth. The whole picture was one of great beauty and simplicity.

As the silence persisted I said, "This is a beautiful room."

The young woman smiled faintly, but the man replied, "The cottage will fall down one of these days—it is four hundred years old."

Then he said nothing more and I hardly knew what I could say to him. We stood motionless and silent. Outside the rain was threshing at the open door.

"I am in the Australian Air Force," I said at length.

The young woman answered slowly, "We had an airman from New Zealand here."

"Walking, too?"

"No." It was the man who answered. "He crashed on the mountains in an Anson."

"By the two lakes?"

"Yes, by the two lakes. He was blind in one eye and his head was injured. It took him seventeen hours to reach our cottage. There were two other men in the wreck."

I looked at him, waiting for him to go on. His eyes were somewhere beyond me.

"It was winter, you see, and his hands were all torn from feeling his way. He went to two cottages before he reached us, but they were empty."

I remembered Hafod-y-gorswen and Hafod-y-garreg, and thought of this man stumbling to them in darkness.

"And the other two?"

"One lived and one died. We were long reaching them in the mists."

"The New Zealander?"

"He lived."

The rain had eased. I saw that the young woman was setting the table for the evening meal. She gave me a glass of fresh milk while the three of them sat down to eat. I drank the milk and only paused a moment longer to ask the way.

The man was vague. He said that directions were really impossible. He could only point out the general line; I would have to go across country. So I thanked them and went out, and within a hundred yards or so found myself high above a stream, the water rushing angrily among slippery boulders about sixty feet below. I slithered down to it under dripping trees, marvelling that the man had not given me directions round it. Alone with the roar of water and the overhanging branches, I stepped gingerly from boulder to boulder, then scrambled up the other side into flat fields. When I looked back I could see the cottage, white against its hill, and beyond it the retreating storm.

That was my one brief contact with Rowlyn Uchaf. It was strange that it should have come to mean to me what it did.

For years after the war I used to imagine how fine it would be to go back to Tal-y-cafn, and walk into The Ferry, and after a good meal to climb among the hills and find my way back to Rowlyn Uchaf. But the notion was impossible.

Twenty years passed and I had given up all hope of returning when, in the summer of 1963, an unexpected opportunity took me to Britain, and for one week-end I was able to go alone to Tal-y-cafn.

As I came at evening through the narrow lanes on the west side of the Conway a feeling of incredulity swept over me, as if I had imagined that my absence might have caused the valley's dissolution.

It lay unchanged, only more beautiful, perhaps, than I had believed.

By the time I reached The Ferry it was dusk. My room—and this was strange—was the one I had occupied before. Standing there in half light I had the fleeting impression that the earlier "I" was still there, looking from the window to the river and its bordering woods. Out there in greyish, gentle light rose the high escarpment on which I had so often sat at this time of evening, a shape so familiar that the enthusiasm of those days seized me and I vowed I would reach its crest before darkness set in.

I turned out of the door without even unpacking, and found myself leaving the hotel behind and crossing the bridge towards the woods. By now all the remaining light was in the river and the sky, enough to recognize landmarks familiar from the earlier days. Here they lay unchanged, while I—I had married and aged and raised a family and had cherished these places in memory.

Where I entered the wood the lane rose steeply, a tunnel-like lane, its roof torn to the sky. At once my feet began to find their way, driving me breathlessly upwards. On either side I saw the same ivy-embossed beech trunks and heard the same bird sounds.

Gradually—and I do not know when it began—a delirium possessed me, a conviction that time had not passed, that I was not middle-aged and out of condition, that I was not in fact alone. The person beside me I knew at once, even though I had imagined her forgotten; I even knew what would happen next. Round this corner, by a stone cottage, we would come on a farmer urging a pair of horses in a dray. He would be crying, *"Tyd! Tyd! Tyd onna!"* and *"Gwas tyd, tyd!"* and as we passed I would ask, "What is it he is saying?" She would answer, "Come! Come! Come on, chaps!"

As I approached the corner my heart protested against the pace, but I laughed at it. This was 1943; no heart or lungs could deny it! I swung my arms against the reluctant air, breathing swiftly and deeply.

As I breathed I became aware of the cause of my delusions: all through the hedges honeysuckle was in bloom, just as it had been then, its scent caught on the enclosed air. . . .

So she was not forgotten then. A whiff of honeysuckle and she was back unchanged, as if choosing to dislocate my plans. She had been like that—mocking, persistent, full of pretended deprecation—mocking gently even now.

When I left the lane and cut across open fields, sanity and age crept back. Near the escarpment my mind was turned from her; for there, across the valley, lay the unchanged hills, and below them the Conway in the last pale light.

It still looked, I thought, as if long ago a wave of humanity had washed far up the slopes and in receding had left white cottages and woods and small fields. Above the cottages rose bare summits, asleep and grey, Carnedd Llewelyn the highest of all. The only sound was of water flowing over stones, and the bleating of ewes and lambs along the flats.

My eyes sought dim creases of the hills for places I had known: the few buildings of Tyn-y-groes and Roewen; the cell-like church. Ah, tomorrow I would go up the valley facing me, then strike over the hills to Rowlyn Uchaf by the route I had taken then. As befitted a man of middle years, I would turn my mind from honeysuckle, however importuning.

In the morning I started between hedges to Tyn-y-groes, but part way was lured a mile or so across fields to the hidden church at Caerhun. I saw the Roman mounds first and then, between its yews, the church itself. There inside were the sloped white walls and the blackened beams and Mr Williams's silent lectern.

From outside I presently heard a woman saying, "They call it 'the old font'."

"To me," said a man's voice, "it is unmistakably a stoup." I went out and saw an elderly man and woman examining a derelict piece of masonry. I asked them if they knew anything of Mr Williams who had been vicar there.

"Mr Williams? Mr Williams? How long ago was that?"

"Twenty years," I said.

"Ah, I have heard of him, but where he is now or whether he has passed on I could not tell you."

Vaguely disappointed, I retraced my steps and went on to Tyn-y-groes—"House on the Crossroads" as Jones Police had explained. There were more houses to it now than I remembered. I asked a man if Mr Jones the policeman still lived in the village. Ah no, he had long gone, he said. Been decorated by the Queen for bravery, too. A fine man, Jones Police, but long gone; long, long. . . .

I frowned. A pity, this. There were meanings of place-names I still had to ask him, and besides, he was a man to know.

As we spoke, I noticed a derelict hearse leaning on its shafts. It had holders for plumes and intact glass panels. As a reminder of passing time it cast a chill over me, as if it had said, "The country is unchanged, it is true, but the people you seek have gone a long, long time."

But soon enough I forgot these forebodings, for I found the lane to Roewen and shut myself between its hedges for the first part of the long walk to Rowlyn Uchaf.

There is no lane in all the world more beautiful. Cows in steep
fields behind hedges munch at one's ear, and more distant cows stand
on steep knolls like tapestry animals on green tapestry grounds,
twenty yards off, or perhaps a quarter of a mile; no one can tell, for
there is optical trickery in the air. It was always a silent lane. Certainly there were cottages, but I had seldom seen anyone about them
or even heard anyone. It was one of those places where I had felt as
though I were a Roman intruder, observed by dark eyes out of woods,
yet unable to detect observers.

After a mile the road plunged into Roewen. All through the street
of white cottages I could hear the bass sound of the stream that gave
the place its name. About here had been that pleasant café The
Shirley. I would go to it again and order morning-tea and would
linger over it. I asked a passing man to guide me.

"The Shirley? No indeed, I do not know." A dark shaking of the
head. Then recollection. "Ah, you don't mean the café across the
stream?"

"Yes, across a narrow bridge."

Mournfully, "It has gone now; long gone. I don't know how many
years."

"And the people?"

"The people too. I don't know where."

I walked away. If so much had vanished, to what degree had I too
wasted? How was I going to find the climb from here to the hills and
on to Rowlyn Uchaf?

I started upwards, breathing deeply, using my energy sparingly.
It was better at that pace; I could listen to runlets coming off the
hills and look up into hedges. They were high hedges rooted somehow in rock walls.

Farther up, the runlets became more numerous and more urgent;
they fell into pockets of stone with hollow sounds and passed under
the road. Sheep soon outnumbered cows and the lush growth began
to fail.

My heart was pounding a great deal more than I remembered it
doing. I stopped at a break in the left-hand wall and sat there, head
in hands. I could hear my heart gradually slowing, but still I sat on.
I had no schedule to keep; only a self-imposed goal of a cottage. The
only ones interested in my comings and goings were ten thousand
miles away.

When I looked up I saw the whole Conway valley open below,
all the complex stitches of lanes and hedges woven into the fabric
of its hills. And there beyond it, much shrunken, was the escarpment
above the river calling faintly of the past night. I could smile indul-

gently now. Anyway she would be—How old? No, no; that was unfair!

I stood up stiffly and began climbing again. Before long the hedges vanished and gave place to high stone dikes; the country became almost bare; cows gradually disappeared and the few oaks looked battered and sickly. Then there were no trees and I became conscious of ponderous clouds voyaging from Snowdon to Anglesea.

Beyond a derelict cottage I came to a gate I remembered well. After that the way was unmade, but it was marked on my map "Roman Road". I began to watch for two tall stones thrust vertically into the ground, left there, it was said, by a giant who had intended casting them into the Menai Straits.

When I found them I knew I must soon climb to the left. I began with legs already aching. The going was steeper and more difficult underfoot than I remembered; bilberry bushes sank like cushions as I stepped on them and the hill appeared to have no end.

I began to think that when I reached the top I would rest for ten or fifteen minutes, then would cut straight across country to Rowlyn Uchaf. I would not attempt Foel Fras or Drum after all, and certainly not Carnedd Llewelyn.

But as I laboured on, I realized that Rowlyn Uchaf was physically beyond me, that it had been absurd to imagine that I could still follow my old route to it. Perhaps I might find a place from which I could see the cottage at a distance where I could sit awhile and from a few miles absorb something of its peace.

I continued to the east side of Drosgyl, but even from there Rowlyn Uchaf was beyond sight. Distances were greater than I had remembered; much greater. That day in 1943 I must have covered thirty miles, perhaps more.

I gave up at that and started disconsolately back to the Roman Road. I had failed to reach Rowlyn Uchaf, had even failed to see it. Probably I would never have an opportunity of reaching it again. I walked slowly toward Tal-y-cafn.

When I reached The Ferry it was dark. I lay on my bed, tired and aching. I had less than eighteen hours left. With Rowlyn Uchaf beyond reach, what did I do now? I shall go, I thought at last, to the farm Esgairheulog; I shall run the gauntlet of the honeysuckle to get there. And when I get there I shall ask for the farmer. . . .

By day the honeysuckle was less insistent; even at the corner where the man had cried, *"Tyd onna!"* to his horses, I was able to smile again indulgently. At the farm gate I stopped. There was the name *Esgairheulog*, "Place on which the sun does not often shine". "For you see," the farmer had said, "my cottage is in a dingle."

We had stood on either side of this gate, he and I, and had talked for an hour or more. He had just asked me to his church at Eglwys-Fach to hear the singing when a wizened, bandy little man had come from the house calling, "Master, your supper is getting cold!"

I had left then. On the Sunday evening I had arrived before the farmer had finished dressing. The wizened little man had shown me to a chair in the living-room. The fireplace was hung with brass harness ornaments which he had been polishing. A stove was open at the top and firelight reflected on the polished surfaces. Just over our heads the floor creaked as the farmer dressed. Presently, he came downstairs and stepped from behind a curtain, a bowler hat squarely on his head, a heavy watch-chain across his snuff-coloured waistcoat.

Together we had descended through woods to Eglwys-Fach. The street there was full of people seriously bent on church. The whole village was closed, every house and shop of it, each window shuttered against the world and the flesh. As the bell began to ring we crossed a stream, stepping on one enormous slab of slate, and presently we were in the church and I was caught up in soaring, uninhibited singing. . . .

Twenty years since then. And there now was the gate. I paused, wondering whether to go down the drive and knock at the door. After all, how old had he been? Not very old, perhaps; all men over forty had seemed old then.

I saw a man in a field up the road—he was beating the bounds in his best clothes, since this was a Sunday—and I walked along the hedge until I could speak to him.

He cast me an anti-Roman glance, but when we had exchanged good-days, I said, "Years ago I met a farmer from the cottage there. . . ."

"Ah, he is dead," he interrupted. It seemed to afford him a melancholy satisfaction to tell me. "A long time—perhaps six years. . . ."

There it was again: "A long time", or "A long, long time", or "Gone many years". I left the man shaking his head and walked on despondently. Very well then, I would find the rough path the farmer had shown me to Eglwys-Fach and would limit myself to recollection. To attempt to re-establish links after so many years was futile.

I followed the lane between field and woods, walking slowly. It was a strange day. A warm, heavy mist had lain along the river like motionless smoke. Up here the trees of the woods were softened. It had rained during the night and moisture was steaming from the earth. Somewhere miles away I heard thunder.

Near a right-angle turn a barn abutted on the lane and close by was a stone cottage. About here I believed was the turning place.

I took out my map and studied it. I became aware then of a young man watching me, standing motionless. I turned and faced the rapier of his eyes.

"Is it possible to go down this way to Eglwys-Fach?"

"Yes," he said, relaxing. "On foot you can go right through."

It came back to me then. "This barn," I said, "was once a church —"

"Why, yes," said the young man. "I myself did not know until last year, when some gentlemen interested in historic buildings came here. How is it that you knew?"

"I was brought here by the farmer from Esgairheulog during the war."

"Ah yes," said the young man sombrely. "He has gone now; died several years ago—heart I believe."

I diverted him quickly. "There is something peculiar about the construction of this barn; something done to evade an English law—"

But before we could discuss this there was an extraordinary call, so high that it was like the whistle of a train. This was apparently to summon him to lunch. Repeating that I could get through to Eglwys-Fach, the young man left me.

I picked my way downhill past a second farmhouse, a derelict place with windows staring into the valley. Down there the mists thickened. I entered under a canopy of leaves, following the rough path steeply down. Its surface was strewn with chippings of slate flung there over the years, impacted now in mud.

Farther on the path looked as if it might have lain unused for a generation. A trickle of water ran down the middle of it and leaves hemmed it closely. The leaves were still and the air was grave and watchful. What had the Druids done but give voice to these places, I thought, these strange places that by some means took one back to the roots of man's being?

Through a break in the trees I saw at last the church at Eglwys-Fach, the "small church", its weathercock sharp against the mists. I emerged near the bridge we had crossed those years before, a slab of slate measuring, I judged, fifteen feet by three and a good eight inches thick. There was a second bridge, a slightly smaller slab, by which twelve geese sailed, holding themselves against the current. There was not a soul about, and the only sound was the coughing of a sheep.

In the deserted street I heard a discreet, sabbath humming from the refrigerator of Jones Butcher, but nothing else at all. I went into the empty church and subsided in a seat at the back. There it was,

I remembered, in the fifth row, that I had sat with the farmer.

And there, a memory prompted, you sat again—remember?—beside you a young, flexible soprano—

True, I admitted.

I saw again her sidelong glance and heard her whisper: "What will they think? A single girl with an Australian airman! A Welsh girl! What will they say?"

"Listen and tell me," I had said.

I said it again to the empty church: "Listen and tell me."

And then I added, "Very well, sweet ghost; since you alone of all I knew seem closest to substance, perhaps you will walk back with me the way we went then."

I fancied she smiled at that and looked at me with mock deprecation. But she came; I am sure she came. And I forgot my failure to reach Rowlyn Uchaf.

We went out past the roll of vicars from 1537, out of the church and into the street. The geese sailed still and the sheep coughed.

"How beautiful it all is!" she said.

"Yes, beautiful," I replied.

Perhaps no one had seen me; perhaps everyone had, watching from behind blinds. "Peculiar the way he came and went so soon. Why now? A stranger and on foot?"

"And I heard him speak—as if another had been with him."

How beautiful was the lane with the valley in mist below—like a Chinese print.

"That other time," I said, "it was moonlight and cold. Remember?"

It came back clearly. Gloved and scarfed we had walked quickly, singing as we climbed.

"A long time ago," I said at length. "A very long time."

She laughed lightly at that, secure in her niche of twenty years past.

The haze thickened. We were in the Chinese print ourselves now, part of the rising mists. We passed an ancient cottage with a wavering gable and turned into the valley of the Conway—but somewhere there I lost her. It may have been the sight of the railway waiting below to bear me away; it may have been that I had passed her ghostly boundary. At all events she had gone and no effort of will could summon her back.

As I walked across the Conway bridge thunder sounded again, this time like boulders rolling down invisible heights. I felt oddly lonely. What had led to it, this strange visitation, when I had thought her gone from my memory, when I had come only to see a cottage? Perhaps she was indeed dead and haunting these places—anything was possible in that Celtic country.

I thought then, I shall ask. It will sound foolish of course, but I shall ask at the hotel if there is anyone who knew her. There was, after all, a woman who had worked there for many years. Perhaps she could tell me.

When I came in I said to the woman, "Did you ever know a girl —a woman from Rhyl—tall, fair-haired." I gave her name.

"Yes, yes; of course."

"You knew her?"

"I know her still," I stopped breathing. The woman was nodding to herself. "A hard time she has had too. Perhaps you heard that her husband had left her?"

No, I said. No, I had never heard.

I waited for something more. She said then, "She lives alone with her two children. I could tell you where—it is not at all far from here."

I stood for a moment without speaking. "My train leaves in fifteen minutes," I said at last. "I have to go."

She smiled faintly. "Shall I tell her?"

"Yes," I said. "Yes, do tell her."

It was raining softly as I left. The train came and I journeyed twenty years to Llandudno Junction, London and Melbourne.

HAL PORTER

Mr Butterfry

WHEN, after eighteen years, I spot him at the Lion Beer Hall, Shim-bashi, Tokyo, I suspect he is someone I knew somewhere before, but it is hard and unimportant to be certain whether he really is that unplaceable someone or merely a unit cut from the template of his type. It is a type instantly familiar because ubiquitous as sinners and dandelions, and almost invariably wears the nickname Blue, despite the fact that, in some tinkling and seemly year, 1922 or 1923 say, a working-class mother has fruitlessly attached to an already wily clown of a baby the ticket Oswald or Arthur or Francis Xavier. Here, in the Lion Beer Hall, forty-odd years after conning his way into and out of the womb, he resembles his template brethren to the last blackhead. He is short, welter weight, discreetly bow-legged, topped with ginger-and-grey curls. Nickname? Guess!

Blue's nose is snub as an *ingénue's*, and as immodestly open to the delicious wickedness of the world as a rocking-horse's. His lips, too pliant, scorched-looking, agitate themselves non-stop to eject, in a falsetto of extraordinary harshness, an overflow of obscenity, boast-ings not to be believed and not expected to be believed, lies too Munchausen to arouse anything but irritated pity, fly-blown witti-cisms, and just enough tiny and tasty (and deliberately planted?) truths to make him bearable, forgiveable, even lovable. His every clause—truth or tarradiddle or downright delusion—is accompanied by a *non sequitur* gesticulation itself in need of exegesis. His water-pale eyes, nailed into all this restlessness and garrulity, are immobile as an umlaut, unwinking as a merman's. An Australian, a refractory, Depression-toughened, war-jangled, Occupation-debased, he is the oldest inhabitant of the Lion Beer Hall.

For years—eleven? fourteen? sixteen?—the Lion has been the weekly rendezvous of expatriate Australians in Tokyo. No need, of course, for a sign BLOKES ONLY. Kangaroo-pelt koalas squat on the newels of the staircase and on top of the 1908 cash-register ornate as a tsarina's jewel-casket. Qantas posters and elderly photographs of Sydney Harbour Bridge and Murray River paddle-steamers hang on the walls between dust-furred sprays of salmon-pink plastic cherry-blossom and the other-year calendars of Hong Kong tailors.

It is behind waitresses of implausible homeliness, and sluts with impasted faces, frowsy false eyelashes, and Elicon-inflated breasts that one queues for a telephone-booth-sized lavatory of which the urinous reek unselfishly mingles with the grey and hunger-discouraging odours from the kitchen. Here, to the behind-scenes yowling of transistor Beatles, are manufactured Japanese mock-ups of spaghetti and tomato sauce, curry and rice, or genteel isosceles sandwiches, or dim-sims composed of elements better not thought about. The food's one merit is its thank-God tastelessness. Skilfully combining Wild West Saloon dash and oriental finickiness the barman flourishes a spatula to slice the foam from the glass jugs of draught beer the Australians order.

Successive proprietors, and successions of Japanese customers meekly and long-time nibbling at the surface of a pony of beer as though it were an inordinately pricy and singular liqueur, have year after year concealed their contempt for the heavy-drinking invaders who, every Saturday morning from eleven o'clock on, crowd into the Lion with an almost delinquent bravura, louder-mouthed than they are, twice as Australian as they could ever be in Australia. Fog or shine, a flannel sky tenderly vomiting down grouts of soiled January snow, August giving its imitation of a sauna bath, Plum Rain weather or suicide month, the Barbarians from Without come roaring in—public-relations men, backroom boys from the Australian and New Zealand Embassies, ABC employees, foreign correspondents, traders' agents, tourists who have heard of the Lion on the grapevine, and members of that clan of confidence-men and near-confidence-men who are the flower of Australian *haut cynicisme*. They come, particularly the dyed-in-the-wool expatriates enmeshed throughout the week in webs of native dissimulation and duplicity, to re-enact themselves among their kind, to refresh their evaluations, to exchange home truths in the cryptic patois, at one and the same time profane and subtle, self-mocking and sensitive, brutal and compassionate, merciless and stingless, that only Australian men can use and understand.

Although the Shimbashi immediately surrounding the Lion presents to the polluted upper air of Tokyo its architectural crosswords of plate-glass and ferro-concrete, its vulgar rooftop fairgrounds and beer gardens, its rooftop golf-driving and baseball-pitching centres encaged in green nylon netting, down below, level with the Lion, near the fissured and buckled footpaths silkily gleaming with spittle, are the pinball parlours, noodle stalls, flop-houses, homosexual bars, and the hole-in-the-wall haunts of herbalists, astrologers, palmists, face-readers, acupuncture quacks, cut-rate abortionists, and third-rate cosmetic surgeons, all jammed together behind booths displaying vegetables and ex-vegetables, azure plastic buckets, and mechanical toys in the shape of prehistoric monsters called Gappa or Godzilla or Gommola. In the mean square which separates the Lion from Shimbashi railway station one steps over rows of *rumpen*, no-hopers, vagabonds, prone and sodden with their ferocious tipple of *shochu*, the grappa-like dregs of rice wine. They and their prophet's wild manes, their gnarled feet and lice-populated beards are wrapped in tatters of straw matting like parcels of stale meat. The whole area is squalid, stinking, respectably vicious, and unremittingly raucous.

Across a lane from the Lion, tucked, like a never-emptied commode beneath a bed, under the Dickensian arches of the overhead railway, its foundations vibrating in the roof of the subway, is the dive New Yorker, an ear-splitting inferno of juke-boxes, red lighting, and rough-as-bags hostesses, earthy creatures from the dwindling rural hinterland, who have scented, painted and adorned themselves as aphrodisically as the law allows in cheong-sams of conjunctivitis-inducing crimsons and verdigris-greens and bale-loader oranges split to their peasant buttocks. Hefty Hokusai hussies all, as well as Hogarthian whores, their laughter is so shrill as to have almost another hideous colour of its own. After a matriculatory grog session at the Lion there I am, in the New Yorker, sitting numbly as a haunch of venison on a banquette of bum-worn magenta plush at a table awash with spilt ale, and doubly repulsive with the spiny rubble of a Japanese meal. I am not alone. Opposite is Blue. The others have, one by one, like the ten little nigger boys, lurched off—"Hooroo!" "Seeya, mate!" "Hooroo!" "Seeya, mate!" Blue and I are the last two of the Mohicans. Of the two I, at least, am incontestably shicker, at the stage where the slightest gesture, the mildest slip of the tongue, or the sliver of a side-glance from a repulsive stranger seems fraught with significance. One drink more, one only, and the garish curtain of hullabaloo will lift to reveal the mountain of white gold and precious silence exploding slow-motion upwards to the knees of God. I am perfectly capable, I feel, of the look-no-hands! feat of singing in Icelandic, rattling off the Koran, understanding what moths gently semaphore with their powdered antennae. It is not to be. Blue, with an extra glaze on his eyes that makes me think of farm-house axe-murderers, says in his desecrating voice, "You don' remember me, y' bastard."

Oh dear, oh dear, dear, *dear*.

Having indubitably waited to say it, he says it flatly, flatly just this side of hurt vanity, flatly just this side of a perceptible necessity for bitterness. I am airborne enough to get this, but neither sozzled enough nor sober enough to do a *passata sotto* by something like, "Are you sure, mate?" or "Watch it, watch it!" Instead, I sit mute as mud, and this silence reveals all. No, it states, I don't remember you. Icelandic, Kalmuk elegies, and a fraternal understanding of what lies behind the caprices of all alligators may, at the moment, be well within my scope. Re Blue, alas and alack, my receiver is off the hook.

He perceives this. It is not not not to be borne. Dead certain, Blue is, that he is not really invisible, right *now*, and also never was in lost-to-me *then*, some yesterday, some foundered year. With a sudden shocking violence he uses his execrable voice and unmatching gestures to have the morass cleared from the table by one suety trollop, fresh beer brought by another. Then, his eyes mesmeric, he settles down to the self-resurrecting stint of putting me s-t-r-a-i-g-h-t. As his own apostle he is pretty vivid, and not to be side-tracked. The trains above the roof, the trains under the floor, the killer traffic outside the bead curtain, the delirious juke-boxes and the god-damning Yankee matelots inside, none of this means a thing, could be silence. He lowers his voice as if just to show. He hangs on his every word. I, too, hang, fighting down an impulse to fold my hands on the table between us like a good little kindergartener. Patiently, truculently patiently, he lifts stone after stone from my memory and, my God, suddenly, presto, lo and bloody behold, abracadabra, the crocuses spike through, spire up, unfurl, and, in the pandemonium and fetid volcano-red gloom of the New Yorker, part of a past unhibernates. A reconstituted he and I are eighteen years younger. The scene is Kure, Occupation Japan. He is a corporal wooing the oh-so-sweet-and-cute housegirl of a Seventh Day Adventist major in the Officers' Mess I also live in.

I seemed, in those days, to be always bumping into him. There he was, any five-thirty, waiting for the major's housegirl by the sentry-box at the Mess gate, meantime not wasting time by third-degreeing or selling short the giggling and cross-eyed guard. There he was, as invariably as though the fates had spun some pretty plot to cross-pollinate us, in whichever of the beer-kiosks, or trinket-shops, or tea-houses I had arbitrarily chosen to give my custom to. There he was in the pathetic two-room brothel behind the White Rose Souvenir Shoppe, where the drinking of luke-warm Asahi beer and the relief of lust took place on the threadbare matting of a room furnished with a pre-Raphaelite sewing machine, a cheval glass sheathed in frayed brocade, and an elaborate Buddhist altar of mildewed gilt in a lacquer cabinet that also contained two bottles, one of Suntory whisky, the other of a murky purgative. Cut-out magazine photographs of Betty Grable and Moira Shearer were pinned to the walls. The room was often aesthetically misted by the fumes, very Art Photograph, of smouldering mosquito repellant. Stenches of varying felicity corkscrewed their tentacles through rents in the paper shutters from God-knows-what putrescence or cess-pit out there in a tatterdemalion town slapped together from the charred boards and singed tiles of wartime bombings.

Blue had, then, an unfailing cheeky *savoir-faire* which was engaging, but so intense that it made my mind behave like a merry-go-round it was impossible to descend from. His quips and cracks were machine-gun but not fresh, not fresh. Whenever we parted after one of these apparently predestined hook-ups he was unable to stop himself squalling out not only "Au reservoir, amigo!" but also, never a miss, "Auf wienerschnitzel, chico!" He badgered me, with the fervour of Mephistopheles, to come in on his Black Market beat: my blunt refusals seem to him crass, my lack of enthusiasm scandalous, if not perverted. He drooled romantically about his housegirl in the goody-goody tones of a Sir Lancelot, his hot little hand meantime virtually well up the kimono skirt of one or other of the three spaniel-eyed White Rose harlots.

Although our natures were, by and large, absolutely opposite, recurring encounters, destiny-engineered or not, led us to exchange little snippets of unwanted truth about ourselves. None was important, and I have a hazy impression that we were drifting apart out of mutual boredom, when it came out that we both knew Gippsland well. Home-town-I-want-to-wander-down-your-back-streets stuff was on. Our relationship now had a different climate and background, both deformed. It began to seem that we had not only lived in Gippsland but had, as well, in a terrain without horizon, outline, language, or name, together participated in an initiation ceremony esoteric to the last degree, and eternally binding. In the oriental chaos and misery and speeded-up corruption of the time it was sufficient for us to recite the names of Gippsland places—Rosedale, Bunyip, the Haunted Hills, Herne's Oak— to make us feel we were members of the one tribe. In a way, of course, we were. Our senses had been similarly baptized, and the shared memory of beige summer paddocks speckled with raisins of sheep dung, of regiments of ring-barked eucalypts St-Vitus-dancing in the heat-ripples, of ravens carping and cursing as they probed the sun-split acres for crickets, of Princes Highway telegraph wires shrilling in Antarctic winds that smelt of brine and seals and lost floes, provided us with enough tribal counters and nostalgic cards to play a childish and empty-headed game of Strip-Jack-Naked neither of us won.

In short, in the tawdry-gehenna of the New Yorker, he recalls us as we are tipsily deceiving ourselves into thinking we were. Like a belligerent warlock he conjures up the ghosts of our younger ghosts. The dusk of drunkenness deepens. It is nevertheless meteorite-clear that what happened in Kure is happening again. That year, it was a common Gippsland past which decorated our cut-and-come-again relationship. Now, it is to be the common past of Occupation Kure that is to handcuff us together again. Since a conclusion must be drawn from the increasingly domestic quality of our tosspot exchanges at the New Yorker, it is as sure as nightfall that the relationship is to continue. Indeed, when I wake the next morning with a mouth that has the taste and texture of tinfoil, and start to put into order the jigsaw of now-blurred, now-blinding bits cumbering my hangover, it is obvious that the relationship has already begun to continue. His business card is in my wallet. Written on its back are the time and place of a tryst. The proper side of the card indicates that he is a sales representative for a variety of commodities: Canadian margarine and tinned milk, New Zealand frozen lamb, Japanese beef and plastic vessels, an English gin, an English rum, American sporting equipment, Australian pineapple juice. His honest-to-God name? Gregory R. Patience. R? Ronald? Ralph? Roger? Reginald? Richard? It no longer matters.

Even his nickname, although I continue to use it to him, is not what my mind uses because, after we leave the New Yorker, I discover that he is Mr Butterfry, the foul-mouthed, uncouth, embittered, loathed Mr Butterfry.

I do not remember leaving the New Yorker, but do remember feeling Anzac-tall and commando-masculine as we buffet our way along beneath the barrel-sized lanterns and sickly stripling willows of the narrow Shimbashi streets, through gaggles of squat and unripe boulevardiers with louts' jaws, and eye-brows like moustaches, who are picking *their* delicate way, puma-like, in cruelly pointed non-leather shoes, among the pools of footpath water which blaze and jerk about with the violet and saffron and venom-green and raspberry of reflected and ever-stuttering neons.

I remember a solitary geisha, outside the Shimbashi Registry Office for Geisha, entering the leatherette door of a jinricksha, and being sealed in like a fabulous idol behind its little isinglass window by her two-legged horse. She is herself already sealed in layer upon layer of opalescent kimono, bound about by a sash stiff with metallic threads. Swaddled, girdled, constricted in her almost hieratic attire, her ludi-

crous burden of a wig flashing like a huge orchid of black glass, her
face and hands thickly frosted with white paint, her vermilion lips
and jet eyebrows glistening like wet enamel, she is borne off by the
man-horse, upright as a clockwork effigy, anachronistic, immoral,
elegant and artificial, exquisitely grotesque.

I remember swaggering after my guide into a number of smallish
night-places alive with hostesses of a coquettishness so defined as to
be nearly bellicose albeit nauseatingly saccharine, each ready to mulct
any man for every yen he has. Since each drink makes me seem taller
to myself, each new batch of harpies in sequins seems shorter, more
and more like plucked monkeys in make-up and drag. Any moment,
oh any moment, they will one and all scamper up the posts of the live
combo platform, or up the fluted pillars of the bar-counter, take to
the rafters, and swing indolently there by spangled milk-white tails
among the fake maple leaves and Gifu lanterns depending from the
ceiling. I remember with a faultless and absolute clarity that, in night-
spot after night-spot, it is these simian women with the raw-fish hali-
tosis of seagulls who, baring their teeth in smiles so deliberately brilliant that one senses they abhor him, call my companion Mr Butterfry.

I step aside to make comment. Most Japanese find it vexing and
difficult to distinguish between l and r sounds. In their mouths Mr
Butterfly becomes Mr Butterfry, a term of particularly incalculable
insult when pronounced with howsoever incandescent a smile, by
bar hostesses. Spoken behind the back the expression is contemptuous
enough. Spoken to the face it is an appalling insult, saturated with
malice. Its open use suggests that whatever incited the use has been
priced as seriously appalling, also. Unforgivable loss of face has been
caused. Only one step away is the offer of the arsenic-spiced *gâteau*,
the jug of petrol thrown in the face, and then ignited. From women
as low in the social scale as bar hostesses any insult is trebled in
value. Nearly all hostesses are essentially prostitutes in that they
accept money for sexually satisfying men. This is not how they see
themselves. Because they reserve the right to refuse a man, however
rarely, and even if never, they view themselves as non-prostitutes—
prostitutes are women without a nay. That this snobbish hallucination
of superiority is no more than a distinction without a difference would
never enter their heads.

Hostesses are, however, not only on the lookout for a well-heeled
male as husband, love-nest sugar daddy, or one-night stand. As
hostesses, as cigarette-lighting animals, drink-orderers, table-com-
panions, hand-holders, and ego-boosters, their presence is heavily
charged for by the hour. As well they get a percentage on every
drink drunk in their company, on every dish of salted peanuts, celery

curls, dehydrated sardines, or seaweed-infested biscuits they can
wheedle onto a customer's table. They prefer, therefore and naturally,
regular clients, feckless clients, mug clients, who will dally for hours
nibbling and sipping and tipping, and who, when the inflated bill is
presented at the evening's end, will pay it without question. *Noblesse
oblige!* Face must not be lost!

Mr Butterfry has only a drink or two in each clip-joint. Why not?
We are ladder-drinking, pub-crawling. He is showing me the many
bars he is familiar with, the same many bars in which he is loathed.
He is not loathed affectionately or off handedly. Just inside every
satin-quilted or rustically bamboo or abstract-adorned bar-restaurant
door he is met with simon pure loathing, naked hatred. There is no
mistaking, though sloshed I am, what the deadly eyes display above
the switched-on smiles. I arrive at the idea that he is execrated not
only because he rebuffs, in tonally offensive Japanese, any attempt
to clip him, not only because he scorns the rules of the game to pay
as he goes, and pocket the change. It is rather elsewise—the vehemence
of his manner, the malevolence of his unnecessary candour. It is his
own hatred. It smells of murder. With no idea of what he is saying, I
can hear that his voice brandishes knives, and flourishes vitriol. When
we leave, the Japanese rules of duplicity require that we are fare-
welled with a facsimile of politeness (anyway, *I* am doing nothing
outrageous), with bows that must be hell to make, with cooings
that must scald the larynx.

"Auf wienerschnnitzel, y' bandy bitches!" shouts bandy Mr Butterfry and, on the way to the next duel of hatreds, bedecks the theme
of Bloody Jap Women are the Bloody Scum of the Earth with "Pox-
ridden bloody sluts! Bloody blood-sucking jealous bloody *tarts*, everyone of 'm! 'N' they've all got false bloody tits! Bloody gold-diggers!"
and worse, far worse, on and on, until the last bar shuts, and another
Saturday disappears down the sewer dealing with days that have
no history.

Where, meantime, is the vivaciously boring Blue who waited by
the sentry-box with a *presento* of chocolate biscuits and Black Market
stockings? Where is the Blue who punned abominably, and unceasingly chattered (and acutely chaffered), in the back room of the
White Rose Souvenir Shoppe?

My hangover still surrounding me in the fashion of a saint's nimbus, I keep the business-card tryst, and discover from a Mr Butterfry
far less injured than I that there should be an overnight bag with me
because it was arranged in the New Yorker that I am coming on a
commercial-traveller foray into the country. Not daring to reveal that
I have no memory of this, I lie that all I need is a toothbrush which

I shall buy at the chemist's in the underground town at Shinjuku, where I also propose having a draught of bottled oxygen to vaporize away my nimbus, which is steadily turning dog-coloured. Presently, nimbus-free, I and a toothbrush with a mauve handle enter Mr Butterfry's Nissan Gloria, and we take off on the first of the many meaningless, fascinating, and revelatory trips we are to make together.

"Y' little mate" is how the Lion Beer Hall mob talk of Mr Butterfry to me when it becomes apparent, after several more Saturday booze-ups, that we are spending much time together like a transmogrified version of Abbot and Costello. True enough: for a couple of months he is my little mate—coarse, sore of spirit, restless as a maggot, and perpetually steeped, even at his gayest and bawdiest, in a rage against something he has not, although he never stops talking of himself, got to the point of directly revealing.

As we drive about the countryside to get orders for margarine or pineapple juice or plastic watering-cans, miles of autobiography stream from him, a mish-mash of superhuman sexual feats, quasi-criminal triumphs of diddling and putting-over, and decelerating happinesses. I come to see that he has been unable to betray his type, his gift of the infirmities and spivvish vigours accompanying Blueness, that his life is movement but not progress and that, just as he drinks with the ritualistic appetite of children and drunks, which has nothing to do with thirst, so he snatches (or used, when younger, to snatch) with ritualistic fever at the unworthiest of satisfactions. He has, I more and more suspect, built a life not to be built on and added to but burned down, a life without consolations or myths.

When I knew him in Kure, long before he had swopped himself and cheekiness for Mr Butterfry and his strange choler, he was one of the shrewdest and most successful of Black Market operators. Myself a non-starter, I was embedded in operator friends and acquaintances: ungentlemanly officers from my Mess, colonels' la-di-da wives, cow-eyed mothers-of-three, acne-embossed children from the school for officers' offspring, fluke-ridden houseboys, virgin canteen assistants from the YWCA, devirginized nurses from the Army hospital. Mr Butterfry, not yet out of his chrysalis, outshone them by many watts. His rocking-horse nostrils objectified his genius for smelling out. Even more zealously than he sniffed around the White Rose, the amateurish strip-tease shows of the Naka-dori, and the major's housegirl, whom he courted with *presentos* of skeins of wool, lengths of Habutai silk, and scanties of imitation black lace, he sniffed around and into the Black Market heart of the back alleys, his face boyishly crinkled and winningly freckled, his eyes motionless as sixpences, his gruesome voice inexorably sawing away at any branch in the way. He had come to a dishevelled country which seemed to make promises, to drop hints. He had ears to hear and, having heard, the skill to turn promises and hints into lovely filthy money.

How he was able to stay on in Japan after Occupation troops withdrew is a triumph he missed telling me of. He became rich. At a time when the starving natives were making hashes of cats and sacred temple deer, suburban Tokyo houses could be bought for the proceeds from the Black Market sale of a couple of cartons of Lucky Strike cigarettes. Mr Butterfry owned five such houses as well as a beach house at Atami, and a mountain retreat at Chuzenji. He married the major's housegirl, who was able to lady it over housegirls of her own. Two children were born, two girls.

He had, so to speak, come all the way from Gippsland and boyhood to catch his unicorn, had caught, and corralled it. He could have consented to be mollified by being some kind of expatriate *rentier*. Not he. Con-men outwit themselves. Maybe there were events outside himself, outside idiot extravagance and jettisoned commonsense, outside his own lack of foresight, which led to downfall. The lusty Black Market, for instance, sickened, grew worse, died. This is not entirely as he understands it or, rather, as I understand he understands it.

As he drives through the Progress-devastated hills and dales littered with bulldozers and concrete-mixers, now and then interrupting his high-pitched and blasphemy-larded monologue to gulp rum from the bottle we share like unholy infants, it gradually becomes patent that he regards himself as having a mystical bond with catastrophe. Some It or They beyond conventional mishap has had it in for him since before he was baptized Gregory R. Patience, and long before he was the scorned Mr Butterfry. I should like to say, "For God's sake, you've got a job, a house, a car, an air-conditioner, an Omega watch, and a gut full of rum. Relax, mate, relax!" or "Look here, you've been crimming around just this side of the law for years. What did you expect to expect?" Instead I plug my mouth with that of the rum bottle.

He finds no repose in the absurd Victim of Fate verdict he has come to. His dismay at being down to his last house and last car has the quality of hostility. With an impercipience so incredible that it dazzles me as if he were a genius moron, he has designated himself a martyr —and a furious one.

The martyrdom, I notice, habitually has Japan as its backdrop or, rather, always seems always to have its climax at the core of a *contretemps*, twilight and sinister, which had been magicked in a jiffy out of radiant high noon by an ectoplasmic but evilly Japanese agency.

I suspect, however, that the faceless fate, the voodoo in the woodheap who or which enrages him, is bandily biped, *homo sapiens*, common as dirt, Mr Butterfry himself.

When his bouts or railing become too strident and dotty I want to say, "For God's sake, Blue, give it a rest. Why don't you just shut up shop here, and shoot back home before you get too decrepit to be racing around flogging frozen mutton and Pommy gin?" This is out of the question, and not to be done because it is not the thing to do: I have no licence. His having, despite the autobiographical incontinence, not stripped away all the rinds from his privacy—and, surely, deliberately—seems a warning to come no closer, to keep my shut mouth shut. It is an attentive ear he has invited to accompany him on his trips to sell condensed milk, not a questioning tongue.

Perhaps I could safely, during his maudlin outbursts of it's-just-a-little-street-where-old-friends-meet home-sickery, have asked why he does not cut the Japan painter, and whip his wife and daughters off to Australia. Per-haps. I decide, however, not to ask, and listen to the one-after-umpteenth edition of his dreamlike passion (he does not know how dream-like, and I have no right to tell him) to retire and settle down—his words—in a little Gippsland fishing port he was last in over twenty years ago. Because I knew this Sleepy Hollow place as he knew it, I understand—at least, as much as someone who has no daydream at all can understand—his fantasy of playing the well-to-do beachcomber there, the weather forever halcyon, the fish always biting, the weatherboard pub never closed. I see what Mr Butterfry sees: the palsied red gum wharves stacked with crayfish pots, the indolent reed-fringed river seething with bream, the Shylock-bearded goats under the Norfolk Island pines, the sandy side-streets of bluestone cottages behind hedges of looking-glass shrubs and lad's love. Yes, I should like to say, "Go back!" but dare not, cannot. If he is trying to change himself into something else, he must use his own wand.

Anyway, whatever nebulous but vindictive force he accuses of hounding him into a cul-de-sac, I incline nearer to a certainty that inertia of will is to blame, that he is his own victim, his own chained and captious mongrel. From my seat there is little else to see.

Then, one night, as if he has—flash! boom!—become clairvoyant about my unput questions and secret judgment or as if he has been profoundly considering them for weeks, and has reached a decision, suddenly, utterly apropos of nothing external to his own mind, he says, with electrifying and ugly vehemence, "Yeah, by Christ, *yeah! I will*. Yeah, I'll showya; I'll bloody showya, mate."

He is drunker than I have ever seen him, maybe because I am so many undrunk drinks more sober than is usual in his company as to be practically maiden. We are well within the outskirts of Tokyo, driving back from Atsugi and the United States Naval Air Station where, having got much larger orders for gin and Kobe steaks and plastic baseball-team jackets than he foresaw, he has over-celebrated in the officers' bar.

Now, early night, eight o'clock, seventy miles an hour, out of the blue: "I'll bloody showya, mate."

With not the wispiest notion of what he is getting at, "Good for you; I can hardly wait," I say, and, "Show me what?" I expect no more than some super-dive as yet unknown to me, some special coven of bedizened monkey-women with unflinching snow-white smiles whose hatred of Mr Butterfry is at the peak, who are already lined up with their tumblers of petrol and an Esper electronic cigarette-lighter. "Show me what, master?"

"You'll see. You'll see." For the first time I realize that the adolescent falsetto, grating and grinding, is old, older than he is, as the noise of the glacier starting to move is older than the glacier itself. "You'll see. I'll bloody showya what it's bloody like." He stops. The primeval sound stops.

Silence . . . and silence.

Silence from him is another first-time experience, and an unnerving one. Momentarily I am aghast. The ventriloquist has left the scene. No matter, the doll drives on. The doll, worn-out and voiceless, with its ginger curls and flat glass eyes, drives on, robot-perfect, at perilous speed. I am host to a nightmare fancy: he and I, the mute residue of Mr Butterfry and I, are to spend eternity together, alone together, fixed side by side in the front seat of a runaway Nissan Gloria which he will steer violently around corner after corner, cutting deeper and ever deeper into a maze of unnamed streets, a labyrinth of catless alleys, all utterly deserted and silent—locked houses, shuttered shops, unlit street-lights, blind walls, smokeless chimneys, telegraph poles propping up the dead filaments of a vast cobweb that has no edge and no centre.

It seems unreal, therefore, when he pulls up in a suburban street of real-seeming passersby, with overhead lamps, and the television gabble of "I Love Lucy" in dubbed Japanese. The street is not much chop, but not seedy, rather claustrophobic from the eight-foot walls of grey concrete on each side in which are set the fake rural gateways leading to the houses behind. As Mr Butterfry gets out at one of the gates he speaks again.

"Home," he says. "Home sweet bloody home." This has the intonation of Hell sweet bloody hell. "Get cracking, y' bastard. Y' gonna meet the wife." In such situations I am the Pavlov rat—my hand fossicks for the comb.

As he opens the gate I ask, "What's her name?" I ask because, in the Kure days, she was one of the Mess housegirls, and it seems possible that she might expect from me the politeness of remembering if she were Fumigo-san, Kiyoko-san, Setsuko-san, or Whatever-san. I am simply after rainy day material to play the game of being well-mannered with.

Mr Butterfry behaves as though I am asking for my own name. He goes immobile and pensive and, after a pause, turns his head, arranges that his eyes are on me, as on a defective, and after an unbelieving examination of something behind my face, says fretfully, "I married the bastard, di'n't I?"

What does he mean?

"Whattay' think her bloody name is? Mrs Hirohito? Mrs Duchess of Windsor? It was for real, amigo. She's Mrs Patience all right." Ah well. Next, as though the name is other and more than authentic, as though information is not the true centre of the circle, he says it again, "Mrs Patience". His burnt-out lips make the two words the filthiest I have ever heard. His face is that of a vole in a trap. Had I any trust in imagination I would accept, right there, outside the gate of crooked branches, the catalogue of answers which has flashed on the screen of my mind, and would dramatically remember any appointment anywhere, and excuse myself to hurry off in the direction of anywhere with his "Auf wienerschnitzel, chico!" gimletting my eardrums. I have no trust in the imagination. I follow Mr Butterfry toward Mrs Patience, and the living-room.

The Japanese living-room with its floor of padded matting, its paper shutters, inconspicuous shut cupboards, sole ornament, and no furniture, has a spartan and spurious refinement. In attempting the affectation of making an art of the skeletal and parsimonious, it imposes the harrowing discomfort of poverty. It is a sort of fragile hut that can quickly become a pigsty hut, kept scrupulously shipshape, ungarnished as an empty bird-cage, it gives the illusion of being the acme of abominably good taste. Of such a room, a large one obviously the total of two former rooms, Mr Butterfry and Mrs Patience, and their half-caste daughters, Lana, seventeen, and Shirley, thirteen, have made an illustrative and crudely gorgeous museum of their lives. It is the very zenith of abominably bad taste.

The area set aside, as it were, for Mr Butterfry's exhibit is dominated by a cocktail bar as flashily outrageous and sparkling as the altar of a Mexican cathedral, and his treasures are arranged near the monstrosity, or festooned above and about it; scores of goliath or obscene bottle-openers; scores of needlessly ingenious and fantastic cigarette-lighters; the stencilled felt pennants of Australian Navy ships, life-saving clubs, and football teams; several richly framed oil-paintings of Gippsland landscapes by old-fashioned, once esteemed Impressionist artists; and a squad of atrocious Made-in-Japan statuettes, all either offcolour or self-consciously pornographic—Pis-Manneken, Leda and the Swan, Europa and the Bull, Cupid and Psyche, that sort of thing. It is the bazaar of a rich little poor boy.

In his unpunctuated soliloquies about himself Mr Butterfry has repeatedly let fall, maybe as incidental self-tribute, that his half-breed daughters are popular as photographic or commercial television models. I have taken popular to mean used twice or thrice rather than once. How wrong. In the junk-shop congestion the most discomposing objects are the overlapping posters which, from ceiling to floor, cover the walls with bar-hostess smiles, and eyes and eyes and eyes. On every hand Lana toys with, holds up, or archly indicates Mikimoto pearls, an Instamatic camera, a deer-skin purse, a Hi-Cook Fryer, a stereo-monaural tape-recorder, or a goblet of Mercian wine. Elsewhere she emerges from a scarlet Compagno Spider roadster or a mink coat, or is discovered in the company of a comely young man amid the *art nouveau* conceits of Maxim's de Paris de Tokyo. Meantime, dozens of poster Shirleys enact, from under a tar-black fringe, or from between horizontal pigtails, childish rapture over tinned beef curry, effervescing cordials, bottled tangerines, homogenized milk, seaweed drinks, and lurid sorbets.

In appearance—the posters prove it over and over again—Lana and Shirley are unsulliedly Japanese, racially untainted. No physical trace shows of the blue-eyed Mr Butterfry with the paprika-tinted freckles blotching his forehead, and sprinkled among the red-gold grass on the backs of his hands. He might never have impregnated, never have set foot in Japan, never even have existed. His daughters could be copy-cat versions of an infinity of ancestresses as they are copy-cat versions of the oh-so-sweet-and-cute housegirl one used to see mincing pigeon-toed between the canna-beds of the mess garden towards the sentry box where her Black Marketeer lover bobbed up and down like a Jack-in-the-box. Visually, the daughters are amoeboid breakaways from no one except Mrs Patience.

Her indubitable contribution to the museum is a perfect illustration of what happens when the Japanese move one millimetre off the strait of their national taste into the complex cross-currents of non-Japanese taste. Richelieu-work antimacassars hang on obese settees of glossy brocade; the carpet arabesques of unsubdued colours pulsate and twitch beneath the light of a plethora of frilled lampshades; two

china cabinets and a glass-fronted sideboard are stoked with the
white-hot brilliance of cut-glass vessels; urns of blue velvet roses are
disposed on pedestals of fictitious marble; little lace-shrouded tables
are burdened with trinkets and figurines. The lean woman standing
erect at the centre of this intemperance is, Mr Butterfry says, *her*,
Mrs Patience. He could be introducing me to a leper.

She acknowledges me by making a cryptic minor adjustment to
her expression, no more. Her eyes are on her husband, as on a snake.

Out of context I should never have recognized the ex-housegirl
any more than I recognized Mr Butterfry at the Lion, and it can only
be illusion that, in the taut creature in its dusky kimono, I think I
discern vestiges of what I think she was once like. I do instantly
recognize something else. How could I not? Outside the gate of
tortured branches my mind had in a flash warned that, just as in all
the bars with their inimical hostesses, so in the last of Mr Butterfry's
seven houses, so in this preposterously bizarre room. Here, too, the
captive air is wounded by the vixen's smile, radiantly bitter, by the
eyes implacable and pitiless. Does she, too, call him Mr Butterfry?

He is behind his bar, under the stalactites of football and life-saving
pennants, pouring this and that to make some show-off interfusion
he calls his Special. Without looking at her, without faltering in his
mixing, "Y' bloody rude Nipponese bitch," he says. "Why di'n't y'
say something to m'mate, eh? Eh? Who d'ya bloody think you are?
Y' know how to behave. She knows bloody well how to behave, mate.
She knows all right." He illustrates that he does, too. He pours a final
jigger of Parfait Amour into the turbid Special and, his mask of
malice merely slightly tempered by hostliness, lifts one of the brim-
ming pilsener glasses: "Come an' get it! It's curl-a-mo, chico. Lead
in the old pencil." As I take the glass, he continues his hostly good
behaviour. "Not t' worry, mate. It's not you she's shitty at. A-a-ah,
no no no! Home sweet bloody home, this is. I told y' I'd showya."
He has fulfilled his obligations, and abandons me to his Special,
and returns to his sheep. "You s-l-u-t. Y' hate me, don'tya? Don'tya?
Don'tya, eh? Answer me, y' scungy bitch. Answer me!"

She has been standing as she was standing when we came in,
unshakable, unshakably in the middle of the implausible emporium,
she and her quarter-smile of well-bred repugnance, her dark-robed
trimness, her iron-still hair riveted around the invisible sorcery of
her mind, her half-seen hands holding nothing with the waxen dead
calm of hands in control of some monstrous engine of destruction.
Disdain surrounds her like an element nothing can fog, splinter, or
melt. A future as yet uncorked, she will, at any moment, in a voice
pure and angular as quartz, utter a lacerating profundity, produce

the flash of a lightning-blue sentence which will erase Mr Butterfry in a sprig of smoke.

"Answer me!"

She speaks. Her lips writhe, as lips in novelettes used to, and she speaks: "Watta y' doing home here at this hour? Get thrown outa somew'ere?"

The battle is joined. The brawl is on. The tainted leaves explode away from the branches. The branches snap and shatter like the sticks of a terrible fan.

At my time of life to be embrangled in the who's-afraid-of-Virginia-Woolf improprieties of a husband and wife savaging each other is still dismaying and spirit fatiguing but no longer shocks and sickens as once it did. Too many ex-glazed lovers and ex-glossy couples have played typhoon and bloody murder under my nose. Perhaps, to be certain of double murder without murdering, they shamelessly require the brake and safety of a bystander or, at least, as exhibitionists do, the presence of a dumbstruck audience. Mrs Patience and Mr Butterfry deny me nothing. The dirty leaves and rotten branches rain down—subtle mischief, flagrant deceit, betrayal, double-dealing, and malevolent chicanery.

Regarding myself as beyond shock, I am nevertheless shocked, and it takes a while to decide why. I am certainly startled and fascinated when it comes out, piecemeal, that most of Mr Butterfry's misfortunes have not been caused by his own moral or mental debility nor by a fateful mis-mating of Japanese stars but by a gluttonously ambitious Japanese mother, the former oh-so-sweet-and-cute housegirl bred on rice slops and pickled radish in a penurious and primitive village in a cleft of the hills behind Kure. It is by her machinations that, one by one, Mr Butterfry's clutch of houses and, I learn, a motor-launch and a racehorse have evaporated as bribes to buy continuing prominence for Lana and Shirley in the careers she has chosen for them. It is easy to see that, to herself, she appears conventionally maternal: thousands of Japanese parents, for example, feed examiners the heavy bribes which ensure a son's or daughter's place in a university. Her bribes will have been indecently heavy for, although Japanese in appearance, the daughters are authentic half-breeds and, as such, so near to untouchable that unusual largesse can have been the only means of getting them within cooee of the limelight let alone smack in the middle of it. Yes, I am startled by the knowledge of what really happened to Mr Butterfry's ill-got riches, but not shocked.

What does shock, and so totally, so physically, that the searing Special laves my gullet like milk, is the quality of Mrs Patience's

self-defensive shrillness, the freakishness of her accent and verbal
obscenity. If the poster daughters, whose magnified china smiles and
multitudinous immense opaque eyes glimmer all around and above
the mêlée, have inherited not one perceivable scintilla of himself
from Mr Butterfry, not so the wife. She has, mantis, eaten his voice
from him—inflection, pitch, discordancy, the lingo itself with its oaths
and mutilations. Her self-justifications match his accusations in every
degraded particular. Acrid and bowelless though they are they even
have the wheedling spirit of the con-man, and I stand convinced that
it all, to the last and most contemptible betrayal, serves him right,
that it is absolutely just that his chickens have come home to roost
defeathered and septic. At the same time—and not merely because
I am shocked by the *lusus naturae* effect of a burlesque Australian
working-man's voice spurting from a pocket-edition foreign woman
in a tastefully dour kimono—I feel that she, rigid and free of warmth
as a doll, is charged with power and evil, with all the glib treachery
and rancorous lunacy of her race, and that Mr Butterfry is doomed,
unjustly doomed.

The mind's cigarette-lighter flicks up a single-flame glimpse of
him as he was, as Blue, in those White Rose and Black Market days,
chipper, impertinent, disarming, as cock-a-hoop as the village idiot
boy at one of his own wretched sallies in the whiffy backroom of the
Souvenir Shoppe, lecherous and unfaithful as a tomcat yet faithful
as a mongrel to his idea of love for his housegirl, his oriental Daisy
Mae, of whom "I love the poor little bastard, chico. Mate, I'm tellin'
ya, she's the only bloody sheila'll ever get me by the short hairs."

Let there be no doubt that it is the fiery and filament tributaries
of the Special suddenly overrunning their levees, and inundating
my brain, that cause the lighter-flame to expand into a wide-screen
fantasy. Despite the din of the quarrel, the strident soundtrack, I
see the whole lurid vision. The down-at-heel castle, Arthurian, Dis-
neyish. Battlements bearded with weeds. A raven hunched on each
and every pennant pole. Pennants like old tea-towels. Dawn—cold
and cheap. Far up, in the highest turret, the faceless King of Con-men
at an embrasure, behind the cobwebs, behind the smoke of a gangster
cigar. Far below, just beyond the portcullis, the rabble of mounted
knights on the drawbridge, Knights of the Unholy Grail waiting the
J. Arthur Rank gong that will unleash the ratbag mob on its quest
of swindling and duping: Sir Jeroboam the Purple Knight, Sir Jocu-
laris the Chequered Knight, Sir Jackanapes the Pin-striped Knight,
a scruffy host of others, spivs all, and . . . there! . . . younger than
any, freckle-peppered, ginger-haired, *retroussé*, tirra-lirra-ing in a
lamentable falsetto, our man from Gippsland, Sir Juvenilis the Blue

Knight. The nags fret and caracole. Each knight, waiting there in the bilious sunrise, secretively polishes a platitude or two, practises a snide and hypnotizing smile. Ah! the ravens stir, hunch their shoulders, look down their beaks—the gong sounds. They're off! Watch the Blue Knight. Follow Sir Juvenilis, and see him by-pass the perils that topple the others. The Forest Forlorn, the Hazardous Crags, the Mere of Thin Ice, the Marsh of False Steps. Hear him whistling past Dungeon Grey where Giant Wideawake has clapped Sir Jeroboam and Sir Jackanapes. Now he gallops down the last avenue (trees of tinsel and fake crystal), radiant with his rake-offs, and shining like a prince, toward the Maiden of the Eastern Hills. In a flash the bells are ringing, the champagne bottles foam at the mouth, the maiden has become his oh-so-sweet-and-cute princess, and the screen shudders and shimmers with intimations of happy-ever-after.

It is a pity, it is always a pity, that even if one is shrewd, or lucky enough to leave in time, while the champagne and *hors-d'oeuvre* are being gulped and gutsed, that circumstances—the dropped glove, the library book left under the seat—bring one back, reluctant and fuming, in the middle of another instalment, a later reel. In this case the dropped glove can be said to be the Shimbashi Lion Beer Hall or, more pinpointedly, Blue saying, in the tones of an aggrieved and deserted deity, "You don' remember me, y' bastard". The later instalment, the latest instalment, is the one in which the Maiden from the Hills, promoted to the princess with her surfeit of antimacassars, and cabinets of cut-glass salad bowls and sandwich trays, turns out to be no more than the wicked witch, the run-of-the-mill dangerous dam, with her casque of iron hair, her stranger's mind, and the stolen voice which quadruples her power since she can annihilate her victim with his own bird-of-prey accent and tricks, his own brutal oaths.

It is time to leave again, and finally, no dropped glove. If nothing else the soundtrack, the who's-afraid-of-Virginia-Woolf discord, is too boring, on and on and on. More boring than anything is the truth. The truth? Mr Butterfry, my little mate, Blue, Gregory R. Patience, Sir Juvenilis, foul-mouthed, desperately yelping behind his cocktail bar and a palisade of on-the-nose statuettes, has really found what the Unholy Grail contains. He has come as far as he can, and that is that. Now that he has, as he said he would, bloody shown me, perhaps I can, at last, partly agree with him: a fatigue like the fatigue of metal has incurably affected whatever brand of luck he may be said to have had. There is no chance of its reviving, and no way back for Mr Butterfry, no escape hatch, secret tunnel, air-lift, exit of any kind, none, and nothing.

It is just as well. It leaves him with at least one dream, one Teddy

Bear to tote around, or cuddle as he ranges the country to sell Pommy gin and Yankee running-shoes. The Teddy Bear dream is the retiring and settling down one. What I had no voucher of permit to tell him is better not told. The dream is no longer worth dreaming. The Sleepy Hollow fishing village in Gippsland, where he sees his dream self fishing and lazing and earbashing and shouting drinks for well-kippered old-timers with fish scales in the salty folds of their sweaters, has been wiped off the board of reality. Goats and Norfolk Island pines, sandy streets and lad's love hedges, crayfish pots, and weather-board pub, not any of these is there. Offshore, oil-drills straddle the former fishing grounds. The village has become a geometric townlet of metal and cement. The blue-stone cottages, one of which he pic-tures himself buying for a song, are contemporarized, added to, and reverberate to the habits and hallucinations and accents of Americans, and cost the earth. Ferro-concrete hostels, gardenless, glassy, glaring, enclose the institutional male horseplay and immigrant odours of escapees from the neurotic and dirty Old World, the riff-raff of degenerating civilizations.

It does not matter how I escape the costly chaos of the living-room and the walls papered with depthless eyes and shallow smiles. As a ghost does from the ignobilities of the living, escape I do, slipping away so inconspicuously that the two engaged vehemently in the drama of hatred notice nothing. The soundtrack of their vilifications does not falter or blur. I close the gate of artistically deformed branches as one closing a book never to be opened again. The long long street of secluding and imprisoning walls, ill-lit, and medievally winding in and out of a plexus of sunless other medievally winding and ill-lit streets, unravels before me, and instantly and darkly ravels and reravels itself behind me. Back there, farther and farther back, lies the room, a gaudy and inferior star caught in the meshes, enclosed in the night just as the geisha, meretricious, bizarre, and blinding, was in the black leatherette cabin of her jinricksha. Back there—caught and enclosed in the room—Mr Butterfry, the Mr Butterfry who must, tonight and any night, sooner or later, flag, run down, crack up, give in again, the Mr Butterfry with whom one has shared the fascinating exhaustions of mateship, and on whom alternately squandered contempt and pity. Not until I am almost out of the tangle of suburban criss-crossings and convolutions does it seem clear that the contempt is useless and that, even if he has to suffer alien constellations and outlandish ethics, the pity is not needed at all.

Whatever anyone thinks life is for or about, whatever fatuous prophecies are attributed to scientists, whatever abnormal skills are wished upon poets, musicians, actors, etchers, sculptors and others of the non-man-in-the-street sect, Nature has not once indicated that life is for or about anything more than an arcane necessity to breed, before one dies, others to breed and live and die. The rest is side-line, mere decoration—Rembrandt oil-paintings, penicillin, Big Berthas, graven images, Lanner waltzes, top-hats, asceticism, pacifism, football-club pennants, cut-glass salad bowls, take your pick—side-line decoration, no more. Nature's suckers are, in a final generalizing count, left one only wry consolation: to love their spawn even if the spawn detest them.

I cannot tell whether, off the posters, Lana and Shirley Patience, mobile and nubile, the flames of their smiles turned down or utterly put out, love the Mr Butterfry whose relation to them, in a country of racial snobbism, makes them nearly untouchable. A guess that they do not love him is beside the point. Whether, in a melodramatically changed form (Act Sixteen, Scene Ninety) from the Kure one, Mr Butterfry still loves the transformed housegirl is most doubtful. A surmise of not is also beside the point. He has decided to bloody show me something of why he viciously hunts bar-creatures through the neon nights. They are creatures of the same sex and jungle as the one he long ago foretold would have him by the short hairs. Only a tithe of his excessive despair is, in private, uselessly usable against the combination of her alien inscrutability and stolen accent and vocabulary. He has, therefore, so much to spare that a prodigality of public venom has become inevitable.

He has, as well, either by accident or with elemental subtlety, bloody shown something else.

Paper smiles and eyes, bought with other houses, remain lining the walls of his last house. In the centre of its bazaar-room, she, the classic dam as much a dupe of nature as he, remains, witch-neat in a sombre kimono, black-tongued as an Australian alley virago. He has not thrown her out. He has thrown out no one, not even himself. He has not torn down the seductively grimacing posters.

If the last house must finally go so that there is no wall at all on which to tack the extra posters the house has been bartered for, his condition of imprisonment would not alter. A beat-up Sir Juvenilis, an aging terrier of a spiv snarling and sniffing in the daily darker corners of the prison, he is not to be pitied, neither for losing his Black Market riches nor the fishing village which no longer exists.

How else than by pretending to hate such showy losses can Mr Butterfry really and truly con himself—as con-men such as he must finally do—into accepting that he hates his guilt, and deeply loves his daughters, all smiles, safe for a year more, a week more, a moment-before-the-deluge more, on and behind their gaudy paper posters?

THELMA FORSHAW

The Grand Passion

"Come in, dear—we are all ready and waiting for you," Mrs Nesbitt carolled, meaning, of course, Zelda supposed, the afternoon-tea and general air of expectation—the way people graciously clear a space in their lives for a visitor and his tidings.

Zelda had not seen her aunt since she was fifteen; now she was twenty-two and going the rounds of her relatives like a town-crier, telling of her recent betrothal. She had considered the matter with her mother and they had decided that the clan was too ill-assorted and the feuds too subtle and complex to bring all together at an engagement party. It was not wholly because they were of Irish extraction and might fight. It was better to see them separately, that's all, Zelda's mother pointed out rather sombrely. She did not want a donnybrook in *her* home.

Zelda held up her left hand and, smiling, wiggled a flashing ring-finger before her aunt's eyes like a ticket of admission. Mrs Nesbitt's mouth opened and her eyebrows lifted in the impressed way expected of her. She admitted Zelda and led her into the sitting-room where infra-red strips were glowing on two walls, warming their air, and Mr Nesbitt sat in a crouching position on the divan, his elbows on his knees like a statue of "The Thinker". He stood up and shook her by the hand after she had flashed the ring at him, too.

"Hooked someone, eh?" he said. "What does he do?"

Zelda said that he was a mining engineer and was away at present mining—or engineering—whatever it is such people do. Neil had never really explained it to her and she did not know. One day she would ask him about it, she believed it was essential for a wife to understand a man's work to a certain extent . . . she trailed off vaguely. She was not sure why.

"How delightful you are," Mrs Nesbitt said bitterly, as she wheeled up the tea-trolley laden with cups and scones and cakes. "I'm pretty

certain that's how men prefer one—not *quite* understanding what
they are up to. *Not* knowing what makes them tick."

Zelda's eyes widened at this sudden swathe of analysis her aunt
had cut through the pleasant, sleepy Sunday afternoon where she was
ready to tell, with a pardonable touch of triumph, all about her prize
and his capture. She took her cup with a murmur and glanced at
her uncle. He had the look of a mandarin. Bland and inscrutable.
She thought of a burglar with a stocking pulled over his face, blur-
ring the features. She could not remember if he always looked like
that or if he had just pulled the stocking over his face when his wife
spoke. He had grinned peculiarly on her arrival. Crookedly, as if
trying to convey ruefulness through the welcome.

"Is he mean?" asked Mrs Nesbitt, squatting down on a pouffe and
balancing her cup and saucer on the points of her knees.

"Mean?"

But it had not been a question—Mrs Nesbitt wanted to pronounce:
"Romance cannot live with meanness. It dies the death."

Mr Nesbitt stuck his little finger into one ear and shook it rapidly
as if *vibrato* speech affected his eardrums.

"No, he's not—he's, in fact, very—"

"*He* used to send me to his sister's clothing factory when I needed
a dress or coat and there I had to choose 'seconds' or remnants at a
lower price than if I went to a store like other women. We hadn't
been married a month. The honeymoon barely over and I mad with
love of him!"

Zelda was aghast. "Mad with love" was an expression she had
never heard spoken before. Still, it was true that "mad with love"
and "remnants" did not sound right together. She imagined that
"seconds" ought to come later, a year, two years . . . perhaps after
the children . . .

"It's not as if he was poor," said Mrs Nesbitt. "That one could
understand. No, he was never *poor*."

Mr Nesbitt smoothed a balding head and tried not to seem like a
robber-baron. However, the idea did not repel him and he could not
avoid a somewhat sleek look. Zelda felt he had received as a compli-
ment what was intended quite otherwise.

Her aunt said: "We are now living in opposition to his old régime.
Now that he 'has it', as he calls it, he would like me to dress up and
show off. I refuse. It's too late. And I will not be bought. Futhermore,
I will not advertise his success for him."

And, indeed, Zelda noticed that her aunt was wearing a pair of
baggy old slacks ("seconds" she wondered) and a scruffy sweater,
her hair pulled back into a queue with a rubber-band. She did, in

fact, have an I-don't-care-a-hang look. It was a shame, as she had heard that her aunt had been rather stylish once.

She drifted off a little, gazing at the white blaze of her ring, then said, because she wanted to talk about Neil—that was what she had come for, after all: "*We're* very much in love. I know it's true love because I've never felt the same with anyone else."

This seemed to act as a detonator, for her aunt burst out: "*No one* could have had more than we had. I fell for that man hook, line and sinker." Her voice trembled and deepened. "I gave him everything. Everything. Ah, God, I thought it was going to be so wonderful."

Mr Nesbitt hunched over his spread thighs and sipped his tea with eyes squeezed shut as if unnerved even by the memory.

"But what happened?" demanded Mrs Nesbitt, as if Zelda might know. "Mammon! Mammon! Mammon! That was *his* god—not Eros. The pursuit of hard cash. Business. Business. Business. And I on fire for him."

Zelda had never heard the words "on fire for him" spoken either. She had read an old book of her mother's called *The Sheik* at one time, and her aunt seemed to be emanating rather sheik-like feelings.

"He was always deep and secretive," Mrs Nesbitt went on. "I think that is what got me in. Attracted me—you know. He *seemed* very passionate—" she paused significantly, "—a bit of the actor in it, I often think now. But I'm not taken in any longer. I prefer celibacy. But there was a time—we would lie with our lips glued together each striving to drink the other in. Oh, don't tell *me* about sex."

Mr Nesbitt looked up alertly, ears pricked, like a dog hearing the rattle of the biscuit-tin. Then subsided.

Zelda flushed, and her aunt went on fierily: "That's what he's lost. That's what he traded for his miserable business. Don't get the idea we're past it. The heart has its reasons," she said with a cryptic air.

Zelda said with great calm and an air of commonsense—she was always good at critical moments——"Neil and I are very compatible."

She had not intended to challenge, but her aunt pounced: "Compatible!" She laughed: "Oh, ho!" then said: "There is compatible —*and* compatible. Those who get on and those who *prefer not to get on.*"

Zelda digested this profundity with a quick glance at Mr Nesbitt who, ever so slightly, lowered his eyelids at her, perhaps inscrutably as he once did to her aunt, enthralling her with his mystery. She had the feeling that he specialized in silence and inscrutability, preferring to communicate by mime. She did not find this particularly attractive herself—she liked a man to "come straight out with things". She wondered if he had teased Mrs Nesbitt into her grand passion with his mystery. If so, her aunt had fought back, all guns blazing, to breach the wall. It had apparently come as a great blow to her that an inscrutable man could in the end be so *mundane* as to choose business instead of spending his life romantically mystifying her. Her aunt had yearned while Mr Nesbitt totted up figures with absorbed satisfaction.

Zelda said peaceably: "We believe, Neil and I, that tolerance counts a great deal. Fortunately, we both like the same things. We share the same feelings, so—"

"*No one* could have had more than we had," Mrs Nesbitt retorted. "We were complementary—I, the outgoing one, he reserved and introverted—not to say *sneaky*," she qualified, replacing with scorn her old enchantment.

"That's often a good combination," Zelda said tactfully. "The attraction of opposites. Only, Neil and I are very much alike." She found herself sounding apologetic.

"Alike, eh?" Mrs Nesbitt seemed to consider this with grim tolerance, then she waved a finger, Zelda was not sure at whom. "Better a dinner of herbs where love is than a stalled ox without," and before Zelda could think of a polite response to this: "Make no mistake, I love that man!" Mrs Nesbitt said, pointing.

Her husband cringed.

"But he has had to realize that spiritual values come before the material. I have had to teach him. He is learning it slowly and— mark my words—*painfully.*"

Zelda, by now acclimatized, said tranquilly: "Of course love conquers all, and Neil and I find our little differences just melt away when we—" she dropped her eyes and smiled warmly, "Well, we are very much in love—romantically in love," she added, perhaps to correct a false impression, or with a touch of reproof.

Mr Nesbitt, condemned to spirituality for the materialism which had spoilt his wife's grand passion, looked wistfully at this gentle girl who would never, it seemed, offer a man more than he could tackle.

"A dinner of herbs," repeated Mrs Nesbitt, "than a stalled ox without. I've said it to him down the years. Now he offers me a stalled ox."

Mr Nesbitt looked surprised.

"But *I* say I don't want your bounty—I have had to pay too dearly for it."

Zelda looked at her admiringly and would have liked to commend her principles, but just then noticed Mr Nesbitt peeking hungrily at her bare knees, and she drew her skirt down as much as she could and said quickly, with faint defensiveness: "We are being married in November. You're both invited. It's at St Adrian's. An all-white wedding."

"I was married in a miserable registry office," her aunt flung at her. Zelda felt like a capitalist reproved by a communist. She said: "It's just a simple wedding. Only two bridesmaids."

"I had no bridesmaids," Mrs Nesbitt went on communistically. "And a so-called honeymoon locked up in a flat for which he had paid key-money—locked up because he thought if we left it someone might come and squat in it. I was not a honeymooner but a *care-taker*."

"We've bought a block of land at Seaforth," Zelda said very gently, "but it will be some time before we can afford to build on it."

"But the whole point is this—" Mrs Nesbitt stood up, her slacks bulging below the knees where they had stretched. She collected their empty teacups. "The thing holds together like steel. No one could part us. No one on earth."

Mr Nesbitt looked doubtful.

"I shall love him till I die in spite of everything. *That* will show you the power of *mature* love." She nodded oneupmanship at Zelda. "When you have no illusions left, when it has all been stripped down to the bare bones, and there it is still—shining like the Curies' minute speck of radium—" she lifted her face ceilingwards, exalted, while Mr Nesbitt, miming wry puzzlement, scratched his head.

"See my hand." She extended her left hand. It was bare of rings. "Lost in the surf years ago. Never replaced. Same with anniversaries. They mean nothing to me. What is the point when you *know*."

Zelda did not think she would enjoy getting quite so far down to bedrock. She turned to Mr Nesbitt to ask why there were no rings. He said: "I have offered her an engagement ring, wedding ring, eternity ring—the lot. All brand new." He seemed haughty with affront.

Mrs Nesbitt gave them both a triumphant glare as if they had ranged themselves (albeit hopelessly) against her merely by exchanging a few words. Fiercely, Medea-like, she gazed at them. Mr Nesbitt looked upward with raised brows, his eyes bulging with wonder. Zelda thought of a bird and snake rapt in mutual fascination. Feeling extraneous, she considered if it might be time to go.

"Wait!" cried Mrs Nesbitt. "There's something I want to give you." She vanished into some other room, while Zelda was left to gaze uncertainly at her uncle who lowered his eyelids at her again inscrutably, without effect. It seemed to devastate only Mrs Nesbitt.

Mrs Nesbitt returned and said: "Stand up."

Zelda and Mr Nesbitt both leapt to their feet.

"Not you," she said, waving him down. "*Never* you," she added significantly, thrusting him back into his cell. She held out to Zelda a silver disc suspended from links on either side by a thin silver chain—a disc the size of a cent on which were inscribed curious characters which for some reason Zelda took to be Arabic. She nervously asked her aunt what they meant. She herself felt they might well mean "All hope abandon ye who enter here". Mrs Nesbitt pursed her lips and, holding the disc between two finger tips suddenly spun it before Zelda's eyes. The rapidly spinning disc clearly spelled out I LOVE YOU and, as it ceased to spin, once more resumed its indecipherable markings.

"Take it for luck," urged Mrs Nesbitt cynically. "I forget where I got it—I've had it so many years. It's of no value to *me*."

Mr Nesbitt looked chastened, even crushed. He had given it to her as a courtship gift twenty years ago, in the days of the grand passion. Pure silver, too.

Zelda allowed her aunt to fasten the silver chain around her neck and deftly drop the disc behind the collar of her frock. She felt uneasy . . . even itchy.

"Thank you very much," she said, "but are you sure you don't want it."

"Why should I want it? What is the need for signs and symbols when you *know*? It is no use to me. It means nothing when you have extracted the essence." As if love had been a marrow-bone she had gnawed through.

Zelda took up her handbag and murmured good-bye to her uncle, who got to his feet and scraped them at her in farewell, a man condemned to spirituality.

Mrs Nesbitt drove the girl before her through the hall with brilliant smiles: "Good-bye and good luck—and I *mean* good luck." Zelda wondered at the fury of her farewell. She had come to display her ring and recount the lore of young love, but her aunt had, instead, showed her the lean and stoic gleanings of what people tend to call "an unhappy marriage". "Look! We have come through!" she might have shouted, flashing the badge of a wounded veteran, finer than any engagement ring.

Zelda turned, as well as she could with Mrs Nesbitt close on her heels, and waved towards Mr Nesbitt's robber-baron face hovering in the background. She went away feeling thoroughly trumped, not to say routed.

JOHN DURACK

The Road

FLUNG back by the speeding car, a gust of grit-laden wind tore at the clothing of the solitary figure by the highway.

The young man shrugged, and, dropping his outstretched arm, squinted into the afternoon rays of the winter sun, following the disappearing car down the gaunt grey trunks of ringbarked trees, till distance swallowed the scream of its tyres.

His first lift from near the university had been easy but he had been standing here now for an hour and had long been wondering why he had forsaken the anonymous security of the train trip for this conspicuous isolation.

Already a dozen or more cars had hurtled past him, momentary impressions of curious blank faces at windows or of offended propriety in the disapproving shake of a head. Safe in their little cages of tin and chrome, they could afford to ignore the hesitantly extended arm and awkwardly cocked thumb. Tasting the bitter rejection of their passing in the grit of their dust, the youth felt he was no more real to them than his scarecrow shadow on the highway. Wheels whirred and he strained his ears once more to hear them but they were only the still-departing tyres of the last car faintly persisting in the quiet air.

Squatting now beside his grimy port, he studied the shiny pebbles of the road's gravel verge and, as the dust settled slowly, he thought longingly of home and family—of a home he had not seen since he left for the university three months before in mingled exhilaration and fear. He remembered the knot of anxious anticipation that had tightened in his stomach as the train clack-clacked through Brisbane's outer suburbs. A symptom of inexperience and unease, it was to stay with him for most of his first term. But when he had left Brisbane early that afternoon he was already beginning to enjoy the arrogant surety of the young.

Home seemed very far away and his new-found liberty a challenge and an adventure. Secure in his niche as a student, he never imagined that a few uncaring faces in speeding cars could crumble his sense of identity and leave him with such a feeling of outcast desolation.

The faint whisper of tyres on bitumen made him lift his head, his eyes quickening, to the spot where the road appeared round a bend through trees. The pitch of the sound was lower, less frantic than those that had gone before and there was nothing aloof about the old blue utility which now slowed and rolled off the road towards him.

"In you get son, 'nd throw that in the back."

The door opened, "Watch out for Dot here though. She's a bit 'ev a crock so just mind her leg. You c'n sit between us."

The speaker was a heavily built man, his face tanned and battered by years of sun and weather, the eyes permanently slitted against the Queensland glare. The woman beside him was almost as deeply tanned but by comparison seemed small. She wore a grey cardigan and from under her nondescript dress a plaster-covered leg protruded stiffly. He clambered over her awkwardly and as he settled back on to the worn upholstery, became conscious of the vaguely pleasant smell of beer and tobacco.

" 'n where 're you heading, son, might a man ask?" The words from the big man were slow and cheerful and as the old utility rumbled up through the gears, the youth told them he was on the way home for the university holidays. Always a little wary of people's reactions to his being a student, he was relieved when the woman glanced at him, smiled and said, "Ah, you're one of them, then. We used to have a couple staying with us. Chinks, they were, medical students. Always cutting up bits of bodies and stuff and leaving them in the fridge . . . real well behaved though . . . but we never got any more when they left, did we, Bert?"

"No, Dot, we never. Funny pair though. Pretty quiet lot them Orr-i-e-ntals." He dragged the word out. "Never would have a beer with a bloke. . . . You'd be having the odd one or two now, wouldn't you, son?" This was a point about which the youth was a bit uneasy since he had promised his mother not to drink in first year and so far the promise had been kept.

The man was obviously disappointed. "Smoke though, eh?" hopefully. He could not disappoint him again. "Well, roll him a fag, Dot, why don't you?" It was useless to protest now and he watched uneasily as expert brown fingers rolled one, first for him and then for Bert. Relieved that they did not watch him as he smoked, he relaxed gradually against the old springs and tasted the unfamiliar strong flavour of tobacco.

The sun was still well above the horizon and the car seemed to

float along the road through a landscape in which every detail of
tree and grass and farm house showed up with clarity that made it
unreal. Hardly a car passed and they were the only thing moving
in a world where all motion was suspended. Except for the muted
purr of the engine it was very quiet, the man driving with the
unhurried assurance of one who was part of the vehicle, sensing the
road under the tyres with his own body.

As they drove westward the boy saw the sun suddenly transform
his two companions. Their faces were ageless and yet a thousand
years old, wrought of the same beaten gold as the mask of an ancient
Egyptian king he had seen in a book on archaeology. Every line of
experience and life was deeply carved as if by some master craftsman
intent on preserving his image to last for ever—stylized for eternity.

They were just the sort of people whose ignorance and complacency
the University was teaching him to despise, but the frenetic activity
of the city he had just left was now another world away. He began
to wonder at the almost tangible bond of trust which existed between
them, trying to guess where such a pair could be going this winter
afternoon with no baggage and apparently no destination.

"What're you doing at the University, son?" He told them he was
studying law, steeling himself as he did so for the usual inanity about
Perry Mason but then not surprised when it did not come. Instead
the woman turned to him.

"You'd have to work pretty hard for that, I'd reckon, and your old
man too. What does he do for a crust?"

"Solicitor." The youth was obscurely embarrassed.

"Is he, eh?" The man sounded interested. "Now, he'd rake in a
bob or two I'll bet. What 'ed he make, now? Forty odd quid a week."

The curiosity might have irritated him at any other time but the
question was put so matter of factly that he could not possibly take
offence.

"I dunno really." He slurred his accent purposely. "About that, I
suppose." He had a pretty fair idea forty pounds would barely pay
his father's income tax for a week, but went on, "We're a pretty big
family, though, and it never goes far," which was true enough anyway.

"We never had any kids, me and Dot. Wouldn't 've minded a few,
but you can't have everything, can you? And anyway I got Dot here.
Haven't I, Dot?"

He smiled and quickly passed on. "We got a cat 'nd a canary,
though. Poor old Mouser's getting a bit past his prime, but Squeaker's
still a noisy bit of fluff. They get on pretty well too, don't they, Dot?

"Mouser got kicked by the old bitch who lives downstairs a while back, and you could see Squeaker was real upset."

"That was when I got this leg here, son." The woman's voice was tobacco soft. "Wasn't very bright of me!" she laughed.

"I'd been out with some of the girls, see, and we'd had one or two for old times sake, walked straight in front of this bloomin' car. Didn't stop either. Bert only got me out of hospital a few weeks ago. Took his holidays so's he could look after me. Didn't you, Bert?"

Bert, slightly embarrassed, watched the road. "Well, I didn't have much else to do. The building trade was a bit slack. Couldn't have Dot here crashing around the flat on her own, just out of hospital."

"I'd 've been all right, Bert. There's always the TV, but I'm glad you did stop home. The flat gets lonely sometimes."

The youth had a sudden vision of the two of them, alone with the cat and the canary and the flickering shadows of the TV screen. The vision was so painful he asked abruptly, "Where are you going?" The woman looked quickly from him to the man, who answered solemnly, "We're going to Utopia."

Taken aback, the young man stammered, "Where's that?"

"You ought to know, son. You're at the University . . . It's where everything turns out all right. And this road's taking us there."

Confused, the boy tried to excuse himself. "Yes, but I didn't know it was anywhere near Toowoomba." His irony was unconscious, but the woman saved him from blundering further.

"She'll be jake, son." She laughed, patting him on the knee. "Me and Bert's just going for a drive."

"Right now we need a beer," said Bert, slowing down at an old weatherboard hotel by the roadside.

They all got out, the man taking the woman's arm up the few steps on to the verandah, leaving her with the boy as he went in to the bar. They sat, not speaking, savouring the silence and the air growing colder as the grey country began to lose its harsh outlines in soft scallops of shadow. The man rejoined them with two beers and a lemonade and, as the boy sipped the cool drink, he knew they had forgotten him, immersed in a communication he could never share; an understanding built on a lifetime of common experience, of problems solved together, of mutual hopes and despair, and the boy, thinking of his own short-lived affairs and moments of illusory contact, was envious.

Even when they returned to the car the silence was unbroken, and they drove for another half hour without speaking, the road now a stream of glistening silver merging into the golden haze of the setting sun. The trip had become something more now to the lad than just an episode, but when Bert stopped at the next hotel and went in for a drink the woman, sensing his unspoken anxiety, said, smiling: "He's all right, son. Take a lot more than what he's had to put him under . . . Bert'll do me any day." Then she got out of the car and hobbled awkwardly on one crutch to the ladies'.

The man returned to sit beside the youth, not speaking, his face suffused in the sun's dying glow. Then suddenly he said: "She's a great woman, you know, son. You'll likely never find a better, but she's going to die." He spoke without emotion.

"The doc. at the hospital told me. Cancer of the lungs, he reckoned. She doesn't know. A year to die in, and I won't be able to look after her."

The lad said nothing; the man talking into the west's incredible gold. Black shapes of ring-barked trees and a motionless windmill stood in harsh silhouette. The woman came back. Bert helped her in.

As he closed the door she looked at the youth and he knew she knew. She smiled.

Half a dozen miles farther on they dropped him by the side of the highway, twenty miles from home. He thanked them and waved as they took the road which would take them over the black mountains of the divide, but he knew they had forgotten him even as they stopped waving and had returned to that private world which only they could share.

A lonely figure, he shivered in the chill evening air as he watched the utility begin to climb towards the black mountains. But even as he turned away it crested a rise and, caught in the last rays of the sun, it blazed for an instant against the dark hill and then was gone.

He stood for a minute watching the place where it had been, then turned back to the road and listened.

PATRICK WHITE

Five-Twenty

MOST evenings, weather permitting, the Natwicks sat on the front veranda to watch the traffic. During the day the stream flowed, but towards five it began to thicken, it sometimes jammed solid like: the semi-trailers and refrigeration units, the decent old-style sedans, the mini-cars, the bombs, the Holdens and the Holdens. She didn't know most of the names. Royal did, he was a man, though never ever mechanical himself. She liked him to tell her about the vehicles, or listen to him take part in conversation with anyone who stopped at the fence. He could hold his own, on account of he was more educated, and an invalid has time to think.

They used to sit side by side on the tiled veranda, him in his wheel-chair she had got him after the artheritis took over, her in the old cane. That old cane chair wasn't hardly presentable any more, she had torn her winter navy on a nail and laddered several pair of stockings. You hadn't the heart to get rid of it, though. They brought it with them from Sarsaparilla after they sold the business. And now could sit in comfort to watch the traffic, the big steel insects of nowadays, which put the wind up her at times.

Royal said: "I reckon we're a shingle short to'uv ended up on the Parramatta Road."

"You said we'd still see life," she reminded, "even if we lost the use of our legs."

"But look at the traffic! Worse every year. And air. Rot a man's lungs quicker than the cigarettes. You should'uv headed me off. You who's supposed to be practical!"

"I thought it was what you wanted," she said, keeping it soft. She had never been one to crow.

"Anyway, I already lost the use of me legs."

As if she was to blame for that too. She was so shocked the chair sort of jumped. It made her blood run cold to hear the metal feet screak against the little draught-board tiles.

"Well, I 'aven't!" she protested. "I got me legs, and will be able to get from 'ere to anywhere and bring 'ome the shopping. While I got me strength."

She tried never to upset him by any show of emotion, but now she was so upset herself.

They watched the traffic in the evenings, as the orange light was stacked up in thick slabs, and the neon signs were coming on.

"See that bloke down there in the parti-coloured Holden?"

"Which?" she asked.

"The one level with our own gate."

"The pink and brown?" She couldn't take all that interest tonight, only you must never stop humouring a sick man.

"Yairs. Pink. Fancy a man in a pink car!"

"Dusty pink is fashionable." She knew that for sure.

"But a man!"

"Perhaps his wife chose it. Perhaps he's got a domineering wife."

Royal laughed low. "Looks like the sort of coot who might like to be domineered, and if that's what he wants, it's none of our business, is it?"

She laughed to keep him company. They were such mates, everybody said. And it was true. She didn't know what she would do if Royal was the first to pass on.

That evening the traffic had jammed. Some of the drivers began to toot. Some of them stuck their heads out, and began yarning to one another. But the man in the pink-and-brown Holden just sat. He didn't look to either side.

Come to think of it, she had noticed him pass before. Yes. Though he wasn't in no way a noticeable man. Yes. She looked at her watch.

"Five-twenty," she said. "I seen that man in the pink-and-brown before. He's pretty regular. Looks like a business executive."

Royal cleared his throat and spat. It didn't make the edge of the veranda. Better not to notice it, because he'd only create if she did. She'd get out the watering-can after she had pushed him inside.

"Business executives!" she heard. "They're afraid people are gunna think they're poor class without they *execute*. In our day nobody was ashamed to *do*. Isn't that about right, eh?" She didn't answer, because she knew she wasn't meant to. "Funny sort of head that cove's got. Like it was half-squashed. Silly-lookun bloody head!"

"Could have been born with it," she suggested. "Can't help what you're born with. Like your religion."

There was that evening the Chev got crushed, only a young fellow too. Ahhh, it had stuck in her throat, thinking of the wife and kiddies. She ran in, and out again as quick as she could, with a couple of blan-

PATRICK WHITE   105

kets, and the rug that was a present from Hazel. She had grabbed a
pillow off their own bed.

She only faintly heard Royal shouting from the wheel-chair.

She arranged the blankets and the pillow on the pavement, under
the orange sky. The young fellow was looking pretty sick, kept on
turning his head as though he recognized and wanted to tell her
something. Then the photographer from the *Mirror* took his picture,
said she ought to be in it to add a touch of human interest, but she
wouldn't. A priest came, the *Mirror* took his picture, administering
what Mrs Dolan said they call extreme unkshun. Well, you couldn't
poke fun at a person's religion any more than the shape of their head,
and Mrs Dolan was a decent neighbour, the whole family, and clean.

When she got back to the veranda, Royal, a big man, had slipped
down in his wheel-chair.

He said, or gasped: "Wotcher want to do that for, Ella? How are
we gunna get the blood off?"

She hadn't thought about the blood, when of course she was all
smeared with it, and the blankets, and Hazel's good Onkaparinka.
Anyway, it was her who would get the blood off.

"You soak it in milk or something," she said. "I'll ask. Don't you
worry."

Then she did something. She bent down and kissed Royal on the
forehead in front of the whole Parramatta Road. She regretted it at
once, because he looked that powerless in his invalid chair, and his
forehead felt cold and sweaty.

But you can't undo things that are done.

It was a blessing they could sit on the front veranda. Royal suffered
a lot by now. He had his long-standing hernia, which they couldn't
have operated on, on account of he was afraid of his heart. And then
the artheritis.

"Arthritis."

"All right," she accepted the correction. "Arth-er-itis."

It was all very well for men, they could manage more of the hard
words.

"What have you got for tea?" he asked.

"Well," she said, fanning out her hands on the points of her elbows,
and smiling, "it's a surprise."

She looked at her watch. It was five-twenty.

"It's a coupla nice little bits of fillet Mr Ballard let me have."

"Wotcher mean let you have? Didn't you pay for them?"

She had to laugh. "Anything I have I pay for!"

"Well? Think we're in the fillet-eating class?"

"It's only a treat, Royal," she said. "I got a chump chop for myself.
I like a nice chop."

He stopped complaining, and she was relieved.

"There's that gentleman," she said, "in the Holden."

They watched him pass, as sober as their own habits.

Royal—he had been his mother's little king. Most of his mates called him "Roy". Perhaps only her and Mrs Natwick had stuck to the christened name, they felt it suited.

She often wondered how Royal had ever fancied her: such a big man, with glossy hair, black, and a nose like on someone historical. She would never have said it, but she was proud of Royal's nose. She was proud of the photo he had of the old family home in Kent, the thatch so lovely, and Grannie Natwick sitting in her apron on a rush-bottom chair in front, looking certainly not all that different from Mum, with the aunts gathered round in leggermutton sleeves, all big nosy women like Royal.

She had heard Mum telling Royal's mother: "Ella's a plain little thing, but what's better than cheerful and willing?" She had always been on the mousy side, she supposed, which didn't mean she couldn't chatter with the right person. She heard Mum telling Mrs Natwick: "My Ella can wash and bake against any comers. Clever with her needle too." She had never entered any of the competitions, like they told her she ought to, it would have made her nervous.

It was all the stranger Royal had ever fancied her.

Once as they sat on the veranda watching the evening traffic, she said: "Remember how you used to ride out in the old days from 'Bugilbar' to Cootramundra?"

"Cootamundra."

"Yes," she said. "Cootramundra." (That's why they'd called the house "Coota" when they moved to the Parramatta Road.)

She had been so dazzled on one occasion by his parti-coloured forehead and his black hair, after he had got down from the saddle, after he had taken off his hat, she had run and fetched a duster, and dusted Royal Natwick's boots. The pair of new elastic-sides was white with dust from the long ride. It only occurred to her as she polished she might be doing something shameful, but when she looked up, it seemed as though Royal Natwick saw nothing peculiar in Ella McWhirter dusting his boots. He might even have expected it. She was so glad she could have cried.

Old Mr Natwick had come out from Kent when a youth, and after working at several uncongenial jobs, and studying at night, had been taken on as a bookkeeper at "Bugilbar". He was much valued in the end by the owners, and always made use of. The father would have liked his son to follow in his footsteps, and taught him how to

keep the books, but Royal wasn't going to hang around any family
of purse-proud squatters, telling them the things they wanted to hear.
He had ideas of his own for becoming rich and important.

So when he married Ella McWhirter, which nobody could ever
understand, not even Ella herself, perhaps only Royal, who never
bothered to explain (why should he?) they moved to Juggerawa,
and took over the general store. It was in a bad way, and soon was
in a worse, because Royal's ideas were above those of his customers.

Fulbrook was the next stage. He found employment as bookkeeper
on a grazing property outside. She felt so humiliated on account of
his humiliation. It didn't matter about herself because she always
expected less. She took a job in Fulbrook from the start at the "Dixie
Café" in High Street. She worked there several years as waitress,
helping out with the scrubbing for the sake of the extra money. She
had never hated anything, but got to hate the flies trampling in the
sugar and on the necks of the tomato sauce bottles.

At weekends her husband usually came in, and when she wasn't
needed in the shop they lay on the bed in her upstairs room, listening
to the corrugated iron and the warping whitewashed weatherboard.
She would have loved to do something for him, but in his distress
he complained about "wet kisses". It surprised her. She had always
been afraid he might find her a bit too dry in her show of affection.

Those years at the "Dixie Café" certainly dried her up. She got
those freckly patches and seams in her skin in spite of the lotions
used as directed. Not that it matters so much in anyone born plain.
Perhaps her plainness helped her save. There was never a day when
she didn't study her savings-book, it became her favourite recreation.

Royal, on the other hand, wasn't the type that dries up, being
fleshier, and dark. He even put on weight out at the grazing property, where they soon thought the world of him. When the young
ladies were short of a man for tennis the bookkeeper was often
invited, and to a ball once at the homestead. He was earning good
money, and he too saved a bit, though his instincts weren't as mean
as hers. For instance, he fancied a choice cigar. In his youth Royal
was a natty dresser.

Sometimes the young ladies, if they decided to inspect the latest at
Ryan's Emporium, or Mr Philup, if he felt like grogging up with
the locals, would drive him in, and as he got out they would look
funny at the bookkeeper's wife they had heard about, they must have,
serving out the plates of frizzled steak and limp chips. Royal always
waited to see his employers drive off before coming in.

In spite of the savings, this might have gone on much longer than
it did if old Mr Natwick hadn't died. It appeared he had been a very

prudent man. He left them a nice little legacy. The evening of the news Royal was driven in by Mr Philup and they had a few at the Imperial. Afterwards the bookkeeper was dropped off, because he proposed to spend the night with his wife before leaving by the early train to attend his father's funeral.

They lay in the hot little room and discussed the future. She had never felt so hectic. Royal got the idea he would like to develop a grocery business in one of the posh outer suburbs of Sydney. "Interest the monied residents in some of the luxury lines. Appeal to the imagination as well as the stomach."

She was impressed, of course, but not as much as she should have been. She wasn't sure, but perhaps she was short on imagination. Certainly their prospects had made her downright feverish, but for no distinct, sufficient reason.

"And have a baby." She heard her own unnatural voice.

"Eh?"

"We could start a baby." Her voice grew word by word drier.

"There's no reason why we couldn't have a baby. Or two." He laughed. "But starting a new life isn't the time to start a baby." He dug her in the ribs. "And you the practical one!"

She agreed it would be foolish, and presently Royal fell asleep.

What could she do for him? As he lay there breathing she would have loved to stroke his nose she could see faintly in the light from the window. Again unpractical, she would have loved to kiss it. Or bite it suddenly off.

She was so disgusted with herself she got creaking off the bed and walked flat across the boards to the washstand and swallowed a couple of Aspros to put her solidly to sleep.

All their life together she had to try in some way to make amends to Royal, not only for her foolishness, but for some of the thoughts that got into her head. Because she hadn't the imagination, the thoughts couldn't have been her own. They must have been put into her.

It was easier of course in later life, after he had cracked up, what with his hernia, and heart, and the artheritis taking over. Fortunately she was given the strength to help him into the wheelchair, and later still, to lift him, or drag him up on the pillows, and over, to rub the bed-sores, and stick the bed-pan under him. But even during the years at Sarsaparilla she could make amends in many little ways, though with him still in his prime, naturally he musn't know of them. So all her acts were mostly only for her own self-gratification.

The store at Sarsaparilla, if it didn't exactly flourish, gave them a decent living. She had her problems, though. Some of the locals just couldn't accept that Royal was a superior man. Perhaps she had been partly to blame, she hardly dared admit it, for showing one or two "friends" the photo of the family home in Kent. She couldn't resist telling the story of one of the aunts, Miss Ethel Natwick, who followed her brother to New South Wales. Ethel was persuaded to accept a situation at Government House, but didn't like it and went back, in spite of the Governor's lady insisting she valued Ethel as a close personal friend. When people began to laugh at Royal on account of his auntie and the family home, as you couldn't help finding out in a place like Sarsaparilla, it was her, she knew, it was her to blame. It hurt her deeply.

Royal of course could be difficult. Said stockbrokers had no palate and less imagination. Royal said no Australian grocer could make a go of it if it wasn't for flour, granulated sugar, and tomato sauce. Some of the customers turned nasty in retaliation. This was where she could help, and did, because Royal was out on delivery more often than not. It embarrassed her only when some of them took it for granted she was on their side. As if he wasn't her husband. Once or twice she had gone out crying afterwards, amongst the wormy wattles and hens' droppings. Anyone across the gully must have been able to hear her blowing her nose at the back of the store, but she didn't care. Poor Royal.

There was that Mr Ogburn said: "A selfish, swollen-headed slob who'll chew you up and swallow yer down." She wouldn't let herself hear any more of what he had to say. Mr Ogburn had a hare-lip, badly sewn, opening and closing. There was nothing frightened her so much as even a well-disguised hare-lip. She got the palpitations after the scene with Mr Ogburn.

Not that there was anything wrong with her.

She only hadn't had the baby. It was her secret grief on black evenings as she walked slowly looking for the eggs a flighty hen might have hid in the bracken.

Dr Bamforth said, looking at the nib of his fountain pen: "You know, don't you, it's sometimes the man?"

She didn't even want to hear, let alone think about it. In any case she wouldn't tell Royal, because a man's pride could be so easily hurt.

After they had sold out at Sarsaparilla and come to live at what they called "Coota" on the Parramatta Road, it was both easier and more difficult, because if they were not exactly elderly they were getting on. Royal used to potter about in the beginning, while taking care, on account of the hernia and his heart. There was the business of the lawn-mowing, not that you could call it lawn, but it was what she had. She loved her garden. In front certainly there was only the two square of rather sooty grass which she would keep in order with the push-mower. Until the artheritis took over, the lawn seemed to get on Royal's nerves. He had never liked mowing. He would lean against a veranda post and shout: "Don't know why we don't do what they've done down the street. Root the stuff out. Put down a green concrete lawn."

"That would be copying," she answered back.

She hoped it didn't sound stubborn. As she pushed the mower she bent her head and smiled, waiting for him to cool off. The scent of grass and a few clippings flew up through the traffic fumes reminding you of summer.

While Royal shuffled along the veranda and leaned against another post: "Or pebbles. You can buy clean river pebbles. A few plastic shrubs, and there's the answer."

He only gave up when his trouble forced him into the chair. You couldn't drive yourself up and down a veranda shouting at someone from a wheel-chair without the passers-by thinking you was a nut. So he quietened.

He watched her, though. From under the peak of his cap. Because she felt he might still resent her mowing the lawn, she would try to reassure him as she pushed. "What's wrong, *eh*? While I still have me health, me *strength*—I was always what they call *wiry*—why shouldn't I cut the *grass*?"

She would come and sit beside him, to keep him company in watching the traffic, and invent games to amuse her invalid husband.

"Isn't that the feller we expect?" she might ask. "The one that passes at five-twenty," looking at her watch, "in the old pink-and-brown Holden?"

They enjoyed their snort of amusement all the better because no one else knew the reason for it.

Once when the traffic was particularly dense, and that sort of chemical smell from one of the factories was thickening in the evening air, Royal drew her attention. "Looks like he's got something on his mind."

Could have too. Or it might have been the traffic block. The way he held his hands curved listlessly around the inactive wheel reminded her of possums and monkeys she had seen in cages. She shifted a bit. Her squeaky old chair. She felt uneasy for ever having found the man, not exactly a joke, but half of one.

Royal's chair moved so smoothly on its rubber-tired wheels it was easy to push him, specially after her practice with the mower. There were ramps where necessary now, to cover steps, and she would sometimes wheel him out to the back, where she grew hollyhock and sunflower against the palings, and a vegetable or two on raised beds.

Royal would sit not looking at the garden from under the peak of his cap.

She never attempted to take him down the shady side, between them and Dolans, because the path was narrow from plants spilling over, and the shade might have lowered his spirits.

She loved her garden.

The shady side was where she kept her staghorn ferns, and fishbones, and the pots of maidenhair. The water lay sparkling on the maidenhair even in the middle of the day. In the blaze of summer the light at either end of the tunnel was like you were looking through a sheet of yellow cellophane, but as the days shortened, the light deepened to a cold, tingling green, which might have made a person nervous who didn't know the tunnel by heart.

Take Mrs Dolan the evening she came in to ask for the loan of a cupful of sugar. "You give me a shock, Mrs Natwick. What ever are you up to?"

"Looking at the plants," Mrs Natwick answered, whether Mrs Dolan would think it peculiar or not.

It was the season of cinerarias, which she always planted on that side, it was so sheltered and cold-green. The wind couldn't bash the big spires and umbrellas of blue and purple. Visiting cats were the only danger, messing and pouncing. She disliked cats for the smell they left, but didn't have the heart to disturb their elastic forms curled at the cineraria roots, exposing their colourless pads, and sometimes pink, swollen teats. Blushing only slightly for it, she would stand and examine the details of the sleeping cats.

If Royal called she could hear his voice through the window. "Where'uv you got to, Ella?"

After he was forced to take to his bed, his voice began to sort of dry up like his body. There were times when it sounded less like a voice than a breath of drowsiness or pain.

"Ella?" he was calling. "I dropped the paper. Where are yer all this time? You know I can't pick up the paper."

She knew. Guilt sent her scuttling to him, deliberately composing her eyes and mouth so as to arrive looking cheerful.

"I was in the garden," she confessed, "looking at the cinerarias."

"The what?" It was a name Royal could never learn.

The room was smelling of sickness and the bottles standing on odd plates.

"It fell," he complained.

She picked up the paper as quick as she could.

"Want to go la-la first?" she asked, because by now he depended on her to raise him and stick the pan under.

But she couldn't distract him from her other shortcomings. He was shaking the paper at her. "Haven't you lived with me long enough to know how to treat a newspaper?"

He hit it with his set hand, and certainly the paper looked a mess, like an old white battered brolly.

"Mucked up! You gotta keep the pages *aligned*. A paper's not readable otherwise. Of course you wouldn't understand, because you don't read it, without it's to see who's died." He began to cough.

"Like me to bring you some Bovril?" she asked as tenderly as she knew.

"Bovril's the morning," he coughed.

She knew that, but had wanted to do something for him.

After she had rearranged the paper she walked out so carefully it made her go lopsided, out to the front veranda. Nothing would halt the traffic, not sickness, not death even.

She sat with her arms folded, realizing at last how they were aching.

"He hasn't been," she had to call after looking at her watch.

"Who?" she heard the voice rustling back.

"The gentleman in the pink Holden."

She listened to the silence, wondering whether she had done right. When Royal called back: "Could'uv had a blow-out." Then he laughed. "Could'uv stopped to get grogged up." She heard the frail rustling of the paper. "Or taken an axe to somebody like they do nowadays."

She closed her eyes, whether for Royal, or what she remembered of the man sitting in the Holden.

Although it was cold she continued watching after dark. Might have caught a chill, when she couldn't afford to. She only went inside to make the bread-and-milk Royal fancied of an evening.

She watched most attentively, always at the time, but he didn't pass, and didn't pass.

"Who?"

"The gentleman in the Holden."

"Gone on holiday," Royal said. He sighed, and she knew it was the point where a normal person would have turned over, so she went to turn him.

One morning she said on going in: "Fancy, I had a dream, it was about that man! He was standing on the side path alongside the cinerarias. I know it was him because of his funny-shaped head."

"What happened in the dream?" Royal hadn't opened his eyes yet. She hadn't helped him in with his teeth.

"I dunno," she said, "it was just a dream."

That wasn't strictly honest, because the Holden gentleman had looked at her, she had seen his eyes. Nothing was spoken though.

"It was a sort of red and purple dream. That was the cinerarias," she said.

"I don't dream. You don't when you don't sleep. Pills aren't sleep."

She was horrified at her reverberating dream. She said: "Would you like a nice coddled egg?"

"Eggs all have a taste."

"But you gotta eat something!"

On another morning she told him—she could have bitten off her tongue—she *was* stupid, *stupid*: "I had a dream."

"What sort of dream?"

"Oh," she said, "a silly one. Not worth telling. I dreamed I dropped an egg on the side path, and it turned into two. Not two. A double-yolker."

She never realized Royal was so much like Mrs Natwick. It was as she raised him on his pillows. Or he had got like that in his sickness. Old men and old women were not unlike.

"Wasn't that a silly one?" she coaxed.

Every evening she sat on the front veranda and watched the traffic as though Royal had been beside her. Looked at her watch. And turned her face away from the steady-flowing stream. The way she bunched her small chest she could have had a sour breath mounting in her throat. Sometimes she had, it was nervousness.

When she went inside she announced: "He didn't pass."

Royal said—he had taken to speaking from behind his eyelids: "Something musta happened to 'im. He didn't go on holiday. He went and died."

"Oh, no! He wasn't of an age!"

At once she saw how stupid she was, and went out to get the bread-and-milk.

She would sit at the bedside, almost crouching against the edge of the mattress, because she wanted Royal to feel she was close, and he seemed to realize, though he mostly kept his eyelids down.

Then one evening she came running, she felt silly, her calves felt silly, her voice: "He's come! At five-twenty! In a new cream Holden!"

Royal said without opening his eyes: "See? I said 'e'd gone on holiday."

More than ever she saw the look of Mrs Natwick.

Now every evening Royal asked: "Has he been, Ella?"

Trying not to make it sound irritable or superior, she would answer: "Not yet. It's only five."

Every evening she sat watching, and sometimes would turn proud, arching her back, as she looked down from the veranda. The man was so small and ordinary.

She went in on one occasion, into the more than electric light, lowering her eyelids against the dazzle: "You know, Royal, you could feel prouder of men when they rode horses. As they looked down at yer from under the brim of their hats. Remember that hat you used to wear? Riding in to Cootramundra?"

Royal died very quietly that same year before the cinerarias had folded, while the cold westerlies were still blowing, the back page of the *Herald* was full of those who had been carried off. She was left with his hand, already set, in her hand. They hadn't spoken, except about whether she had put out the garbage.

Everybody was very kind. She wouldn't have liked to admit it was enjoyable being a widow. She sat around for longer than she had ever sat, and let the dust gather. In the beginning acquaintances and neighbours brought her little presents of food: a billycan of giblet soup, moulded veal with hard-boiled egg making a pattern in the jelly, cakes so dainty you couldn't taste them. But when she was no longer a novelty they left off coming. She didn't care any more than she cared about the dust. Sometimes she would catch sight of her face in the glass, and was surprised to see herself looking so calm and white.

Of course she was calm. The feeling part of her had been removed. What remained was a slack, discardable eiderdown. Must have been the pills Doctor gave.

Well-meaning people would call to her over the front fence: "Don't you feel lonely, Mrs Natwick?" They spoke with a restrained horror, as though she had been suffering from an incurable disease.

But she called back proud and slow: "I'm under sedation."

"Arrr!" nodding thoughtfully. "What's 'e given yer?"

She shook her head. "Pills," she called back. "They say they're the ones the actress died of."

The people walked on, impressed.

As the evenings grew longer and heavier she sat later on the front veranda watching the traffic of the Parramatta Road, its flow becoming syrupy and almost benign: big bulbous sedate buses, chrysalis-cars still without a life of their own clinging in line to the back of their host-articulator, trucks loaded for distances, empty loose-sounding jolly trucks. Sometimes women, looking out from the cabins of trucks from beside their men, shared her lack of curiosity. The light was so fluid nobody lasted long enough. You would never have thought boys could kick a person to death, seeing their long soft hair floating behind their sports-models.

Every evening she watched the cream Holden pass. And looked at her watch. It was like Royal was sitting beside her. Once she heard herself: "Thought he was gunna look round tonight, in our direction." How could a person feel lonely?

She was, though. She came face to face with it walking through the wreckage of her garden in the long slow steamy late summer. The Holden didn't pass of course of a Saturday or Sunday. Something, something had tricked her, not the pills, before the pills. She couldn't blame anybody, probably only herself. Everything depended on yourself. Take the garden. It was a shambles. She would have liked to protest, but began to cough instead from blundering into the powdery mildew. She could only blunder at first, like a cow in a garden, or runty starved heifer. She had lost her old wiriness. She shambled, snapping dead stems, uprooting. Along the bleached palings there was a fretwork of hollyhock, the brown fur of rotting sunflower. She rushed at a praying mantis, a big pale one, and deliberately broke its back, and was sorry afterwards, it broke so easy.

As she stood panting in her black, finally yawning, she saw all she had to repair. The thought of the seasons piling up ahead made her feel tired but necessary, and she went in to bathe her face. Royal's denture in a tumbler on top of the medicine cabinet, she ought to move, or give to the Sallies.In the meantime she changed the water. She never forgot to change the water. The teeth could look amazing.

All that autumn, winter, she was continually amazed at the dust, for instance, she had let gather in the house, at old photographs, books, clothes. There was a feather she couldn't remember wearing, a scarlet feather, she *can't* have worn, and gloves with little fussy ruffles at the wrists, silver piping, like a snail had laid its silver round the edges. There was, she knew, funny things she had bought at times, and never worn, but she couldn't remember these. And books. She had collected a few, though never a reader herself. Old people liked to give books, and you took them so as not to hurt anybody's feelings. *Hubert's Crusade*, for instance. Lovely golden curls. Could have been old Mr Natwick's, Royal's father's book. Everybody was a child once. And almost everybody had one. At least if she had had a child she would have known it wasn't a white turnip, more of a praying mantis, which snaps too easy.

In the old box she had a coloured picture, *Cities of the Plain*, she couldn't remember seeing before. The people escaping from the burning cities had committed some sin or other nobody ever thought, let alone talked about. As they hurried between rocks, through what must have been the "desert places", their faces looked long and wooden. All they had recently experienced could have shocked the expression out of them. She was fascinated by what made her shiver. And the couples with their arms still around one another. Well, if you were damned, better hang on to your sin. She didn't blame them.

She put the box away. Its inlay as well as its contents made it something secret and precious.

That autumn was still and golden, the winter vicious only in fits. It was what you could call a good winter. The cold floods of air and more concentrated streams of dark-green light poured along the shady side of the house where her cinerarias had massed. She had never seen such cinerarias: some of the spired ones reached almost as high as her chin, the solid heads of others waited in the tunnel of dark light to club you with their colours, of purple and drenching blue, and what they called "wine". She couldn't believe wine would have made her drunker.

Just as she would sit every evening watching the traffic, almost always about dusk, when the icy cold seemed to make the flowers burn their deepest, purest, she visited the cinerarias. And the evening when, for some blissfully confident reason she hadn't bothered to ask herself whether she had seen the car pass, he came towards her along the tunnel. She knew at once who it was, although she had never seen him on his feet, she had never seen him full-face, but knew from the funny shape of his head as Royal had been the first to notice. He was not at all an impressive man, not much taller than herself, but broad. His footsteps on the brick sounded purposeful.

"Will you let me use your phone, please, madam?" he asked in a prepared voice. "I'm having trouble with the Holden."

This was a situation she had always been expecting: somebody asking to use the phone as a way to afterwards murdering you. Now that it might be about to happen she couldn't care.

She said yes. She thought her voice sounded muzzy. Perhaps he would think she was drunk.

She went on looking at him, at his eyes. His nose, like the shape of his head, wasn't up to much, but his eyes, his eyes, she dared to think, were filled with kindness.

"Cold, eh? but clean cold!" He laughed friendly, shuffling on the brick paving because she was keeping him waiting.

Only then she noticed his mouth. He had a hare-lip, there was no mistaking, although it was well sewn. She felt so calm in the circumstances. She would have even liked to touch it.

But said: "Why, yes—the telephone," she said, "it's this way," she said, "it's just off the kitchen—because that's where you spend most of your life. Or in bed," she ended.

She wished she hadn't added that. For the first time since they had been together she felt upset, thinking he might suspect her of wrong intentions.

But he laughed and said: "That's correct! You got something there!" It sounded manly rather than educated.

She realized he was still waiting, and took him to the telephone.

While he was phoning she didn't listen. She never listened when other people were talking on the phone. The sight of her own kitchen surprised her. While his familiar voice went on. It was the voice she had held conversations with.

But he was ugly, real ugly, *deformed*. If it wasn't for the voice, the eyes. She couldn't remember the eyes, but seemed to know about them.

Then she heard him laying the coins beside the phone, extra loud, to show.

He came back into the kitchen smiling and looking. She could smell him now, and he had the smell of a clean man.

She became embarrassed at herself, and took him quickly out.

"Fair bit of garden you got." He stood with his calves curved through his trousers. A cocky little chap, but nice.

"Oh," she said, "this," she said, angrily almost, "is nothing. You oughter see it. There's sunflower and hollyhock all along the palings. I'm famous for me hollyhocks!" She had never boasted in her life. "But not now—it isn't the season. And I let it go. Mr Natwick passed on. You should'uv seen the cassia this autumn. Now it's only sticks of course. And hibiscus. There's cream, gold, cerise, scarlet—double and single."

She was dressing in them for him, revolving on high heels, and changing frilly skirts.

He said: "Gardening's not in my line"—turning his head to hide something, perhaps he was ashamed of his hare-lip.

"No," she agreed. "Not everybody's a gardener."

"But like a garden."

"My husband didn't even like it. He didn't have to tell me," she added.

As they moved across the wintry grass, past the empty clothesline, the man looked at his watch, and said: "I was reckoning on visiting somebody in hospital tonight. Looks like I shan't make it if the NRMA takes as long as usual."

"Do they?" she said, clearing her throat. "It isn't somebody close, I hope? The sick person?"

Yes he said they was close.

"Nothing serious?" she almost bellowed.

He said it was serious.

Oh she nearly burst out laughing at the bandaged figure they were sitting beside particularly at the bandaged face. She would have laughed at a brain tumour.

"I'm sorry," she said. "I understand. Mr Natwick was an invalid."

Those teeth in the tumbler on top of the medicine cabinet. Looking at her. Teeth can look, worse than eyes. But she couldn't help it, she meant everything she said, and thought.

At this moment they were pressing inside the dark-green tunnel, her sleeve rubbing his, as the crimson-to-purple light was dying.

"These are the cinerarias," she said.

"The what?" He didn't know, any more than Royal.

As she was about to explain she got switched to another language. Her throat became a long palpitating funnel through which the words she expected to use were poured out in a stream of almost formless agonized sound.

"What is it?" he asked, touching her.

If it had happened to herself she would have felt frightened, it occurred to her, but he didn't seem to be.

"What is it?" he kept repeating in his familiar voice, touching, even holding her.

And for answer, in the new language, she was holding him. They were holding each other, his hard body against her eiderdowny one. As the silence closed round them again, inside the tunnel of light, his face, to which she was very close, seemed to be unlocking, the wound of his mouth, which should have been more horrible, struggling to open. She could see he had recognized her.

She kissed above his mouth. She kissed as though she might never succeed in healing all the wounds they had ever suffered.

How long they stood together she wasn't interested in knowing. Outside them the river of traffic continued to flow between the brick and concrete banks. Even if it overflowed it couldn't have drowned them.

When the man said in his gentlest voice: "Better go out in front. The NRMA might have come."

"Yes," she agreed. "The NRMA."

So they shuffled still holding each other, along the narrow path. She imagined how long and wooden their faces must look. She wouldn't look at him now, though, just as she wouldn't look back at the still faintly smouldering joys they had experienced together in the past.

When they came out apart and into the night, there was the NRMA, his pointed ruby of a light burning on top of the cabin.

"When will you come?" she asked.

"Tomorrow."

"Tomorrow. You'll stay to tea."

He couldn't stay.

"I'll make you a *pot* of tea?"

But he didn't drink tea.

"Coffee then?"

He said: "I like a nice cup of coffee."

Going down the path she didn't look back, or opening the gate. She would not let herself think of reasons or possibilities, she would not think, but stood planted in the path, swayed slightly by the motion of the night.

Mrs Dolan said: "You bring the saucepan to the boil. You got that?"

"Yeeehs." Mrs Natwick had never been a dab at coffee.

"Then you throw in the cold water. That's what sends the gravel to the bottom." This morning Mrs Dolan had to laugh at her own jokes.

"That's the part that frightens me," Mrs Natwick admitted.

"Well, you just do it, and see," said Mrs Dolan, she was too busy.

After she had bought the coffee Mrs Natwick stayed in the city to muck around. If she had sat at home her nerves might have got strung even tighter waiting for the evening to come. Though mucking around only irritated in the end. She had never been an idle person. So she stopped at the cosmetics as though she didn't even have to decide, this was her purpose, and said to the young lady standing behind one of the counters: "I'm thinking of investing in a lipstick, dear. Can you please advise me?"

As a concession to the young girl she tried to make it a laughing matter, but the young person was bored, she didn't flicker a silver eyelid. She said: "Elderly ladies go for the brighter stuff."

Mrs Natwick—my little Ella—had never felt so meek. Mum must be turning in her grave.

"This is a favourite." With a flick of her long fingers the girl exposed the weapon. It looked too shining-pointed, crimson-purple, out of its golden sheath.

Mrs Natwick's knees were shaking. "Isn't it a bit noticeable?" she asked, again trying to make it a joke.

But the white-haired girl gave a serious laugh. "What's wrong with noticeable?"

As Mrs Natwick tried out a little on the back of her hand, the way she had seen others do, the girl jogging from foot to foot behind the counter. She was humming between her teeth, behind her white-smeared lips, probably thinking about a lover. Mrs Natwick blushed. What if she couldn't learn to get the tip of her lipstick into its sheath?

She might have gone quickly away without another word if the young lady hadn't been so professional and bored. Still humming she brought out a little pack of rouge.

"Never saw meself with mauve cheeks!" It was at least dry, and easy to handle.

"It's what they wear."

Mrs Natwick wouldn't have dared refuse. She watched the long fingers with their silver nails doing up the parcels as though they would never touch anything but cosmetics, probably not even a lover.

The girl gave her the change, and she went away quiet without counting it.

She wasn't quiet, though, not a bit, booming and clanging in front of the toilet mirror. She tried to make a thin line, but her mouth exploded into a purple flower. She dabbed the dry-feeling pad on either cheek, and thick, mauve-scented shadows fell. She could hear and feel her heart behaving like a squeezed rubber ball, as she stood a little to look. Then she got at the lipstick again, still unsheathed. Her mouth was becoming enormous, so thick with grease she could hardly close her own lips underneath. A visible dew was gathering round the purple shadows on her cheeks.

She began like to retch then, only dry, and rub, over the basin, scrubbing with the nailbrush. More than likely some would stay in the pores and be seen. Though you didn't have to see, to see.

There were Royal's teeth in the tumbler on top of the medicine cabinet. Ought to hide the teeth. What if somebody wanted to use the toilet? She must move the teeth. But didn't. In the present circumstances she couldn't have raised her arms that high.

Around five she made the coffee, throwing in the cold water at the end with a gesture copied from Mrs Dolan. If the gravel hadn't sunk to the bottom he wouldn't notice the first time, provided the coffee was hot. She could warm up the made coffee in a jiffy.

As she sat on the veranda, waiting, the cane chair was shifting and squealing under her. If it hadn't been for her weight it might have run away across the tiles, like one of those old planchette boards, writing the answers to questions.

There was an accident that night down at the intersection. Two cars, head on. Bodies were carried out of the crumpled cars, and she remembered a past occasion when she had run with blankets, and Hazel's Onkaparinka, and a pillow from their own bed. She had been so grateful to the victim. She could not give him enough, or receive enough of the warm blood. She had come back, she remembered, sprinkled.

Tonight she had to save herself up. Kept on looking at her watch. The old cane chair squealing, ready to write the answers if she let it. Was he hurt? Was he killed, then? Was he—what?

Mrs Dolan it was, sticking her head over the palings. "Don't like the accidents, Mrs Natwick. It's the blood. The blood turns me up."

Mrs Natwick averted her face. Though unmoved by actual blood. If only the squealing chair would stop trying to buck her off.

"Did your friend enjoy the coffee?" Mrs Dolan shouted. Nothing nasty in her. Mrs Dolan was sincere.

"Hasn't been yet," Mrs Natwick mumbled from glancing at her watch. "Got held up."

"It's the traffic. The traffic at this time of evenun."

"Always on the dot before."

"Working back. Or made a mistake over the day."

Could you make a mistake? Mrs Natwick contemplated. Tomorrow had always meant tomorrow.

"Or he could'uv," Mrs Dolan shouted but didn't say it. She said: "I better go inside. They'll be wonderun where I am."

Down at the intersection the bodies were lying wrapped in someone else's blankets, looking like the grey parcels of mice cats sometimes vomit up.

It was long past five-twenty, not all that long really, but drawing in. The sky was heaped with cold fire. Her city was burning.

She got up finally, and the chair escaped with a last squeal, writing its answer on the tiles.

No, it wasn't lust, not if the Royal God Almighty with bared teeth should strike her down. Or yes, though, it was. She was lusting after the expression of eyes she could hardly remember for seeing so briefly.

In the effort to see, she drove her memory wildly, while her body stumbled around and around the paths of the burning city there was now no point in escaping. You would shrivel up in time along with the polyanthers and out-of-season hibiscus. All the randy mouths would be stopped sooner or later with black.

The cinerarias seemed to have grown so luxuriant she had to force her way past them, down the narrow brick path. When she heard the latch click, and saw him coming towards her.

"Why," she screamed laughing though it sounded angry, she *was*, "I'd given you up, you know! It's long after five-twenty!"

As she pushed fiercely towards him, past the cinerarias, snapping one or two of the most heavily loaded, she realized he couldn't have known that she set her life by his true time. He wouldn't have dawdled so.

"What is it?" she called at last in exasperation from her distance.

He was far too slow, treading the slippery moss of her too shaded path. While she floundered on. She couldn't reach the expression of his eyes.

He said, and she could hardly recognize his faded voice: "There's something—I been feeling off colour most of the day." His misshapen head was certainly lolling as he advanced.

"Tell me!" She heard her commanding voice, like that of a man or a mother, when she had practised to be a lover, she could still smell the smell of the rouge. "Won't you tell me—*dearest*?" It was thin and unconvincing. As a girl she had once got a letter from her cousin Kath Salter, who she hardly knew: *Dearest Ella* . . .

Oh dear. She had reached him. And was all strength. The strength of a lover.

As they straddled the path, unequally matched—he couldn't compete against her strength—she spoke with an acquired, a deafening softness, as the inclining cinerarias snapped.

"You will tell me what is wrong—dear dear." She breathed with trumpets.

Hanging his head he answered: "It's all right. It's the pain—here —in my arm—no, my shoulder."

"Ohhhhh!" She ground her face into his shoulder forgetting it wasn't *her* pain.

Then she remembered, and looked into his eyes and said: "We'll save you. You'll see."

It was she who needed to be saved. She knew she was trying to enter by his eyes. To drown in them rather than be left.

Because, in spite of her will to hold him, he was slipping from her down amongst the cinerarias, which were snapping off one by one all around them.

A cat shot out. Once she had been so poor she had wished she was a cat.

"It's all right," either voice was saying.

Lying amongst the smashed plants, he was smiling at her dreadfully, not his mouth, she no longer bothered about that lip, but with his eyes.

"More air!" she cried. "What you need is air!" hacking at one or two of the cinerarias that remained erect.

Their sap was stifling, their bristling columns callous.

"Oh! Oh!" she panted. "Oh God! Dear love!" comforting with hands and hair and words.

Words.

While all he could say was: "It's all right."

Or not that at last. He folded his lips into a white seam. His eyes swimming out of reach.

"Eh? Dear—dearest—darl—darlig—darling love—*love*—LOVE?" All the new words still stiff in her mouth, that she had heard so far only from the mouths of actors.

The words were too strong she could see. She was losing him. The traffic was hanging together only by charred silences.

She flung herself and covered his body, trying to force kisses—no, breath, into his mouth, she had heard about it.

She had seen turkeys, feathers sawing against each other's feathers, rising afterwards like new noisy silk.

She knelt up, and the wing-tips of her hair still dabbled limply in his cheeks. "Eh? Ohh luff!" She could hardly breathe it.

She hadn't had time to ask his name, before she must have killed him by loving too deep, and too adulterously.

MARGOT LUKE

Old Man Running

THE DAY he had the shock Trader turned into an old man and a stranger to himself. Sixty-four is not so very old when you keep your figure and your teeth. He had vaguely looked forward to a never-ending middle-age, with his doctor saying once a year, "I don't know how you do it." But then the shock came. Some incomprehensible scandal involving one of his students; and Hella, his wife, glad of it. The ground shifted under his feet, rocked by her malice. He had to keep walking to stop himself from tottering, crumbling and disintegrating. Walking, on and on, away from himself, and the farther he walked the less he understood. A blind fool—echoes of Lear, and he had not even bothered to count the money in his pocket or chosen the way. No need for thought. His feet undemandingly marched him on and on, with his skull taking photographs through the eye-sockets. Trees, trams, parked cars, houses being smashed and then stacked up again.

He rejected the hills, his usual refuge, and avoided solitude, his natural inclination. He wanted the ugliness of the city to overwhelm and drown out the vileness of the afternoon, and now jostled with the peak-hour crowd in the raucous pubs. Six o'clock closing was a legend of the past, but the habitual swill went on, in direct continuation of his own heavy drinking years more than a decade ago. Once again he tasted the bitter wholesomeness of fresh beer and breathed the sour stench of uncollected dregs. Hoarse, blurred voices, half-buttoned clothes, glazing reddened eyes. A fury boiled in him, a need to blot out the scene in his study, and he now toiled to destroy all that kept him alert and separate from the other drinkers. Even as he emptied one glass after another, purposefully and unceasingly, he could not ignore the intrusion of great literary binges swirling through his mind. With the memory of eighteen double whiskies he accelerated his drinking until even the clichés would be obliterated, and nothing left but a spinning giddiness.

Partial success, that's what it was. Only partial. "Only partial success, you understand," he told the man with the big elbows, standing next along the bar.

"That a fact?" the man marvelled obligingly.

"Meant to get away from him, and here I'm catching up with him fifteen years ago."

"She'll be right, mate," the man consoled him. It was obvious he didn't understand, and Trader knew he'd have to find the others. Working his way up Swanston Street, dragging against the ebbing stream of busy and sober shop assistants, he searched for the pub of the old days, the Swineherd's Familiar, staggering from corner to corner, unable to find it. He hunted for other landmarks and found he had strayed into a strange city bearing the old street names. Wherever he looked, the old places had turned into tall smug giants of concrete and glass, banks, that now flashed their closed glass doors at him, blinking in the orange-coloured evening sunshine.

His bush-walking days had given him a stamina which now kept him on his feet. The internal drowning had been unsuccessful but the theme of drowning persisted. He reached the river, only to find that its muddy depths struck no answering chord in his imagination. Much later, or perhaps the next moment, he became aware of giant cactus plants and palm-trees, and the ringing of a distant bell. He eased his back against the smooth muscular trunk of a Moreton Bay fig-tree, and gazed down the softly rolling green slope at a lake choked with water-lilies. It was a good drowning lake. Hazily he wondered whether he was in the Botanic Gardens, or in one of the half-dozen millionaire estates modestly burgeoning behind suburban hedges. Either way, he had complete privacy, and would be able to drown at his leisure, when he felt the moment was ripe. The deepening green of the trees, and the urgent bird-calls of evening gave him enormous satisfaction; a foretaste of the deep green of the water and his own last incoherent calls to the world. The sharply serrated fronds of the palms stood out clearly against the chamois-and-green sky and he regretted that such clarity of vision should come to him at a time like this, when it was irrelevant. By the time darkness had fallen, he was fast asleep beneath the Moreton Bay fig, and entirely unaware of the occasional splashes of the fat eels in the lake, who might have shared his last sleep.

When he saw the setting sun again, it was over the sea. He knew he could not spend another night in the open air. His bones ached, and he was hungry but too sick to eat. Although he had walked to the beach in the early morning and spent the warm day sleeping off the worst of his hangover on the sand among the bottles and beer-

cans, he felt incapable of thought. It was getting late and cold, and
the air was still and clear. The façades of the houses along the beach-
front stood out in sharp detail in the setting sun. Dark and foolish
architectural hyperboles alternated with stark square boxes iced over
in Mediterranean blues and pinks. All had names like Seaview or
Marine Parade. He headed across the street towards them. He shook
the sand out of his shoes and clothes, and in the window of an ice-
cream kiosk caught sight of his unshaven face, suddenly aware that
no guest-house would welcome him. He trudged past the follies and
the mansions, down into the side streets with their crumbling terrace
houses and broken cast-iron balconies. Passers-by failed to see him.
Italian children with Australian voices let their long skipping-rope
hang idle long enough to let him pass, and then continued with their
game.

He began to read the cardboard signs in front-room windows and
nailed to balcony posts. "Twin room and Kichan to let." "Rubishis
removed." "TV's fixed, any time any place." In front of the next
house with a room-to-let sign he stopped. Darkness was falling now
and the forbidding and dusty look of the house gave him hope that
the inside too would be dark enough to hide his dishevelled state.
He lifted the door knocker, shiny brass on a door scarred with peeling
paint, and tapped.

The door opened. A hunchbacked creature the size of an eight-year-
old girl peered up at him. "Yes?"

"I believe you have a room to let. According to the card in the
window . . ."

"Please come in." She limped ahead into the dark house and he
followed. There was no light in the room they entered, but as the
curtains had not yet been drawn he could dimly make out the
shapes of dark heavy furniture.

"You will excuse me if I lie down while we talk. Sitting tires me
out so."

"Of course." He groped for a chair.

She settled herself slowly and painfully. He could only guess at her
movements. In the background he became aware of a faint tracery of
sound—Brahms's first symphony.

"You'll have to wait till mother gets back. She's having her treatment tonight."

"Oh. I'm sorry . . ." he contributed inadequately.

"Poor mother. She suffers dreadfully. What do you look like?"

Torn between truth and expediency, he finally suggested that
perhaps if he turned the light on . . .

"That won't be any use. I'm blind, you see," she said with simple
pride.

Even as he registered his own feelings of shock and guilty relief, he was aware of her own deliberate dramatic manipulation of shock effect.

"I'm sorry. I didn't realize."

"Yes. People notice that I'm a cripple and they don't look any further. Everybody's the same. They don't expect lightning to strike twice in the same place. But it does. Often. Have you ever noticed how many people win first prize in Tatts when they get second as well?"

"I hadn't given it much thought." He had to escape to the refuge of the room before the mother returned.

She cackled. "You're just dying to fix up about the room, aren't you?" Proud of the effect she created with him, she confided. "I've got a sixth sense, you know. Cripples often have remarkable gifts. Do you know what E.S.P. stands for?"

Obediently, fascinated, he murmured something about extra-sensory perception.

"That's right," she praised. "Nobody else in this house would have known a thing like that. And you speak like an educated man. Like a radio announcer. ABC of course, not commercial stations."

"Thank you." Brahms was reaching a majestic finale, although on the small transistor it sounded as though the symphony was being played on a comb and tissue paper.

"Switch that off, would you please?" she ordered him daintily. "The best part is over, where the violins climb up to the top and towards the sun. After that it gets boring. The rent is three pounds ten plus gas and electric." She corrected herself. "Seven dollars, I mean." Then, repeating a well-rehearsed speech, "And no visitors after ten, no noises on the stairs, radio to be kept low, no washing of clothes in the bathroom, cleaning and morning cups of tea extra charge."

"That'll do very well. Shall I pay you now?"

She held out a small twisted paw. "Seven dollars, thank you."

He could hear her tuck the money under her pillow, as she said mockingly, "You haven't even seen the room and you haven't asked for a receipt."

"I'm very tired."

She believed him. "Up the stairs," she directed, "turn left, up three steps, the door to your right. The bathroom is opposite. The convenience is down the backyard. And please don't flush after ten, it wakes mother. What did you say your name was?"

"F-Finnegan."

"Oh, Irish. Ah, well, it can't be helped. If you are one of those that go to mass at crack of dawn, please be very quiet opening and closing doors. It wakes mother."

"I'll be quiet."

"Good. I'll see you later then." She dismissed him.

He opened the door to the room and it was like entering an oven. The window was tightly closed and the roller blinds drawn. Dark brown furniture, shabby lino, threadbare mat and bedspread had all been roasted crisp for some mad gourmet. Clumsily he wrestled with the window, gasping for air. He let himself fall on to the chiming rustling bed, and listened to the thundering and buzzing in his ears. Giving in to discomfort seemed a luxury. He breathed in the brown airlessness of the house and felt himself obliterated more effectively than the day before. Like a lizard sitting motionless on the rocks that match his colouring, he too felt himself growing invisible, becoming transformed from Trader to Finnegan. The ugliness of the furniture swept over him like a sudden strong wind. He could not remember when he had been so intensely conscious of objects. Objects so hideous that it seemed unbelievable that human beings should have created them deliberately and gathered them together for permanent possession. Darkly bulging wood, stained and battered, ornamented with thick laboured scrolls, and at floor level cloven hooves concealing castors. The devil on wheels concealed in dry cracked wood and musty upholstery.

The women, mother and daughter, like two unevenly matched spiders, lay in wait for him when he had to go downstairs later. The way to the toilet led inexorably past their living-room.

"Is that you, Mr Finnegan?"

"Yes."

"I'd like you to come in and meet mother."

The dim brown light had been intensified by a small swathed lamp clipped to the marble mantelpiece. The older woman remained motionless in one of the large straight chairs. "I'm Mrs Kilmeny," she introduced herself without getting up, "and this is my daughter Nairee. It's a New Zealand name, you must know."

"Yes." He felt they could see him more clearly than he could see them. Some special evolutionary process affecting the eyes. "I hope you are feeling better," he ventured, as an offering suitable to either mother or daughter.

"A visit to the herbalist always does mother the world of good," Nairee informed him.

"Better than the masseur," Mrs Kilmeny agreed. "I hate Thursdays. They're a little rough with you at times. Really they're used to footballers, you see."

"I see." Wondering.

"And what's your occupation, Mr Finnegan, if it's not a rude question?"

"I'm—retired."

"Ah!" Mrs Kilmeny seemed at a loss, but Nairee took over with aplomb.

"And before your retirement, Mr Finnegan?" She grew more animated. "No, don't tell me, let me guess."

The two women concentrated their dimly luminous faces on him, and for a moment he felt weightless, non-existent, while they invaded him. Until they pronounced their findings he would be a mere shadow in this brown-tinted room, less substantial than the furniture.

"Something to do with books," Nairee said.

He coughed gently.

"Ah, I'm right. Printer? Librarian? Bookseller? Give me your hand."

He crossed to her bed and took her hand. It was cold, clammy and seemed boneless. He repressed a shudder as he felt her spider fingers exploring his own firm hand.

"Too smooth for a printer. And you don't walk like a librarian. Bookseller then," she concluded. "And you are still an active man. You'll want at least a part-time job. Mother will look out for something."

"The old bookstall at the market might do . . ." Mrs Kilmeny mused. "Leave it to me, Mr Finnegan."

They had created him. Finnegan, the lizard man, quite indistinguishable from his surroundings, went to bed, a part-time bookseller elect. In his dream that night he arrived in the Town Hall, ready to start his Wyatt to Wordsworth lectures and found that the course had been changed to Plumbing with Electronics. The students, Engineering and Agriculture to a man, had brought flour-bombs, and he woke up, suffocating in brown wholemeal flour.

The house was still wrapped in a brown sleep when he padded out to the little corner shop and returned with basic camping provisions, also some shaving equipment. But even when he was dressed and shaved and fed, reality refused to become graspable. Even though he was now sober and rested, he found himself incapable of clicking back into the mechanism of responsibility.

Once more he let his feet take over, but lack of food had made him weak. A few blocks away the street turned into a small park with dusty palm-trees. Here and there sat old men dozing in the morning sun, newspapers drooping over their knees. He found a free bench and sat down. The curious feeling of weightlessness persisted. He was nothing. Just an old man on a park bench, exactly like the others, except that he had no newspaper to give him the appearance of purpose. The deadness of the park and the motionless old men on the other benches filled him with sudden panic that he might in fact be dead himself. The movement of a myna-bird, stalking importantly four feet away from him, reassured him that there was life close at hand. All he had to do was move his feet and the bird would fly away, confirming his own existence. Trader kicked up a cloud of dust and the bird flapped a few paces instead of walking them. A feeble reassurance of life.

But then, Trader was dead. Long live Finnegan. Finnegan holed up like a nocturnal animal in a brown burrow, gradually being created by Mrs Kilmeny and Nairee in their own image.

One of the men from the other benches got up laboriously, dusted himself, straightened his newspaper slowly and walked up the path towards Trader. "Would you care for this morning's paper? I have finished with it."

"Thank you."

"Would you have the correct time, I wonder?"

Trader looked at his watch. "Ten to twelve."

"Ah! Time I went. Best to get there early, you see. I haven't seen you there, have I?"

"Where is that?"

"The midday soup at the Mission. No, I'd remember if I had. Very good soup they give you. Especially on Wednesdays. And it's not charity, you understand—it's our right as senior citizens. Our right." He seemed reluctant to go without Trader. "I was too proud to go once, you know. But they explained it. There's no shame in it."

"No. I'm sure there's not. Don't let me keep you."

The man looked pained, but then brightened. "I'll see you there one of these days," he predicted triumphantly, and went off in a stiff-legged jerky hurry.

The paper featured bushfires and sharks. On page five, tucked between shop-lifters and suburban stabbings, a small paragraph informed him that nothing further had been discovered in the Trader case. He was believed to be suffering from amnesia, and the public was requested to keep a look-out for him. Evidently the big story, if there had been one, had been in the previous day's edition. Readers' letters gave him more prominence. There were demands that his textbooks be banned, a suggestion that tape-recorders be used in tutorials to safeguard the morals of students, and finally a no-nonsense inquiry regarding the necessity of university study for young women anyhow. The possibility that Trader might have been accused unjustly was not envisaged.

While reading, the fog of unreality lifted for a few minutes, and Trader could admit the irresponsible—insane even—quality of his present flight. Logically he should have stayed, and proof of his innocence would surely have been found. But it went deeper than that. His daily habit of escape, his small avoidances of human contact, had prepared him for this moment. It was easy after living a shadow life to step out altogether. Finnegan was growing more real than Trader, was hourly gaining in substance. Now, for the first time, he was overwhelmed by the answer to the question he had refused to ask before. Why the girl's accusation, why Hella's malice, why his welcome of defeat? What kind of guilt was it, he admitted? Coldness, an emotional exhaustion that had overtaken him ten years ago was surely his misfortune, not his fault? But trading on the goodwill established by the earlier man, and raising expectations—that had been fraud. Dimly he perceived that both Hella and the hysterical student were making him pay for his failure to live up to their expectations. Why would they not let him be? All he wanted was peace. Or did he? The visions of death and nothingness that had come to him in the green cool evening and in the stifling brown room had been extreme, but unsatisfying. He had gone on. And having jettisoned Trader, he found that Finnegan was no more safe from the demands of others. Already the park had changed from a landscape of death, numbing in its withered desolation, into a place of living, suffering, fellow humanity. Back in the safety of his burrow Mrs Kilmeny and Nairee were waiting to trap him in the brown gloom of their web, speculating, touching, manoeuvring. Finnegan had come into existence only yesterday, and already the world was making its demands.

Slowly, painfully, he got up from the bench, dusted himself off and folded the paper. Stiffly he walked along the path, and threw the paper into a litter basket. Almost immediately it was retrieved by a new arrival who took over his bench. A sea of demands battering and gnawing at the old hulk that was himself, and he was more fitted by training and experience to deal with the old demands. He found himself smiling. Welcoming Trader back. Slipping into his skin.

He walked more quickly, straightening up, leaving the dusty park behind him. In the distance he could hear the grinding whine of a tram, and he walked towards the sound.

The bored stares of his fellow passengers promised him safe conduct. He curved his body to the hard and shiny wooden seat, and wondered at his choice. Finnegan obviously took trams, while Trader either walked or rode in taxis. There had to be a phase of transition, and he felt the briefest time of panic in his uncertainty. Would he know when Trader finally took over again? Would the people in the tram notice? And even in his present turmoil he knew that it was a smoke-screen of his own creation, to hide the moment of his homecoming. Now the demands would have to be met, because he was not ready, he found, to die.

ALAN MARSHALL

The Three-legged Bitch

TIM SULLIVAN was seventy-five years old. He was a thickset, powerful man with a crown of grey hair. His face had weathered wind and sun and rain and bore the character of an old rock. He had calm blue eyes and spoke slowly, gathering words from a mind that had been given few opportunities to express itself in speech.

He lived in Jindabyne at the foot of the Australian Alps. Everybody knew him. He had been a dogger, a dingo-trapper, and the years of his youth and manhood had been spent with packhorses and dog-traps amongst mountains and hills.

He had lived by killing. The death of dingoes brought him prestige, friendship, praise and sufficient money to live on. With the scalps of those he killed bagged on his packhorse he would come down from the mountains to collect his bounties and replenish his stores. He would ride down the main street of Jindabyne, his traps clinking from the back of the packhorse following him. Man standing at the hotel doorway would wave to him as he passed.

"How are ya, Tim?"

The station-owners with their broad-brimmed hats and Harris tweed sports coats shouted for him in pubs, threw him a fiver when some notorious dingo from whose raids they had suffered fell victim to his traps. They listened to his stories with interest, an interest born of an involvement with his successes and his failures. When on mustering rides they met him on lonely mountain tracks they reined in their horses to yarn with him.

They vied with each other in offers of hospitality should he visit them to trap the dingoes that harassed their sheep.

"Spend a few weeks with me at Geehi."

"There's a room for you at Khancoban."

He was a good fellow, an honest bloke, a chap you could rely on.

Upon the attitude of these men towards him Tim Sullivan built a framework of confidence and pride in himself.

For fifty years he hunted dingoes. He followed them into remote valleys, along ridges few men had trod. He knew every cattle- and sheep-pad that bound the hills. He drove the few remaining dingoes back to the inaccessible places where they lived on wallabies and from where they were afraid to venture down to the sheep country. He acquired great skill and knowledge.

When Tim was sixty-five his wife died. She had been a placid, stout woman with a friendly manner. She wore aprons upon which she wiped her hands before offering one to your grasp. She would then bustle round the kitchen making tea, anxious to please his guest. The glance she sometimes gave her husband affirmed what he was saying.

He had always felt young when she was alive. He could lead his packhorse into the mountains and stay away a month tracking some elusive dingo. But he thought of his wife a lot. He was always happy to return and began feeling a reluctance to leave again, to subject his stiffening joints to the sway of a saddle over miles of mountain tracks.

When she died he suddenly felt old. It was as if a cloak had been removed from him and he felt the coldness of the wind. His movements became slower and from thinking ahead he began thinking of the past.

"I never sleep on Sunday nights. I keep thinking about when Nell was alive. Every Sunday we had a roast."

He sold his horses and his traps. He became an old-age pensioner and hunted dingoes no longer. The attention of those people who noticed him walking up the street carrying a sugar-bag was momentarily arrested by his carriage.

"See that old bloke! He carries his head like he was somebody. I forget his name, but he used to trap dingoes or something. They say he was famous at it. He keeps clean, doesn't he?"

He had been confident in the continuation of his friendships. But he was of no value to the station-owners now. He was finished, out, done . . . He was an old-age pensioner who bored you with tales of your past losses. Gradually the men he had once served began to avoid him. They passed him on the street without a greeting. He began to realize where he now stood in the complex of the district's social structure.

"It sort of hurt me, him not recognizing me. I spent a month at his place once. I was going to say to him, 'Look, I'm not going to bite you for a couple of bob or the price of a drink. I just want to say "hullo", that's all.' But he just kept going."

So it was till the Three-legged Bitch came over from the Snakey Plains to harry the flocks in the Snowy River area.

For eight years the Three-legged Bitch roamed the ranges round the Snow Leases of the Kosciusko country. From the Grey Mare Range to the Pinch River men spoke of her. Her howl had been heard on the Big Boggy and they knew her tracks on the Thredbo. The bones of sheep she had slain lay along the banks of the Swampy Plains River on the Victorian side of the Snowy Mountains. She had crossed the Monaro Range, some sheepmen said.

The Three-legged Bitch was an outsize dingo with a thick, rusty-red coat and a short bushy tail. When she was young and inexperienced she had been caught in a trap and one of her forepaws had been partly severed. Only one toe was left on this disfigured foot, and the track it made was the brand by which she was known to those who hunted her.

She ran with a slight limp, her shoulder dropping a little when the leg she favoured took her weight. It had long since ceased to be the limp of pain or defective action; now it suggested a sinister development of style and her speed and strength seemed to stem from it.

She worked alone. Sometimes her howl brought a trotting male dog to a sudden halt on a valley track and he would stand a moment with lifted nose then turn and make up through the wooded spurs to the treeless uplands where she made her home.

But those wandering dogs who answered and went to her never possessed her cunning or brains, and they either fell victim to doggers or failed to survive long periods of hunger when the snow came.

On the Crown lands above the timber where the tussocky grass grows thick and gentian flowers come in the spring, sheepmen bring their flocks up from the valleys during the summer months and leave them to graze on areas they have leased from the Government— Snow Leases, they are marked on the maps that define them.

When the first horsemen appeared on top the Three-legged Bitch would retire back into the remote parts where they could not follow her. From here she came out to kill.

In March, before winter begins, the sheepmen go in and bring their flocks down to the snow-free valleys round the homesteads where the wild dogs never go.

There are no sheep on top in the winter, and then the snow lies in heavy drifts on the Snowy Plains and the dingoes and wild dogs grow lean with hunger. Yet the Three-legged Bitch always retained her strength. Some said she raided the rubbish dumps of the tourist chalets on those wild nights when her tracks would be covered by morning. A few doggers—those who delayed leaving the high valleys till snow forced them out—suspected she lived on sheep missed in the annual muster. These animals are often buried in the snow, and here the Three-legged Bitch would scent them as she trotted through the still, white world of the surface. When the warm breath of them came to her through the snow she burrowed down till she reached them huddled together in terror. Then she tore the living flesh from their backs.

In the summer she came in about every third night, favouring the boisterous nights when terrified bleating would be lost in the wind and her panting was just another sound. She had been known to slaughter fifty sheep in one run when there was a gale and a full moon was whipped by clouds. She had killed for a week at Thompson's when Thompson was away.

All the sheepmen knew her work. She always revealed her identity in the method of her killing. She was the criminal betrayed by fingerprints. Long before she became known as "The Three-legged Bitch" tales were told of sheep with mangled throats lying in lines on the snow leases of the high country. The unknown dog that slew them ran on the offside of each panic-stricken victim till, in that stumbling moment of weakness for which it awaited, it leapt for the throat, jerking the head backward as its teeth sank deep and breaking the animal's neck as it came down.

Sheep still alive but gasping horribly through torn windpipes were brought in at the muster. Many sheep were never found. Their torn bodies lay in ravines and among rocks where their last desperate run had taken them.

Angry men held quick musters and swore at the count. In the bars of mountain pubs, with the froth of beer on their stubbly lips, they slew the Three-legged Bitch with fury.

"I'll fix her once I get hold of her."

"If she gets amongst my ewes I'll follow her to the Murray."

The kill of minor dingoes was blamed on her; kills twenty miles apart did not save her from a double accusation.

"She killed at Groggin's Gap on Wednesday."

"She came in to Big Boggy on Wednesday."

All slaughtered sheep were hers; the kill of every dog was hers.

She killed for sport, they said. She was blood-hungry, blood-mad . . . She snarled and drove in, she ripped down then back, she leaped like a shadow, whipped round and in again, on to another one. Snarl and rip and slash and on again. This was how they saw her, flecked with blood, her snarling mouth dripping. This was how they described her one to another, from man to man, across bar counters, in sheds and homes. The instinct that drove her to kill as many sheep as she could in a run seemed to them evidence of a creature with the mind of a murderer.

Before sheep had come to this country kangaroos and wallabies had been the dingoes' food. These animals could outrun the hunting dogs. It was only when an unsuspecting mob of wallabies was quietly feeding near trees or sheltering rocks that they were in danger. The hiding dingo suddenly burst into view fully extended and was amongst them with ripping teeth before they had time to gather speed. Two or three would die before the mob bounded away.

Food was life. Survival demanded the seizing of every opportunity to kill, for such opportunities did not come every day. Two slain wallabies were food for days.

Then sheep came to the mountains, helpless animals that could not escape by running. So the dingoes killed till they were tired, driven to slaughter one after another, not by a mind finding a savage joy in killing but by an instinct born thousands of years before when the animals they hunted had the speed to escape them.

The Three-legged Bitch had survived because of her skill in obtaining food, by her skill in avoiding the guns and traps and poisons of man.

She was afraid of men, but there lingered in her some allegiance to them handed down from remote times when her domesticated ancestors had reached Australia with the first dark man. Sometimes from a safe distance she followed men droving cattle or a solitary musterer. She stood far back from the light of campfires howling quaveringly as she watched them.

She was the last of her kind in those parts, the only pure-bred dingo that had survived the hunting of men. Yet she was incapable of feelings of revenge. That feeling marked the attitude of men towards her, the men from whose vast flocks she had taken her food.

For eight years man hunted her. First for the price of her hide, then for the value of her scalp, then for twenty pounds reward . . . fifty . . . a hundred . . . They came up from the farms and the towns and the cities. There were young men with brown faces and strong arms and old men with beards. They came leading packhorses or tramping up through the woollybutt and snow gums carrying guns. Solitary riders with the stock of a cocked gun resting on their thigh walked their horses through the timber, across plains of snow grass, down long ravines, their heads turning from side to side in an eager seeking. Packs of dogs, noses to the ground, followed in the confident steps of owners seeking a final payment. From some of the laden horses stumbling along the high tracks huge dog-traps clanked and swung. Men came with poison, with pellets of dough and ground glass, with stakes and snares. They shot brumbies and with blood-stained gloves upon their hands thrust poisonous crystals into the gashes made in the flanks. They poisoned the carcasses of sheep, cattle . . . Groups of sheepmen rode in lines, shouting through the scrub. On the far side their companions waited with guns.

She watched them come and go.

The defeated men came down from the mountains with tales that made minor triumphs of their failures. They lied to save their pride, they boasted to impress.

"I bowled her over with my second shot," Ted Arthur said. "She was staggering when she got up. I reckon she'd toss it in somewhere round by Little Twynam."

He didn't say how he came on her at a kill on the Grey Mare Range, how he fired and missed. She went down that slope in long bounds, hugging the cover, with his kangaroo dog at her heels then shot into a clump of wattle. When Ted's spurred horse reached the clump the Three-legged Bitch glided out on the far side and disappeared into the scrub. It was then he found his dog thrashing in a circle on the bloody leaves.

She had thrown up three of Bluey Taylor's baits, and Jack Bailey always swore she lost another toe in one of his traps.

But they all came down—Ted and Bluey and Jack and scores of others. They all left the snow leases, left the mountains . . .

Five men visited Tim one day. They left their cars at the gate and stood in a group before his door, waiting for it to be opened to their knock. Tim invited them in. He knew them all. Once he had imagined they were his friends. They were still, it seemed, by the warmth of their handshakes and the tone of their voices.

"We want to talk to you about the Three-legged Bitch, Tim," said one. "She killed seven of my ewes last night, and Jack here lost five on Friday night. We've got to do something about it fast. She scatters those she doesn't kill, and God knows how many we have lost. You are the only man that can get her. We want you to go after her. It won't take you so long, with your experience. Now wait till you hear our proposition," he hastened to add as Tim moved to speak. "We know you have retired from the game, so to speak, but . . ."

They all paid tribute to his skill as a dogger. Everybody said he was the only man who would bring in her scalp. They were all agreed on this. They would stake him, buy his grub, supply him with horses and packs, pay him a hundred pounds for her scalp. He was still remarkably fit. You only had to look at him. They recalled him coming down from the top in snow storms, they remembered the time he had ridden ninety-four miles between sunrise and sunset.

"You couldn't kill him with an axe," one remarked to another.

They continued to praise him but Tim wasn't listening to them.

He was looking at the walls of his hut. Many things hung there all with a tongue—an old bridle, a rusty, broken trap, the skin of a dingo, faded photographs in frames of painted cork, frames of seashells, pictures of horses cut from the pages of magazines . . . How many times had he sat and looked at them! It was his life he looked at and it was a protection. He only had to turn his head and there through the window were the mountains with a thin track winding up into the cold and the loneliness, the loneliness that had often sat with him in this room.

"You couldn't kill him with an axe," he thought.

Their words were sweet to him. The pains, the aches, the digestive troubles his mind had fashioned from boredom and which seemed to lurk within him awaiting the trigger of purposelessness to release them, suddenly vanished and a deep breath filled his lungs with a new strength. He'd show them, these men who could discard a friendship like an old shirt. They needed him now. All the others had failed. He wouldn't fail.

"I'll bring you back her hide," he said.

They took him down to the pub and shouted for him. They gave him advice. They all knew how the bitch could be caught.

"You'd probably bring her into the traps using piss as a lure," said one of the men, a grazier whose wife, sick of life in the bush, was living in a Melbourne flat. "They'll follow the trail for miles."

Tim didn't reply. He knew all the lurks. Tie a bitch on heat so that she has to stand on a sheet of galvanised iron, catch her urine in a tin and bottle it—it would lure a male dog into the traps or within reach of a rifle, but didn't this bloke realize he was dealing with a slut! It had no appeal to her.

His mind even now was planning the methods he would use. He was remembering past triumphs when with unresented patience he followed a dog for months until he knew her every habit, her peculiarities, her weaknesses . . . He would do the same again.

Four days later he was following Barlees Track across Reads Flat. The Geehi flowed near by, fed by the melting snow that still lay in drifts on the Snowy Mountains. He was making for a cattleman's hut not far from Wild Cow Flats where the tracks of the Three-legged Bitch had been seen by several sheepmen preparing to take their flocks up above the tree-line to graze during the summer months.

She had not yet killed, they said, though one of the men who had seen her several times trotting down from the Grey Mare Range said she was in good condition after the winter.

"She knows when you haven't got a gun," he said. "She stood and

watched me one day—only about forty yards away. You could tell
what she was thinking."

For two months Tim camped in the hut. He used it as a base from
where he ranged the surrounding country. He had found her tracks,
listened to her howl as he sat over his log fire.

He thought a lot about her while sitting before his fire. He de-
veloped a strange affection for her. Was she as merciless and cruel as
they said? Was she evil? He had earned his living by killing. And
he had got joy from it. He had looked down on the trapped dog with
excitement. Then he had killed. He didn't like thinking about this.
He didn't like thinking how he loved the admiration of other men,
an admiration earned by killing.

"There's nothing you don't know about dingoes."

"I'll hand it to you; you're the best dogger in Australia."

Then he had seen her. He had been riding back with a load of stores
he had bought at Jindabyne when he came to an outcrop of rock just
off the track. Huge boulders leaning one against the other formed
cavities that would be a perfect shelter for a dog. He dismounted,
left his reins hanging and began searching round the rocks for tracks.
The indentation of each claw was always absent from her tracks.
They had been worn down by age and travel and she only left the
impression of her pads. The claw tracks of young dogs were always
deeply impressed into the ground.

She had been there all right. He looked at her tracks. She was older
than he thought. He noticed the mark of her injured paw. He turned
and looked up the mountain-side as if expecting to see her slinking
through the boulders. Suddenly she shot from a cavity to the left of
him. She bounded on to a flat rock and then stood looking at him
for a few swift heartbeats. His gun was back with the horses. Then
she was gone. She seemed to flow over the rock upon which she had
been standing. She glided through the trees and rocks making of
each one a cover that stood between them.

Tim saw her many times over the next few months. He got to know
her well. She had a deep curiosity. She often studied him from the
shelter of some rock on the mountain-side before slipping quietly
away. He had seen other dogs too, mongrels with her blood in them.
But he was not involved with them. He had set out to destroy one
dog—the dingo bitch. She was famous, so was he.

He studied her for months. He knew she always came in fairly
fast. She trotted along a track, her head low, her tongue dripping.
She never paused, but kept up her tireless trotting for miles. She
always went out by a different track. When making back to the higher
country she went slowly, pausing to roll on the grass or sniff at a

tree-trunk she knew would attract other dogs. She had killed and her hunger was satisfied.

When coming in on wild, moonlight nights, she sometimes stopped and raised her head and her throat would vibrate in a quavering howl, a sound that always gave Tim a disturbing feeling of fear. His reaction to the howl of a dingo had never been removed by familiarity with the sound. The uncomforted voice of the bitch drew him into an experience of utter loneliness. It was the cry of a living thing in isolation and it united his yearnings with her own.

He discovered an old sheep track coming down from the craggy top of the range where it ended on a treeless flat. Here sheep were often grazing. He set two traps on this track. He set them with skill and left them. Some day she would use that track. Months of rain and sun would remove all evidence of their existence. They would wait.

He sought the sheep tracks she had used recently. On one that followed the crest of a spur he found her tracks, clear and distinct, unweathered by rain and wind. She always trotted along ridges rather than through valleys. She liked open country for travel and avoided those tracks that demanded she cross a creek. She was always reluctant to leave a cattle- or sheep-pad on which she found herself. She followed them for miles, lifting her front legs high in a style that had been cultivated on the tussocky uplands above the tree-line. On this track Tim set his traps in the form of a letter "H". He selected a spot where the track was flanked by bleached tussocks that formed a dense cover she would naturally avoid.

The dog-traps Tim was carrying were like oversized rabbit-traps, each with two springs. The teeth of the wide jaws did not meet. This prevented the dog's leg from being severed instead of held.

Tim wore old gloves which were caked with the dried blood of a brumby. He spread a bag on the track, placed a trap beside it, then cut an outline round the trap with an old shear-blade, pushing the blade deep into the soil. He removed the outlined sod by prising it free with the blade till it could be lifted intact and placed carefully on the bag. He placed the topsoil on one corner, the bottom soil on another so that he could return them to their original position in the set. The set trap fitted exactly into the excavation.

He enjoyed doing this. All his past experiences were directing him and they grew in value as he pondered on his skill and knowledge. He suddenly felt linked with all men who knew their craft and worked well, a great army of men with whom he walked shoulder to shoulder.

He never touched the soil. He transferred each root-bound lump with the blade. Beneath the raised plate he thrust dry grass, pushing it carefully into position to prevent soil collecting there. He did not place paper above the plate as in rabbit trapping. It would be likely to rustle when a dog stepped close to it.

He buried the chains attached to the traps with the same care. At the end of each chain a strand of wire increased its length and ended by being fastened to a "drag", a log of wood Tim had selected because of its shape. They were not too heavy and would enable the dingo to drag them some distance without subjecting her leg to a strain that would sever it.

When the traps and chains were covered he carried the bag on which surplus soil was lying and shook it some distance away. He then used the bag to "blow" the set. He waved the bag above the set, blowing away loose crumbs of earth. Using the shear-blade he scattered dry leaves and broken cow manure above the area on which he had been working until all evidence of his work had vanished.

He stood up and looked down at his work with satisfaction. The longer the traps stayed in the ground the better his chance of catching her.

He passed near by to the set two days later, but it hadn't been disturbed. Then on the fourth day after a gusty night of wind he reined his horse beside the track and looked down on the scarified earth over which he had worked so carefully. Two of the traps had been sprung. Dirt and stones had been scratched over them in what seemed to be a gesture of contempt. She had come trotting down the track, following it with her head down. She continued between the arms of the "H", then stopped dead at the bar. Here she stood a moment deadly still—the last four paw marks were deeply indented—sniffing at the polluted air. She then backed carefully out, stepping into the tracks she had already made, until she was free of the enclosure. It was here she turned and ripped up the stones and earth in an attempt to render the hidden steel harmless. Tim sat on his horse and looked at her answer. There was a faint smile on his face.

In the months that followed he tried every trick he knew. Wearing gloves stained with blood, he had dropped poisonous crystals into slashes made in the flanks of freshly-killed brumbies. He had shot only thin horses. He believed a dingo, knowing it had swallowed poison, could throw up the flesh of a fat horse. She had eaten round the slashes. He tried poisoning the carcasses of sheep she had slain. She ignored them.

But still she killed, leaving a trail of dead animals on the Swampy Plain, out by Bogong, on the slopes of the Blue Cow. She was killing with more than usual ferocity as if danger had made her desperate.

He dragged putrid legs of sheep by a rope tied to his saddle, leading her for miles to baits of fresh liver with deadly mouths slashed into them. She often followed these trails, scratching dirt over each bait as she reached it. On one occasion she had carried two of the baits and dropped them on top of a third that lay on an open pad beneath the sun. Beside this pile of poisoned meat she had left her dung.

A symbol of her contempt? Tim kicked it to one side and smiled. She had no mind for such gestures. It was the heavy odour of putrid flesh that inspired her to leave the smell of her presence for the benefit of other dogs.

On a small flat open to the sky Tim found a pool of clear water. The banks were undermined, and matted dry grass clung to these banks and hung over the water, immersing their pale, brittle stems beneath the surface. On one side there was a gap in the encircling grass, and here on a tiny beach of grey mud she had left the imprint of her battered paws.

Tim studied them, then looked around him. The flat was treeless except for a bushy snow gum growing some twenty yards away. He knew that after a dingo drank she would trot to the nearest tree where she would stand or lie down for a while in the shade. There were no tracks to the tree—the grass was too thick—but there was an impress on the grass beneath it that suggested she had lain there.

He set four traps round the tree. When he had finished, the grass, the earth, the littered bark was as if no hand had touched it. He was pleased and stood for a moment anticipating victory.

Two days later he stood there again. She had sprung the traps with scratched dirt. She had drunk at the spring, trotted to the tree and stood there a moment with senses alert while her sensitive nose detected the evidence of his work. Then the fear and the destruction of what she feared. Tim understood her. He loaded the traps on to his horse and rode away, and there was no anger nor resentment in him.

He followed her with the rifle and fired at her from distances that demanded keener eyes than he possessed to hit her. He watched the spurt of dust rise near her feet, then trailed her till her tracks petered out amongst the rocks that littered the uplands.

She became increasingly wary of him—she feared guns—and he began finding it difficult to get within sight of her. He moved from hut to hut on the high country, following reports of her killing and camping for weeks in some remote shelter built by cattlemen and only visited for a week or two each year.

He wintered at the Geehi Hut on the track to Khancoban. He packed in his stores and was never short of tucker. When spring came to the mountains he followed the retreating snow to the top. For a week he searched for her tracks then found them criss-crossing the pitted earth behind a flock of climbing sheep. She had killed one of the stragglers.

There were moments when he felt she was indestructible, that all his skill was useless against her instinct to survive. He sometimes felt there wasn't a trail from the top in which he hadn't buried his traps; no clearing he hadn't baited.

He had made it a habit to make a regular visit to the old trail in which he had set his traps when first he came to the mountains. Almost a year had passed since he had hidden them beneath the track she once had made. Snow had covered them since then; bleak winds had flattened the soil above them, sun and rain and frost had removed all trace of man, and the track wound upwards in an unbroken line that smelt of wild grass and the presence of spring.

His horse knew the way. She moved at a brisk walk through the tussocks while he sat relaxed in the saddle, the reins drooping from her neck. He had no feeling of anticipation. This visit had become a habit.

When he first saw her crouched upon the track, draggled, panting, surrounded by the torn earth of her struggling, he experienced a leap of excitement that was almost a pain so intense it was. He had stopped. The air had no motion, and he sat in a still silence savouring his triumph like a powerful wine. He could hear distant shouts of acclaim from beyond the accusing mountains, cheering. . . .

The moment passed, and his shoulders sagged to the burden of the accusation. He alighted from his horse and walked to her. Two traps held her helpless, their naked jaws clamped on a front and hind leg. They had lain in darkness beneath the track for over a year, and the smell of the earth had become their smell. The chains were taut from the drags which had prevented her from struggling into the concealing grass.

As he approached she wriggled backwards taking up what slack was available to her, then she faced him, crouching low, her muzzle resting on the earth, her fangs bared in a soundless snarl.

They faced each other, the old man and the greying dingo, both killers who had reached a final reckoning. And Tim knew it in a clouded way. Hundreds of slain dingoes marked the trail of his lonely passage. Her pathway was a line of torn sheep lying motionless across the mountain uplands where she was born. He was surprised that she didn't reveal in her appearance the murderer of her reputation. Sheepmen saw her as inspired by an evil joy in slaughter. The mind that directed her was to them the cold and calculating instrument of a criminal. Now Tim saw her as a lonely old dog scarred by pellets of shot, by traps, and the teeth of hunters' dogs. He was a bit like that himself, he thought, but his scars didn't show. They lay beneath the confident smile, the pride in killing; her's denied him his pride.

"I'll bring you back her hide," he had told them. Well, he'd bring it back. He'd given his word.

When I kill her, he reflected, I kill myself. I'll go back to being an old-age pensioner. No more slaps on the back, shouting in pubs. No more invitations to stay at the homes of wealthy people. I'll return to my hut and die in my hut, and that will be the end of it all.

He stood watching her, torn by indecision. He wanted to go on living with himself, he wanted to be able to walk with his head up. When he did act it was with sudden desperation. Reason had bowed its head.

He seized a log of wood from the ground and advanced upon her, his face twisted with an anguish his powerful arms denied. She waited for him, shrinking closer to the earth, her glaring eyes desperate. The snarl she had held in silence now found voice in a vibrating growl of defiance and she sprang as he raised the log aloft. She took up the slack of both chains in her spring, and the blow he brought to the side of her head jerked her sideways as the tightened chains arrested her leap. She fell on her side to the ground, her head thrown back, her four legs taut and quivering.

He hit her again, not with frenzy but with despair, then turned and walked back to his horse. He suddenly felt old and tired, and he walked stiffly. With his head resting against the saddle he drew deep breaths of replenishment till the cold sense of betrayal passed and he could stand erect.

He walked back to her body lying prone on the ground and released her paws from the grip of the traps. He dragged her to one side, her head bouncing loosely over the stones. Even in death she still snarled her defiance. Her worn teeth were bared in one last, horrible grimace from which Tim turned his eyes.

He'd made up his mind. He buried her there beneath the tussocky grass, and he did it with the same care he used in setting a trap. When he straightened himself the grass was waving in the mountain wind above her grave and the sheep track was the same as it was before he'd sowed it with death. Cloud shadows rippled up the mountain-side like the passing of her feet, and an eagle soared down the wind. It was a good place to rest.

KAY BROWN

She Let Them Know

My BROTHER Stuart and me met Mrs Rigby our first day at Copper
Top. She was digging in the bed of the Leichhardt when we went
down there to explore. The bank was high just there, and we saw
this square sort of old woman digging against the side where the
rocks leant over and the sand was shaded. She had a deep hole dug
and the sides were wet looking.

Stu has real nice manners, and he's clever, too. He said, "Goodday.
Can we help you dig?" He went near her to take the shovel, but she
moved away sharply from him and said, "Who's yous boys?" and
peered at us with hard, shiny black eyes, like little winking marbles.
They winked a lot. The glare, I s'pose.

She had on an old felt hat, a man's sort—very shapeless. And her
dress was a faded blue colour, of strong stuff and *square*. Her body
moved around inside it like someone in a tent. And while she was
looking at us and waiting for our answer, she pushed the hat back
off her hair, which was streaky grey and short like a man's too.

Stu told her our names, and that we were the new stationmaster's
boys, and just come to have a look round the place while Mum and
Sis were fixing things up at the house like they have to every time
Dad gets a transfer to a new place.

She said, "I'm Mrs Rigby," and held out her hand to us both, and
we shook it. Then she handed Stu the shovel to dig, and sat on a rock
to fan herself with the hat. She said, "Like I told you, I'm Mrs Rigby.
Not old Ma Rigby, and mindjoo, if ever I catches either of yous boys
calling me that, I'll let you know. See?" She looked pretty fierce then
and I wanted to go, but Stu said "Yes", and dug on for a bit.

I said, "What is the hole for?"

"That's me soak."

Stu and me hadn't seen a soak before. After a bit, she took the
shovel from Stu and dug a bit more, very quickly, so the wet sand
flew out zunk! zunk! in thuds like heavy rain falling. Then she

stood back and said, "There. See?" pointing, and we looked down into the hole kneeling carefully so's not to push the sides in. It was lovely! The water oozed in and filled the bottom gently like the tide at the sea coming in. It was a real little toy well.

Mrs Rigby handed us an enamel pint, and Stu scooped the clear water up in it for us to drink. It was cool, too, and tasted nice.

Then she got a wooden case and lined the sides so the sand wouldn't fall in and then put an old sheet of iron over it and told us to fetch some big stones and put on top—to hold it down in the wind, I thought, but she said, "That's to keep them 'roos and goats off-uv it."

Stu had filled the big, black old billy-can and he carried it up the bank, and I took the shovel for her. A little way from the river was a low, iron humpy sort of building. It had a good strong fence around it, of rusted barbed wire, and the walls were white-washed.

"That's me place," she told us, and we went in the gate.

A big, blue-black dog came to meet us, very old, with a baggy body hanging shapeless and floppy from its backbone.

Mrs Rigby said, "This here's Lucy," and the dog nodded, sort of, and went off again to lie down under some shade.

It was dark inside the place, till she went over and pushed up a shutter with a stick. There was a dirt floor, and in the corner, a bag bunk with blankets on one end and some cases round the walls with newspapers spread on top, and in the middle, a scrubbed deal table.

She made us strong tea in a billy and told us she was a champeen rider and could drive a team as good as her dad. We weren't too sure about teams—only football and cricket ones. She said her dad came up from the Coopa with teams.

"But they's all gone now. But he was a champeen those days." She sighed then, remembering him.

We had to go then, but we thanked her for the tea and she said, "Yous seem decent boys and mindjoo I don't like anything lessit's proper. None of the 'Old Ma Rigby' stuff, or I'll let yous know!"

Mum and Sis didn't bother too much where we'd been. They were tired from the fixing. We had to start school then, and only on Saturdays for sure, and sometimes other afternoons or after dinner, Sundays, we could call on Mrs Rigby. We found out about the "Old Ma Rigby" she didn't like, too. The sergeant and his wife and the people from the hotel, and stockmen who came to the railway office for things, all told Dad and Mum about her.

"Old Ma Rigby's a Holy Terror," they'd say. "You wait till she goes for you." Everyone seemed to think she would just call one day and "go" for Dad and Mum.

Stu and me never said about being friends with her. Stu is clever and he said best not. The yellow kids at school used to tell about chasing her and giving cheek, but Stu said, "Bet I know who does the chasing—not you." So they shut up skiting.

She told us lots of stories about what they used to do "on the roads" with the teams. Some days she'd be cross about something or someone, and tell us how she'd "let them know".

At home we'd hear the sergeant's wife tell Mum "Old Ma Rigby went off at so-and-so today". They all used to laugh a lot about that. Once when we were coming from school for lunch we saw her coming out of Daley's store backwards, and yelling out bad names at the storekeeper. As we passed, we could see him standing well back against the store wall, and Jim the yellow boy who helped him ran out the back.

When she saw us she dropped two stones from her hand. Big ones. I felt a bit scared. She wiped her hands on her dress and came over to where we were walking. But Stu raised his hat and said "Good day, Mrs Rigby."

"Good day, Stoot," she said, and nodded at me. Then she stepped up close and peered into our faces. I felt her breath, and wanted to run, but I could see Stu wasn't scared, and then she said, still peering into our faces and nodding her head one to the other, "Yous boys been good at school today, eh?"

Stu said, "Yes, Mrs Rigby," and then she looked real pleased and said, "That's all right, well," and turned away towards her place.

Everyone at the store and the hotel had been standing still and watching, and Mum hurried to the gate to meet us coming in, and said, "What did that old thing say to you two?"

"Were we good at school today," Stu said, and went in to dinner.

Mum and Sis took deep breaths and then laughed and looked at each other, and Mum said, "Well, can you beat that?"

Then, after dinner, she said, "If that old woman ever speaks to you boys any time, you both be polite and answer nicely. Some of the boys tease her. She's dangerous. Now, do you hear me?"

We said, "Yes."

Some Saturdays we learnt to saw leather and put rivets in. She showed us a little flowery plant that made good yeast, and we went looking for it for her along the river-banks. She would bake lovely bread in a big camp-oven, and the days we knew she had set it we would hurry down after school and watch her knead it up, and wait till she baked it. She never used the table to work on like women do, but cut open a clean flour-bag and knelt in front of it to roll and knead the dough round and round, and in on itself. She showed us how to make the hole for the big old iron camp-oven "that me Dad had on the roads", and we would carry shovels full of coals or ashes and put them carefully on top. We had to be careful and do everything proper, too, my word: if we didn't do a tidy job she'd let us know, she said.

We ate as much of the crisp bread as we wanted to. I don't think she really needed to make it. She just liked to do it, and we liked her to. I expect she got a bit lonely for her own boys, too. There were ten of them, she said, "but they's all gorn over now."

We weren't too sure about that, but anyway she didn't seem to expect them back. Sometimes, Mum worried when we didn't want much tea on bread days, but Stu just said, "We had some pieces." Mum thought it would be at a boy's place.

After Christmas the river came down and the sergeant called for us all and took us up in his car to see the floods. There were a lot up there. Everyone was out to see the river running, and I saw Mrs Rigby watching too. We went to her place next day, and she told us she'd seen us with the sergeant. She said she didn't go much on them fellers. One of them had taken her old man orf. She never said where to, and we didn't ask. We walked down to the river's edge with her and stood watching the water rushing along. It filled the deep hole between the high banks where the soak was, and was up over the end of the town too, and over the railway bridge. "But this wasn't nothing," she said of the roaring waters. "Yous boys should've seen 'er the time my Harry went over 'er."

Harry, she said, was a good boy. She looked at us very fiercely here, and seemed to be waiting for us to say he wasn't. "Harry never done anything wrong," she went on, "just had a lot of spirit in him. Time the river come down that year, them fellers had him locked up. There was a lot of thunder about that night, a real big storm, and my Harry kicked his way out. Fancy that, eh? Kicked down the door."

She looked away into the distance as if she could see Harry back, then: "Strong! My word that Harry was strong," she said. "He come and got tucker and borrowed a horse and swum over." She nodded at the swollen river.

"Did he? In all that flood?" Stu asked, and I stared at the tumbling whitey-brown water rushing along, and the boughs of trees and old logs bobbing in it, and sticks and leafy bushes, and I thought of strong Harry swimming in that with his borrowed horse and I suppose pushing aside the boughs and that out of his road with his strong arms.

"Yes," Mrs Rigby answered Stu. "Just acrorst there." She pointed at the low bank farther along and we waited to hear more. But she seemed to have gone away somewhere for a while, then. So we all watched the patterns of the rushing water and thought of Strong Harry in it in the night.

"Did he go far?" Stu asked.

"No," she said. "No, not Harry. He done a fool thing. Borrowed the wrong horse. 'Corse, mindjoo, it was real black that night, but I reckon I never got over Harry to mistake a horse like that."

"Why? Did the horse buck him off?" Stu asked then.

"No. Drowned itself. Not a swimmer. Lot of horses like that. Look here now." She bent down and put a small twig at the edge of the water. "Yous boys always wants to do that, see? Then watch the water and you'll know if she's rising or falling, see?"

We said "Yes", we would remember what she told us. She'd left Strong Harry, we could see, and it didn't seem proper to ask any more.

Once at breakfast Mum and Sis were talking about her, and Mum said, "I feel a bit sorry for her though, poor old thing. She's had a lot of trouble—and losing all those children."

Dad said, "Has she lost them, though? I heard a yarn or two about a few of them beating the police to the Territory border." So we hoped Strong Harry never drowned with that wrong horse after all.

Then Mr Harris left on transfer, and a new sergeant came. We didn't see as much of him as we had of the Harrises. Dad told Mum he was a New Broom when she asked about him.

We were nearly finished lunch that day when Dad came in and said to Mum, "Hear the sergeant took old Ma Rigby up last night."

"Goodness," Mum said, "whatever's happened?"

"Oh, nothing, I don't think. He's just cleaning up. Hear he's going to ship her to Brisbane on todays' train with young Fletcher. Not waiting for the mail, in case she gets troublesome, I suppose."

We went out quick, without eating any more, and I asked Stu, "Where will they take her?"

"Dunno." The bottom of my stomach felt like when I've told Mum a lie and she's found out. The yeller kids at school said they knew where she was getting taken to but we wouldn't tell them we believed it. Stu was real silly in lessons all afternoon.

The slow train got in at four. We hurried and got through the fence for a short cut instead of going home first and being stopped by anything. We stood up the end of the dirt platform—it was red ant-bed, a bit higher than the other ground. We knew Dad would be in his office till the train came in, and Jelly Neil the porter wouldn't mind us.

The new Sarge—Mum said it was disrespectful to say "Sarge", but I was always going to now, and so was Stu: we made it up at school that day—well, the new Sarge and Constable Fletcher were standing at the door of the waiting-shed. We walked along quietly and saw Mrs Rigby sitting on the bench inside.

We wouldn't have known her. She had on a black dress with a lot of lace stuff at the throat and a big brooch with yellow glass stones in it, pinned on the neck, very high, and as she swallowed it moved up and down and wobbled a bit. There were black cotton gloves on her hands, and a shiny black hat with a funny broken grape on one side of a ribbon band sat on her head. On her lap she had a small basket very neatly strapped with one of the strong leather ones we'd seen her make. When I saw it was the one I put the rivets in too, I just wished her Strong Harry would ride up then and hit that new Sarge.

We went in the waiting-room, and it was dark after outside. Mrs Rigby was looking away like she did after Harry that day. Then she looked at us, peering how she did, and Stu said, "Hullo, Mrs Rigby. Is there anything you'd like us to do while you're away?" Gee, Stu is game!

She sat up straight then, from where she had been kind of slumped and tired-looking, and the sun came in and I saw that the black hat and her clothes were really a kind of greeny colour.

"Well, good day, yous boys," she said, real strong and loud for that old Sarge to hear too. "Yes, now, there is a few things." Her voice got much stronger as she went on, real like the old Ma Rigby they were all afraid of.

"Look after me soak now. Don't let none of them fellers near it." I thought of the water rushing along over it, but didn't say. "And let no one near my place neither, Stoot. Any them fellers goes near it, my word I'll let 'em know!"

The train whistle sounded at the bend. Mrs Rigby got up and handed Stu the basket and me a little box from under the seat. You could see she felt a lot better now. But not the Sarge and the Constable. They came close to the waiting-shed and looked at us hard. Mrs Rigby bustled us down the step and shouldered the two of them aside as we passed. The slow goods pulled up and Dad came out of his office. The train guard got down and, seeing Mrs Rigby, said, "Where to, lady?"

Stu said, real quick, before that old Sarge could say anything, "Brisbane—and a good seat facing the engine, please."

The guard grinned and handed Mrs Rigby in and found her a good seat where she could talk to us from the window while he and

Neil unloaded some stuff from the van. We stood close to the window and Stu talked about Brisbane to her. I felt someone touch my shoulder. It was the Sarge, and he was handing two shillings to me.

"Go and get your friend some soft drink for the train," he said. "You've got time."

I looked at Stu and he nodded. I ran fast to the store for it. On the way I thought, "Oh, I never asked her what sort." But I got lemonade because I like that and anyway she mightn't have known the names of soft drinks. I never saw her have any. I reckon they only had tea on the roads. But I bet she'd like lemonade. When I got back with the soft drink Dad was talking to Mrs Rigby and smiling. She looked real well and proud too—her head kept turning to the other people in the carriage, and she called Dad "Station Master".

"You got two sensible sorts of boys here, Station Master." She nodded at us. "Mindjoo, boys gets out of hand—you got ter let 'em know you want things done proper."

I didn't give the cold bottle to Stu to give her, either. I reached up to her myself. "Here's some lemonade for the journey, Mrs Rigby."

Journey sounded more proper than just train.

She took the bottle and showed it to the other passengers.

"See, eh? Thank yous, boys." Then the whistle had gone and the train was moving before I had time to tell her it wasn't us that bought it for her.

We waved till the train went round the bend, and Stu looked at me so's we'd go through the short cut again and miss Dad and them, and we went quick.

My stomach felt better than at dinner-time. You bet there wasn't anything to worry about. Mrs Rigby wouldn't let anyone get her down at any old looney house like the yellow kids said. Not her. She'd let them know, you bet. And I'm going to say "The Sergeant" again, now. I bet Stu does, too.

JULIE LEWIS

Dry Season

THE *but-but-but* of the engine continued all night. More forceful than a two-stroke, it impinged on the threshold of consciousness to a maddening degree. Occasionally, stronger concentration blotted it out. But not for long. Marg Patching threw back the damp sheet and lay for a moment, the heavy still air pressing on her like some physical thing, intolerably. Across the caravan the other bed was undisturbed, still empty. Marg Patching levered herself onto one elbow to peer at the distant glowing figures on the clock. Nearly three! And still not home. She tried to pin down what she felt. Not longing. Longing, like Bert, had long since ceased to be her bedfellow. Nor disgust. She didn't care enough to feel disgust. Irritation perhaps. And certainly resentment.

She swung her feet to the floor, her nightgown clinging to her in moist limp folds. God, it was hot! She flicked a switch and the rhythmic beat of the engine was thrown into a brief spasm before its throb resumed. The light, in sympathy, flickered and died once or twice before revealing in its yellow glare the glint of chrome and stainless. For a brief moment she was back in the city, in the safe suburban box that had been her home. She tried to recapture the night sounds of the city. The swift start and stop of the milkman's ute, the soft slap-slop of his footsteps, the crash of the milk crates, the clink of bottles. The throaty roar of the incoming jet, the meaningless yelp of a nearby dog, the steady whine of a car far away, but driven too fast.

With swift familiarity born of habit, Marg Patching lit the gas under the kettle, prepared pot and cup and sat to await the kettle's boiling. Nearly six months they'd been here. Six months and not even TV to pass the time. Her fingers left five little pits in the dust on the ledge. Red dust. Always red dust. The kettle boiled and she made her tea. Its steaming well-known fragrance helped put things into a more acceptable perspective. She could even think about the other night without it hurting quite so much. There'd been a crowd of them and they'd all had a few beers. Bert's laugh was louder than most and his jokes were hovering on the blue side. The plump blonde girl, convulsed by giggles, plonked down beside Marg.

"He's a bomb, that Bert, isn't he?" she managed between splutters.

"Depends how often you've heard it before." Marg's voice was flat.

"Go on," persisted Blonde-hair. "Where's y' sense of humour?"

The girl's perfume, a modern version of the tawdry French imitation she'd worn as a girl, sickened her.

"I'm getting another beer," she informed her persecutor.

"I bet a girl could have a bit of fun with him!" Blonde bosom heaved, bottom wriggled.

"That's a point I'll take up with you," said Marg.

The girl looked startled.

Marg pressed her advantage. She'd fix the little twit.

"I'm married to him," she said.

But no. Blonde-hair had the last word after all.

"Oh . . . I didn't . . . I mean . . . he looks so young!"

So it was on again. And here she was sweating out another night. But he'd be back. She ought to leave him. If she'd had the guts she would have done so long ago, but . . . it wasn't love that held her. Habit perhaps . . . or pride . . . or laziness.

She heard the car long before it swung off the main road to the track leading to the caravan park. The tea scalded her mouth as she hurried to finish it. By the time the car stopped with a scrunch of brakes beside the caravan, she was back in bed, tense.

His lumbering footsteps made the caravan lurch as he entered. He swayed slightly on the top step, yawned noisily and switched on the light. This time the engine rejected the load and came to a shuddering standstill.

"Bloody thing!" he muttered.

He stumbled along in the darkness and slumped on the bed. She could hear his heavy breathing as he bent and pulled off one shoe. It clattered to the floor. Then the other. She sensed his scrabbling for the shirt tail, heard it being pulled over his head. She caught a faint whiff of perfume, cloying as a soft gum-jube, and almost overpowered by the strong male armpit smell. Her jaw tightened. She couldn't resist a jibe.

"So you have come home, then?"

He stepped out of his pants and flung them on the end of the bed.

"Can't a bloke ever get out without y' start t' nag?"

"You're always out," plaintively, in spite of herself.

"I want t' live . . . not rot away!"

"You'll do worse than rot, the way you're going."

"Aw go and get . . ." He stopped and gave a short laugh. "Gawd, I'd take m' hat off to anyone that'd stir you up!"

She winced.

"You didn't think so once."

"That was before y' froze up."

"Can't you think of anything else? Ever?"

His bed creaked as he rolled over.

"Shut up will y'. I'm tired."

She sought and rejected a dozen retorts, but the almost immediate rattling snores told her she might as well give up. The unfairness of it all struck her like a blow and she turned her head into the pillow to bite it in her own frustration.

With the light, Marg accepted a return to dreary normality. The toneless *kar-kar* of the crows and the busy chatter of the cicadas were as familiar now as the flat brown land with its shimmering heat-waves. She flopped on aged thongs to the shower block. The water was warm already and faintly brown. As it splashed over her dappled body she studied herself appraisingly. She wasn't bad really. Breasts full, still firm. Stomach flat. But who cared. You'd had it at forty.

Across the strip of powdery orange dust, Bert had his head thrust in the shed housing the engine.

"You've got a hope if you think you can fix it," she called on her way back to the caravan.

"Yeah? Well, you have a go then!"

They picked at each other as a child at a scab.

"For God's sake get one of the blokes from the depot t' come and have a look at it."

He didn't answer, but was soon in for Weet-Bix and tea and a piece of brittle toast. Then he was off, down to the depot and on to the job. The day was hers. She looked distastefully at the beds, the sink, the dust. So many things to do. So much time to do them in. She picked up an ancient magazine . . . *Confessions*. Some people lived! The bed was hot but as tempting to slip into as conversation with an old friend. She wallowed in a dream world of youth and love and excitement.

The sound of a car approaching fast recalled Marg to reality. What was he back for now? But the slam of the car door was unfamiliar. She frowned and peered through the window. A Zephyr. Nobody she knew. As she reached out for the magazine and prepared to lose herself again, from behind the car there came, casually, with torso bare, a young man. A stranger. Wearing brief tartan shorts. Self assured, swaggering almost as his feet sank into the powdery dust, little pools of it squelching up between his toes. He leant in through the window of the car and brought out a packet of cigarettes and matches. With careful deliberation he lit a cigarette, glancing as he did at the caravan. Marg melted back. She slid off the bed and slipped her feet into the thongs, pushing back her hair in an automatic feminine fashion. From the window over the sink she could see him more clearly.

The perfection of his body made her gasp. She'd forgotten how slim a man's hips could be. The intricacy of his muscle structure fascinated her. She remembered studying a picture in one of those family medical books her mother had bought from a travelling salesman. It was a picture of a man, skinned, with every muscle fitting neat and smooth over and under the next like an elaborate piece of weaving.

She put the kettle on.

He was fossicking ineffectually in the engine shed as she left the caravan. He turned and grinned at her.

"Having a spot of trouble?" he said.

"Yes." The turn of that calf muscle, the stretched tendon of the ankle . . . she couldn't raise her eyes.

"I told Bert I'd see what I could do." He stared at her with a familiarity that vaguely disturbed her.

"So long as you can get it going by tonight," she said. "We've got gas for stove and frig."

"Uh-uh," he said, plunging into the gloom of the shed.

"What do you think's the trouble?" she asked, reluctant to lose communication.

He came out, wiping his hands on some old piece of rag.

"Your guess is as good as mine."

His eyes, restless, flickered over her. There was a youthful masculine arrogance about him which unexpectedly excited her.

She swallowed.

"Can you fix it?"

"Dunno," he said and gave her a slow half smile. "But I'd rather put in a day here than be down on the job."

She felt a prickling in the base of her spine.

"Don't you have to get back?"

He drew the back of his hand across his nose.

"Who cares?"

She couldn't meet the challenge of his eyes, but studied instead her fingernails.

"Would you . . ." and hesitated ". . . like a cup of tea?"

He considered this for a moment. Then shrugged his acceptance.

"Sure," he said. "Whatever's going."

She led the way into the caravan, very conscious of him close behind. She turned suddenly at the top of the steps so that he lurched into her.

"Watch it mate," he said, laughing.

"I'm sorry about the place," she replied. "It's very untidy."

He raised both eyebrows slowly.

"Like I said. Who cares?"

The kettle was boiling. She rinsed the cups, and mixed some powdered milk. The spoon clattered against the side of the bowl. The tea was hot and sweet and strong. They drank in silence.

"Another?" she asked.

He shook his head, pushed his cup away. Took out his cigarettes from the pocket of his shorts.

"Have one?" Thrusting the packet towards her.

She took one and leant forward for him to light it, guiding his hand with her trembling one.

"You've got the shakes," he said. "Been on it, have you?"

She inhaled the smoke, not answering.

He studied her under lazy lids.

"Like it up here?"

"I hate it," she said.

He blew a fine stream of smoke towards the ceiling, still watching her.

She searched desperately for the right approach.

"It wouldn't be so bad if . . ." she looked up at him, ". . . if there was something to do."

"Like what?" he asked.

"I'd have thought you knew all the answers."

"Not all." He paused. "Most."

"Well . . .?"

Even the cicadas held their chatter.

He reached for his cigarettes. Suddenly brisk.

"I'd better get that engine fixed."

"There's plenty of time." Her hand groped towards his. "Stay a while."

His fingers crinkled as though they'd spent too long in hot water.

"You've got all day," she whispered.

The insolent eyes stripped her from toe to head and back again.

"Turn it up, Ma." There was a slow shrivelling inside her. "What d' y' take me for?"

LYN DOWSON

Across the Creek

On her way home from school Cathy called in at the shop. Ida was busy. There were customers in all three fitting-rooms and Sandra, her assistant, was coping with two more at the showcase-counter.

Glancing out of the second fitting-room where she was trying to ease shapeless old Mrs Fairweather into a dress designed for a shape, Ida was surprised to see her daughter standing there in the middle of the carpet. Cathy seldom called in of an afternoon nowadays. On Saturday mornings she would come down and lend a hand if Ida asked her. Otherwise she kept away, busy about her own affairs, study-ing, or perhaps just idling and dreaming. Ida did not press her. Cathy had to have some time to herself. And for her own part she didn't want Cathy to become too involved with the shop. Cathy had brains. Ida hoped she would get a scholarship at the end of the year, either to the University in Brisbane, or to the Teachers' Training College.

Yet here was Cathy, in mid-afternoon, to see her mother. Standing awkwardly on one leg, angular hip jutting, looking around at the racks of bright-hued shifts and caftans with a perplexed air, like a traveller from another country trying to imagine what they were for.

No grace, thought Ida regretfully. And the school uniform, dark maroon tunic with white blouse, and that ghastly panama hat, didn't help. Still, she must have something, because she not only had Geoff Bain as a steady escort, but one or two other boys had shown unmistakeable interest. At which Ida marvelled but was pleased.

All the same, she is different from me, Ida thought thankfully, remembering herself at seventeen as a bosomy, bouncing girl already experienced with boys. Cathy's innocent, virginal air seemed to Ida both touching and alarming. She saw her daughter as belonging to a different breed from herself, better, finer, a small aristocracy of women, a natural *élite* whose lives ran straight and true and happy. Not wobbling all over the place as hers did.

She got Mrs Fairweather into the dress and left her to repent while she went out to speak to Cathy. "Not much time," she said rapidly. "Did you want something, sweetie, or is it just a social call?"

Cathy didn't seem at all sure of why she was there. Taller than Ida, she directed her doubting gaze at a point above Ida's mahogany-tinted hair. "I thought I'd just call in." Her mouth had a downward, unhappy curve.

"Well, of course, you know you can any time. But I can't stop to talk just now." Ida dropped her voice to a whisper. "Mrs Fairweather —a real old tartar—won't let Sandra look after her. But if you'd like to wait out the back—"

"It doesn't matter." Cathy raised her thin shoulders in a shrug, turning her palms outwards. It was the fashionable mannerism.

"Yes, well then—"

"All right, I won't keep you," Cathy said, very polite, as if to a stranger. She picked up the school bag she had set down at her feet and half-turned away, still looking around with an undecided air.

"Lovey, I must go," Ida said, hearing impatient noises from the fitting-rooms.

"Will you be coming straight home this afternoon?" Cathy asked, addressing a rack of summer suits marked, From $10.00.

"Yes, I guess so. Yes, why not?" Ida tried not to sound impatient.

"Or round by Bain's?" the girl asked, turning her head now and looking directly into her mother's eyes, the pupils of her own eyes dilating until the grey irises almost vanished.

"Bain's?" repeated Ida. "I don't know. Maybe." There were more noises from the fitting-rooms. "Wait a bit, Cath." She scurried away. When she looked out again Cathy was gone.

Now what was that about? She felt uneasy. Why shouldn't she go home via the Bains' house. She often did. All it meant was getting off the bus one stop earlier, a short walk up the road to Etta's house, then the pleasant walk down through the orchard and across the creek to home. She did it whenever she needed to see Etta for any reason or sometimes for no reason other than that she wanted to see Etta, who was not only the silent partner in the shop but also her best friend and the person to whom she owed a great deal. All of which Cathy knew very well and had never questioned before. Then why call in now to ask that?

She can't, thought Ida, whisking to and fro with piles of garments, she can't have heard a whisper about Vic and me. No, of course she couldn't. There was little enough to whisper about. A couple of times over at the beach, once here at the shop when she had been working back and Vic had dropped in. And only that one other time down by the creek and who could have seen them there? Etta and Geoff were

both out that afternoon and Cathy was staying over at Hartleys' for
a few days. No one else went down there. All the same, that sort of
thing was risky and she didn't care for it, besides the discomfort, the
prickling grass and those damn disrespectful ants. Yet it couldn't be
that—that was a couple of weeks ago.

She was not ordinarily a worrier. Easygoing, pleasure-loving, she
preferred to let things take their course. Whatever was going to
happen would happen. In this way she had allowed her marriage to
slip through her fingers. It still surprised her that it had ended as it
had. She and Des had scarcely had a serious disagreement in their ten
years together. They had drifted amiably along side by side, until
one day Des had packed his bags, driven off south, and written to
her that he wasn't coming back. She had not heard from him since.
She had supported herself and Cathy on her wage as a shop assistant
until Etta bought the shop, gave her the job of managing it, and
two years later made her a partner. After all, she was better off without Des. There were plenty of men to be had, and she liked her free-
dom now that Etta had solved the financial side for her. Why worry?

This afternoon, however, worry was not so easily banished. That
look of Cathy's disturbed her. One thing was certain, she hadn't
come in just to ask which way Ida was going home. I should have
made her wait, thought Ida, reproaching herself. If anyone has said
anything to her about me, what a nasty shock it would be for an innocent kid like her. She was always such a good kid, even when she was
little. Put her on the floor with her dolls and there she would play
for hours. Or she would talk to imaginary playmates. Such a sweet,
quiet little kid.

I'll have to straighten up, thought Ida, not let myself get into these
things without thinking. It isn't as if I care two hoots about Vic really.
If I had been serious about him I'd have avoided him like the plague
rather than get involved. I wouldn't hurt Etta that way. But there I
go, just because it didn't matter very much. Me all over.

When the rush ended she rang the house. Cathy had had time to
get home.

"Yes?" the girl's voice said eagerly. "Oh, it's you, Mother." Her
voice fell away. She had said "Mother" as she did when she was
being formal or putting on dog in front of her friends. Ida felt it.

"Anything wrong, Cath?"

"No."

"If you need a bit of extra cash there's some in the old vase." Ida
infused a jolly note into her voice.

"I've still got some of my allowance, thanks." Cathy was polite
again.

Ida felt aggrieved. Other boys and girls were always running through their allowances. Why couldn't Cathy be just like the rest?

"Sure?"

"Yes."

"Oh, well." If she wasn't going to say what was up then she wasn't. If it was serious it would come out sooner or later. "See you later then."

"Yes," the girl said. Then abruptly, "I won't be seeing Geoff any more."

"What?" Ida fumbled with the receiver. "What?"

"You heard."

"Don't speak like that. It doesn't sound like you. What do you mean, you won't be seeing Geoff any more."

"I just won't."

"You mean you've had a tiff?"

"No. It's all off, that's all. Geoff doesn't want to take me out any more."

Is that all, thought Ida, relieved. That young dope has seen someone else he fancies. It had to happen sooner or later. They were too young to be serious. And she had never fancied Geoff all that much, though she couldn't very well say so. No go in him, no red blood.

"Don't you worry about him, love. He's not the only pebble on the beach."

Cathy said nothing to this. After a few moments Ida said, "We'll talk about it when I get home."

"Yes," the girl said in a dry tone, and the receiver clicked.

That dry monosyllable shook Ida, she did not know why. She put the telephone down and stood looking at it, dismal thoughts flitting through her mind. Pregnancy, abortion, unmarried mother. But no, Cath wasn't like that. Who isn't, the realist in her derided? Oh Lord, if it could just be a kid's falling out! God, you let this be all right and I'll behave myself, I promise.

She came to a quick decision. Sandra could manage till closing time. She would leave now and call in on Etta. At least she would know how she stood there. Etta couldn't hide anything. One look at Etta and she would know if there was anything seriously amiss.

The Bains' house stood on a rise on the outskirts of the town, in an area where building development was making inroads into farming land. Fields of young beans still greened the slopes, and on the steeper hillsides beyond were banana plantations and the geometric shapes of pineapple farms. A tractor hummed not far away. And the air, on this late summer afternoon, smelt of warm earth and grass and an occasional whiff of fertilizer.

Etta was sitting on the patio of her handsome white brick house, wistfully inhaling these fragrances. Born and bred to farm life, she had married a man of no particular bent—he was working in an office when she met him—and had taken him back to the land with her. They had had a pineapple farm a long way out of town for some years, and Etta had worked outside with Vic to make it pay, planting, chipping, picking, packing. They had paid their debts and begun to make money when Etta's father died and left her, his only child, a considerable fortune. Vic had persuaded her to sell the farm and live in town where, he said, she would have a comfortable life and a bit of fun and it would be easier for Geoff to live at home when he was older. Now Etta filled in her time with C.W.A. meetings and ladies' auxiliaries, and with sitting on the patio sighing for the old hard life. The truth was, Ida well knew, it was Vic who had wanted the comfort and the fun.

"Ide!" Etta cried joyfully. "I'm that glad to see you. I've been sitting here for an hour hoping someone'd turn up. Let's have a cup of tea."

Her pleasure in seeing her friend was transparently real. If there was anything wrong Etta did not know of it. Ida's legs were actually trembling. It was exquisite relief to sink into a chair and see Etta's broad, kind, open face as welcoming as ever.

"I need a cool drink, Et, with a dash of something in it." God, she thought, I'll never fool around with Vic again! He can jump in a lake.

She felt that she loved Etta, really loved her. Et was not a bitch like herself, nor was she one of that fortunate *élite* Cathy was to belong to. Et, in spite of all her money and her nice house, was a born victim; and the nicest thing of all about her at this moment was that she didn't know she was a victim.

"What's all this about Geoff not seeing any more of Cathy, Et?" Ida asked when Etta brought the drinks in long glasses, ice cubes pleasantly clinking. Relief had exhilarated her. She could afford to be bold. From where she sat she could look down the long slope where Vic cultivated a citrus orchard as a hobby, to the belt of timber by the creek. The citrus-trees, already well established when Vic and Etta bought these few acres and now fully grown, were planted in contoured rows across the slope. From the patio Ida's gaze could skim the tops of these trees and not much more. It was impossible from here to see anyone down by the creek even before they entered the timber. Even in the orchard it would be possible to see anyone only while they were still near the house. So much for that. She had been making something out of nothing.

Etta's face, deeply lined from too many seasons spent out of doors, had clouded. "I don't know, Ide," she was saying earnestly. I thought you might know. I don't know what's got into Geoff lately, that's a fact." She put her big, square hands on her knees and sat leaning forward in a masculine attitude, looking at her friend. "He isn't himself at all. Now he reckons he's leaving the bank and going south and just when he seemed to have settled in there. You never know where you are with young folk these days. They're all that restless."

"It's a difficult world," Ida said sagely.

"You're right there, Ide. I'm sorry about Cath. I'm sure Geoff thinks the world of her really." Etta was truly sorry. It had all been so nice. She liked everything to be nice. "I hope she doesn't take it to heart."

"At her age?" Ida's smile gently derided. "There's others that'll be glad Geoff's out of the running."

"I'm sure," Etta said. "Geoff's the loser."

"Probably all for the best," Ida murmured, finishing her drink. "Where's Vic?"

"Down in the orchard somewhere. He spends half his time there and the other half at the Lions or the Bowling Club." Etta sighed, then looked guilty. "Of course he has to have something to do. Men need an occupation. I've got the house."

"It's enough," said Ida, who hated housework and did as little of it as need be.

"I guess so." Etta's expression doubted. "Only we used to see a lot more of each other when we were on the farm. We were always together then. I remember—"

"I must go, Et." Ida put her glass down and rose. "I wanted to get home early."

"Have another drink."

"No thanks, Et. I do have to be getting along. I'll go down through the orchard. You'll have to get Vic to put a proper footbridge across the creek. One of these days I'll fall off that damned log."

"You tell him about it yourself, Ide. And if you see him down there now, send him up. We're having early tea because we've got to go over to Whitlows' afterwards."

"I'll tell him."

Ida felt gay, wending her way down through the dark green and gold of the citrus orchard. She could have skipped as she used to do when very young, going on an errand for her mother.

She reached the tall timber by the creek without seeing Vic and was startled when he stepped out behind her and seized her.

"Guess who?" Standing behind her he put his hands over her breasts, pulling her close against him, and kissed the plump curve of her shoulder.

"Cut it out, Vic. Not here. I told you before I wouldn't come at that again. It's too risky." But already he was drawing her down into the long grass and already she was submitting, when something rustled in the bushes and she sprang away from him. "There, you see. There's someone around."

"It's just the Campbell's dog. No one comes here but us."

"What about Geoff?"

"Not these days. Since he got the car he won't go anywhere he can't drive." He reached out for her again. He was a small man, no taller than she was but tough and wiry with something explosive, violent in him that made her a little afraid of him. He had very dark eyes and black hair and his skin, burnt to a dark brown, gave him a foreign look. "Come back here."

"Be your age, Vic. What about Etta? What if she came looking for you?"

"She won't. She never does."

"And what if she did?"

"Then let her. We'll say we're having a chat."

"Some chat, the way you go on." But Ida couldn't help smiling.

"All right then. Let her think what she likes. I don't pry into anything she does."

"Because you know damn well she doesn't do anything that needs prying into."

"More fool her then." He sat down with his back against a tree and grinned up at her. "Come on, love."

"No, I can't, Vic. Don't start being difficult. We've had our bit of fun together, but it's only been fun."

"And I feel like more fun." He made a sudden grab for her ankle. Ida stepped backwards, catching at a bramble to steady herself. The end of it scored a deep scratch down her forearm. Blood flowed, trickling into her hand. Drops fell on her bone linen dress. Ida swore vehemently, rummaging in her bag for a handkerchief to hold against the wound. "Damn you, Vic. Now look what you've done."

"You'll live," he said coolly. "It's only a scratch." He pulled a packet of cigarettes from his pocket and lit one. "What're you being so cagey for all of a sudden?"

"I'm not taking any more risks. We're not a couple of kids. And Etta's been a good friend to me."

"Isn't it a bit late to bring that up?" His eyes flashed and narrowed but he still grinned at her. "Etta wouldn't do a damn thing anyway.

Except cry. And bloody well forgive us. I don't care what she does. It doesn't have to be just a bit of fun between us. I've been thinking, why don't we try to make a go of it. I could ask Etta for a divorce. I've been salting a bit away these last few years. We'd be all right."

Ida stared at him, incredulous. "You're kidding."

"Like hell I am."

"You mean you'd just walk out on her like after the way she slaved for you on that farm?"

"She didn't slave for me. She slaved because she likes slaving. I'm bloody sick of hearing about that pineapple farm and how good life was then."

"You sod!" Ida said. But she said it amiably; because, after all, most men were sods. And the soddishness in this case—for once, Ida, for once—was in her favour. She was flattered but not tempted.

"What about Geoff?" she temporized. "What about Cathy?"

"Geoff's old enough to get along without me. And Cathy can come with us."

A flicker of expression in his eyes gave Ida a flash of insight, as sure as if he had spoken his thought aloud. He was after Cathy too. Oh, he was a sod all right!

"No thanks, Vic." She spoke easily and calmly, afraid of rousing that latent violence. "It wouldn't work out for us. We'd never hit it off. Too much alike in too many ways. I'd better get on home and do something about this arm. It's hurting like hell."

"Vi-ic," Etta's voice called down the slope.

He stubbed out his cigarette, got to his feet and took Ida by the shoulders. His hard fingers dug into her flesh. "You think it over." He planted a rough kiss on her mouth, and another. "I'll be seeing you." There was faint menace in his voice.

"Vi-ic."

Without another word he turned and went up through the darkening orchard. Ida turned and made her way across the creek. Hell, she thought, double hell! Now what? But she was suddenly too tired to think any further. She would have to stall him as best she could. No use trying to work it out now.

She trudged up the opposite slope, all the lightheartedness gone. No longer a girl tripping off on an errand, but a middle-aged woman running to flesh with a corn on her big toe and legs that ached from standing all day. She didn't give much thought now to Cathy's problem, such as it was. Anyone Cathy's age didn't have any real problems. Everyone got turned down sometime. Lucky if it was only once.

She went in by the kitchen door. The house was in darkness, the table was not laid for the evening meal, the vegetables were not done.

She set her basket down, went to Cathy's room, and switched on the light. "So there you are." Cathy was lying on her bed, still in her uniform, with her hands behind her head, looking at the ceiling. She seemed quite calm. At any rate she had not been crying. "Are you all right?" There was a hint of reproach in Ida's voice for the vegetables not done, the table not laid. She didn't ask much, when all was said and done. Wouldn't she like to lie on a bed herself now and do nothing?

"Yes thanks," Cathy said flatly. She had the binoculars beside her on the bed. Des's binoculars that he had left behind eight years ago and were seldom used now. She laid one hand on them and said deliberately, "You took a long time coming over from Bains'."

"You were watching through those?"

"Yes. I saw you leave the house."

Their positions seemed to have become reversed. It was Ida who was being investigated.

Ida wondered in sudden panic how much could be seen through the binoculars. "I stopped to speak to Vic Bain," she said reasonably.

"Like the time you stopped down by the creek a couple of weeks ago? One Thursday when Mrs Bain was out?"

"What of it?" A blush was rising to Ida's cheeks.

"Geoff saw you."

"Jesus!" Ida said. The blush spread right through her. She could feel its crimson glow in heart, liver, lungs, entrails. "Saw what?" she asked, bluffing.

The girl sat up and swung her long legs over the side of the bed. "Enough. I'll say it if I have to. But don't make me say it."

Jesus Christ, thought Ida, shuddering. Watched. Horrible. That rotten little prig must have crept up on them. There was a name for that sort of thing.

Her arm was hurting badly. Didn't people get tetanus from being scratched by bushes? She sat down on the end of the bed, nursing her arm, silent. She didn't know what to say. She was damned if she was going to say she was sorry. That would be worse than anything. Yet she was sorry. Sorry and humiliated and ashamed. She would have given anything for this not to have happened. If only she could stop being herself! "It's hard for you to understand," she said at last.

"I understand all right," the girl muttered. She shrugged that irritating shrug. "I understand a lot more than you think." She turned her head and looked at Ida. "I know about your boy friends. I've known for ages. I don't care about that."

Ida turned and looked into her daughter's eyes. Again she saw the black wells of the distended pupils as she had seen them that afternoon. She had the sensation of looking into the eyes of a stranger. And what she saw was certainly not innocence. "Well—" she stammered, "—what—"

"If only you hadn't picked on Geoff's father." The girl's voice rose in a childish wail. "You've mucked things up for me now."

"I'm sorry about that, Cath." Ida could manage to say that much. Cathy had turned her gaze away now and Ida sat staring at that tender, virginal profile with wonder. This was the daughter she knew; but the other into whose eyes she had looked a minute ago was also her daughter, very much so. Not better, not finer, but cooler, cleverer, more calculating, and much, much more ruthless. "I didn't know Geoff meant that much to you." Yet this was beside the point. It wasn't this Cath should have been grieving for, what Ida herself was grieving for.

"I wasn't in love with him, if that's what you mean," the girl said, with a hint of scorn. "But he was useful and I liked him all right and I could manage him so easily. Now I'll have to get someone else."

"You will." Ida said. Her arm throbbed, her corn throbbed, her heart throbbed. She didn't know whether she wanted to laugh or cry. Except that laughing came more easily.

Welcome! she thought. Welcome, my girl, to the sister-hood.

PATSY ADAM-SMITH

Hot Eyes

THE WATERFRONT at Hobart is open to the public and we all make use of it. The only part of the wharves that is barricaded off is a small part of Princes where the roll-on roll-off ferries come in and this fence is more to corral vehicles in the marshalling yards than to keep us Tasmanians off the wharf. If they hoped to keep people out they would shut the gates or at least put a patrol-man there. As it is we just walk through the gates to that pier. The docks are just so much a part of our life down here that when I went to Sydney once for a holiday I was surprised to find it was like an inland city, not at all like a seaport; life there just did not revolve round the waterfront. And Melbourne! It must have turned its back on the sea a century ago.

We aren't like that at all. Everybody at some time goes down to the wharves here, some people go often, and until my brother Bruce got to be fourteen or fifteen he used to fish down off the piers every Sunday and then come home on the tram with half a dozen fish strung on a string over his shoulder. Now that buses have replaced the trams, those kids and men with fishing-gear are made to use the back seats. Every sunny day girls from the jam factory eat their lunch seated on the stacks of timber near Constitution Dock where the old barges come in and typists go down to look at the passenger ships when they berth and I don't know when the girls who get their names in the society page on Wednesdays go down but they do because the captions under the pictures say, "Miss So-and-so chatting with Lieutenant Such-and-such at a cocktail party on board this or that ship."

My father who isn't interested in anything much drives down during the apple season and tells us over tea about the loading, what ships have got their quota and which are held up because of shortage of pallets or some other things. There are news items in the *Mercury* nearly every day about ships and seamen, and writers and artists use the water and the men on it as their most constant theme; even little old maiden ladies are stirred by this salty climate and us kids doing our final year at High School cut out a misprint of one of their articles about the Hobart waterfront which had been meant to read, "The buildings are still there on Salamanca Place where the whalers and seamen of a century ago rampaged ashore and had a naughty time. . . ." but the paper had left out the word *time* and we left this stuck up on the locker-room wall until the Head found out about it.

Even women like my mother who is forty-four walk around the wharves, but they usually take an excuse like a camera or go in an amateur painting-class and this is how my mother came to be accosted on the Hobart waterfront—well, she called it being accosted but I was with her because it was a Saturday morning and nobody asked me what I thought when the man leaning over the rail of the little ship said, "How about it?" She had just got to the last letter L on the ship's name, painted in white on its green stern, *Speedwell*, and needed only to etch in the lines of her timbers and touch up the mast with chinese white. She had used a pen to scratch in the horse boxes on deck and the crates of groceries with pumpkins and onions in string bags and all the funny bits and pieces those traders take to the islands off the Tasmanian coast.

When that man spoke she left in such a hurry I had to gather up her easel and the hot-water bag in which she carries water to mix her paints and her folding stool and while I was bending down folding this into its stupid plastic cover I looked sideways and up to the man and he was looking down at me and as I watched he put his hand to his mouth and I kept looking at him and he drew his hand slowly away and down a little. He didn't say anything to me but kept looking and I looked all the time at him and then the water-bag slipped and I grabbed it and hurried up to the car and Mum and when I heard that man dying and when he was by himself just before he died and he said he was alone I wished I had gone back to him for a little while when everyone else was asleep that night.

"He had hot eyes," Mum said. She means sexy eyes but she wouldn't say anything like that in front of Bruce and me and we sometimes wonder how she equates this attitude with us studying the reproductive organs in biology. Yet she said "hot eyes" and pasted her *I am disgusted* look over her face to camouflage what those hot eyes had done to her. Does she think she helps us or presents a more memorable picture of herself by appearing to be dead on her feet? And pretending to have done nothing all her life, "nothing of which

I'd be ashamed to tell the world" as she says every time she thinks she's caught us up to something as she calls it and leaves us to wonder what we could have got up to if we'd known and sometimes we get some pretty snazzy ideas this way.

She's just so frightened. I don't know what she's frightened of. Bruce who's at University now says it's because by the time they're able to marry and have kids in our society they are so old they have projected an outside covering, a sort of public image of themselves and they dare not—not even to help their kids—let this covering be pierced by admitting they've gone through all the things we are worried about or even that they still have feelings and even still worry about certain things. This is what Bruce says anyway.

If that's right I don't know why I felt angry with my mother when she gave me her "Let's be women together" talk and she quoted Shakespeare about being true unto thine own self, because she isn't and I can't see how I can be even though I try and I can't ask her about this not because she *couldn't* understand but because she *won't*.

When I cried for that man whose name I didn't know until the day he died I couldn't go to her and I wanted to and I wanted to know why am I crying like this and how does this happen between people and do other girls sometimes feel like this when they've never even spoken to the man or am I queer or am I bad, and how can I stop feeling this awful sadness and mostly I wanted to say I want to put my arms around him and put the side of my face on the side of his face. But I couldn't say anything of course and I stayed in the house all day listening. I heard him by accident first; Bruce had been fooling around with the radio the night before and when I got out of bed and went into the living-room and switched it on to find out the time it crackled and spat and gave out morse signals. I turned the dial along a bit and that's when I heard a voice. I didn't know at first it was his voice; it didn't sound like his voice when I couldn't see his face but he said the name of his ship three times. *"Speedwell Speedwell Speedwell."* Then, *Speedwell* to Melbourne Radio", and I knew it was him.

My notebook and pencil were still on top of the radio where I leave them to practise my shorthand while the news is being read and I began to write and I knew that he was going to die. "I am shipping water, ship is down by the head, fo'c'sle full of water," he said, and the radio crackled, "Are you receiving Melbourne? Over." The static sparkled and he waited for a reply. Then he said, "Melbourne doesn't seem to be there. Any small ships listening in?" Immediately a voice answered, *"Stormalong* to *Speedwell, Stormalong* to *Speedwell,* what's the trouble Johnnie?" Johnnie. His voice came back, "I don't know for sure Mick, I'm shipping water fast. The fo'c'sle was full before we knew about it. I reckon she's spewed her caulking somewhere along the starboard side of the bow." "She's old enough to do that and she's so old she could be nail-sick too," the other man said. "Might have sprung a strake near her stem."

They both were so calm and so matter of fact that when my father shouted out he sounded like an excited lunatic. "Practising shorthand, eh? That's short wave you're on; that's no good to you." He turned a switch and music came on. "I'll kill you," I said, but evidently the sound didn't come out because he laughed and said, "Your lips moved and no sound came out. Engrossed in your work, eh?"

I turned the knobs but all I got was music, then I got static but I couldn't find the voices of the men on the ships. I ran into Bruce's room. "Bruce quick get up and fix the wireless." He's always good to me but when he turned the set to the place he thought it must have been earlier we could only hear static.

I translated my shorthand. "Sounds as though they're goners," he said. He knelt down in front of the set and buttoned his pyjama coat up with one hand and moved the knob a little with the other. I wanted to turn it but he said no. "He'll come on again, that bloke, the man who's in trouble. He'll be busy, he'll be the only man on the ship with experience. Those little tubs carry only one qua' fied seaman —he's captain, engineer, radio operator, navigator, eve: ything."

"Is he alone, then?"

"No, he's probably got three or four labourers to wo.k cargo and take a trick on the wheel but no more than that. He'll come back on the air when he's free."

The voice came through again. "*Speedwell Speedwell Speedwell. Speedwell* to Melbourne Radio. Are you receiving, Melbourne?" And back came the reply, "Melbourne Radio to Speedwell. Come in *Speedwell.*" "*Speedwell* to Melbourne Radio. I'm shipping water and cannot control the vessel. I request a ship to stand by." Quickly Melbourne Radio called, "Stand by please all small ships, stand by all small ships. Go ahead, *Speedwell.*" "My position is due north of Cape Grim. One hundred miles due north Cape Grim." Static crushed his next words. Melbourne Radio called again, "Melbourne Radio to *Speedwell*, Melbourne Radio to *Speedwell*. Repeat your course and weather please. *Speedwell* course and weather please *Speedwell.*"

"There's a sou'-west gale driving big seas in between Tasmania and King Island. Wind force 8. Wind force 8. I'm trying to head her nor'-nor'-east," his voice came.

On the map of Australia on the back of my shorthand exercise book Bruce put a cross where he thought the ship to be. "But if he's heading nor'-nor'-east he's heading to open sea," I cried. "Why doesn't he head for the land?" Bruce told me, "He said the damage was in the bow; well, he's trying to protect his bow by running stern before the gale. If he turned her into the storm to head for land she'd split apart."

Melbourne Radio spoke: "Melbourne Radio to all small ships in the vicinity. Stand by all small ships and report your position, speed and course."

One by one they came in, all the rag-tag and bob-tail we've seen wallowing up the river over the years with their scruffy scabby unshaven crews and ludicrous cargo piled high on their decks. But they were all far away from *Speedwell*. The gale was such they were all sheltering or running for shelter. But they all said what can we do for Johnnie and by the time Melbourne Radio had worked out which two ships were nearest Johnnie these two ships had already worked this out and replied, "O.K. Melbourne. We're already under way." In a little while *Tassie Too* called Melbourne Radio. "We're beating up into the strait into a heel of a sea. Visibility is down to a few yards. We're giving her all we've got but against this sea it's not much over six knots."

'That *Tassie Too*'s got a powerful motor," Bruce said. He knows a lot about ships. "They'll be giving her all she's got all right. *Whoom, whoom, whoom*, I can just about hear her." *Whoom, whoom, whoom*, so could I. Pounding. Like inside me. Johnnie. Mum was up now and worrying about breakfast. It was Saturday and she had to get out by 10 a.m. with the painting-class. We told her about the *Speedwell*. "Oh yes," she said, "I painted her. She's sinking? Well, fancy that." "Well, she's seen her best days anyway," Dad said. "She couldn't have lasted much longer." He was hurrying too. He wanted to go to golf but he had to take Mum to meet the painting-class or he couldn't have the car. "Beats me how they ever get anyone to crew those old tubs." And he ran off to help with the breakfast when Mum called him. "Coming!" he boomed. "At the double. Hup two three four, Hup two three four." And he was hearty all through breakfast.

It was now an hour and a half since Johnnie first called for help. I am very superstitious. Bruce says it's religion but Mum says I'm superstitious. Now I said to God, "If I go away for a full hour and don't listen to the radio he won't sink." I wasn't asking Him, I was telling Him. And as soon as I promised I was furious. I didn't want to leave the radio. But I had to go or I might break the agreement. "How long can he last?" I asked Bruce. "Probably not long in that sea. You noticed nobody else was out in it. All sheltering. Must be some blow." I said, "Why is he out in it?" Mum said, "Him? I wouldn't put anything past him." She turned to Dad, "This is the man I was telling you about. I nearly had him arrested."

"Shut up!" It was me. I yelled at her.

Dad blew up. "Don't you let me hear you speak to your mother like that," he shouted, and stood over me.

"We're off again," Bruce said. Sometimes he can bring Dad almost down to earth. Dad thinks if he and Bruce exchange a knowing smile that will prove they are mates. Bruce grinned at him now and he grinned back and winked at Bruce. I knew if I looked at Bruce he would glower at me to tell me to shut my face in future. I can do that easily with my father. He's been a joke to me ever since I got top marks for an essay on "My Father". I had searched the dictionary for something to impress my teacher and got "Bluff hearty character". My English teacher, who knew my father, said, "Anyone after reading this essay could recognize this man." And this is really what he does look like to most people because he wears it permanently like a skin graft, but I think of him as being like the piece of "mysterious monster" they found washed up from the sea on the West Coast last year, all puffed out or pitted or sluffed so that no matter how you poked at it you couldn't get at the core, the solid bit you presumed most living things built on. Shovels and saws and picks and mattocks were used on the monster but still they didn't get far; they were burrowing in and getting exhausted as they wallowed and slipped and were side-tracked by blubber that was tough and wet and massed together again as fast as it was hacked into. And all the while they were doing this I thought of my father and I thought if they get a big hook, a great big steel hook like you see on a mobile crane and make it fast deep down in a gash in this lard and then pull a whole strip would flense away and I'd see my father and I stopped thinking then because it wasn't fair and he was pathetic and cringing and shamed about the things we saw, and what was so awful was that they weren't awful things at all and I just felt sad for him having felt shame all this time about such shabby little things.

"Don't you worry about me," Mum said. She put her hand on Dad's arm and his eyes broke off their togetherness with Bruce's and slid into Mum's where they'd be safe for a while. "You're a wonderful mother Alice, so patient and forgiving." She lowered her eyes without letting go of his and replied, "That's what mothers are for, George. To take the bitter with the sweet." He patted her hand a few times and nodded his head a few times and gave a few sad smiles which satisfied her and then went back to his toast, which he dipped in his tea. It was nearly half-past nine. Three-quarters of an hour had gone; there was fifteen minutes left. "I'll do the dishes." I started to clear the table; Mum handed her plate across and didn't let go of it until I had to look at her eyes and she had her look ready, patient long-suffering, expecting nothing for all my heartache and aren't you ashamed for causing me this pain?

When they'd gone, she to her Art class, Dad to golf, the hour was almost up. I got out the sketch Mum had done of *Speedwell*—all her paintings were stored in the sideboard—and stood it up on the mantelpiece. I'd never looked at it before and now I was surprised to note that you could *see* the place where he had been standing at the rail, actually *see* that that space had been taken when the painting was done. But why hadn't she painted whatever had filled that space? The rest of the sketch wasn't bad, the horse boxes on the forward deck looming up over the bulwarks, drums, crates, piles of rope and ship's gear in vague suggestive scratches, the single mast, the wheel-house as small as a suburban bathroom and behind this the lifeboat lashed down upside down on the after deck.

"Bruce, why can't they get away in the lifeboat?" He was hammering new stops into his rugby boots and didn't hear me at first. "Bruce!" I couldn't wait now, the hour was nearly up. I switched the radio on. Bruce came in. "Why don't they use the lifeboat?" "I reckon he'll try to save the ship, only use the lifeboat as a last emergency."

We couldn't pick him up on the radio. I went right along the dial. Bruce had brought his shoe-last in and was hammering again. "You won't find small ships down there. You'll only pick them up on the six-megacycle band." He pointed with his hammer. "Do many people switch in to this?" He thought many did. "Wives of fishermen, friends, owners and agents of traders under three hundred tons. Twice a day Melbourne and Hobart Radio have what they call 'Small Ships' Schedule' for fishermen and traders under three hundred tons. Ships are supposed to report only their position and weather and other official information but most men manage to slip in news to the listeners at home such as time of their return and such like. Scores of people listen regularly. News will have got round about this ship in trouble and hundreds will be tuned in now."

"*Speedwell* to Melbourne Radio. *Speedwell* to Melbourne Radio. Here is the information you asked for." Bruce was hammering again. "Shut up." Johnnie gave his position in degrees. "Melbourne Radio to *Speedwell*, what's the situation like now?" "*Speedwell* to Melbourne Radio. Fo'c'sle completely flooded. The collision bulkhead is holed and I've plugged it with blankets. Forward bilge pump blocked, aft bilge can't pick up because of angle of ship. I still think I'll be able to save her." But the operator in Melbourne said he must sound the automatic alarm. Bruce told me about this. It is fitted in many of the larger ships that do not have radio operators on twenty-four hour duty. The alarm can be actuated automatically by a special radio signal in case of emergency and bring the operator to the alert. Now the big ships would be racing to the rescue too.

"Bruce, does this mean they will save him?" He said it all depended whether any ships were nearer him than the two fishing-boats. He took my notebook and pencil and made some calculations. "*Stormalong* and *Tassie Too* would take five hours at six knots to reach him. They've been under way for nearly two hours. Three hours to go." Melbourne Radio came on: "There's no one in the Straits, *Speedwell*. A liner approaching the Heads and a tanker off Port Adelaide are changing course but both report heavy seas and gale force winds and are a good four hours away." "Don't worry too much," Johnnie said, "I think I'll be able to save her."

After a while he came back. "I've got her nicely around running with the gale, making about three knots nor'-nor'-east. She's sweet." His voice sounded gay coming clear out into the living-room. "She's sweet." Bruce hammered again and I screamed at him. "Hell, you can get bitchy," he told me. "And I thought you were going to hockey?" "Well I'm not and shut up and get out." "There's someting about you when you snarl that quite charms me." Since he started at University he makes crummy remarks like that. Anyway it was time for him to go to rugby and he went and I knelt down in front of the radio so I could see it more clearly.

In a little while Johnnie was not so sure. "Conditions deteriorating, seas rising, wind strengthening." It was difficult there in the living-room, kneeling on the carpet, to really feel this. I shut my eyes. I imagined big waves and a wind that screamed and a little ship alone in a wide sea but it was all like a play and when I opened my eyes all I saw were his eyes looking down at me and his hand to his mouth.

The weather gave him hope again. "I reckon we'll see Hobart yet," he laughed. It was a real happy laugh. I closed my eyes. I'd listen to Small Ships' Schedule and be down on the wharf when he came in. I'd go over to the rail. . . . I must have made-believe for a long time, long enough for him to forget the laugh. "I don't think we'll be able to make it now. I've got the men standing by in life-jackets. She's well down by the head even though I've had the deck cargo shifted aft." Melbourne Radio asked him what crew he had on board. He gave three names, "Paul Glover, eighteen, truck-driver making his second trip with us; Lester Harris, sixteen, from MacPherson Reform Farm, first trip; Olaf Gunnerson, seventy-one, donkeyman, been with me three years. You know my name, aged twenty-seven, master mariner for four years, been at sea twelve years." Melbourne then asked about cargo. "I think I see what you're getting at," Johnnie said. "But it's no go. It's dense in the hold. Green timber. It wouldn't keep us afloat. On deck I've got three horses in boxes, fifty drums of petrol and miscellaneous goods." These last, with the help of two boys and an old man he had moved back aft. "We're well down by the head. I can hardly keep her up into it now."

In a while he said, "Our position is very bad. I'm going to fire a rocket. It may guide rescue craft to us." Soon he returned, "*Speedwell* to Small Ships. First rocket gone. Did you see anything of it?" But the little ships were still too far away to sight it. Next, "Bulwarks awash. We won't last long now." Johnnie Johnnie Johnnie Johnnie. *Tassie Too* asked if it was possible to launch the lifeboat in such a sea and with the ship down by the head. Johnnie replied, "We cannot free the dinghy."

I tried to visualize the painting on the mantelpiece heeled over, the lifeboat jammed behind the mast. "It might float off," *Tassie Too* said, and Johnnie said yes, they were depending on that. The ships were now less than an hour away. I had drawn longitudinal lines across the map on my book and marked the hour on each when the rescue ships would pass that spot. "Decks awash. Don't know how long we can last." A minute later. "Position deteriorated even more. Fifty drums washed over the side." On *Tassie Too* the man Ted said, "We're coming fast, Johnnie." Johnnie sent up another rocket. "Did you see anything of it, Ted?" But they couldn't see it; perhaps the spray and huge seas hid the glow from them, perhaps they weren't even near him? God God God. The tacks on the place where the carpet was joined were sticking up so I moved over on to them and the sharp tacks cut my knees. God! God! It was a long time before he spoke again. "I've ordered the crew over the side in their life-jackets."

He was alone. He was there by himself hanging on to the ship and still they couldn't see his rockets. Were the horses still there? Their boxes sliding across the deck, floating, then crashing into the bulwarks. Did the horses scream? And the rigging scratched in with a pen and indian ink—is the sea strong enough to snap these, like bootlaces? And would their snapping let the mast fall down and if the bulwarks were smashed down would it be like his home his whole world deserting, disowning him? I could imagine him nowhere else but leaning over that rail, even in my make-believe when he leant over and lifted me up he didn't move away from that rail but held me while he stood there and looked at me. Oh God, where are those ships? Where are those bloody ships? You bastards, where are those ships?

"I'm still here, but I can't hold her now. The sea has her." He had kept a rocket for the very end. "I'm going to let it go now," he said. The ships didn't call him back. He had to call them. "Anyone see anything of it?" But the two men in the two fishing-vessels could not match his calmness. One said no, and that was all, as though his sob might penetrate the sea wrack and shroud the man he wept for if he said more; on *Tassie Too* the fisherman said, "Christ! Oh Christ, isn't there another rocket?" as though he were appealing to Jesus Christ and I think he was.

I was back in front of the set staring at the place where six mega-cycles must be printed but now I could see the ship and the sea and hear the wind that keened a wake to hasten his going, and he spoke. "It looks as if this is it . . . see you later . . . cheerio." And he didn't speak again. I banged the set, then turned the knob and when I got back to the place, Melbourne Radio was calling, "Melbourne Radio to *Speedwell*. Melbourne Radio to *Speedwell*" over and over and over again. "Come in *Speedwell*. Melbourne Radio to *Speedwell*. Melbourne Radio to *Speedwell*." My arms were right around the radio, "Come in Johnnie come in Johnnie come in Johnnie." My fingers were tangled in wires like rigging round limbs and I dragged them free and when the tip of my finger touched the broken earth-wire the volume of sound increased. I'll be able to hear him now. It was too faint before. I held my finger on the wire. I've fixed this damned bomb of a radio. Johnnie. Come in Johnnie. Come in. But I never heard his voice again.

All afternoon they searched for him, the two small ships that got there half an hour after he said "It looks as if this is it", and the liner and the tanker that came later and the four planes from the R.A.A.F. station, but all they found were a few bits of wreckage. "*Tassie Too* from R.A.A.F. *Tassie Too* from R.A.A.F. There's something about 200 yards ahead on your port bow," and "R.A.A.F. from *Tassie Too*. We're passing through wreckage: one 44-gallon drum, one door, one life-jacket. That is all. That is all."

And when my mother came in from her art class she said, "Not still listening to the drama of the sea!" and she went to the kitchen and put on the jug for a cup of tea and she hummed, "All the nice girls love a sailor" to annoy me. I thought I had never hated anyone so much.

When Bruce came home I told him, "He's gone." Bruce knew. It had come over the news. "They say the ship was so old she'd packed it in twice before and he'd got her home with her fo'c'sle full of water." My father came home and because he'd had a few drinks at the Golf Club he had to be wary of Mum so he turned the radio off and said loudly, "Don't you think you'd do better to go and lend your mother a hand young lady? She can't be expected to wait on you all your life you know." But I went to my room and took the water-colour off the mantelpiece with me although it was no use to me, nothing meant anything to me, not the notes I'd taken down as the men spoke, nothing. All my inside was scooped out, my head was busting, but my inside was gone and I couldn't even cry any more. Mum came in. "That man died," she said and I said "Yes."

I wondered if she thought of his hot eyes now but I couldn't look at her. I didn't need to. She felt nothing and he was under the water and his hand was floating down and away from his mouth. My mother was looking at the painting and she took it and stared at it and then she wet her thumb in her mouth and began to drag it over the painting and then wet it again, a lot, and dragged the spittle across on the ball of her thumb until the paint smudged and smeared right over the place where he had stood by the rail and then she went out and Bruce came in. "What did you do to Ma? I thought she was going to faint." I told him what she did to the picture. Bruce hesitated, then, "Poor old Mum. The poor old thing. And she went off to her Art class as though nothing had happened. That poor old thing."

I lay there and the room got dark and I could hear Dad blustering and Mum snapping at him and he cowering in return. How can he let her do this to him? How can she bear him when he does this? Then, why did she obliterate the space that should have been filled by the man? Surely she didn't think ... surely she wasn't frightened ... of herself? Of her thoughts? Of anything that might make her see Dad as she would never allow herself to see him; of anything that would make him suffer by comparison? Or did she wonder, who did he make a pass at with his hot hot eyes that are now filled with water? And I rolled over and the tears came again and filled my eyes too.

JUDY FORSYTH

For the Good of the People

"Blessed art Thou, our Lord, King of the Universe, who has brought forth the fruit of the vine."

Abie Katzen blessed the wine and the bread in a slurred sing-song and his wife and daughter sang out the customary "A-a-men".

The table was laid as usual for Friday night's dinner with a clean white cloth and two newly-lit candles in brass candlesticks. Set before Abie were a carafe of red wine and twin loaves of white bread, their plaited surface brittle and burnished with egg.

After the prayers Mrs Katzen served traditional fare; tonight it was lokshen soup, chopped herring, veal and carrots with syrup, followed by rich, sticky sweetmeats.

She had been cooking all day, preparing the Sabbath meals. To-morrow she would rest.

Abie had hurried home as usual after the twilight service, first tucking his tasselled prayer-shawl and black prayer-cap into their bag of velvet, embossed with a golden Star of David.

He brushed past the group of elderly men, standing, with ancient wisdom netted in their beards, near the altar, and emerged into the foyer of the synagogue. There young boys, dark-eyed colts, awkward in navy suits, larked it about, with prayer-caps set rakishly on their heads, their voices braying into manhood and echoing to the blue-and-white domed roof high above them.

In the tolerant dusk Abie walked quickly home; a small frail man, his step light to the seraphic descant of the choir boys still lilting in his mind.

As he passed through the front door of his house he touched the small oblong token nailed up high in the jamb, a miniature scroll containing portions from the Pentateuch. It was a defiant emblem of his race, a sign of his piety and a useful deterrent to those confident evangelists so rude with their Good News.

"Blessed be the Sabbath," he intoned, as he closed the door behind him, and the old and the young woman within, always half-awaiting his footsteps at this hour, responded with the same.

Jaffa, his daughter, a thin girl with sharp features, glanced up at her father's face as he came to the table. She had already declared her intention of attending her weekly meeting tonight and hoped to read from his expression the temper of his resistance. Abie ignored her and turned to his wife Rochke, who smiled at him with her mild blue eyes, as she always had since their marriage, and served him, with honour, her delicious food.

Whilst they ate Abie discussed with her aspects of his business affairs. These consisted in some rather undefined transactions with the larger hotels for Matzos, the unleavened bread used during Passover, and in blessings and proper witness for two Kosher butchers. There were other, vaguer activities of varying profit, for necessity had become, for Abie, the stepmother of his halting ingenuity. Since his emigration from Poland fifteen years ago Abie had hung on the fringe of the new colonial economy like a tassel on a tablecloth.

After the meal Rochke superintended the dish-washing by their native servant and Jaffa went to her bedroom. Soon after, she came out, dressed in the uniform of the Zionist Socialist League of Youth of which she was an ardent member. She wore a light blue shirt and tie, a navy skirt, stout brogue shoes and short brown socks.

Her solid brown leather lumber-jacket completed an ensemble suitable both to the climate of proletarian honesty and intellectual refinement.

In one hand she carried a scarf and in the other the "Movement" flag, furled.

She wore no make-up. They did not believe in it.

"I am going now, Papa," she said shortly.

Abie answered her. "Yes, you are going. Where are you going?"

"To our meeting."

He let her stand waiting for his formal consent, then sighed at last with the resignation of continued defeat.

"Oh yes. You will not be home late tonight?"

"No later than usual." She was tart. "You know we always go to Barney's afterwards."

"I know. Can't you bring them home here?" he begged crossly. "We have coffee too, and cakes."

"It's not the same, Papa," she repeated, while they sparred on the familiar routine.

"No, no. No, no. So you said. My house is not good enough for some of your friends."

She covered her head with the white scarf and tied it under her chin. "Well good night," she announced with rough finality.

Then she added gently, as she bent forward and kissed him quickly on the side of his cheek, "Don't wait up for me."

Like many cherished youngest children she vacillated in a staccato rhythm between indignation and guilt.

The front door slammed behind her and the draught flickered the candles—their flames glowed like two amber beads in the long mirror on the wall behind them, and beyond, in the darkening room, reflected the image of Abie, sitting alone, with his hat on, head of his deserted table. He stared unseeing at the slow-spreading blots of wine spilt on the white tablecloth before him, for his eyes were narrow gates to the ghetto within him.

The scarf around Jaffa's head had reminded him of the time when all three of his children were little, Chana, Riva and Jaffa, in Warsaw, playing in the snow with their small faces pink and pointed, framed in white fur-trimmed caps and their little bodies stocky in warm clothing, cuddly and charming. He remembered how, when they all returned from romping outdoors, he would rub their cold blue toes between his hands, teasing and tickling them, whilst the thin film of ice on their boots exploded into shallow craters and dribbled down into tiny pools of water on the floor and their socks lay faintly steaming beside them.

Chana and Riva—they had been gone now for five and three years. They had joined the "Movement" too as youngsters and had each, on turning twenty-one, emigrated to Israel to live and work there in a kibbutz. Chana was married now. She wrote seldom and Riva not much more often. There was no talk of sending him and Rochke the fare to go over there, even for a visit. Abie knew they were afraid to suggest it lest he should want to remain in Israel once he got there. In any event he would never ask them for the money—he was too proud to beg his rights.

If he went for a visit he would have to endure the misery of parting again, and, as for going to live there, he was shrewd enough to suspect that he himself did not want to be "next year in Israel". Yes, a man must have his ideals, but he does not necessarily want them realized. His little suburb of Johannesburg, Doornfontein, a shabby lower-middle-class area, populated mainly by Jews, was the nearest he would ever get to "home" in his fundamentally stateless existence, suspended between a glorious historic past and a messianic future. If not for the loss of his daughter he could have been contented enough, at peace with his philosophy.

His fretted thoughts turned again to Jaffa. What would she be doing now at their meeting?

First they would all stand in a circle around the flag and sing their anthem, then maybe their leader would deliver a lecture on the history of Israel and later they would sing Hebrew songs and dance the "hora" until they were limp and damp. Afterwards some would go on to the tearoom and others—others? Jaffa? It was whispered in the neighbourhood that couples had been found lying together on the ridge near by and—oh God—did she? would she? In her maturity he thought her complexion as richly delicate and her skin as scented as an oleander flower. No—not she!

Yet what about those books she kept on her shelf—*Sex and the Modern Woman*? And where did those conversations lead, of which he would catch snatches, when, hotly debating the individual's need for privacy and self-expression, she and her friends took complete possession of his lounge?

If he went in they would stop arguing and sometimes, with a rueful smile and a twinkle in his eye, he would ask them,

"Carry on, please, carry on; what are you always talking about, explain it to me."

"No, Papa," Jaffa would answer with ill-concealed scorn, impatient for him to be gone, "you wouldn't be interested."

And when he left again he would hear phrases of their arguments about Freud; their dogmatic assertions that no one has the right to make moral judgments, and the endless quarrels about something called "the Marxian dialectic".

He knew he was not an educated man, Abie, but he was not such a fool either. He had learnt a lot from his eldest daughters.

As he brooded the doorbell rang and Rochke hurried to change out of her slippers. She was expecting her sister Leah, with Max, her husband. Their daughter Sophie was newly engaged and she was also coming with her fiancé to receive the Katzens' congratulations. The fiancé was a handsome young doctor. They had met him a few times up at Max's comfortable home in Parktown.

Rochke opened the door to the quartet, which sang out its "Good Sabbaths". She embraced her sister, an older edition of herself, but smarter. Leah was compressed in black, resembling an overfull patent leather suitcase, its soft expensive surface unevenly bulging.

"Oi, Sophka, mine engela," Rochke exulted over her niece, "mazel-tov, congratulations," and taking the girl's face between both hands kissed her exuberantly.

Then she shook the fiancé shyly by the hand.

"Come inside, come inside," she urged them all. "Abie," she called out, "they have come. Max is here."

Abie could put it off no longer and rose from the table as the visitors began to clutter the dining-room.

"Good Shabbos," Abie greeted his brother and sister-in-law, "congratulations."

"Good Shabbos, Abie, thank you, thank you."

Max took off his jacket and carefully dressed the back of an upright chair with it. Then he sat down on the sofa, and pulling the chair close by, for his legs were stocky, put his feet up on the leather seat, careful that his green suede shoes did not touch the edges of his jacket. His corduroy sports shirt was rolled up at the elbows revealing thick black hairs which curled in impudent profusion up his forearms. They nestled also at his chest and pushed out over the open collar of his shirt.

Max waved a stubby hand at the fiancé.

"Make yourself at home, Cyril," he said, "Abie's your uncle now."

When Max smiled he showed four gold-capped teeth; these constituted for Abie the ultimate affront.

"Certainly, certainly," Abie assured Cyril shaking his hand, "and congratulations to you."

Then Abie embraced Sophie tenderly and for a moment tears filled his small eyes. What a lovely girl she was, dark-skinned and brown-eyed, with her heavy black hair hanging half-way down her back. She wore a soft blue nylon dress with a velvet sash and on her elegant feet were strapless high-heeled blue shoes. There was nothing of Max in her.

"Come and sit by me, my darling," he petted her, and drew her to an easy chair where she curled herself up, feline, along the arm of it, and put her hand around Abie's neck.

Her father always called Abie a pedlar, but since a child she had found her uncle consistently gentle and even gallant in an old-fashioned way.

"Well, how's business, Max?" asked Abie, speaking in Yiddish.

"Fine, fine. Can't complain," Max replied in English. "You can't beat plastics in the shoe industry. It's a pity the Kaffers don't eat matzos, Abie old boy."

Abie was silent a moment while he regarded his brother-in-law. Then he answered slowly.

"Just matzo-eaters we have plenty of amongst our own people. Since Joseph, good Jews you can't buy or sell."

"Don't talk to me about good Jews," Max snapped, "I'm as good a Jew as you are, even though I don't go to 'schul' every day. And a good South African too," he added, meaningfully.

"Of course, of course," agreed Abie.

There was a pause.

"How about a game of bridge, Abie?" Max suggested suddenly.

"Oi Vei, Maxie," Leah reproved, "not to quarrel so quick, specially tonight."

Rochke judged this a good time to make tea and the women went into the kitchen together.

Abie ignored Max. He turned to Cyril.

"Well, how goes it at the medical school? I hear you are doing some research work up there. Cutting up cats these days, isn't it?"

He generously attempted humour to give the young man an advantage.

"But they're all Kosher, Abie, don't you know?" Max broke in.

"I should know, Max," Abie retorted quickly with rare sarcasm, "I do the blessings for them, don't I?"

Cyril guffawed suddenly. He warmed to Abie, this little wraith of a man, always so subdued up at Max's, and began to describe the project.

Max turned on the radio loudly and picked up the Yiddish newspaper, which he scanned at arm's length until the women brought in the tea.

It had all been settled in the kitchen that Rochke would make the wedding-dress. Abie was to understand that she had offered. Abie looked at his wife with compassion. She had always been generous to her niece, but he knew that she was doing for Sophie what her own daughters had denied her.

In the kibbutz rumour had it that the girls would doff their khaki jeans and borrow a navy skirt and a ring for the wedding ceremony, which was performed by an itinerant rabbi. True or not, in any case his girls had never written details when they got married, nor had they asked for clothes.

The visitors left soon after tea. On the way home in the car Max vowed that, but for Rochke's sake, Leah would never drag him down there again.

"Can't do a damn thing in that house on or after the Sabbath," he declared. "God wants us to be happy, doesn't he?" Max was emancipated.

"Why, the man is so 'holier than thou', he's a pain in the neck. Of course Jaffa wasn't there, Sophie. I told you she wouldn't be."

"You should feel sorry for him, Maxie," said Leah.

"And why should I feel sorry for Abie? He's asked for it for years. Ramming religion down his kids' throats since they were born. No wonder they want to run off anywhere—let alone Israel."

Max drove contentedly home with his elbow out of the window and his family inside the car.

At the Katzens', Rochke went to bed and Abie sat down again at the table, thinking about Max. What had that oaf done to deserve such a daughter—such a son-in-law—such settled felicity? He visualized Jaffa in a blue nylon dress getting engaged to Cyril. No, instead she would be leaving soon, like Chana and Riva. A pogrom of anguish swept down upon him. Jaffa, his youngest, his angel, his pink-and-white furry-capped darling.

"Oh God, she is my last, you stayed the hand of Abraham upon Isaac, give me a sign to stay mine," Abie prayed, looking intently at the candles on the table; their lambent flames were elongated and almost immobile.

Suddenly they flickered sharply, in response, Abie knew at once, to God's whispered command, and he rose to receive their kindling message of faith within his breast. Where she had strayed Jaffa would be waiting for him. He must go at once and bring her home.

Behind him the curtains at the window billowed softly in the passing breeze.

It was near to eleven and the streets were all but deserted. It was cat and dog time.

He almost ran along the pavement past the small houses of his neighbours until he reached the tram-lines and then turned left to the delicatessen where, behind the lighted windows, the counters were piled high with spicy goods. He did some business with them in Matzos and usually he calculated how many Egg-Matzos and how many Plain they might take this year.

But tonight he saw nothing of that. He was heading straight for Barney's. She would be there, Jaffa; she was a good girl.

Outside the tearoom he paused a second and looked in at the windows. It was crowded inside with late-night customers from the cinema. The "friends" from the Youth Group were there with Jaffa amongst them. They sat at four tables drawn up together and their loud laughter dominated the room as they seriously enjoyed themselves.

Abie walked quickly inside and aproached his daughter. She was absorbed, chatting gaily with her friends and only saw him when he tapped her on the shoulder.

"Jaffa," he entreated, speaking softly in Yiddish, "come home."

She looked up at him and at once blushed deeply. Then her face turned wicked with rage and her chair scraped a wound in the floor as she pushed it back suddenly and stood up.

She began to shout at him at the top of her voice.

"My God! This is the bitter end! Now you've taken to following me—how will I ever get away from you? You should know, you better than anyone, you religious fanatic, that I am not in this for myself. I am doing it, like my sisters, for the good of our people!"

She stalked out alone, while the blot of her fury spread in concentric circles of diminishing strength through the silent tearoom and slowly effaced Abie Katzen beneath them.

For what shall it avail Man to contend with a jealous God?

CLEMENT SEMMLER

Penitence

HE LOVED the sandhills. There was to him at once a symmetry and a
poetry in the shifting dunes, their edges scalloped and furrowed by
winds scampering out of the mallee scrub, the tall tufts of spinifex
forming a rampart at the end of each ridge. In the hot sun the sandhills shimmered white, but on the cold grey days of winter they
seemed to embody the bleakness in a sullen brown.

One Sunday morning a rainbow seemed to end right in the middle
of them and, though dressed for church, he had set off in its direction
with no clear idea of what he expected to find. He trudged through
the shifting mounds, his boots heavy with sand, but the rainbow's
end further and further off still tantalized him. Then when he came
to the edge of a stubble plain and saw that the mocking colours still
beckoned him in the scrub beyond, he was elated rather than disappointed because the sandhills had always been a barrier to further
discovery. Now, sheltered from the winds, overlooking the stubble
paddocks, here was a place of solitude and refuge where, in the milder
autumn days, he could visit when he chose and lie drawing figures
in the sand, imagining he was at the very edge of Arabia.

For a while he sat and watched a stumpy-tailed lizard which, whenever he tossed a stick at it, opened its mouth—more, he thought, in
curiosity than fear. "I won't hurt you, you sleepy old bugger," he said:
Anyway, lizards ate snakes, Ferdie Strank had told him, and this
secret place belonged just as much to the lizard too. He drew triangles
in the sand and watched the tiny coruscating avalanches that followed.
He drew a square beneath a triangle and was thus suddenly reminded
it would be time for church. He jumped up and ran, his heart pounding, back through the dunes.

Touched by the early morning dew the galvanized-iron roof of the
house on the corner with its verandah-all-round glistened its welcome
and warning as it came into view. His father—blue, shiny, serge-
suited, tattered hymn-book in hand—stood at the gate irritably flick-

ing shut his pocket watch. His mother and sisters in their Sunday best were waiting on the verandah.

Dora and Vera screamed: "Where've you been, you naughty boy, we've been waiting for hours!"

"A man ought to take a stick at you." His father gave him an angry shove. But his mother interposed, "Paul, it's Communion today," and his father strode off down the road as the church-bell began to toll.

The girls chattered around Simon: "Naughty boy! Where *have* you been? Pastor Schulz will be *terribly* angry." His mother scolded him too and then quickly walked on to join her husband ahead. She seemed strangely preoccupied and not to have noticed his rumpled and sandy clothes.

Simon dropped behind. He hated Church. He hated the mournful tone of the bell; it reminded him of funerals and black veils and dead flowers. He hated the Sunday morning heat, the stifling atmosphere inside Church, the smell of boot polish, cheap scent, women's under-arms, and bad breath ill-concealed by peppermints. It all seemed to distil into one vast odour so that along with Pastor Schulz in the pulpit, the Holy Trinity scrolled above the altar, the hymns as sung, the blowflies high in the windows, it became church and religion in holy essence.

He was ashamed of the bandy legs of his father stumping ahead. Once he had said as much to his mother and she had rebuked him indignantly. His father was a hard-working man and the best black-smith in Willow Reach, she said. He was bandy because he had ridden horses when he was a boy on the farm and because all the years he had been a blacksmith he had had to bend over with the horses' legs tucked between his own legs so he could shoe their hooves. "Your father had a hard life. You should be proud of him, he fears God. And he started working when he was nine, poor Dad. He minded sheep for five shillings a week."

Simon kicked a stone. "Minded sheep for five shillings a week," he mimicked. On many nights when they sat around the smoking kerosene lamp on the battered and scratched long table, when he was trying to concentrate on his homework, he heard bits of the story. There was occasionally a bitter quarrel, usually about money, when his mother taunted his father about his family, his job, the farm they had once had before they "went through the hoop." (Simon could never work this out but concluded it must be like the rich man in Pastor Schulz's oft-declaimed story who had difficulty in going through the eye of a needle.)

Or when an aunt or uncle came for a visit—there were reminiscences and laughing and story-telling and the muscatel wine was brought in from the cellar. *"Liebe Gott!"*, his *Tante* Clara would mop the tears from her eyes; and she would again tell the story of their neighbour on the farm, the old bachelor Herman Mielich, who grew black grapes round his well and put them when ripe in a small tank, trampled on them with blücher boots, and tapped the juice into kerosene tins. Then, impatient to wait more than a week or so, he would drink it while it was still fermenting and his crazy screaming and cursing could be heard every Saturday night. One Sunday morning they had found him asleep in the pig-sty, and here *Tante* Clara and his mother would exchange knowing glances. Or they would talk of friends and relatives recently *tod* and of the mourning and the funerals and how many cars, sulkies and traps there were in the processions. But Simon looked forward to *Tante* Clara's visits because they were usually after a pig-killing and she brought leberwurst and long thin met-wursts and big hunks of blut-wurst speckled with rice, delicious when they were fried. . . .

The Church stood waiting. Small knots of people shuffled below the steps—the Heinrichs, the Kuchels, the Nagels, the Klugmanns, the Zimmermanns—awkward, gawky in their Sunday best of uncomfortable wing-collars and corsets. Children hung onto skirts, whimpered, scampered, giggled, called to each other. Be fruitful and multiply, the Lord said. Mothers hissed, slapped, pulled roughly—all the while taking their weekly pleasure of gossip and small talk.

"Goitre, Alma! Doctor came three times last week. God be thanked it isn't cancer. . . . Gertie Wundersitz, another at Christmas. Five in four years. *Doch!* And the house not built yet, only the barn already. And the mud. The Pastor was there last week already. . . . *Och ja* . . . today the girl, it is sad for them, adopted, so nice and big and strong and pretty. But those men on the swamps. . . . Shh Max! Your father will strap you when I get you home—quiet now!"

Apart, the menfolk talked of rain, crops, work—elaborately avoiding responsibility for their children's behaviour, fierce scowls daunting offspring who came too near.

"Bill, how is the business?"

"No good, Carl. A man oughter give it up, work for wages. Only the shoeing and tyring pays. Nothing in the township for a blacksmith."

"Well, next week I'll have the front wagon tyres for you. Spot cash. Hey Bruno, how are the crops at Nildottie?"

Bruno Wundersitz, picking his teeth with the end of a match, joined the group. Simon was fascinated by the tufts of hair growing out of his ears.

"No rain, only in the township. We're giving stock bore-water. Drinkin' it ourselves, too. And the wife expecting again. . . ." He screwed his mouth disgustedly. His father caught Simon's eye and scowled, motioning him away.

"Well," Simon heard Carl Zimmermann say, "better that way than this silly bitch of. . . ."

The rest was lost as he walked slowly over to his mother. Dora and Vera made faces at him. Bronchially the organ began to wheeze *The Church's One Foundation* and the groups straggled into a queue at the door. Simon at the top of the steps looked despairingly back at the sandhills in the distance and followed his parents and sisters down the aisle. The Church law was that males and females sat separately on either side, so Simon sat with his father next to the huge bulk of the stertorously breathing Bruno Wundersitz. Simon hated Mr Wundersitz—his piggy eyes, wide red face, fleshy bulbous lips, the hair growing from his ears and nose. And he stank from his mouth so that every time he hawked in his throat the evil smell came to Simon's nostrils.

"In the name of the Father, the Son and the Holy Ghost," intoned Pastor Schulz, black-gowned, short and fat, his bald head glinting in the light that came through the vestry windows. The congregation sang "Amen" and sat down.

Annie Klugmann, gawky and spindly, but always with a kind smile for Simon, coaxed rending chords from the aged organ on the platform, swaying forward and backward in simple ecstasy as the tortoise congregation sang swiftly to catch the organ hare.

> *We all believe in one true God,*
> *Father, Son and Holy Ghost,*
> *Present helper in our need*
> *Praised by all the heavenly host.*

Annie stretched and turned, her knees bobbing above the wind pedals. Pastor Schulz, stern with salvation, stood at the altar. The congregation rose. Simon was mesmerized by a streak of sunlight that danced on Pastor Schulz's bald head; perhaps it was the Pentecost and he would begin to talk in a strange tongue. But Pastor Schulz faced his flock.

"Beloved in the Lord! Let us draw near with a true heart and confess our sins unto God our Father beseeching him in the name of our Lord Jesus Christ to grant us forgiveness. . . ."

His voice quavered into song, re-echoing mournfully around the Church walls,

"Glory be to God in the Highest,"

and dutifully, untunefully, the congregation responded:

"And on earth peace and goodwill to all men."

Mr Wundersitz between gales of foul breath essayed, Simon noticed, a tenor accompaniment, reaching uncertainly for his notes and trailing into silence before the response had concluded.

The congregation thumped into the seats and after an indifferent beginning Annie persuaded from the unwilling organ the opening strains of *A Mighty Fortress is our God*. The congregation sang with lusty but hallowed zest; as well it might, for Martin Luther, whose enlarged portrait hung on the left-hand wall of the altar (a thorn-wreathed Christ decorated the opposite wall) had written the hymn, and at Sunday School (held on Saturday mornings) the deeds and virtues of Luther as the Father of the Church and the Scourge of the Priesthood were regularly extolled.

Simon, shifting uneasily in his seat, reflected unhappily on the time when Clarence Macnamara, who was a Catholic dog and attended the Convent School past which all Lutheran children were admonished to hasten with averted eyes, had taunted him by screaming, "Yah! Luther stinking swine! He had the pox!" Simon, feeling some retort was expected of him, had yelled in return "Old bugger Pope pokes the nuns!" Stones had been thrown, honour satisfied and the episode concluded. But at Saturday School, presided over by Pastor Schulz and Frau Pastor Schulz (moonfaced and with a behind like a working bullock), Simon had asked: "Please Pastor, Clarence Macnamara said last Tuesday that Martin Luther had the pox."

There had been a stifled shriek from Frau Pastor and a bass groan from the organ on which her paralysed hands involuntarily pressed. Pastor Schulz had rushed forward, his face redder than a rooster's comb, the veins standing from his bulging neck, his lips working soundlessly, dribble starting at the corners of his mouth. He had seized Simon by the collar, hissing in German:

"Junge! You have sinned by repeating this accursed blasphemy!" He had rained blows with his clenched fist on Simon's face, ears and shoulders. Simon, shocked at first into silence by the onslaught, had burst into tears and whimpered with fright and then pain as Pastor Schulz, still in ungovernable rage, cuffed and punched him. And threw him finally back into his seat so that his head banged on the pew and almost stunned him. The children, hushed and in dry-mouthed terror, had watched as Pastor Schulz tottered, gasping from his exertions.

"You will never, children"—he had stopped, gulping for his breath

—"you will never repeat the lies of the Catholic heathen! This stupid boy has made himself the tool of the Pope, the Antichrist."

Simon, choking his sobs, had looked fearfully through his fingers at Pastor Schulz.

"That way lies the burning fire of hell," shouted Pastor Schulz, "those fires where all Catholics will roast and scream in agony, spitted on red hot spikes, and be given not one drop of water."

The children had listened with awful visions of screaming Catholics roasting like so many legs of lamb, along with Clarence Macnamara and Simon (unless he was forgiven, which seemed at this point unlikely), and being tortured by devils with pitchforks. For hell was a favourite theme of Pastor Schulz and rarely a Saturday went by that he did not warm to his subject. Hellfire was especially reserved for those who bet on racehorses, adulterers and fornicators (Simon could only assume that one word meant men and the other women), and in the hottest centre of it, for Catholics and Freemasons and like members of Secret Christless Societies.

Pastor Schulz, his rage partially subsided and his breath returned, had continued:

"Martin Luther was chosen by God to lead the Reformation and to deliver us all from the bonds of the Pope and the Devil and to show us the way to Eternal Life. He was . . . he is next to Christ, he sits now at the right hand of God."

Simon even amid his tears and pain, had wondered how the Holy Ghost would feel about this arrangement. But when in bed that night his mother had spoken gently to him:

"Pastor told me what happened today, Simon. He was sorry he had to punish you, but he had to do that because God expects it of him. The Devil lives in the Convent, Simon, you must never listen to what those poor sinful children say."

Slowly, with the weight of the enlightenment of his flock pressing on his shoulders, theatrically, solemnly, Pastor Schulz mounted the pulpit in the left-hand corner of the Church. With resignation and love he faced his congregation, then bowed his head in silent prayer. The congregation shuffled uneasily, collectively tallying its sins. There was a clearing of throats and sporadic coughing. A fretful baby was shushed.

"May the true God, the Father, the Son and the Holy Ghost be with us," suddenly exclaimed Pastor Schulz. "Our text from Holy Writ is found in St Matthew, chapter sixteen, verses three and four. *O ye hypocrites, ye can discern the face of the sky, but can ye not discern the signs of the times? A wicked and adulterous generation seeketh after a sign, and there shall no sign be given unto it, . . ."*

Mr Wundersitz shifted and squirmed in his seat. The blowflies seeking the warm upper parts of the windows buzzed welcome to the consciences rising about them. Annie at the organ crossed her legs primly, smoothing down her skirts with averted sex-slumbering glances at Willie Schumacher, who sat near her in the choir and only last night had caressed those very legs to her thighs and beyond. Slowly a tingle of gratification arose within her but it was suddenly jolted away as Pastor Schulz, using his familiar technique, suddenly changed from his soporific, cooing, soul-winning voice to the thunder of declaimed damnation impending.

"Yes, sex! It is true that Christ Jesus our Lord and Saviour asked of his disciples who would throw the first stone. But that must *never* be taken as an excuse for licence! Sin lurks everywhere around us. In the ballroom, in the wine-bottle, look not upon the wine when it is red, thine eyes shall behold strange women. And in our cities, Sodoms and Gomorrahs that they are—read the newspapers. See the vice and fornication daily, leading into the sad corridors of the divorce courts, the abortionists"—Pastor Schulz lowered his voice— "the homes for unwanted children. Verily whatsoever a man soweth that shall he also reap!"

Annie at the organ gulpingly sought forgiveness for Willie Schumacher's straying fingers. Simon, screwing up the corner of one eye, saw his father sternly, sinless as one who had minded sheep at the age of nine, staring midway between Martin Luther and Jesus Christ. Across the aisle his mother adjusted her Sunday hat with Christian foreboding. Dora and Vera played patacake with their hands, silently.

Pastor Schulz, with the eternal flames of hell flickering sulphurously at his back, now billed and cooed his listeners to the cool havens of salvation. Safely he transported them past the licking fires, so that they became plastic in his hands.

"*Come to me ye that labour and are heavy laden, all ye repentant sinners, saith the Lord.* My friends, out of His boundless love and mercy He forgives us all." Small clouds momentarily dimmed the forgiving sunshine of Pastor Schulz's salvation-proffering countenance as he frowned and raised his voice a little. "Yes, dear friends. He forgives us, even the bearers of false witness, the unbelievers, the whoremongers. . . ."

Simon, peering down the aisle, could see Stan Weinert chewing gum unconcernedly next to his florid-faced father, neck bulging above celluloid collar, who ran Willow Reach's only butcher's shop. Stan was the oldest boy in the Saturday School. Simon wondered if he were asking God for forgiveness at that very moment; but it didn't seem so as Stan pulled the gum out of his mouth in a long strip and then sucked it in again. Stan was undoubtedly a whore-monger. Simon thought how Frau Pastor would scream and faint if she heard the things Stan muttered to him during Saturday School. He had felt twenty-three girls so far, he said; he had frigged seven of them. The last had been Bertha Schmidt only two weeks ago. Bertha, dark, plump, rosy-cheeked with swelling breasts and big swinging behind, sat sheltered under a large hat with red cherries next to haggard, harassed-looking Mrs Schmidt near the front of the Church. Mrs Schmidt had five other daughters.

"She sleeps in the sleep-out," said Stan. "I crept in the window last Tuesday night. Fixed it up with her after school. They'd all gone to bed. The old bugger is always boozed to the eyeballs. Boy, was she willing!" Stan was nicknamed Dinger because he had the biggest ding of the boys. In morning recess-times Dinger frequently gave demonstrations in the boys' outhouse. One morning he had it stand-ing up so big that "Hocker" Slade and Herman Zimmermann hung their boots on it.

Stan was a whoremonger for certain. But Simon shifted uneasily in his seat. Perhaps he was, too. Hadn't he gone down to Weckert's bakery with a couple of other boys and in the shadows behind the bakehouse paid Olga Weckert threepence to put his hand down her bloomers. It was wet and sticky, and he wished afterwards he had kept his threepence. He could have bought some licorice blocks and musk sticks from Mrs Drogemuller's shop. Now God had him re-corded for certain in that Book that Frau Pastor talked about at Saturday School. His heart pounded and he hardly dared look at Martin Luther and Christ on the Cross. Both stared accusingly back at him.

The congregation stood for the Benediction in sweaty ranks.

"The Lord make His face to shine upon you and be gracious unto you and give you peace. . . ."

But after they had sung *Praise God From Whom All Blessings Flow*, the congregation did not move out. In straggling hesitation it sat down instead. There was a hushed silence. Pastor Schulz, Bible under his arm, strode slowly to the altar. Simon noticed that even the blowflies seemed to be quiet. Perhaps God had done this. Or Martin Luther.

For a long time Pastor Schulz faced the altar in prayer. The congre-gation waited. Someone near Simon scraped his boots; Mr Wunder-sitz blew his nose with a horrible snotty sound; a baby cried and was hissed to silence in the women's part. Pastor Schulz spoke solemnly and awfully.

"Dear friends in Christ. Our Lord Jesus as you know wants us to confess our sins to Him. We can seek His forgiveness at all times in our prayers. We do not publicly seek his forgiveness except that in the custom as instituted by our church father, Martin Luther, we collectively ask forgiveness of our sins before partaking of the holy sacrament."

Pastor Schulz's brow darkened.

"But we do not as the Catholics and their Antichrist the Pope do —have confessionals with their heathen practice of paying money for forgiveness of sins."

The congregation sucked in its breath in collective horror. Pastor Schulz now spoke even more slowly and awfully.

"But our Church elders have ordained that whenever a member of our congregation has committed Public Sin whereby he or she has thus offended his or her fellow members of the Church, then the member must make true and penitent confession before the congregation as in the presence of Almighty God."

He paused as if waiting for a sign. Slowly, after some shuffling in the back of the women's side, a handkerchief to her face, Edie Olsen walked uncertainly down the aisle. She wore a loose white frock— her stomach still protruded, and Simon felt the blood rush to his face for he could see that Edie was soon to have a baby. Next to Simon, Bruno Wundersitz half stood. His eyes bulged, he seemed to quiver all over, his large fleshy lips were parted and moist and often he passed his tongue over his lips. Simon moved closer to his father. Mr Wundersitz gripped the pew in front so that his knuckles were white. He watched, breathing short and fast, his eyes riveted on Edie as approaching the altar she seemed to walk more slowly and painfully. At the back of the other side of the Church Simon could see Mrs Olsen crying silently. Several rows down in front of him he saw Mr Olsen rigid, stony-faced, chin thrust forward, staring at the altar. Mr Wundersitz, breathing faster and faster, moving his thighs together, watched Edie Olsen as she knelt in front of Pastor Schulz.

The river banks and Edie Olsen were together in Simon's mind— the banks of the great, green-watered, tranquil Murray flowing in silent mutter past Willow Reach. Edie was a Saturday School teacher, and Stan Weinert used to drool about her in Simon's ear.

"Boy, those tits! She's only a coupla years older than me. Wouldn't I like to pull her pants down. She'd know a thing or two, I bet!"

Simon, unconcerned, liked Edie. She always walked down the road with him when Saturday School was over. She lived down near the irrigation settlements along the swamps on one of the low bare hills overlooking the reclaimed areas where her father had his dairy farm.

"But I'm only an adopted child," explained Edie one day. "Of course, they're very good to me, and Mum couldn't have kids of her own. Dad's awfully strict. He beats me for the littlest thing. Always on my bum. Gosh he makes it sore. But still, I've got a home with them."

She looked sideways at Simon. "Do the boys at school tell you jokes?"

Simon nodded. "Some of them do. They scrawl things on the out-house walls, too."

"What things?"

"Oh well, things, you know." He was embarrassed. "They draw things, you know, a girl's and a boy's."

"Big ones?"

"Aw . . . yair."

"With, you know, everything?"

"Yair . . ."

"Any words, you know, for doing it?"

"Yair, but Mr Hempel said he'd cane the life out of anyone he caught writing them. He whitewashed them off last week."

Edie touched his arm with her finger.

"But . . . was there that one word, you know . . .?"

All of a sudden Simon had a funny feeling in his stomach.

"Well, yair . . . someone wrote it in indelible pencil and it spread all over the wall and that's why Mr Hempel had to use whitewash. Crikey he was mad!"

"But did they draw the boy's right in the girl's?" Edie persisted.

"Gosh, I don't remember, Edie."

"How about the jokes?"

Simon remembered a rhyme Stan Weinert had recited all through Saturday School. He stumbled through it. Edie trilled and clapped her hands.

"Oh Simon! Say it over again!" As they walked down towards Simon's house Edie repeated it several times.

"Simon, ask your mum if you can come over on Sunday afty and have tea with us. We can walk round a bit on the swamp. And Dad'll drive you into Church with us in the trap."

Simon thought it would be a good idea.

It was a hot Sunday afternoon and it was a long walk down to the irrigation settlement. Mrs Olsen was pleased to see him, gave him a glass of home-made ginger beer to cool him down, and asked after his mother and sisters. Mr Olsen sat on the verandah with a sheepdog sleeping at his feet. He was reading a book which Simon thought looked like a bible. Now and then he looked down towards the criss-cross of green and yellow irrigation paddocks on the swamp, with the willows shimmering blue-green in the heat and the muddy green river beyond. He didn't seem to notice Simon.

"Mum, Simon and me are going for a walk down on the swamp past the cliffs. I'll show him the new quarry."

"Well, I'm setting tea at half-past five so we'll have plenty of time to get into Church. You be back sharp then. You know what your father will do if you're late. And watch for snakes on the river banks."

Edie's legs were inclined to plumpness but she moved actively and slid and scrambled down the sandy banks leading to the swamp below. She had no stockings on and wore a pale blue cotton frock without sleeves, its pattern of dots washed out. A frog croaked in the reeds, and in the afternoon heat haze the river flies buzzed in clouds as they walked by.

"Simon, do you think we all go to Hell if we do things wrong, like Pastor Shulz says?"

"I dunno. Dad and Mum always say so. I can't see how Hell could be big enough, you know, with all the people in the world, the Chinese and the Africans, they all have to go to Hell 'cause they ain't Lutherans. And all the ones that are dead and that."

Edie kicked a clod of dried mud which splashed down into the irrigation ditch.

"I've thought about it too. And where does God keep it. I said somethink like that one night and Dad gave me a terrible hiding. He said it was time I learned you shouldn't argue about what it says in the Bible."

"Mmm," said Simon sympathetically.

"But who can say what's wicked and what isn't?" persisted Edie.

"Well, I suppose it's in the Ten Commandments." Simon switched at a frill-necked lizard gaping up at him from the embankment. "Thou shalt not kill, and covet thy neighbour's goods and all that."

Two men scything lucerne hailed them as they walked by.

"Hullo, rosy bum," one of them called. "How about that tumble you promised me!"

"Oh them Ross boys," said Edie, crimsoning. "The things they say. That Len. He's always asking me to come down in his shed and see his prize packet."

"Prize packet?"

"Go on," said Edie impatiently, "about what is wicked."

"Well, the Commandments aren't always about what is evil. Like sanctify the holy day. And thou shalt honour thy father and thy mother."

Suddenly Edie began to sob hysterically. She sat down at the side of the embankment, her shoulders heaving, her head on her knees. Simon knelt beside her, terrified at the sudden change.

"Oh Simon, Simon . . ." she cried. Her face was streaked with tears as she looked at him piteously. "It says that, doesn't it? Thou shalt honour thy father and mother. . . ."

"Yes it does . . . but. . . ."

"Even if he isn't your real father?"

"That's right," Simon assured her, "but you don't have to cry about it, Edie. . . ."

"But then it says . . . it says . . . thou shalt not commit, not commit. . . ."

". . . adultery," said Simon greatly puzzled. "But that's nothing to do with honouring thy father and mother."

"Oh yes, Simon," she wailed, and Simon was sick at the sound of her despair. "I don't know whether it's in the Bible or the Commandments. I don't know whether it's wicked or not. But . . . but if he was my real father and he . . . you know . . . got into my bed, would it be wicked. . . . Oh Simon, would it?"

Edie seemed shrunken as Pastor Schulz prayed over her.

"God in His infinite mercy has brought this erring daughter of the congregation to the altar of His holy love. Cast not the first stone, our Lord Jesus said of the woman taken in adultery. But Edie Olsen, who has sinned in the eyes of God, who has known the carnal lust of man and is now with child, seeks forgiveness at her own request and at the request of her grieving father Brother Olsen and his wife."

Pastor Schulz placed his hand on Edie's bowed head.

"Do you Edie Olsen confess that you have sinned in the sight of God and man and earnestly seek the forgiveness of your Lord and Saviour Jesus Christ who died for you on the Cross? And answer I do."

Faintly came the reply, "I do."

"Do you believe that the forgiveness I will pronounce upon you as an ordained minister of Christ is the forgiveness of our Saviour, and answer I do."

Faintly again, "I do."

"And do you promise with the help of God and the Congregation to amend your ways, never to sin in shameful adultery again, to create a new heart within you with clear and pure thoughts, and to raise the child which your sorrowing parents will care for in the nurture and admonition of the Lord?"

Softly, agonizedly, like the breeze whispering through the reedbeds when Edie had sobbed before him on that summer afternoon by the river, Simon heard Edie's painfully uttered "I do." Suddenly she fell forward on the altar and Pastor Schulz jerked her back on her knees, muttering something in her ear as he did so.

"The congregation," he said, "will rise in prayer."

Bruno Wunderlitz, eyes bulging, hands in pockets, his whole frame shaking, suddenly and furtively looked around him and awkwardly rose to his feet. But Simon, the tears streaming down his cheeks, knew not what he could say or think except that, with his heart pounding, it came to him blindingly and desperately that the God of whom Pastor Schulz talked was not just and merciful. And that forgiveness was mockery. And that Pastor Schulz's God would never be his God.

DAVID POCKLEY

Tell About the Rice

He was a tall old man, lean and stringy, bald, lined, scarred and weather-beaten. He was dressed in a clean, faded, long-sleeved blue shirt and frayed khaki pants; dirty once-white sandshoes without laces were on his sunburned feet. He was sitting comfortably on the low sea-wall and he was talking to the small girl standing in front of him.

"Well," he said, "there were two of them; the *Koopa* and the *Beaver*. The *Koopa* was a pretty nice ship, but the old *Beaver* was a bit of a wreck. She had a funny sort of whistle. All us kids could tell when the *Beaver* was coming in."

The girl said, "Like a train?"

"Well no; sort of *Who-o-o-op, Who-o-o-op!* We used to think real beavers made that sort of noise."

"What sort of noise *do* they make, Grandpop?"

"Search me," he said, "the only beaver I ever saw was stuffed"— At the foot of the stairs in the old Russel Hotel he thought. The night we got on the grog in Johnny Kent's speakeasy: Doug Pouchard and the stuffed beaver and that little dark Vancouver girl, all finishing up in the same bed together.

The girl said softly, "*Who-o-o-op, Who-o-o-op,*" then, "What are you laughing at, Grandpop?"

He brought his wandering thoughts back. "Eh?" he said, "I guess I was thinking about beavers. They gnaw trees down and when it's just about ready to fall, they sit back on their tails and yell '*Timberrrr!*'"

She covered her ears and laughed delightedly. "Mum says you're silly," she said.

"That's right," he agreed; "silly and getting sillier. The older I get the sillier I get. Did I ever tell you about the *Olivene* and the *Beryl*?"

She shook her head.

"Well," he said, "there were two launches used to run between Sandgate and Woody Point; the *Olivene* and the *Beryl*. We used to come down from Brisbane to Sandgate on the train and cross over to Woody Point on one of them. We used to like the *Olivene* best."

"Why?"

The old man thought. "Blowed if I know; I think we liked the name. My grandfather used to meet us at Woody Point jetty with the sulky. God help us," he said, "that'd be your great, great grandfather."

He fell silent and his faded blue eyes took on the remote and withdrawn look of age. Tess, he thought, Tess. That was the pony's name; a creamy, what they called nowadays a palomino. All this Yankee influence; too much TV. He remembered sitting up beside his grandfather and the pony's fat quarters working, and the dust.

The little girl said, "You *did* tell me. You told me about the rice."

He looked vacantly at her. "What?"

The girl was patient. "You *did* tell me about the *Olivene*," she said, "and you told me about the rice. Don't you remember?"

"The rice? What rice? Oh, the *rice*!" He laughed suddenly.

"Tell me about the rice, Grandpop."

"I told you before," the old man said; "you just said so."

"Well, tell me again, tell about the rice."

The old man straightened his leg and groped in his trouser-pocket for his pipe. He tapped it on the sea-wall, put the much bitten stem between his teeth and reached for his tobacco. "Well, Okay," he said, "I'll tell you again."

His granddaughter said, "Mum says you're not supposed to smoke before breakfast."

"I had breakfast," he told her, "hours ago. Long before you were up."

"Was Mum up?"

He shook his head.

"Well, who cooked it? What did you have?"

"Bit of fish."

"Grandpop," her cry was anguished, "you didn't eat my fish?"

He laughed at her. "No, I didn't eat your fish; your fish is in the fridge, right where you put it. We'd better get home before your mother gives it to the cat."

"Mum wouldn't," she said positively. "She's going to fry it for my breakfast."

"Well," he said, "don't you think we'd better get home and organize it? Aren't you getting hungry?"

She thought about it. "Pretty hungry, but tell about the rice first."

He laughed again. "That's right," he said, "the rice."

He took a new plug of tobacco and an old, ground-down, two-bladed knife from his pocket and shaved flakes of tobacco into his palm as he talked. "Well," he said in the slow, reminiscent voice of age, "my grandfather, your great-great-grandfather and I were on the *Olivene* going over to Sandgate. The old feller was a bit of a dandy and he was always very proud of his feet. I remember he used to get his boots made to order—some little place on Queen Street."

He snapped the knife shut and returned it and the plug to his pocket. He began to rub the tobacco between his palms, the dry tobacco whispering between the dry, old hands. He was remembering the tall, thin, upright figure of his grandfather. The high-buttoned, grey coat, the carefully tied black satin stock with its pearl pin, the tight trousers strapped under the varnished, shiny boots.

His granddaughter said, "You're the only man I know that smokes a pipe."

He grinned at her. "There's very few of us left."

"Don't you ever smoke cigarettes, like Dad?"

He shook his head. "I used to. I used to smoke cigarettes and cigars and I used to chew tobacco."

The child's voice was horrified. "Chew to*bacco*?"

"Some places," he said, "it gets so cold that if you take off your mits to make a cigarette or to fill your pipe, you get your fingers frost-bitten, so most people chew tobacco. Or snoose," he added.

He fell silent; his faded eyes squinted into the early morning sun and across the sparkling waters of the bay, his mind going back, remembering the logging camps in the Queen Charlottes. Those snoose-chewing timber beasts. Oh, my arthritic old bones, he thought! Oh, my lost youth, when I'd rather drink than eat and rather fight than drink. Those trips down the Inside Passage in one or other of the old Black Ball ships with a hundred newly paid off Scandahoovian loggers going out to spend their cheques. The poker and blackjack schools; the fights. God, those fights when the hootch was in and all sense gone; the swinging peaveys and the flying calks. Unconsciously his thin old hand traced the thin white line of an old scar that crossed his bald head. The brawl in that camp on the Inlet; that *was* a fight. He remembered the giant Nordska, drunk—as they used to say—as forty-seven naked savages, standing, swaying in the moonlight, his macinaw shirt on the hard-packed snow at his feet, a half-empty aquavite bottle in one mighty fist, a hickory picaroon handle in the other; arms thrown wide, head back, bellowing that damfool song, while Swedes piled out through the bunkhouse doors and windows like ants. That song, how did it go? The tune was "Maryland my Maryland". His fingers tapped on the wall beside him and he sang the words in his head, singing in heavily accented Scandinavian-English, just as the drunken, big Norwegian had sung it all those years ago.

> *Ten t'ousand Svedes*
> *Run t'ru de veeds*
> *At de battle of Copenhagen;*
> *Ten t'ousand Svedes*
> *Run t'ru de veeds*
> *Chasing vun Norveigen.*

That's how she started, he thought, and before it finished there wasn't a man in camp didn't have a bone broken. The Norwegians fought the Swedes and the Swedes fought the Danes and the Danes fought the Finns and the Finns fought everyone—even each other. And then that ratty little high-rigger from Quebec pulled a knife.

Ancient prejudices stirred his mind. "Horse's ass of a pea-souper," he said aloud.

The little girl was shaking his knee. "What's that stuff?" she asked.

He brought his mind slowly back. "What stuff, Honey?"

"That stuff you said people chew."

"Snoose," he said. "It's snuff. Sort of powdered tobacco. They pack a wad of it inside their bottom lip and suck at it all day."

"Did you ever do that?"

"Not me. You have to be brought up on that stuff. I used to chew plug tobacco. What was the brand?" he pondered. "Mail box? Mail bag? Mail pouch? That was it, Mail pouch chewing tobacco."

The child had lost interest. "Aren't you going to tell about the rice?"

"Well, blister my belly," the old man said extravagantly, "haven't I told you about the rice yet? I'll tell you right now. Are you ready?"

The child standing in front of him nodded expectantly, her bright pony-tail dancing.

"Well, then." Her grandfather reached into his shirt-pocket for matches. He held the box in one hand and his pipe in the other. "My grandfather and I were crossing on the *Olivene* and there was a lady and her little boy on the same seat. The boy was next to my grandfather."

"How old was he?" the girl interrupted. "Was he as big as me?"

"About your age," he nodded; "I was a bit bigger. I was around six or eight I guess. Anyhow, there must have been a bit of a sea running because suddenly this little kid threw up all over my grandfather's boots."

Sitting hunched on the low wall, his thin, corded forearms resting on his thighs, his pipe and matches in his scarred, gnarled, old-man's hands, he was gazing straight at her but he wasn't seeing her. He was seeing, as plainly as if it had happened yesterday, the windy deck of the battered little passenger launch, his grandfather's high-nosed, tight-mouthed, disgusted face, the vomiting, tearful child, the flustered, apologetic mother.

The girl had heard the story before and was waiting now for the punch line. "Then what?" she asked.

"Then my grandfather turned to the woman and said, 'Madam, if you must give your child rice, the least you can do is to see that it is properly cooked'."

The old man laughed, as he had laughed at the telling many times before, but the little girl said seriously, "I wouldn't have been seasick on the *Olivene*."

Her grandfather lit his pipe, cupping the match and sucking so hard that hollows formed in his cheeks. He put the matchbox back in his shirt-pocket and lowered himself down from the wall. "No?" he said. "How about that time I took you to Bribie, you got sick that time."

"But, Grandpop!" She was indignant. "I wasn't even four then."

"That's right," he said, "you *were* pretty young." He dusted the sand from the seat of his pants. "Come on, let's go home and you can get stuck into that fish."

They walked along the sea-wall to the low flight of steps; they climbed them side by side and he held her hand as they crossed the road; then the little girl walked in front of him and stopped him. She stood looking up into his face.

She said, "You know Teddy?"

"Teddy!" he asked, "Teddy who?"

"Teddy," she said impatiently. "You know Teddy. My Teddy."

"Oh sure," he said, "I know your Teddy, what about it?"

"Well," she said, "his name isn't Teddy now, he's got a new name."

"What are you going to call him?"

The little girl was suddenly embarrassed. She looked down and dragged her bare foot along the kerb, muttering something inaudible.

"Eh," he said, "what was that? What are you going to call him?"

She looked up into his eyes. "Oliv*ene*," she said clearly. "His name's Olivene."

PETER BENNETT HILLS

Thicker than Water

SHEM, day-dreaming, eyes half slit against the sun, suddenly became aware of the approach of his father. A guilty glance at the flock assured him all was in order, and he stretched to his feet. The old man covered the ground at a remarkable pace, but reached him intact in dignity, and scarcely out of breath.

"Shem! I need fifteen hundred gopher-trees."

Barely awake, Shem thought he had misheard.

"You want *what?*"

"Fifteen hundred gopher-trees," said Noah, "perhaps more."

For a moment Shem's eyes and the valley were as one, desolate from rim to rim.

"Pop, you must be kidding!"

"Certainly not," said Noah. "Certainly not. I am going to build a boat."

The sun has reached him, thought Shem. The sun has finally melted his weak old brain. He's getting on a bit. Been very pre-occupied lately. I'd better take him home. He said gently:

"Pop, what kind of a boat are you going to build with fifteen hundred gopher-trees?"

Noah thought for a bit.

"A big one," he said.

"That," said Shem heavily, "is for sure. What do you need a boat for? A thousand miles of sand—who needs a boat? If we had any wood, which we haven't, I could make a boat out of one tree trunk. If we had an ox, which we haven't, I could haul it down to the Euphrates within two or three weeks. Also, if launched it would sink like a stone on account of I have never built a boat before." As an afterthought, he added, "Also, I would have fourteen hundred and ninety-nine trees left over."

"There will be no trees left over," said Noah. "This boat will be four hundred and fifty feet long."

"*What!*"

". . . And forty-five feet high."

"What!!"

". . . And seventy-five feet wide."

"Absolutely impossible!"

"Nothing is impossible. It is necessary that we build such a boat."

"We would have to cut down all the Cedars of Lebanon."

"No cedar," said Noah. "It has to be gopher-wood. It's in the specification."

"Specification! What specification? When we build this liner four hundred and fifty feet long, does it say what we have to do with it?"

"Pitch it," said Noah simply.

"A very good idea," said Shem with feeling.

"Pitch it inside and out," said Noah. "I estimate we shall need ten or twelve tons of hot pitch."

"Ten or twelve *tons*!"

"Give or take a ton."

"Let's walk back to the tents and have a drink."

"Shem," said Noah urgently. "I want you to go back and explain to the boys. I hurry now to the tents of Eli to trade with him for oxen. Tomorrow you and Ham must take a team north, looking for gopher-wood. Japhet I shall need here to tend the herds, and later to trim the trees as you haul them back. Gather up your goods and make ready. You must be my left arm. Persuade you Ham, for he must be my right."

"He'll love it," said Shem. "He'll just love it."

Noah sped on. Shem, more slowly, moved down the slope of the hill, thoughtfully scanning the valley as he went. As he drew near the first tent, he could see them under the sagging goatskin. Ham, lanky, confident, was resting easily on one elbow. Japhet, still boyish, was tossing and catching pebbles. Grinning, he skimmed one at Shem's approaching feet.

"What's new, man!"

"When I tell you," said Shem, squatting inside the tent shade, "man, will you get a surprise!"

Ham raised an eyebrow. "Tell me more."

Shem told them. Japhet said, "I don't dig you, man!" Shem told them again. Japhet's mouth was hanging open. Ham had his head to one side, eyes hard. "So—tomorrow we take a team and start north!" Then they were both speaking together.

"The old man's flipped his lid!"

"He's blown his stack!"

"He's crackers!"

"How much wood?"

"How long?"

"How high?"

"He's gone stark, raving bonkers!"

"Better tell the old lady."

"How long?"

"How high?"

"Build what?" said Ham. "Build *what*? Listen, Jack! A hundred and seventy years I've lived in this desert, and I can't even build a sandcastle!"

Shem said, "O.K.! O.K.! You sort it out with him. Just remember that around here his word is law."

They suddenly realized he was standing in the opening of the tent. A sly breeze ruffled the magnificent beard, and he washed them with his soft, tender eyes. "My boys," he said. "My boys. The chosen ones. The fountainhead of a new humanity. I see the questions in your faces. Why must we build a boat? Because, gentlemen, at the appointed hour will come a Flood. A Flood so great, the whole world will be laid to waste. A volume of water that will stagger the imagination. We alone have been given the honour of surviving that catastrophe, gentlemen. But we must build a boat."

Only Ham dared to speak. Ham, the loner, the rebel. He said, "Pop, don't you think that for five people a four hundred and fifty foot boat is kinda big?"

The full majesty of the noble head was turned fractionally in his direction. The eyes crystallized to pure quartz, and Noah cowed him with a moment of icy silence.

"Shem, you will be ready to leave in the morning."

"Yes, father."

"Ham, you will leave with him."

"Yes, father."

"Japhet, you will attend me at first light."

"Yes, father."

He was gone. Japhet said, "I don't wanna build no crummy boat." Ham said, "It's the same with all these old guys. When they get around five hundred years old, they start to act funny." Shem said, "Rain, eh! Well, of course, that could make it a bit different." Their heads came together, and they conversed rapidly in low tones.

At dawn, two teams of oxen moved off the valley floor, and by mid-morning had breasted the last rise of the hills. Moving downhill, unseen below the rim of the high land, they changed direction from

north to north-east, and began skirting the valley. At noon the party
rested.

"How far do you think we have come?" asked Shem.

"About five miles."

"The idea," said Shem, "is O.K. We circle around for a couple of
days, keeping out of sight. Then we head home when the old man
has cooled off. But supposing he hasn't cooled off?"

"He'll cool off," said Ham.

"The bit that worries me is this rain angle. Do you remember rain?
I saw rain once, when I was a boy. Must be a hundred and fifty years
ago. Japhet's never seen rain. He's too young. Do you remember
rain?"

"Yeah," said Ham.

"First he told me about the boat. Then he told us about the Flood.
He didn't mention a flood that first time. D'ya think he just made
it up about the Flood to make us build a boat?"

"Yeah," said Ham.

"But that wouldn't be like the old man. He's never told a lie in his
life. He wouldn't be in the position he is today if he told lies. Suppose
we go out to Mount Zefferon and have the story checked."

"You're joking," said Ham. "You know the kind of country it is
out there. I should eat dust for three days out there just because the
old man's got a touch of the sun."

"So we circle around for three days, or we sit here for three days.
That's going to be just great. We may as well go somewhere definite
for three days. What have we got to lose?"

"You must be nuts," said Ham, but he got up and turned the team
back down the slope.

On the second day they entered the foothills, and on the tenth hour
were climbing Mount Zefferon proper. The cave was higher than they
remembered, but the Prophet sat, as he had always sat, a goatskin
bundle in the shade of a rock. As they drew close, the Prophet spoke.

"Greetings, my sons. How goes the world with you?"

"We were hoping," said Shem, "that you could tell us."

There was an uncomfortable silence. Presently the Prophet spoke
again. He said, "What is it you seek?" Shem squatted on his haunches
and said nothing. Ham fiddled with his crook, then took the plunge.
"Do you have anything in the nature of a long-range weather fore-
cast?"

The Prophet looked blank.

Shem said, "Could you sorta give us the weather pattern, local-wise
and world-wise?"

The Prophet looked at Shem. He said, "I have looked into the future many times, my son. It is always the same. Oh, miserable sinners! The wage of sin is death. The wages of sin are death." He looked embarrassed. "I can never get that darn quotation right." He leant forward confidentially. "Anyhow, I can tell you fellows that in a couple of thousand years, things are going to get mighty tricky."

"Possibly," said Shem. "Possibly. However, we should appreciate something a little more current." The Prophet looked into the middle distance. His eyes glazed. He fell asleep. He woke up. They leant forward anxiously, waiting for him to speak. He said, "I'm sorry, fellas."

"What did you see?"

"I'm sorry fellas, I can't tell you."

"Why can't you tell us?"

"Something pretty big is going to happen. Something in the pretty near future. But I can't get a clear picture."

"Why not?" they asked.

"Too much damn rain!" said the Prophet.

Shem leapt to his feet. "Let's go," he shouted.

"Good enough for me, man!" said Ham.

They struggled to U-turn the patient oxen on the rocky track. "North!" shouted Shem, "North, and don't mess around." The coal-black hooves made little patterns in the dust.

Nothing punched home the seeming impossibility of the whole project more than the drawing. Shem and Ham first saw it as they battled the exhausted teams over the valley lip. Sketched across the valley, deeply etched in the sand, was the Ark. It was a masterly composition. The straights were correctly economical and faintly superior as straights must be, and the curves, robustly swelling at bow and stern, would have delighted the heart of Rubens. It was also monstrous and alien, as though it had swallowed the little huddle of tents which lay in its belly. It seemed scarcely credible that this baked-earth draughtsmanship could have been executed in the bare two weeks that they had been away.

When Shem could tear his eyes away, he saw that Ham had been seized by the thought that was presently in his own mind. Ham was looking over the shoulder of his lead ox at the trunks. They looked like a bundle of twigs. Against that endless mural, the trunks they had fought and sweated and slaved to cut shrunk to a handful of splinters. It was so ridiculous he almost laughed, but he and the oxen stood patiently on the hilltop until Ham stopped cursing and beating his fists on the rock. Presently, Ham let his arms fall slackly to his sides. "That does it! Rain or no rain, I quit!" He kicked the lead ox in a sudden relapse of frustration, and the surprised animal jerked and set off down the slope with its load. Shem was still studying the drawing.

"It's got a little window in it; about half-way up."

"Oh, shut up!" said Ham savagely. They started down after the team, coughing in the swirling dust.

Shem met Noah standing defensively at the prow, busily diverting the lead ox who was threatening to erase a portion of the boat. Noah clapped him cheerfully on the shoulder, "Well done, my boy." The ox wandered off aimlessly with its log. Noah waved his arm airily at the valley in general, "Not bad, eh?"

"Tremendous, Pop," said Shem. He meant it. For an old guy five hundred and fifty years old, it really was tremendous. Noah was counting, estimating. "We shall need a lot more logs," he said.

"Please don't mention that to Ham," said Shem.

"You will have to make lots and lots more trips."

"Please don't mention that to Ham."

"You may have to go several hundred times."

"I wanna go and say hullo to Mum and Japhet," said Shem. He moved down the curve of the bow, taking care not to smudge the line. As he turned under the flap of the tent, he could hear Ham's upraised voice. Shem kissed his mother on the cheek. He said, "How come you haven't talked Pop out of this crazy idea?" He nibbled at a crust of bread. Mrs Noah was mixing something in a bowl. "You know how your father is. When he gets these ideas, there is no stopping him. Besides, for some reason, this time I think he is right." Japhet came in through the tent flap and slapped Shem heartily on the back.

"Hi, man! What do you think of the crazy drawing?"

"Great," said Shem dryly.

"What's with Ham—yelling up there?"

"It's the wood," said Shem. "We brought back enough to make two deck planks and a window frame."

Japhet said, "Do you have to go back for more?"

Shem said, "You've got to be joking!"

It was no joke. No joke, no rest, no peace. The hot winds blew, the sun climbed higher through the days, and the seasons died. The sheep grazed, and lambed, and passed away, and new generations of goats lived through their time. Here and there on the dusty basin a little grass would grow, and sometimes a bush, and occasionally the seed of an olive would root, and spread, and climb. And with them grew the Ark. It climbed through a hundred days on its hardwood keel. It spread through a framework of formers and spacers and uprights and bulkheads and risers. It grew until it towered above them, brooding and impossible. They still needed the wood long after Eli's oxen had grown old and crumbled into dust. Through the ten, the twenty and the thirty years, they still needed the wood. The hill-sides were scoured with the coming of it, and the floor was thick with the chippings of it, until Japhet was grown to a man, and Ham's thick beard was streaked with white, and Mrs Noah had grown pale in the shadow of it, and suddenly it was done.

It was the biggest thing in the world, and Noah was very pleased. He was slow, and old, and bent, and it took him half a day to walk around it. They lost him in the depths of it. He would descend into the bowels of it, and they would have to send Japhet to find him. In the fortieth year following the commencement of the Ark, he called them all together and made his pronouncement.

"It meets the specification."

Ham said he was very gratified. He said a lot of other things as well. He discussed at length his possible reactions if the Ark had *not* been to specification. Shem was pleased, too. He was pleased with the silence. He was filled with a delicious sense of peace. They had finished the hammering. There would be whole mornings to even-ings devoid of somebody banging something on something. They lay on the sand in the shadow of the Ark. They lay under a million stars in a silver sky. Shem lay with his hands clasped behind his neck, drinking in the peace.

Ham said, "Tomorrow, we don't have to harness no oxen." They were happy in the prospect of it, and allowed him to be ungramma-tical. "No more wood. I never want to see another tree."

Japhet said, "I wonder when it will start to rain?"

Shem said nothing. Forty years ago they didn't want the rain. They certainly didn't want to build a boat. Now they had the boat, and they wanted the rain. They wanted to make the boat worth-while, and the building of it to mean something. They did not think their father was so crazy, either. He knew that secretly even Ham conceded they had achieved something wonderful. He thought: we're all rather proud.

Ham said, "In the morning, we get to lie in."

In the morning, Noah said, "Now we assemble the animals." The cold winds of a thousand northern winters clamped around their hearts. The sun froze in the sky. The birds stopped, and the sheep stopped, and the sons of Noah stood very, very still.

"What animals?" asked Ham, soft as silk.

"All the animals," said the old man, waving his arms about vaguely, "all the animals in creation."

Japhet said, "Let's not exaggerate, Pop. Exactly how many animals?"

"Two," said Noah.

The softest of relaxing sighs.

". . . of each," he added.

There was a catch in it, but they could not see where it lay. Japhet said tentatively, "Two oxen, two goats and two sheep?"

Noah said, "Those, certainly. Those—and all the others."

Shem said, "What others? There aren't any others! Are there?"

"Certainly there are others. Do you, for one moment, imagine the whole world is contained in this miserable valley? Of course there are others. Did you think, for one moment, the Flood would merely submerge the land of Ur? Why did we build the Ark? If man can cover great distance in a season, how far could we have walked in forty years? How great is a Flood that in forty years we could not reach the edge of it? Beyond the deserts and mountains and valleys are more deserts and mountains and valleys. Each contains its complement of creatures. Two of each sort must be gathered up. I charge each of you with this task. I shall remain here, and take care of the birds."

"What birds?" said Ham. "Waddya mean, the birds?"

"The birds," said Noah, "will come of their own volition. At the appointed time, they will come. This is quite outside our jurisdiction."

"Never mind the birds," said Shem. "Let's get back to the animals. What animals?"

For answer, Noah led them to a little cave in a hillside. The cave was stacked from top to bottom with slabs. "I have faithfully recorded all the animals," said Noah. "The library covers several thousand tablets. Enumerating briefly, to the south are antelopes, lions, monkeys, rhinoceros, hippopotamus and giraffe. To the north are wolves, bears, reindeer, horses and foxes. To the east are elephants, tigers, camels, . . ."

"Hold it!" said Shem. "Hold it! I've heard enough."

Japhet said, "A hippowhat?"

Ham said, "This is going to be another timber deal. I can feel it in my bones."

"How big?" asked Shem. "How big are these animals, sizewise?"

"Which one, for instance?" asked Noah.

"F'rinstance—elephants?"

It was an unlucky choice. Ham was quite put out. He shouted, "I knew it! I knew it!" It was some time before they could calm him. "Whatever happens, I don't go east. Somebody else can go east. Definitely no elephants. I'll take west. What's west?"

Noah told him about the west, taking care to mention chipmunks and ring-tailed possums first. Ham was somewhat mollified, but suspicious. Noah said, "Now there is only just enough room on board for the quota. I don't want you boys bringing back more than two of each."

They just managed to contain themselves until he was out of ear-shot. They filled the next few minutes with a spectacular display of massed invective. It was an impressive pile of masonry, and they considered it with studied disgust. After a while, Japhet selected a tablet and studied it. He said, "Tiger—Bengal (meat-eating). Length ten feet. Weight five hundred and fifty pounds."

Ham tried to look disinterested. "What was the weight again?"

Japhet said, "Five hundred and fifty pounds."

Shem said, "Four times bigger than me, and it eats meat!"

"I betcha it lives in the east," said Ham. "Yeah, in the east I betcha. Now you all heard what the old man said. I get the west. Let Japhet go east. All he's done for forty years is chop little twigs off logs. Let him do some work!"

"I hauled logs, too," said Shem mildly.

Japhet said, "Relax man! I'll take the east. You guys don't know what you're missing. Listen to these. 'Monkey—White-tailed Guer-eza, Monkey—Colobus Angolan, Monkey—White-collared Man-gabey'. Man! Imagine me seeing all those."

Ham said, "You won't if Tiger—Bengal (meat-eating) sees you first." He had two tablets in his arms, one marked "Wolf—Grey Timber" and the other "Wolf—Prairie". Both tablets were embossed at the top with a crudely chiselled capital "W", and he reluctantly piled them to one side of the cave mouth. After a while they were all busily sorting the tablets into points of the compass.

They were not to meet again for many years. The huge Ark sat in the silent valley and waited. High on the prow, Mrs Noah affixed a little goat-skin awning, and in the tenth year Noah took to sitting in the shade of it, while watching the horizon. In the summer of the twenty-second year, the old man grew restless, and refused to leave his station day or night. He sensed their coming, and the tremendous import of it wrapped his shoulders like a mantle. He did not feel helpless and alone, as he had when Mrs Noah made her little trip to Kish, or overawed as he had when the birds had come blackening

the skies. He felt uplifted. His destiny was upon him, and his soul
sang. The morning sun unveiled a puff of dust in the east, no bigger
than a man's hand. The old man, bent as a bow, struggled to his
feet, and threw his arms in the air.

"Japhet comes!"

Daily the dust cloud grew, until it was a column a mile high in
the sky. On the fourth day, a second cloud of dust appeared out of
the north. The old man was trembling with joy, and Mrs Noah
came and sat with him, in the shade of the little awning. "Shem is
coming," she said. They held hands.

Two weeks later, the animals started pouring over the rim of the
valley, an endless chain stretching back as far as the eye could see.
Two by two they came, but meeting with the Ark they broke forma-
tion and began milling about, until they formed a sea of black, brown
and stripe, fur, hair and bristle. By the time Shem had worked his
string into the valley, it was near full from end to end. He met up
with Japhet, and they embraced.

"Have a nice trip?"

"Fair, man! Dragged a bit on the last five years, when I turned
them for home. You know, last mile home is the longest, and all that
jazz."

"You've said it," said Shem. "How come you weren't walking?"

"It's a great new idea I had, man," said Japhet. "Like I was riding
on this animal's back. Riding is gonna be all the rage. Walking is
out, man, like finished. Pick a tough, chunky animal like I had, 'Pig
—Malay Babirusa'—absolutely ideal, man."

"It's got a round back," said Shem, doubtfully. "Why not pick an
animal with a flat back, like 'Horse—Arab'?"

Japhet said, "You're having me on. What, sit right up there! That'll
never catch on. The secret is to have your feet touching the ground."

Noah said, "Who went south? No creature must be missed."

Japhet said, "I went south, Pop, then worked my way around to
the east." He caught Shem looking at him sheepishly, and added
quickly, "Well, I'm younger than you guys. It wasn't far out of my
way. I like keeping busy."

Mrs Noah said, "I've been busy, too. I went over to Kish to invite
some of those nice young girls to pay us a visit. I've talked it over
with your father, and we might let three of them take the trip with
us. Do you remember Rebeckah, Japhet?"

Japhet said, "Do I remember! You mean the swinging chick I met
at the well in Kish, one Tishri about a hundred years ago? You mean
she's on board!"

Mrs Noah said, "I think you had better have a wash first, dear."

Shem said, "I wonder what's keeping Ham?"

Noah was jumping about, happily patting the shorter animals on the head. "Well done, boys, well done. I think we had better start the loading as soon as possible, Shem. As they go up the plank, Japhet can check them off against the tablets."

"I was planning to wash up, Pop, and take a stroll around the deck."

"Time is against us, boy. Time is running out. Events of great moment are upon us."

So spoke he, and as always he must be obeyed. The loading went well, with only one distraction. On the thirteenth day, Ham trudged into the valley at the head of his herd. He walked purposefully, as would a man who has simmered for sixteen years. He seized Noah by the shoulders, and shook him like a leaf. He said, "O.K., wise guy —how come you didn't tell me about the Bison? These bison got minds of their own. You just try turning around eight hundred pounds of bison when it's facing in the wrong direction." They restrained him with great difficulty. Noah went up and sulked under the goatskin awning. For the rest of the week Mrs Noah trotted soothingly among them, pointing out the sooner they finished the loading, the sooner they could rest. Noah was six hundred years old. They did not know, but it was Zero.

Shem was pushing a small goanna up the gangplank with a piece of stick when a large drop of water struck him on the hand. For a moment it did not register.

Ham said, "Well that does it, apart from two wart-hogs and a bison. I tell you now, I'm gonna put a wart-hog under each arm, and once I'm up that gangplank, I'm all through, boy!"

Japhet said, "Like you brought in the bison, man. I say you should get him up the plank." A large drop of water splashed over his ear. "Hey, what's this stuff?"

High above them, a snowy head appeared over the side of the Ark. The voice was high and quavery, but the message was clear. "I think the time has come, gentlemen. Kindly come aboard and pull in the gangplank." Several large drops splattered on the sand.

Shem shouted, "You heard what the old man said! This is *it*! Get this crummy bison up the plank."

Japhet stood up horrified, and dropped the last tablet. He said, "Holy Cow! I think I forgot to bring a dodo." Mrs Noah appeared from nowhere and grasped the bison by one ear. It followed her obediently up the plank. Relieved of responsibility, Ham put a wart-hog under each arm and followed her. Shem and Japhet pulled the gangplank inboard amid a flurry of heavy rain.

It was the forty-seventh day. The Ark rode on the face of the waters, and Noah was six hundred years old. Shem, Ham and Japhet were stretched out on the deck, dozing in the sun. Noah came upon them and smiled. He had a dove in his right hand, and a leaf in his left. He said, "If the signs are right, gentlemen, I shall soon have work for you to do."

Japhet said, "You name it, Pop. We can handle it."

Noah moved on, chuckling.

Ham said, "He ain't such a bad old guy. How many people could think up an idea like this, and get away with it?"

Shem said, "I asked him once how he knew this thing would float. He just said, 'I have it on the highest authority'. What can you say about a faith like that?"

Japhet said, "Well, he sure got me in shape, man. Starting a new civilization is going to be a breeze. I can handle any animal known to zoology, and you should see my muscles, man!"

Shem said, "You think you built this tub single-handed or something? If there is anything I don't know about gopher-wood . . ."

They lay contented in the sun.

Ham said, "Did I ever tell you guys about the time I personally manhandled an eight-hunnerd pound bison?"

The Ark sailed on.

DAL STIVENS

Sanctuary

HE DIDN'T like me being there and I can't say I blamed him. I wasn't included in the great plan and there had been no provision for me. I was an extra mouth and I had no special skills.

Now that it was achieved and there was nothing more to do but wait he had relaxed; the strain of the days before which had stalked him persistently had now overwhelmed him. He sat for hours in his big chair, arms in lap and his heavy greying head slumping forward. Sometimes he closed his eyes for minutes; at other times he stared into space beyond me as though he was trying to pierce the emptiness that lay outside the immense black hull. I'd seen the same look in the great golden eyes of the black-ruffed male lion in the hold as he searched for antelopes that were not there on a non-existing thorn-clothed plain.

Curiosity killed the cat, they say, but it had saved my life. I'd heard about the ship and gone aboard to see for myself. No one stopped me and afterwards it was too late to off-load me. They'd been instructed not to open the hatches and besides it would have been casting me to my death and they couldn't do it. But all the same, they resented my being saved. I hadn't been chosen and I was saved. The men resented me, too, because I was young.

Only the old man didn't feel this but then he didn't seem to feel anything. He was looking past me when the lion in the hold roared suddenly and brought his eyes back to mine.

"How long?" I asked. We had been shut up now for many days.

"Some time yet," he said. We had lights; otherwise we would have been in darkness. They danced on the white tips of his beard and on the pitch-black hull. "I will know when we can land. I have my orders."

"What's out there?" I asked although I knew.

"Emptiness," he said. "Nothing. The void and below—death. Everything that lived is dead. Perhaps the plants will live—some of them."

His voice had no emotion. He wasn't elated that he still lived or sorry that all the others had died. He had known it was coming and he had time to get used to the idea. But it still numbed my mind.

"All the cities," I said. "The children and their mothers, the strong young men and women, the old frail ones. . . ."

He nodded. The macaws in the hold screeched and set the apes jabbering. "It'll all happen again," he said. "The destruction of cities. They'll not be able to help themselves. This ship is believed to preserve the seed of life but it is the seed of death—"

I wondered then, as I had before, why he should have been chosen. He read my thoughts.

"I was given my orders," he said. "I do not question orders. I did not ask why or wherefore. I don't even now though you might think so, my friend. I merely know my own kind—" and with a smile—"myself. The plan may intend it all." He added after a pause, with a faint smile, "I didn't even ask why I had been chosen."

"Where are we going?" I asked, glancing at the sealed window

"Nowhere," he said. "We'll drift and when it's safe we'll land— and start it all again. And see the rainbow in the sky."

I asked suddenly, "The others—do they think as you do?" I did not know because they would not talk to me.

"They are younger, and that, I suppose, is why they were chosen," he said. "I am tired now and wish to sleep." He closed his heavy hooded eyes and was asleep almost before I'd left him. I went down to the bottom hold and the animal noises and the ammoniacal stench stormed the senses. They had taken aboard everything they could in the animal world. Great cages and enclosures filled the two bottom holds.

A towering elephant languidly flicked a trunk over my head while its mate stuffed a pink maw with straw; a hyena thrust a nauseous snout through the bars and its mate sniffed at its hindquarters; an eagle buried its beak in rotting horse flesh while its mate slumbered, defecating once as it did so; two chimpanzees picked each other's skins and then took to hurling excreta at each other. . . .

The girl I liked now approached me. One task I had been allotted was to help with the feeding of the animals and birds. The others were glad of my help though only the black-haired girl ever said so. The feeding kept them busy in the "afternoons" for we tried to keep count of the days and, moreover, the animals' stomachs kept the old time. The lions roared always in the late afternoon. The girl nodded to me and inclined her head for me to follow her along the passageway. Away from the others—and her husband—she chattered as was her habit but only about the animals.

"The poor things. They miss the sun."

"Like us," I said.

"The strange thing is the lion," she said. We'd now approached his cage. He stood there firmly on his great thewed legs, his head nobly uplifted. His eyes looked far beyond us. "We thought we'd have trouble with him, the caged king of beasts and all that sort of thing. Restless and raging. But not a bit of it. He just eats and sleeps and wants for nothing more."

"Like some of us—the first part anyway," I said. The shadow crossed her face as it always did when she sensed I was talking of what was forbidden.

"You'll be fat and out of practice when we land, poor monarch," she addressed the lion. "You won't be fit to earn your living at first." She laughed gaily. "And perhaps the doves won't be able to fly."

"You're anxious to land, aren't you?" I asked. "In spite of the death and destruction?"

I saw her eyes light up with the seed of life. Some of the others came by then. On the men's faces was hostility for me, the unchosen, the unpaired, the rival. I laughed happily and then began feeding the rank chunks of horseflesh, streaked with golden fat and dripping dark sacrificial blood, to the pompous lion and his mate.